EVE'S DAUGHTER

Lizzie Bishop, full of romantic dreams, finds fulfilment with Ben Kite. Two former rivals for her affection, Stanley Dando, her enigmatic second cousin and Jesse Clancey, the likeable and handsome son of a prosperous neighbour, remain secretly in love with her. Then Ben, with the noblest of intentions, makes the biggest mistake of his life, and everyone is caught up in the spiralling consequences.

Set in a Black Country community in the early 20th century, and encompassing obsessive desire and deceit, Lizzie's story is by turns tender, sensual and often hilariously funny.

EVE'S DAUGHTER

EVE'S DAUGHTER

by

Michael Taylor

Magna Large Print Books
Long Preston, North Yorkshire,
BD23 4ND, England.

British Library Cataloguing in Publication Data.

Taylor, Michael
    Eve's daughter.

    A catalogue record of this book is
    available from the British Library

    ISBN   0-7505-1727-1

First published in Great Britain 1997
by Peacock Publishing Ltd.

Copyright © Michael Taylor 1997

Cover illustration © H. Moseley by arrangement with
Allied Artists

The right of Michael Taylor to be identified as the author of this work
has been asserted by him in accordance with the Copyright, Designs
and Patents Act, 1988

Published in Large Print 2001 by arrangement with
Michael Taylor care of Marjacq Scripts

Magna Large Print is an imprint of Library Magna Books Ltd.

Printed and bound in Great Britain by
T.J. (International) Ltd., Cornwall, PL28 8RW

AUTHOR'S NOTE

Although Kates Hill exists today, and is a thriving community with modern tree-lined cul-de-sacs, the narrow streets, the terraced houses, the many pubs and corner shops, the pits, the forges and foundries of yesterday have all disappeared. St. John's church, however, remains a focal point, still a warm and welcoming place.

To Linda and Joseph, who have been remarkably tolerant of me in the preparation of this book.

ACKNOWLEDGEMENTS

I offer special thanks to the Archives and Local History Department of Dudley Libraries, to the Black Country Living Museum, and to my mother for her excellent memory.

Chapter 1

When he was alive many decent folk had wished him dead. Now, Isaac Bishop lay on his back, silent, unmoving, at last obliging them. His head was a gory mess of dark, red blood, drying, matted into his grey hair. The dented, old bowler hat he wore for work, Tom Dando had placed appropriately on his crippled chest like a black cairn. Elderly Doctor Clark had been summoned to the scene of the accident to attend Isaac as he lay in a heap at the crossroads where two public houses and the Bethel Chapel outfaced each other. And some would say it was poetic justice, profoundly ironic, that being hurled against the stout iron railings of the chapel should have ensured Isaac's death.

Tom Dando pushed Isaac homewards on a squeaking handcart the greengrocer had lent, keeping behind the doctor, who headed the procession through the narrow terraced streets on his antiquated dog-cart. A growing band of morbidly inquisitive children drew up the rear in instinctive silence.

Tom Dando had always felt obliged to make sure that Isaac, his cousin and workmate, got home if they'd been drinking together; for Eve's sake. Usually, the fool ended up draped across somebody's wheelbarrow, incapable of remaining upright, comatose, snuffling contentedly like

God's dog. Tom regretted making that promise to Eve all those years ago. He would happily have left Isaac anywhere, at any time, to sort out his own salvation, for his respect for him was lower than everybody else's. At least, this time would be the last, Tom pondered with some satisfaction.

When they arrived at the house, the doctor insisted on breaking the news to Eve himself, and to Lizzie, Isaac's doting youngest daughter. He'd had greater experience of such things. He knew how best to convey news of sudden death. And he would do it without Tom's help, despite Tom's assertion that it might be better coming from him. So he hobbled up the entry alone, holding on to his hat with cantankerous defiance lest the ferocious March wind took it, and braced himself for the barrage of grief he imagined would ensue.

Tom waited apprehensively in the horse road with the hushed entourage, watching for Eve. A minute or two later she scurried down the entry, already pale and in a daze. Young Lizzie, equally bewildered, clutched her mother's billowing, long skirt. Wife and daughter stopped by the handcart and remained still, like two shrubs frozen in midwinter. They stared incredulously at the bloody corpse that had been husband to one and father to the other, while the growing crowd of onlookers shuffled in respectful silence, waiting for somebody to speak.

First to do so was Tom. 'Eve, my flower, I'm that sorry.' Eve instinctively cupped her right hand to her better ear and leaned towards him. 'Beccy Crump witnessed it all. I knew nothin'

14

about it till they fetched me out o' the "Loving Lamb". Did the doctor tell yer as it was Jack Clancey's hoss what bolted and smashed him into the railin's at the Bethel?'

Eve nodded, sighing gravely. 'He told me... But does Jack Clancey know?'

'He knows now. He was in "The Four Ways" having a drink. Sammy Hudson fetched him out.'

'And what did he say, Tom? Did he say anything?'

Tom sighed, not knowing whether he should tell Eve what Jack had said. But he'd never tried to hide anything from her before, and now would be an inappropriate time to begin. 'He said as how sorry he was. That he'd pay you his respects later... But he said as he wouldn't grieve over Isaac...'

'Like as not.' Eve looked at her husband's broken corpse and shook her head. 'Best bring him in the house, Tom. I'll see if I can open the front door.'

A few seconds later, they could hear the key turning inside, and reluctant bolts being coaxed to slide on their layers of rust. It seemed to Eve that the only times this door was opened was to let a coffin out ... or a corpse in.

Motionless, Lizzie looked on at her poor father, at first unable to accept that he was dead; that the man lying on the handcart was no longer the father she knew and adored, but just a heap of dead flesh and broken bones. She drifted behind the random cortege as it contrived to station his body in the house, her adolescent mind in turmoil. She wanted to cry, but she dare not yet,

15

not while there was a chance that this was simply some terrible nightmare from which she would be released in a minute or two.

But this was no nightmare. It was happening now.

People were beginning to speak more freely; quietly giving instructions to each other on how best to manoeuvre the handcart; to shift the rag-filled stocking that kept the draught out; for somebody to put their foot on the oil-cloth to hold it down; to prise the door open wider. But the handcart could not go through the door. Tom and the doctor would have to carry poor Isaac.

'Eve, where's your screwdriver, my flower?' Tom asked. 'I'll get the middle door off to lay him on. I've already sent for Annie Soap to come and lay him out.'

Eve hesitated, perplexed, unable to contemplate the whereabouts of such as a screwdriver. When she'd collected her thoughts she went to the brewhouse, ignoring a hen that was strutting the back yard with defiant composure. She returned with a screwdriver.

While Tom Dando was inside, removing the door between the whitewashed scullery and the seldom-used front room from its hinges, Lizzie gazed into the open, unseeing eyes of her father. The thought of him dying had never crossed her mind. She at least did not want him dead. She wanted him alive. She wanted him to call her on a Sunday morning to get ready for church; to bring her toffee apples on Friday evenings when he returned from work. She wanted him to ruffle her nut-brown hair whenever he walked past her, even though it always infuriated her. She wanted his fatherly squeeze from time to time. Now all that was gone; gone forever. Nobody could ever take his place. Nobody could ever be to her what he had been. Never again would she see his hearty, laughing face, or hear his hoarse chuckles. Never again would she see him enjoy a meal, then fall asleep in his chair. Eve moved to Lizzie's side and wrapped her arms about her and held her tight, reading her daughter's thoughts. Lizzie turned and buried her face in Eve's ample bosom. Tears stung her eyes, and she let out an involuntary whimper, then a great angry scream of grief that seemed to gush out of her in frantic escape.

Her father was dead, and Jack Clancey's horse had killed him. It was Jack Clancey's fault. If he had driven the milk float into her father deliberately it would have been no greater murder. Where was Jack Clancey when it happened? Why wasn't he looking after the animal? It was Jack Clancey who deserved to be knocked down, not her poor unsuspecting father. It was Jack Clancey who should be lying lifeless, laid out on a door.

That was four years ago. Lizzie Bishop still resented Jack Clancey. But four years is a quarter of a lifetime to a young lady of sixteen. And in a quarter of a lifetime, many of the prejudices that are diligently nurtured by refusing to forget the wrongdoing that once hurt you, can be conveniently shifted or overlooked when nature diverts your attention. Thus it was one summer

Sunday in 1906.

Lizzie Bishop's thoughts were much removed from her father. Her self esteem was high. With her white leather-bound prayer book clasped demurely in front of her she felt special, and knew she looked her best. Love, she was certain, could not be long coming. She had begun dreaming of love, and longed to taste it; to experience the potent emotions that drove others to behave in ways that ordinarily seemed totally out of character.

She stole another glance at Jesse Clancey, Jack's only son. He was tall and fair, with a lovely drooping moustache that widened enormously when he smiled, which was often, and his steel-blue eyes radiated sincerity and compassion. He was amiable, unassuming and well liked. The low sun behind him glinted off his blond hair, and Lizzie contemplated how magnificent he looked. Her own dancing hazel eyes, if only he were perceptive enough to read their expression, hinted at a stimulating inner turbulence, a vivacious adolescent desire. Jesse was standing just a few feet from her; close enough for her to touch, close enough for her to hold. But so maddeningly out of her reach.

She swung her shoulders to and fro self-consciously, feeling Jesse's eyes on her. She ought not to, but she glanced at him from under her long lashes. She could not help it. It taxed her diminishing willpower too much not to admire him and, as she returned his hopeful smile, she felt herself blush. With a casualness she did not feel she turned away and, to hide her blushes, looked down with contrived composure at her best shoes. Why did she have to colour up so vividly? Why did she have to show her partiality by blushing.

He smiled again. 'Nice outfit, Lizzie,' he said privately, so that nobody else could hear. 'Suits you.'

She sensed his shyness, and understood the courage he'd had to summon to say it. 'Thank you,' she replied with equal diffidence, but retaining her smile.

Her outfit was in the Gibson Girl style. It used to belong to her older sister, Lucy, and was a bit out of date, but that was forgivable: there was no money these days for new, more fashionable clothes. Besides, Eve had altered it to fit, and it fitted perfectly. It fitted so well that Lizzie hoped it would turn not just Jesse's head; Stanley Dando was equally desirable. The long, navy skirt with the belt drawn in tight, accentuated her small waist, and neatly tucked in it was the white striped shirt that emphasised her firm, young bosom, gently rising and falling with each smiling, eager breath. The girlish set of her head was enhanced by a tilted, straw boater with navy hatband that sat on top of a mound of lush, piled-up hair, an errant wisp of which contrived to caress her elegant neck.

Jesse's mother, Ezme, overhearing her son's compliment, scornfully gave Lizzie the once-over, scrutinising her lovely second-hand outfit for faults, mismatched seams, an uneven hem, poor finishing; anything to decry Eve's handiwork. But she would find no such fault. Eve was Ezme's rival and equal when it came to mending and dressmaking. The Clanceys lived near the Bishops in Cromwell Street, but neither Ezme nor Eve ever had a kind word to say about each other, even before Jack's horse caused Isaac's death.

Lizzie was convinced that the dressmaking was the cause of this acute rivalry. Ezme was an adept seamstress and supplemented the family's income by it. And, although she was no better at it than Eve, she certainly believed she was. It galled Ezme that Eve did not do it for money; that she did it out of kindness. So they sustained a senseless antagonism; antagonism that had pervaded even Lizzie's own easy-going attitude. It was all the more difficult therefore, all the more futile, to respond in the way she would dearly love to respond to Jesse, should he ever pluck up the courage to defy his mother and the prejudice invoked by that fatal accident four years ago. What a dilemma it would create! But it was a dilemma she would welcome with all her heart.

Ezme was a big, intimidating woman, almost masculine, though it was said she had not always been so. As a young woman, when she moved to Dudley from Darlaston to marry, she was said to have possessed striking looks. She was also headstrong. Certainly she was too much of a match for Jack, who hovered about her like a mere accessory.

The group, conscious of the ever-present tension between Eve and Ezme, were conversing blandly, discussing the imminent departure of the vicar, the Reverend Mr Nelson Crowshaw, and wondering whether they would approve of the new incumbent.

Beccy Crump, Eve's next door neighbour, said, 'I hear as old Dr. Clark's about to retire, an' all.'

'Fancy,' Eve replied with interest, her hand to her ear.

'They say as he's handing over his practice to his son.'

Eve sighed her approval. 'To Donald? Oh, bless him. He's a lovely lad, is Donald. A good doctor, an' all, they reckon.'

Jesse Clancey meanwhile could not take his eyes off Lizzie. She was as exquisite as a young princess and frisky as a foal, but he was painfully aware she was nine years his junior. Nine years that he perceived as an obstacle. Nine years that were inhibiting him from making a fool of himself. The family dairy business depended on the goodwill of its customers, so any disparagement through foolish encounters with girls, who were dangerously young, would be unprofitable. More significantly, this nine years forestalled any wrath and derision from his mother, for he, too, was aware that she held Eve, and thus Lizzie, in huge contempt.

Lizzie discovered Jesse's age by casually asking neighbours. Socialising was not encouraged, so she could never ask him directly, of course, even though they lived so close. But she could dream of him, yearn for him; and they could exchange secret smiles. Lizzie was flattered to receive the admiring glances of a man so much older. It somehow confirmed her own womanhood, her own desirability. If only he would pluck up the courage to ask her out.

Church on a Sunday evening was a social as well as a religious affair, and it wanted at least five minutes yet before they would go inside. So Lizzie, not harkening to the soft Sunday voices of her mother and the others as they stood gossiping, tilted her face towards the sun's deepening, yellow glow, which was falling warm on her face. Momentarily, she closed her eyes, savouring the pleasure of it. Silver birches were casting long, cool shadows over the monolithic graves of wealthier families, and the doves that dwelt in the bell tower flapped fussily as they vied for best roosts. A bee, hindered in its flight home by its own diligence, hummed with optimism around a final bunch of tulips on one of the lesser graves. Lizzie imagined herself standing outside some country church immersed in rural stillness. But, tomorrow, the forge close by would violate this enviable peace. The ground would tremble to the thud, thud of massive board hammers, as if a giant's heart were pounding beneath your feet. In adjacent streets, the cupolas of hot, sulphurous foundries would roar more terrifyingly than the furnaces of Bedlam. Pit heads with their big, rumbling wheels, and the clanking, hissing steam engines that powered them, were also within sight and earshot; and men would be calling to each other over the din of it all.

Yet all was so serene now.

Aunt Sarah Dando arrived at last, with Sylvia and Stanley. Sylvia was quite the young lady now, twenty years old with dark, wavy hair, and an inch or two taller than Lizzie; her face was thinner, but her eyes were bright. She walked and stood proudly, and when she smiled she revealed a lovely set of even teeth. Lizzie noticed how she, too, kept glancing at Jesse, smiling coquettishly when he chose to look her way.

Lizzie calculatingly detached herself from the group, which by now had granted token observance to the perennial walnut of women's suffrage, and was discussing Bella Dowty's ulcerated legs. One sure way to divert Jesse's interest away from Sylvia, she reckoned, was to make him jealous. A ploy she'd learned some time ago. So she moved to talk to Stanley, her second cousin, with whom she enjoyed an easy friendship. She flirted openly with him, touching his arm with agonising familiarity when she spoke, tormenting Jesse.

Stanley was eighteen, tall and wiry, with dark curly hair. He had a clear complexion, a pretty face for a lad – even prettier than his sister – and a mouth that Lizzie increasingly considered was extraordinarily kissable. As children they used to play games that involved stealing a kiss or two. But now she was older and growing inexorably more interested in kissing, the notion of doing it properly had appealed for some time, but with increasing intensity lately. And if she could not be kissed by Jesse Clancey with his lovely moustache, who better than Stanley?

Stanley, for his part, was entertaining similar fantasies about Lizzie. Six months ago he wouldn't have given her a second thought; after all, they were so familiar; like brother and sister almost. But, lately, she'd blossomed into such a desirable young woman, and he regarded her now in a different light. He'd not met any girl he would rather see undressed. Her beautiful eyes seemed to sparkle with vitality, and always with a taunting frolicsome look, and he was sure she was thinking thoughts as impious as his own. It was certain she would allow him to undress her if he applied himself sensitively.

'Where's Uncle Tom, Stanley?' Lizzie enquired.

'In "The Freebodies". He wanted a quick pint before the service. Said he was thirsty.'

She felt Jesse's eyes on her again, but she could afford to disregard his admiring stares now she'd found less controversial company in Stanley. She said: 'We'll see the new vicar tonight, Stanley. That's why a lot have come, I daresay. There's folk here I haven't seen for ages. If ours don't hurry up and finish their chinwagging, we'll never get a seat.'

'How about me and you going in now, Lizzie? We could sit by ourselves. We needn't wait for them. We needn't sit near 'em, come to that.'

'Oh, I don't know, Stanley. I shouldn't leave my mother.'

'Aunt Eve'll be all right. My folks'll keep her company. Hang on, I'll tell 'em we'm going in without 'em.'

Lizzie smiled and said all right, then turned away self-consciously. It all seemed to be happening tonight. The two men she was most interested in were as good as dangling on her string. The realisation excited her. She fancied Stanley more each time she saw him, and it was just as easy to turn to him as to Jesse. Probably easier; at least he was attainable without controversy. A bird in the hand and all that.

As Lizzie moved away she turned to make sure that Jesse Clancey had noticed. He had, but concealed the fact, striking a casual pose and laughing extra-heartily at something Sylvia had said. Lizzie smiled contentedly. Two men patently interested in her; two gorgeous, dashing men. If only she could have both. She had the capacity to handle both until she finally decided which one to marry.

But who to choose? It was so confusing.

Now, with Stanley's hand in the small of her back guiding her into church, she felt another flush of excitement at the thought of sitting with one admirer while the other yearned jealously for her. She allowed Stanley to lead her into the back pew, the prime location for courting couples. They would have it all to themselves, for it wasn't a full length pew; one of the massive columns supporting the vaulted roof occupied much of it.

Stanley gallantly opened her *Hymns Ancient and Modern* and found the first hymn for her. 'I've wanted just the two of us to sit together for ages.' His smile was devastating. 'I've never been able to pluck up the courage before to ask you. I thought you might laugh at me ... being second cousins and all that.'

Lizzie hunched her shoulders with delight, and an exhilarating warmth surged through her at the prospect of a romance so unexpected. 'Being second cousins doesn't matter, Stanley. I'm glad you did.'

25

'Even first cousins can marry, you know, Lizzie.'

His very words made her hot. Funny how romance could be so spontaneous.

Their folks walked down the centre aisle. Tom Dando, back from 'The Freebodies', acknowledged Lizzie and Stanley with a nod, and courteously allowed Eve to enter the pew before him. When the women had settled their long skirts and taken off their gloves, and the men had placed their best hats under the pew, they all knelt down and prayed. Lizzie smiled at Stanley over the success of their spontaneous assignation, and with increasing regularity as the service progressed. During the sermons – for there were two; the first, a valediction from the exiting Mr Crowshaw; the second, a greeting from the new vicar – Stanley shuffled close and shamelessly took her hand. Lizzie felt her heart start pounding at the contact, and she blushed once more, in half a mind to withdraw. It was, after all, a liberty and, besides, it could surely never be proper to hold hands in church. But she brazenly allowed her hand to remain in Stanley's, and a dangerous glow of pleasure enveloped her.

After the service, everyone filed out through the main door. While Mr Crowshaw thanked all for their support in the past, the Reverend Mr John Mainwaring and his wife met his parishioners for the first time, shaking their hands warmly. Many lingered in the churchyard afterwards, chatting, saying what a nice man the new vicar seemed. Since Ezme Clancey was the relief organist, she and Jack and Jesse were expected at a welcoming party at the vicarage, along with other church dignitaries. As were Beccy and Albert Crump. Albert had taken the pledge years ago and was secretary of the Band of Hope in the St. John's Church of England Temperance Society. Despite Albert, however, Tom Dando claimed defiantly that he and his family were going for a drink or two at 'The Shoulder of Mutton'.

'Why not come with us, Eve, and bring young Lizzie?' Sarah suggested. 'It'll be a bit o' company.'

Eve automatically cupped her hand to her good car.

'I daresay Eve's got other things to do, Sarah,' Tom chided. 'Leave her be.'

Eve glanced at Tom. She had not caught his words, but his expression alone forbade her accepting. It was unlike him.

'No, we'll go home, Sarah. Our Joe and May'll be expecting their suppers.'

'Let 'em get their own suppers,' Sarah scoffed.

'And I've gotta be up early to light the fire under the wash boiler... Anyway, while I'm here I want to tidy up Isaac's grave.'

Albert and Beccy bid them goodnight and joined the other group that included Ezme and Jack Clancey, ready to leave to attend the welcoming party at the vicarage.

Lizzie and Stanley deliberately lingered by the lych gate meanwhile, teasing each other and laughing in their new-found understanding that had transmuted them into another kind of relationship; more adult; more thrilling; where emotions could suddenly run amok; where your heart thumped ever so often, and for a long time.

'Shall you come to our house with your mother and father on Wednesday night?' Lizzie asked him, her eyes alight.

'I don't know,' he teased. 'Think I should?'

''Course. Why not?' Her enthusiasm was fuelled by the witnessing of Jesse's apparent shift of interest twenty or so yards away. He was talking intently to Sylvia again, and Sylvia was laughing coyly. 'We could go for a walk. We could go for a walk over Oakham fields. To the Dingle.'

As they drifted out into the street through the lych gate Stanley foresaw the possibilities...

They made their way over to the rest of the group standing on the pavement outside. Lizzie felt quite breathless after her encounter. Eve was saying her goodbyes to Tom and Sarah, when Sylvia came flouncing towards them. As she approached in the reddening light she tried to act normally, but there was no hiding the self-satisfied look on her flushed face. She smiled self-consciously and, despite Stanley, Lizzie felt acutely aggrieved that one of her admirers might have defected to her pretty cousin.

'You'd best go and fetch some fresh water from the butt for these flowers, our Lizzie,' Eve said, and poured what remained of the stale water out of the enamelled grave vase onto the ground. 'They could do with a drink, it strikes me.'

She handed Lizzie the vase and watched her step back towards the church up the steep slope, picking her way between the other gravestones in the lengthening shadows, lifting the hem of her skirt to avoid getting it dirty. A blackbird swooped down and perched on the arm of a stone cross surmounting another grave, and began its persistent song.

Eve contemplated Isaac. His grave lay on the north side of St. John's church. Every time Eve visited it she had vivid recollections of the funeral more than four years ago that sometimes stayed with her for days afterwards. On the day of the funeral the wind had freshened, blowing in rain from the west, rustling the tops of the hawthorn trees and the bright bunches of daffodils that had been lovingly arranged on surrounding graves. Family and friends had stood around the hole in the lee of the church, each thinking their own thoughts, she reckoned, each recalling some moment of pleasure or pain Isaac had brought.

She'd tried hard to shed tears that day, for she felt she ought; but no tears would come. God knew she'd spilled enough already over the others. Nearly thirty years ago her second son had died of peritonitis at only five years old. Helplessness and grief had sickened her then. Why her child? The anger and frustration she'd felt was overwhelming, as was the seeming futility of loving and caring for a life that was tenuous and so easily snuffed out. Fifteen years ago her eldest son died at the age of twenty-one in a preventable pit accident at the Bunns Lane Colliery; another cherished life wasted. Two years later, her eldest daughter, unmarried, died in childbirth, and refused to name the man who devised her ruination. Another son died of typhoid in a field hospital in South Africa barely six years ago, his tragic reward for volunteering to aid queen and country in the Boer War. Had he died in battle, she could have accepted it more readily. And then there was the daughter she carried full term but was stillborn.

Eve resented more than anything this useless waste of life; those sudden, unexpected ends that had made a nonsense of all her striving. Little wonder she had not been able to weep for Isaac.

Eve recalled that as the funeral service drew to a close she at last felt a tear roll down her cheek. But it was not a tear for Isaac; it was for herself. It was for all the doubts, the misgivings, the love she'd been prepared to give him which so often had been spurned. Yet in more recent years, since the birth of Lizzie, he had mellowed. He became more attentive, more appreciative of her efforts; life with him became easier and more agreeable, as if he was finally repenting of his waywardness. She was glad of the change in him, and had embraced it with all her heart.

Now she looked across the valley towards the castle on the next hill, as she had done that grey, gusting March day in 1902. A billowing cloud of white steam, spouting from a locomotive as it emerged from the Blowers Green tunnel in the middle distance, was instantly dispersed in the wind. So, too, was life itself dependent on the unpredictable consequences of other people's whims, Eve pondered; and on events that do whatever they like with us.

Lizzie returned with the vase filled with fresh water. 'Is it true that cousins can marry, Mother?'

Eve put her hand to her ear. 'What say, our Lizzie?'

'I said, is it true that cousins can marry? I mean, for instance, Stanley and me might start courting by the looks of it. Could we marry? He says we could.'

'Our Stanley?' Eve's expression was one of concern. 'Stanley Dando?'

Lizzie nodded.

'Oh, I wouldn't want you to marry Stanley, our Lizzie. I definitely wouldn't want you to marry him. You can do much better for yourself than Stanley.'

Lizzie was disappointed at her mother's response, so decided it best to say nothing more. At least not yet. She picked up a flower and broke an inch off the bottom of its stem before stooping to replace it in the vase. She did another. Then another. Thinking about Stanley and what might come of a romantic interlude with him, it was some time before she stood up and spoke again to her mother.

She said, 'Why did we come here to Father's grave so soon? It was only Friday after tea we came last time and put some flowers on.'

'I didn't fancy going to "The Shoulder of Mutton" with your Uncle Tom and Aunt Sarah.'

'Oh.' Lizzie pondered the lost opportunity with bitter regret. 'I'd have liked to have gone,' she pouted. 'I'd have loved to have gone.'

Eve did not hear, but she saw the disappointment in Lizzie's eyes. Silently, between them, they rearranged the carnations and Lizzie picked up the ends of the stems she'd broken off, then

31

stood up again. She read to herself the inscription on her father's headstone; an inscription she knew by heart.

'In loving remembrance of Isaac Bishop who died tragically and unexpectedly 15th March 1902, aged 59 years. They have sown the wind. Thy Will be done.'

Chapter 2

Sunday's fine weather continued into Monday. Lizzie Bishop walked to work without her coat, her head swimming with dreams and fantasies. The brief, romantic adventure last evening with Stanley Dando was devouring her. It had been so unexpected, but she had relished every minute. In a flash, her emotions had been relentlessly stirred like leaves in a gale, and it was heart-stopping. Now she could hardly wait to see him again, especially after they'd been so abruptly parted when the families went their separate ways. If only she could summon the patience to wait till Wednesday, when they would walk together across the fields by the Oakham farms to the Dingle, where it would be quiet and secluded. She hoped more than anything that he would have the courage to kiss her.

Stanley had set something in train that excited her beyond all expectations. Now she was determined that nothing could stop them or divert them. Strange, she thought, how she'd known Stanley all her life; but not till recently had she thought of him as anything other than family. His dark curls, his even teeth, and his lovely, lovely lips would surely break the hearts of a good many girls. It was up to her to make sure no one else had a chance. Stanley was drawn to her, too, just as surely as a buck is drawn to a doe; that much was obvious. And her eager appetite had been whetted enough.

The clatter and whine of an electric tram travelling through the Market Place roused Lizzie from her daydreams. Stallholders were loading their trestles beneath the red and white awnings with everything from fruit, vegetables and rolls of velvet, to brass fenders, lamp oil and crockery. Horses clip-clopped over the cobble-stones drawing rumbling carts, and a motor car spluttered as it passed circumspectly in the direction of St. Thomas's tall spire at the top of the town. A man riding to work on a bicycle took pains to avoid getting his narrow wheels caught in the tramlines. Already, awnings were out over many of the shop fronts and Lizzie could see others being drawn down. A hawker was selling fly papers outside the front door of E. C. Trentham's, Ironmongers and Cutlers, where she worked, and bid her good morning.

She saw May Bradley walking towards her from the opposite direction, and waited. They entered the shop together and headed for the passageway at the rear where they generally hung their coats. Today, they had only their baskets to deposit before entering the small back-room to titivate their hair. May looked at herself in the mirror and rearranged a wayward wisp. Despite their age difference the girls got on well. They first met when Lizzie started this job, some couple of years ago, and soon they began to meet socially.

May was down-to-earth, with a ready smile, and a wit that was at first beyond Lizzie. She was an attractive girl with a slender waist and an ample bosom, and she had an abundance of dark, wavy hair that framed a pleasant but hardly striking face. When Lizzie invited May home to tea one Sunday afternoon to meet her mother, it was Joe Bishop, her brother, then twenty-two and looking more like his late father every day, who monopolised the conversation, amusing May with his humorous quips. Later, when it was time for May to leave, Joe offered to escort her home, since it was dark. He insisted there was no need for Lizzie to trouble herself accompanying her friend. May accepted bashfully, thanked Eve for her hospitality, and that was the beginning of their courtship. Eve was hopeful that Joe had found himself a nice, homely girl, at last.

May turned away from the mirror to speak to Lizzie. 'When you was at church last night with your mother, me and Joe went for a drink in "The Junction", and while we was in there, we saw Arthur Dowty, your next door neighbour. He says as how him and Bella am a-flittin'. He reckons it's 'cause of Jack Hardwick's pigs. Anyroad, when we got back I said to Joe as we ought to think about rentin' that house ourselves. If we could have it, we'd get married. That way, we'd still be close to your mother.'

Lizzie fastened the ties of her pinafore behind her. 'Wouldn't the pigs bother you as well?'

'Oh, I'm used to pigs. Me father always kept pigs. He's a pig himself. Anyroad, if the pigs was there afore we, we couldn't rightly complain.'

Lizzie shrugged. 'I suppose not. But how soon are Bella and Arthur flitting?'

'As soon as they find somethin' else, they said.' May continued to fiddle with her hair in the mirror. 'There's plenty houses to rent. It shouldn't be long.'

Lizzie's smiling eyes lit up her face. 'Another wedding to look forward to. Oh, I'm that happy for you, May. I'm sure that our Joe'll make you a lovely husband, though I say it myself.'

'Yes, and if you get him a big enough piece of wood, I daresay he'll make you one, Lizzie.' May tried to keep a straight face.

'Oh, I think I'm a bit too young yet, May,' Lizzie replied innocently, not having caught the humour in May's comment. Then she said coyly, 'I think me and Stanley Dando might start courting, though.'

'Oh, young Stanley, eh? What's brought that on?'

Lizzie sat down and explained excitedly how Stanley had all but abducted her to the back pew in church, even held her hand, and told her that cousins could marry. But she failed to say that her mother seemed not to approve.

'Well, he seems a pleasant enough lad. He's nice lookin', an' all, there's no two ways. But remember you'm only sixteen, Lizzie. It's no good courtin' serious at sixteen.'

'I know that. But when I'm eighteen, I'll be old enough to get wed. That's less than two years off.

35

A good many girls get wed at eighteen.'

'Not if they've got any sense they don't. It's generally 'cause they've got to if they'm that young. You'd break your mother's heart if that happened, you know. Just remember she's been through all that before with your sister Maude. And look what happened to her.'

'Oh, May, I wouldn't do anything like that. What sort of girl d'you think I am?'

'Like any other, I daresay, so liable to get carried away.'

When Lizzie left school at twelve years old she had found a job at the Dudley Bucket and Fender Co-operative and made a friend of another girl, roughly the same age, called Daisy Foster. They soon bettered themselves at another firm, operating small guillotines, cutting coils of brass into lengths ready to be pressed into parts for paraffin lamps. They stayed for two years, not just learning the job, but learning about life, listening to the other women gossiping over the hollow rattle and thumps of hand presses, and the fatty smell of tallow. Most of the girls they worked with were older, and Lizzie was amazed at the unbelievable things some of them used to tell her about their men, the amazing antics they performed with them and, most surprisingly, how often. Lizzie didn't know such things were possible, but it all sounded intriguing. Those girls told her things she would never have known about had she stayed at home. By autumn, however, the girls had tired of the oil lamp factory, and found jobs at Chambers Saddlery in Hall Street. Lizzie, however, did not take to working with leather and its dark, sickly odour, whereas Daisy did. Thus the two girls split up when Lizzie left to seek other employment.

'I know a lot of girls *do* do it, May ... you know? ... before they get wed I mean... But I wouldn't, even if I wanted to. I'd be too afeared of getting caught.'

'Yes, well... It's somethin' you need to bear in mind, Lizzie.'

'Do you and our Joe do it, May?'

May registered no outward change in her expression, continuing to preen herself. 'That's between Joe and me.'

'Well, have you ever done it? With anybody, I mean?'

'Lizzie! Honestly!'

'It isn't that I'm being nosy,' Lizzie persisted, trying to justify her questioning, 'but I can talk to you about things. I've got nobody else to talk to, and I want to know about things like that. I want to know what it's like, and everything. I need to talk to somebody about it.'

May turned round and grabbed her pinafore from the hook on the back of the door. 'You'll learn soon enough when you do get wed, Lizzie, and not before if you want my advice. There's no rush... Tell me about Stanley, eh?'

Lizzie smiled again, modestly. I keep thinking about his lips, May ... and how much I want him to kiss me. I only have to think about him and my legs go all wobbly. D'you think I'm falling in love?'

May shrugged. 'So you'm not interested in Jesse Clancey any more?'

37

'Well I would be if he'd asked me out. But he seems more interested in our Sylvia.'

Kates Hill lay about a mile south east of Dudley town centre, overlooked only by the old Norman castle on the next high ridge. It was a warren of narrow cobbled and muddy streets, each like a gorge, lined with rows of red brick terraced houses and little shops. Some of the streets were steep, others only gently inclined. Not one could you claim was flat, and few failed to host at least one public house. The houses, many of them back-to-back, were built during the early part of the nineteenth century to house the influx of workers who came seeking jobs in the burgeoning foundries, forges, coal mines and ironworks. There were many other factories tucked away, small concerns, some squeezed between houses, some crammed at the back of them, or down alley-ways that the ever-present wind funnelled heedlessly through. Most were concerned with the shaping of metal. Furnaces still glowed in many streets after dark as workers toiled on, striving to earn a few pence extra to bring some comfort to their spartan lives. Three brass foundries and a forge all stood within shouting distance of each other, so there was always the sound of hard work within earshot; the ringing of metal; the steady, reassuring gasps of Boulton and Watt steam engines built practically next door in Handsworth. Everywhere a great confusion of chimney stacks volleyed columns of grey smoke up into the obliging sky.

The Bishops' house was roughly in the middle

of an unbroken terrace that ran the whole length of Cromwell Street on one side. It was not a regular terrace, though. Some houses, those inhabited by better off families, stood further back from the horse-road than others, with iron railings at the front and long flights of stone steps up to the painted gates of their entries. The Bishops', however, was none such; their front doorstep directly met the footpath with its criss-crossed, blue, paving bricks.

There were three bedrooms. Two were on the front, one of which was a box-room where Lizzie slept. At one time she and her sister Lucy used to share it, till Lucy found a job at the Station Hotel which meant her living-in. Her three brothers used to share the bed in the other little front bedroom, to raucous guffaws and irreverent cursing, especially at bed time in winter if they were arguing over who should warm his feet first on the wrapped fire brick. She could hear just about everything through the thin wall of wooden laths that separated her from them. But, nowadays, all was quiet. Ted and Grenville had wed and moved out, which meant that Joe had the bed to himself.

When she parted her curtains in a morning, Lizzie could see St. John's church in the middle distance in the gap between 'The Sailor's Return' public house and the brass foundry opposite. Beyond the church was the castle keep looming grey over the trees at the top of its steep, wooded hill.

To Lizzie, the castle seemed no higher than Cromwell Street. Indeed, tradition had it that

Oliver Cromwell himself had supervised its destruction from that very spot, because of its elevation; hence the street's name. Certainly, Cromwell's forces besieged the castle from these heights.

The back bedroom, overlooking the yard, was where Eve slept in her big, brass bed. The scrubbed, wooden stairs rose directly from the scullery into that bedroom, so access to the others was through it. When Isaac, their father, was alive they all had to be home and in bed before it was time for him to retire. If any of them came home after he went to bed, they were condemned to sleep all night on a chair in the scullery, or face the verbal equivalent of a firing squad for disturbing him.

Downstairs, the scullery seemed all cupboards and doors, from floor to ceiling, of brown varnished wood; doors to the stairs with a single stair jutting out, and the cellar door. There was the middle door as well, to the front room that seemed only ever to be used for weddings, for funerals, or at Christmas time. A chenille fringe adorned the edge of the mantel shelf, and Eve laid a matching cloth on the table every Sunday, without fail.

Isaac had always ruled the roost. Because he was the main breadwinner, his needs and desires came first, though none of the family ever wanted for anything. His job had always paid a steady wage, and with other sons working many neighbours envied their standard of living. Meals were regular and substantial, and they always had good clothes and stout shoes to wear, even if they were shared from time to time.

It was not until some time after her father's funeral that Lizzie began to miss him and his death started to have any real meaning. The evenings at home in their small house were quiet as she and her mother sat companionably in front of the coal fire that burned agreeably. Joe, her youngest brother, was nineteen then and, whilst he had a steady job in a forge and handed over his money every Friday night, it was hard work, and to relax he was out drinking with his friends most evenings. Lizzie missed her father's wit. She missed his presence; the little things, like his cursing if anyone accidentally nudged him while he was shaving with his cut-throat razor in front of the fire, and his mug on the mantelpiece. She missed the aroma of Turner's Brass Foundry that used to linger on him when he came in from work. She missed him polishing her boots at night. She missed all sorts of things.

After the funeral she would daydream, reading by candle light in the prevailing silence but, when she glanced at her mother sitting quietly in her high-backed chair, she would sometimes see the firelight reflected in tears rolling down her cheeks. She would watch Eve lift her spectacles without a murmur and wipe her eyes with a dainty handkerchief, then return to her newspaper, which she always scoured from front to back, whispering every word she read. Lizzie began to understand even then that those tears were not just for her father; they were for all the other loved ones lost, perhaps for opportunities lost. Sometimes, she was moved to weep herself,

41

but she would stifle the tears and put on a brave smile, then go over to her mother and give her a hug.

Lizzie had been confused by her mother's reaction, though. She had grieved more at the loss of Major, the son who died of enteric fever in a field hospital in Bloemfontein during the Boer War.

On the Wednesday, May came to tea, as was lately her custom. She arrived with Lizzie during the afternoon, since every Wednesday they were both given a half day off. May liked to spend time with Eve, black-leading the fire grate for her before lighting the fire, and peeling potatoes while sitting out on the yard in the sunshine on chairs taken from the scullery. When Joe returned from his chainmaking, Eve served up liver faggots and grey peas with boiled potatoes. When they had finished eating and everything had been cleared away, they informed Eve that the Dowtys' house might become vacant over the next week or two.

'If the landlord agrees to rent us the house next door, we'll do it up and get married. What d'you say to that, Mother?'

Eve smiled, a self-satisfied smile. 'It's about time, our Joe. And you won't find e'er a nicer wench, either.'

He looked proudly at May. 'So we've got your blessing?'

'Yes, you've got me blessing. Be sure to look after her.'

Lizzie looked at the clock on the mantelpiece.

42

It was just after eight. If the Dandos were coming they should arrive at any minute.

'Well, one thing about it – we shan't be a million miles away so, if I don't look after her, you can always come round and give me a good hiding.'

Eve caught every word. 'And you can be sure as I would. There's ne'er a chap living that's too big for a good hiding off his mother, specially if he knows he deserves it. Anyroad, I'll have a word with the landlord for you.'

'You'll be needing some furniture,' Lizzie suggested.

'Yes, and I've been thinkin',' May said, 'our Travis has got a table and chairs he wants to get shut of. It'll be all right to start off with.'

'You'll get a few things as wedding presents,' Lizzie said. 'I'll buy you something nice if you tell me what you want.'

Joe got up from his chair to poke the fire. 'Don't go spending your money on us, our Lizzie. You'll need all you can get for yourselves, you and mother. We can fend for ourselves. We'll pick up a bargain or two at any decent pawnshop.'

'Pawn shop? I don't want other folks's left-offs, Joe. I'd rather have new.'

'We'll buy some new things, May. We'll buy a new bed. But as regards the rest, we'll have to see how we'm fixed for the old spondulicks.' He peered into the coal scuttle as an afterthought. 'Bugger me, this blasted thing's empty again. Every time I look it's soddin' empty. Our Lizzie, fetch some coal up, my wench, and I'll give yer a

43

silver threepenny bit.'

'Go yourself and keep your silver threepenny bit.' There was sisterly contempt in her voice. 'Why should I get all mucked up? Aunt Sarah and Uncle Tom will be here in a minute.'

May raised an eyebrow. 'Not to mention Stanley.'

Lizzie glanced guiltily at her mother, but Eve had heard nothing. It was then that they heard footsteps in the entry, and Lizzie's heart started to pound.

'Aye up. Sounds like they'm here now,' Joe said, disappearing into the cellar with the coal bucket.

The back door opened and in walked Tom and Sarah. Tom sat himself in the armchair and Sarah sat on its arm, her back towards her husband while they talked. Joe returned from the cellar, heaving the bucket of coal. He set it down on the hearth and made up the fire while Lizzie waited for Stanley to come in. But there were no more footsteps in the entry. No more opening of the back door. The flutter of excitement under her rib cage became an ache. Usually, either Stanley or Sylvia accompanied their mother and father. Tonight, there was neither. Lizzie felt a perfidious desire to cry out. Where was Stanley? Why hadn't he come? But conversation about May's and Joe's plans was already in full spate, so she let it be.

'Well, I reckon as we should go and have a drink on it,' Tom suggested. 'Let's pop up "The Junction" and celebrate.'

'That's all you think about,' Sarah complained. 'Beer, beer, beer. I wonder as you don't drown in it.'

44

'No, that's a bostin' idea, Tom,' Joe agreed. 'Gi' me a minute to wash me hands. Come on, Mother. Get your lid on. We'm off for a drink to celebrate.'

So everybody, except Lizzie, began sprucing themselves up and smoothing the creases from their clothes. When they were about to leave, Tom asked her why she wasn't joining them.

'I'm not old enough to sit drinking in public houses.' She felt desperately sorry for herself.

'You can sit in the children's room, my darlin'. I'll bring you some pop.'

'The children's room? No thanks, Uncle Tom.'

'But it's a celebration.'

Lizzie preferred to stay at home. Stanley was sure to arrive sooner or later. After all, he'd promised. She would wait, and be alone with him when he did arrive.

But Stanley broke his promise. He did not come to see her that evening; nor the following Sunday evening at church; nor on the Wednesday after that when his parents came visiting again. Stanley wasn't even mentioned. His continued absence stung Lizzie. If he cared anything at all he would surely have appeared by this time and apologised for not being able to see her before. His feelings on that first Sunday evening of July were too obvious for her to be mistaken. And yet she must have been mistaken. She must have misinterpreted his signals. Something did not add up. Something was wrong, and she couldn't fathom it out. Had he been merely stringing her along? Was he practising on the nearest girl to see

45

how she might respond to his advances? Perhaps he was. But she could have sworn...

Lizzie decided that next Wednesday when the Dandos came round she would be out. She would be out returning the compliment, visiting their house in the hope that Stanley would be at home. She had to see him; this not knowing was driving her mad. The least she deserved was an explanation. Besides, she knew Stanley well enough to be able to visit him uninvited.

Or did she? This intimacy, which had befallen them so easily, had changed everything. Somehow, it complicated accessibility to each other; accessibility they could have freely enjoyed before. Lizzie was no longer sure of her ground. But she just had to know whether he loved her.

By the time Wednesday came round again, the weather was uncomfortably hot and humid. The whole country was sweltering in the grip of an intense heat-wave. Lizzie wore a cotton shirt and light cotton skirt. Her long underskirt seemed to stick to her moist, bare legs in the heat, and she wished the day would come when cooler, shorter skirts might be considered seemly. In this sort of weather they would certainly be more comfortable. She stood talking to Gert Hudson and Ida Wassall in Cromwell Street, her hair elegantly done, while she discreetly awaited the arrival of Tom and Sarah. When she saw them she waved but, as she'd anticipated, neither Stanley nor Sylvia accompanied them. So she took her leave of Gert and Ida, and made her way to the Dando's house.

Certain that this contrived meeting would sort

things out and thus settle her mind, Lizzie strode purposefully on. As she turned into Pitfield Street, where Phyllis Fat lived, half a dozen small children were playing in the gutter, throwing stones at a passing cat. One of them was naked, the rest in rags, their faces grubby, their hair matted with filth. The street was long and narrow, with a long line of crumbling back-to-back terraced houses on each side. Chimneys leaned precariously, slates were missing from the roofs, and paint peeled from faded front doors and window frames. A few people, mostly elderly, sat on the steps of their open front doors in open-mouthed, toothless silence. In some houses the floor was dirt – no quarries, no floorboards, no linoleum. Coal was heaped under the table in those houses that had a table. Often, Eve had warned Lizzie not to venture down Pitfield Street alone, but no ill had ever befallen her. It cheered her to see the occasional house with sparkling windows bedecked with pretty curtains and a bunch of fresh flowers, and a front step conscientiously whitened at those houses where respectability defied poverty.

As she left it all behind her and walked on to Dixons Green Road, the contrast was marked. Dixons Green was where the well-to-do merchants of the town had established substantial homes. And, although there was a malthouse opposite 'The Shoulder of Mutton', it did not intrude.

Lizzie walked on, past 'The Bush Inn', an old public house with a wooden porch on the front that reminded her of a pigeon loft. Men wearing collarless shirts and braces were leaning against the wall and railings outside, drinking beer, laughing, swearing, enjoying the warm weather, and several of them whistled and hooted after her. From here you could look west and, on a clear day, see the green Clent Hills, but the humidity and stillness of the last few days made sure that the atmosphere was thick and hazy now. You could see no further than the old mine workings and pit mounds of Mudhall Colliery, grey and foreboding against the reddening sky; and the old Buffery Clay Pit at the bottom of the hill. And this scarred and barren landscape, relieved only by the tower of St. Peter's church, a hazy silhouette in distant Netherton, was overlooked by the Dandos.

As she turned into Grainger Street, Lizzie's pulse was racing. She had arrived. The Dando's home was fairly new, built only in 1903. The windows gleamed and an aspidistra sat majestically in a shining, brass pot in the centre of the front room window. They had their own gate at the top of the entry and a private back yard, too, with a garden and flowers that Sarah tended with loving care. Nervously, Lizzie tip-toed through the entry, quietly opened the gate on the right, and walked onto the foreyard. She tapped tentatively on the back door, feeling weak at the knees, wishing now she hadn't come and hoping that even though she had, Stanley would not after all be at home. After all, there was still Jesse Clancey. She could still turn her attentions to Jesse.

She waited, and was just about to turn tail and

run, when the door opened a fraction. Sylvia's flushed face appeared, bearing a sheen of perspiration.

'Lizzie!' She stepped outside and Lizzie could see that her hair was untypically ruffled. She held her stomach in to tuck her blouse into her skirt. 'What brings you here? Mother and Father have gone up to your house. Is there anything wrong, Lizzie? D'you want to come in?'

'No, no, Sylvia.' She was retreating backwards slowly down the entry. 'I ... I just thought I might see Stanley, that's all... If he's not in, it doesn't matter.'

'Our Stanley went out, Lizzie. I expect he's out with his mates for a last drink. Can I give him a message?'

Still retreating, Lizzie shook her head. 'No, it's all right, Sylvia...'

At that moment, a man appeared at Sylvia's side, and peered intently into the entry. Lizzie gasped. It was Jesse Clancey. His blond hair was tousled also, his shirt crumpled. As soon as he could make out Lizzie in the dimness of the entry, he ran his fingers through his hair to try and smarten it up.

'Oh, it's Lizzie Bishop,' he said. 'How are you, Lizzie?'

'I'm all right, Jesse, thank you.' She was bitterly disappointed to see him there. She noticed he had no shoes on.

'Good. Fancy a glass of beer with us?'

'No, Jesse... Thank you. I'd best be getting back.'

She made the conscious decision then to turn

and walk away with as much dignity as she could muster. The sound of her own footsteps seemed deafening as they echoed through the entry. Now her frustration was complete. Not only had she failed to see Stanley, and broadcast to his sister and to Jesse Clancey that she was actively seeking him, but she had also discovered that Jesse was intimately involved with Sylvia. What could he possibly see in her? He couldn't possibly be in love with her.

Lizzie felt foolish. It was evident now to even a blind man that Stanley was not interested in her. She had made a big mistake by allowing herself to be enticed by his insincere show of interest in the first place. And what did Sylvia mean by saying that Stanley was out having a *last* drink?

What if she'd been just a bit more responsive to Jesse that Sunday evening? What if she'd plucked up the courage to actually strike up a conversation with him instead of smiling coquettishly and making stupid cow eyes at him? Would he have asked her out, even though she was so much younger? Or would he still have arranged to see Sylvia? But he had not asked her, so it hardly mattered. In any case he could never really be a serious contender since his father was indirectly responsible for her own father's death. She could never justify it. And their mothers, with their insane rivalry, would never allow it anyway. Nobody would condone it. There were just too many impediments.

She climbed Buffery Road's steep incline, feeling hot, uncomfortable and miserable. She felt like crying when she arrived home, fraught and in despair. Her skin was clammy, sticky with the humidity, and she wanted to lie in a bath-tub full of cool water. She hoped that Sarah and Tom might have taken her mother to 'The Junction', so she could have some time to herself for a while, to cry, to think, to calm down, to sort out her bewilderment. But, as she opened the back door, she could hear her Uncle Tom's booming voice. She groaned inwardly, but forced a smile.

'Oh, I'm that hot,' she declared flatly, trying to hide the turmoil inside her. 'I'd give anything to stand in the cut for half an hour.'

'Where've you been?' Eve asked. 'We was wondering what had happened to you?'

Lizzie shrugged. 'I called to see Stanley.' It was a reckless admission, but she was too hot and too miserable to care. 'He wasn't in, though.' She resisted the urge to mention that Sylvia and Jesse Clancey were having an intimate evening of it.

'You won't be seeing much of our Stanley in future, Lizzie,' Tom said. 'He's took the king's shilling and signed up. I was just telling your mother as he's off to start his training tomorrow. He's got to be up at the crack of dawn to catch the train. I reckon as he'll be sent to the Cape, you know.'

The Cape? South Africa? But Stanley had mentioned nothing about joining the army.

'Or India,' Sarah suggested with a hint of discontent.

'Or India. Either road, it's one way of seein' the world. It'll mek a man of him. We'll miss him, though.'

So that was what Sylvia meant when she said

51

he'd gone out for a last drink. 'What made him decide to do that, Uncle Tom? Was it sudden?'

Tom glanced at Eve. Sarah in turn looked at him, awaiting his answer.

'Well, you know what young chaps am like, these days.'

Chapter 3

May Bradley and Joseph Asa Bishop were married on New Year's Day, 1907. Only a few guests – close family of the bride and groom, the Dandos, and Beccy and Albert Crump from next door – were invited to their new home for some liquid refreshment afterwards. Albert uttered not one word about the evils of drink, in deference to May's family, whom he did not know and had no wish to alienate, while he supped cups of tea. But, while he anxiously listened to his wife singing raucously after drinking several glasses of port, he believed it might behove him to register his avowed disapproval. So he gave her a glance conveying notice of the divine retribution about to be visited on her if she did not shut up and regain her dignity. At about midnight the newly-weds were left to enjoy their first night together, after Grenville and Ted had made an apple-pie bed for them, with biscuit crumbs liberally folded in for good measure.

So Eve and Lizzie were finally left to themselves in their little house, which had, over the years, been so crowded with family that there was barely room to move. Lizzie soon took advantage of Joe's departure by moving into the larger of the two front bedrooms. Eve reflected that as each year passed, so the population within had decreased; as each in turn left, or was taken by the good Lord, the quieter it became. No day passed, though, when Joe or May would not call to see them. Because May continued to work, Eve took on the extra task of doing their washing, for which Joe paid his mother handsomely. He was aware that the loss of his wage would hit them hard. Lizzie was the only one now earning any money at number 48, and her wage was barely enough to keep them in starch. His mother, approaching sixty, could hardly be expected to find a job, though many women her age worked. In any case, Joe vowed he would not allow her to. As far as he was concerned she'd done a lifetime's labour rearing her children and looking after a husband whom Joe, these days, was not sure had been everything that a husband should be.

May, too, was considerate. She would buy an extra couple of chops, or an extra half dozen eggs, especially for Eve and Lizzie. It pleased her to do so, since she felt closer to her mother-in-law than to her own mother. In any case she could afford it. She would pay for a quart of lamp oil from Trentham's whenever Lizzie said they needed any, and send round two plated dinners of a Sunday, to save Eve the trouble and expense of a Sunday joint.

Ted and Grenville usually called to see their

53

mother at a weekend, Grenville on a Saturday when Wolverhampton Wanderers were playing away. Ted's day was a Sunday when his shop was shut. Between them, they donated what they could to the welfare of their mother and youngest sister.

Even their kindness, however, was insufficient to maintain them in anything like a comfortable existence, and it was especially hard on Eve. Although Isaac had been nothing less than a swine in many respects he always turned his money up. Consequently, they'd always lived well, though he'd never saved; gambling and drink had devoured all his spare cash. Now, things were different. Eve thought she might be entitled to some parish relief, but the indignity of having to ask precluded her from getting it. So she struggled on, managing with what they had, with what was donated, and with what could be bought cheaply.

New clothes were out of the question. Fortunately, Eve could mend and alter the old clothes that remained in the house in abundance, cast-offs from the departed members of the family. Shoes were more of a problem, though; Lizzie wore out shoes quickly, having to walk the mile or so to and from work every day. During the summer, Eve took care of every last penny, conscious that come the winter, they would need extra coal to keep warm.

Lizzie realised she was destined to live with her mother for the foreseeable future, even when she eventually wed, and the man she married would have to accept it. Indeed, it would have to be a condition of marriage.

It surprised Lizzie that Tom Dando was so consistently kind to her mother. His Wednesday evening visits with Sarah continued with a regularity that was almost monotonous. Fridays also, on his way home from work, he would hand money to Eve and tell her it was a bit of pension from Turner's Brass Foundry. Tom's own family were all grown up and gone, with the exception of Sylvia, so he evidently felt he could afford to help Eve.

Lizzie asked her mother why it was that Tom seemed to favour her so much.

'Oh, when we was young, your Uncle Tom was sweet on me.' Her eyes smiled distantly at the recollection of it. 'In fact, when I married your father it broke his heart.'

'But they were cousins, Mother.'

'Well, that was neither here nor there, our Lizzie.' Eve folded up the newspaper she'd been reading. 'Me and your Uncle Tom was sweethearts afore ever I met your father – I was a handsome fleshed madam in them days, though I say it meself, and I had one or two nice, young men after me. Tom's two years older than me and I knew then what a lovely chap he was, even though I was only just eighteen.'

Lizzie leaned towards her mother's better ear. 'So how did you meet my father?'

'At their old Uncle Eli's funeral. Tom took me to show me off to his family. We'd been courtin' a long while. It was there as I met your father all done up in his best black suit and best bowler. Oh, our Lizzie, I only clapped eyes on him and I knew as I'd marry him. He was a lot older than me – about twenty-six at the time – but they said as how he was still a bachelor and a right one for the women, an' all. Well, when we'd gone back to their uncle's house for the wake, Isaac come a-talking to me and Tom. After a bit, Tom went to get himself another drink, and Isaac told me how lovely I looked and how as he'd love to kiss me. I remember I blushed to me roots, but there was something about him as took me fancy. After that I kept on thinking about him, even when I was with Tom. Anyroad, afore long I met him again, and I was all of a tiswas. Well, he asked me if I'd meet him one night. So I did, unbeknowns to Tom. I enjoyed meself that much I said I'd see him again and, afore I knew what'd hit me, I was in love – well and truly ... and I reckoned I could cure him of his womanising. Anyway, when I told Tom what'd been going on he was heartbroken.'

'So were they friends after that, Uncle Tom and my father? I wouldn't have been very pleased if a cousin of mine had stolen my man.'

'Well, they weren't very friendly when it first happened, our Lizzie, I can tell you, but they still worked together. They had to. Jobs was scarce in them days and they had to put up with one another, 'cause they worked as a team. But, when Tom met Sarah, they patched up their differences. Tom never forgave your father, though, for pinchin' me off him. Even the day I got married he told me as he'd always love me.'

'And did you cure my father of his womanising?'

Perhaps Eve did not catch Lizzie's question, or

pretended not to, but it struck Lizzie how convenient deafness could be at times. 'You know that lovely Coalport China tea set what's at the top of the cupboard up there? That was Tom's weddin' present to me. When I'm dead and gone it's yours, our Lizzie. But I want you to promise me now as you'll cherish it.'

''Course I promise. 'Course I'll cherish it, if it means that much to you.'

Eve nodded and remained with her thoughts for a few minutes, till she picked up her newspaper and began reading again. Lizzie smiled to herself. Evidently she was to be told nothing more. But what she'd been told did not surprise her. Often she heard Uncle Tom and her mother laughing about some incident or some person from the old days; she'd seen the glances that flashed between them, conveying some private understanding. Lizzie wondered whether her mother ever felt she'd married the wrong man. If she'd married Uncle Tom instead, she, Lizzie, would not be sitting here now, contemplating it all. Lizzie was curious how her Aunt Sarah viewed all this; since she must know about this relationship of decades ago. It was so long ago that surely it must be a joke now; regarded benignly as some folly of youth. Certainly Tom and Sarah seemed content. They'd reared a family, too.

Uncle Tom must have looked a lot like Stanley when he was young, Lizzie thought. He was dark, too, and tall, and slender as a lath. He must have been very handsome as a young man with his twinkling, blue eyes and his roguish laugh.

Lizzie's thoughts turned inevitably to Stanley. She'd heard nothing from him since he joined the army, though she knew he'd been back home for a few days when his training finished. She often thought about him, wondered whether it was because of her that he joined? Was it to get away from her? Was it because he'd started something he didn't feel inclined to finish? She hoped not; the thought of him being hurt in some skirmish of war, when he might otherwise have been at home, she could scarcely countenance. She would always feel responsible. Or was it collusion between Uncle Tom and her mother, after she had asked if it were true that cousins could marry? But she and Stanley were young; little more than children; lots of things might have happened to part them, even if they had started courting. There was nothing to say they would ever get married. So why should he have gone away?

Such thoughts plagued Lizzie from time to time. Stanley lingered in her heart, and because she could not have him she wanted him all the more. Boys were interested in her; she could tell that from the way they looked at her, but no one with Stanley's good looks. Jesse Clancey was beyond her reach anyway because he was courting Sylvia Dando, as Aunt Sarah was always at pains to remind them. Sylvia couldn't have picked a nicer chap, and Jesse couldn't have picked a nicer girl, she told them proudly every time she visited. They were a perfect couple. And with Jack Clancey talking about retirement, Jesse would take over the dairy business and eventually inherit a tidy nest-egg.

It was in June of 1907 that Jack Hardwick's standing in the community was highlighted. Jack lived next door to May and Joe, and they not only shared the privy at the top of the yard with the Hardwicks, but also the stink and the squealing of his pigs. Like Jesse Clancey, Jack was an only son, and the Hardwicks identified with the family from the dairy house, aspiring to success, too, in their own small business. Their way of going about it, after many family discussions, had been to set up Jack in their own converted front room as a butcher, a trade he'd learned well. Business had been brisk ever since the venture started and Jack was growing in confidence daily.

Another trader, Percy Collins, a stout old man with a drooping moustache, watched Jack's scheme with envy. He owned a general stores at the bottom of Hill Street. Percy had a son as well, Alfred, a core-maker at the Coneygree Foundry in Tipton, who had no interest at all in the family business. It galled Percy, therefore, to see Jack Hardwick enthusiastic in his butchery, and his own son apathetic to greengrocery.

Despite the envy, Percy had to admire the Hardwicks's enterprise and success, especially in view of the number of butchers' shops already on Kates Hill. He was content to patronise him by encouraging his wife, Nora, to buy their Sunday joint from him every week. However, each time she returned, she felt Jack had overcharged her.

One Sunday dinnertime, Percy returned home with their joint of beef, roasted to perfection as usual at Walter Wilson's bakery, after the last bread had been baked. But, on the way, Percy had called in 'The Junction' for a pint or two of ale.

'I'll just goo and tek the dog a walk afore I have me dinner, Nora,' Percy suggested.

'No, leave her be,' Nora replied curtly, prodding cabbage leaves into a pan of boiling water. 'Her's on heat. You'll have every dog for miles sniffin' after her and piddlin' up the front door. Carve the joint instead.'

So Percy took the carving knife, sharpened it and strove manfully to cut the meat. But it was so tough the knife would barely cut through it. He took the knife outside and sharpened it again on the front door step. When he returned and tried once more, he imagined the beer had sapped his strength, so didn't complain as he hacked half the joint into small bits. The remainder he left intact, having too little patience to continue. Soon Nora served up their Sunday dinners. Again Percy had difficulty cutting through his first slice of beef, and so vigorously did he try that the said slice slid off the plate and ended up in his lap, along with a potato, some cabbage and a goodly dollop of thick, brown gravy.

'Oh, Perce! For Christ's sake, what the hell yer doin'?' Nora scolded. It was another mess for her to clear up. 'Yo'm wuss than a babby.'

Percy scraped his errant dinner back onto his plate with his knife and mopped his trousers with a dishcloth, fetched from the scullery. Undaunted, he sat down and attempted to cut the beef again.

'Look at the state o' this meat, Nora. I defy

60

anybody to cut it.'

'It is a bit 'ard, I agree, Father,' Alf mumbled, chewing determinedly, encountering similar, though less spectacular, difficulty.

'Hard? I should say it's bloody hard. The damn cow as this lot come off must've been weened on sand and cement.'

'I noticed yo' had a bit o' trouble carvin' it,' Nora commented wryly, 'but I reckoned as it was the drink. The price it was it ought to be as tender as a bit o' chicken.'

'How much did he charge you for it?'

'Two an' nine.'

'How much? My God, it was dearer than bloody gold. He ought to be ashamed, that Jack bloody 'Ardwick.'

So the Collins family ate what they could and, afterwards, Percy fell asleep in his chair. He awoke some two hours later, still troubled by the irreconcilable difference between what Nora had paid for their joint and its quality. Then an idea started to take shape and Percy smiled to himself. Yes, he would do it. He would show up that Jack Hardwick for what he was – a robbing charlatan. Tomorrow dinnertime would be the perfect time, just as the workers from the brass foundries were turning out. In the scullery, he found the meat, cool now, hidden under a muslin cloth to keep the flies off, and set about carving two thick slices.

Monday dinnertime seemed a long time coming. But just before the 'bull' whistle was due to blow at the brass foundry at the top end of Cromwell Street, he donned his working boots, tied the laces and strutted down the steps of his shop, carrying the remains of the offending joint wrapped in newspaper under his arm. A black and white mongrel, which had been rooting round the allotments opposite, instantly caught a whiff of meat and trotted over to investigate, sniffing eagerly at the footpath. At that moment, the hooter blew and, in just a few seconds, a throng of people were released from the three brass foundries and sundry other establishments into Cromwell Street. Some headed towards 'The Junction', some in the other direction towards 'The Dog and Partridge' and 'The Sailor's Return'. Another dog, a cross between a Jack Russell and a Scots terrier, picked up the same scent and joined the first animal sniffing at Percy's feet. Yet another emerged panting from Granny Wassall's entry in Cromwell Street. Soon there was a whole pack of dogs yapping at Percy's heels, and his own labrador bitch escaped by jumping up onto the ledge of the lower half of the stable door and over the back wall, to join the hunt.

Most of the workers bid Percy good day, and some asked why he was accompanied by so many excited dogs. Percy was happy to tell them, so it was with great anticipation that those walking in his direction lingered at Jack Hardwick's little butcher's shop to watch the sport, gathering more dogs as they went, all crazed at the scent of the beef.

As Percy mounted the steps to the shop, the dogs tried to gain entrance with him. He kicked out to fend them off, but they interpreted it as a sort of game and were greatly encouraged to try harder. Jack Hardwick rushed round his counter to shut the door, but two of them got in and were up at the sides of bacon and the sheets of lights hanging from the walls.

Jack hated dogs. Relishing the sudden opportunity to inflict some harm on the first, the Jack Russell cross, he seized it by the scruff of its neck and hurled it outside with a kick between its back legs to help it on its way. Percy tackled a bigger animal that bore a faint resemblance to a sheep dog, but was bitten for his trouble. While this commotion was going on, Jack's mother, Amy, alerted by the barking, whining and shouting, came in from the brewhouse where she was rinsing out her bloomers, wielding a wooden maiding dolly. She had the presence of mind to grab a couple of bones, which she threw out to the dogs in the street to create a diversion.

By now, a sizeable crowd had gathered outside Jack's shop, watching with amusement as the dogs fought and snarled over the bones. Jack Hardwick, still unsettled, and fearful that they would invade his shop again, bounced out with his mother's maiding dolly and began flailing at the dogs, but it had no effect.

'This is all your bloody fault, Percy Collins,' Jack yelled angrily. 'Fancy bringin' a pack o' dogs into a butcher's shop. Yo' must want your head lookin'.'

Percy laughed. 'It ai' me what's attracted 'em, it's the mate yo' sell, Jack.'

'Well, it's good mate. It's the best.'

'It's the bloody dearest. Though these dogs

mightn't know the difference.' The animal that had some sheep dog ancestry decided that squabbling over a couple of bones was a lost cause and headed again for Percy's boots. 'See what I mean?' he said, kicking out at it.

'I doh know what yo'm on about, Percy Collins, but I wish to God as yo' and the bleedin' dogs would sling your 'ooks.'

'Listen, you. I'm on about the mate yo' sold my missus.'

'What about it?'

'What about it? I should've thought it bloody obvious.' He raised his boot, showing the sole to Jack. 'That's it, there, on the sole o' me shoe. It was that damned 'ard it was good for nothin' else.' He handed Jack the parcel he carried under his arm. 'And if yo' doh believe me, here's the rest of it. Yo' try it, and if yo' can eat it, I'll gi' yer a sack o' taters for your trouble. But yo'll need a wairter-cooled jaw.'

'There's nothin' wrong with my meat. It's the way it's roasted.'

'Then you'd best tell Walter Wilson, Jack, 'cause he roasted it in his bread oven, same as he does for a lot of folk.'

Suddenly, there was a loud collective guffaw from the workmen gathered round, but the butcher and the greengrocer, engrossed in their impassioned dispute, ignored it.

'Fancy askin' a baker to roast a joint o' beef. What the 'ell's he know about roasting beef?'

'Whether or no, I want me money back,' Percy countered. 'Yo' ought a be ashamed chargin' what yo' charged for this rubbish.'

Another cheer went up and hoots of encouragement, inciting Percy to greater things. He was evidently doing well in this argument; better than he'd anticipated.

Then someone called out from the crowd. 'Is this your dog here, Percy?'

Percy turned. The man who called him pointed to the group of baying and panting animals. The sheep dog derivative had mounted another animal and was thrusting into her wholeheartedly, his eyes glazed with determination, hell-bent on relief of some sort, if not his hunger. Percy's labrador bitch was on the receiving end of all this canine passion, and it suddenly dawned on Percy that this was why they were all cheering.

'Oh, Jesus Christ. That's all I need. Jack, lend me the dolly to part 'em, afore it's too late.'

'You must be joking,' Jack replied vindictively. 'Mother's gorra do the washin' with that.'

'Fetch us a bucket o' water, then, so's I can chuck it over 'em.'

Jack shook his head, walked back into his shop, smiling, and closed the door behind him.

Next morning, workers noticed that the sign over Jack's shop, which the day before bore the legend 'J. F. Hardwick, High Class Butcher', had been whitened out, and altered to: 'J. F. Hardmeat, Purveyor of Shoe Leather'.

Chapter 4

Old customs prevailed. Eve's abiding routine of looking after a family continued unaltered. Nothing changed, even though there was no longer a house full to worry about. Saturday night remained the start of the week, when she mixed the Sunday fruit cake after tea and put it in the oven at the side of the grate, so there was something to offer any visitor who might drop by. That in its turn meant a roaring fire, which would get the room nice and warm for bath time. They would fill the bath with hot water carried from the boiler in the brewhouse and top it up as required. The back door bolted, Lizzie would be first to bathe, but her thick hair seemed to take ages to dry after Eve washed it for her.

On Sunday, it was best clothes, and friends or family often invited round for tea; then church in the evening. Years ago, for convenience, Eve would fry up vegetables left from Sunday dinner for when the children came home from school on washing day. Nowadays she was satisfied with a cheese sandwich, by herself, and there was no need to hurry because what little there was to launder was usually finished by dinnertime. Eve always used to do her ironing on a Tuesday, but often now she could manage it on Monday afternoons if it had been a good drying day.

She had a day for cleaning the bedrooms and

scrubbing the stairs, for polishing the best furniture and the linoleum in the front room, for cleaning the windows and the front door step. On Wednesdays, the fire wasn't lit till late because that was the day the grate was blackleaded. To her credit, May still called round and did the job for her on her Wednesday afternoon off, assisted by Lizzie of late.

Eve was feeling her years and, though she was by no means old, all this housework was getting harder. The joints in her hands were becoming lumpy; when she walked any distance her legs ached, and she found herself out of breath doing tasks she would have found easy just a year or two ago. Because of a persistent thirst, she was drinking noticeably more water than she used to and visiting the privy umpteen times a day in consequence. Once or twice, too, she found herself wobbly at the knees well before meal-times. She put it down to hunger, since eating seemed always to alleviate it.

While Eve felt she was withering, she only had to look at Lizzie to see that she was blooming. She said nothing, but regretted that Lizzie should reach this state of optimum physical womanhood when she was in no position to make the most of it, for the finest looks faded over the years. The girl needed good, fashionable clothes to show herself off to best advantage; to enhance her self-esteem; as did every young woman. But financial constraints precluded it. Her other daughters, Maude and Lucy, had blossomed when the family was comparatively well off; when Isaac was earning good money; when Ted and

Grenville were bringing home a wage.

Yet the lack of money never stopped Lizzie looking her best. Although many of her clothes were old, they were always spotlessly clean and immaculately ironed. Eve made some admirable creations from old garments, and Lizzie took pleasure in wearing them. She only wished that she, too, had a similar talent, rather than none at all.

Eve silently worried about Lizzie. The girl was sensitive and easily hurt, and she wanted so much for her to meet the right man; not necessarily a rich man, but a kind and loving one. If he turned out to be comfortably off as well, then so much the better. But no Jack-the-lad who fancied his chances with other women, like Isaac. A decent, honest, ordinary sort of chap who was prepared to do an honest day's work would do nicely, so long as he would cherish Lizzie. As yet, though, there was no sign of any young man in her life; but she was young yet. Oh, Lizzie was sweet on Stanley Dando and no two ways, but his joining the army had thwarted that.

Eve could also see that her youngest daughter was not without admirers. She was most aware of it when they walked to church on a Sunday evening in summer. Not only men's heads would turn but women's, too, and Eve would feel so proud. There were one or two eligible young men at church every week who went out of their way to speak to Lizzie, but they must surely be tongue-tied or over-awed when it came to asking her out.

Not least of the admirers, Eve could see, was

Jesse Clancey. Even though he was courting Sylvia Dando he still had eyes for Lizzie. But Eve did not wish to encourage that. She did not wish to encourage it at all. It would not do for Lizzie to get mixed up with him. It would not do for Lizzie to be upset by Ezme's evil tongue. Not at any price. Sylvia Dando was fine for Jesse. Perfect, in fact. She hoped they would stay together and get married.

It was in September that Lizzie renewed her friendship with Daisy Foster, the girl she used to work with when she first left school. They met again when Lizzie went out with May and Joe one sunny, Sunday afternoon to hear the Cradley Heath Prize Band playing in Buffery Park. Seats had been specially laid out around the bandstand and they were early enough to find three together near the front. Come the interval and Lizzie stood up to stretch her legs and smooth the creases out of her best skirt, when, on the opposite side, facing her, she espied Daisy with another girl and two lads, aged about nineteen. She went across to say hello.

'You look ever so well, Daisy.'

Daisy was slender and nicely dressed in a loose-fitting green dress, and a wide straw hat adorned with flowers. Her ready smile was marred only by two slightly crossed teeth, which seemed more noticeable now, but which didn't detract from her prettiness; rather they were the imperfection that added to it.

'And so do you, Lizzie. You look lovely.'

'It's been ages.'

'I know. We should get together and have a rattle. Are you working in Dudley now?'

'At Trentham's.'

'Trentham's? Fancy. And I only work in the Market Place. Why don't you meet me one dinnertime?'

'How about Wednesday? I have Wednesday afternoons off.'

'That's my afternoon off as well. I could meet you at the Midland Café, if you like.'

Lizzie smiled, a broad smile of pleasure at re-establishing contact with her old friend. 'Yes. About ten past one? I couldn't get there before then.'

'I'll keep us a table.'

Meanwhile, the lads occupied themselves in conversation with the other girl, though Lizzie couldn't help noticing one of them. He was wickedly handsome, with sparkling blue eyes and almost black hair that was immaculately trimmed. And he kept looking up at her, trying to catch her eye with an interested smile when the other girl wasn't aware.

On the appointed day, the two girls turned up for their reunion under umbrellas, for the weather had turned. A steady drizzle all morning had been drenching everything. Market stall holders were packing everything away, loading their carts with unsold merchandise ready for the next day; for there would be few, if any, customers this dreary afternoon.

When they had let down their brollies and shook them they entered the café and took a vacant table in the window. They ordered a pot of tea, with tongue and cucumber sandwiches.

'It was such a shock to see you on Sunday,' Lizzie said, beaming, tucking a strand of hair under her hat. 'You were the last person in the world I expected to meet.'

Daisy shuffled and leaned forward expectantly. 'I know, but it was a lovely surprise. Did you say you're working at Trentham's now?'

Lizzie nodded.

'I was in Trentham's just last week. It's a wonder I didn't see you. It must've been your dinner time or somethin'. I work in the Public Benefit Boot shop. I left Chambers's Saddlery ages ago. Pullin' on the leather and stitchin' and that played havoc with me hands, I couldn't stand it. Then I found this job, and I like it. Besides, I get me shoes cheap.'

'That's handy.'

'Oh, anytime you want some new shoes cheap come and see me, Lizzie.'

'I'm desperate for some new shoes, Daisy. I'll have to come and see you... Are you courting now, then?'

'Oh, nothin' serious.' Self-consciously she wiped condensation from the window with one of her gloves.

'Oh, I bet! Is it one of those chaps you were with on Sunday?'

'Yes, the fair haired one.' Daisy peered through the patch she had cleared at passers-by trying to avoid stepping into puddles on the uneven pavement outside. 'His name's Jimmy Powell. I've been goin' with him six months now. But it's nothin' serious, honest... He's nice, but...'

'Where's he live?'

'Tividale. That was his mate, Ben, who was with us. He's a nice chap, an' all.'

'Mmm, I noticed him. He looked ever so nice, Daisy. I could've taken to him myself. He kept smiling at me, but I pretended not to notice.'

The two girls laughed easily.

Daisy said, 'Fern – that's his sweetheart – she noticed. She was ever so funny with him after you'd gone. I think she was jealous.'

'Oops! But I did nothing to egg him on.'

'You didn't have to. Looking the way you did was enough. I thought you looked smashin' in that outfit with your hair done up, an' all.'

Lizzie smiled, acknowledging the compliment. 'I've had that outfit ages. It's due to be made into dusters.'

A rickety, old waitress brought their tea and sandwiches. They thanked her and continued talking; comparing their lives since last they worked together; laughing over the meetings they had with two lads they used to see after work, and wondering what had become of them. They talked about the other girls they worked with, and chuckled when they recounted the escapades with men they'd bragged about. They wanted to know about each other's families; about births, deaths, marriages. There was such a lot to catch up on. It was two pots of tea later that the girls emerged from the Midland Café, still laughing.

'You'll have to come to tea one Sunday, Daisy. Mother would love to see you.'

'That'd be nice.'

'What about a week on Sunday? You could

bring your sweetheart, if you wanted to. Mother wouldn't mind. She wouldn't mind at all.'

Daisy smiled. 'All right then.'

Eve was indeed pleased to learn that Daisy Foster and her young man were coming to tea. It would be a nice change to entertain somebody different.

'I wish I could have a new frock,' Lizzie said. 'I can never wear that outfit again.'

'I wish you could, as well,' Eve replied, having caught every word and understanding Lizzie's frustration. 'I'll see if I can make you something new for then. Perhaps May's got something as I can alter.'

'There's a frock in me wardrobe I never wear, Lizzie,' May said, stirring her tea as she sat at the scrubbed table. 'Have it with pleasure if you want it.'

Lizzie smiled. 'Ooh, May, thanks. Can I see it after?'

''Course. If you like it, bring it back with you.'

'I could do with a new coat, as well, Mother,' she said with a plea in her eyes. 'I've got some money saved. Enough to buy a new coat. Can I?'

Eve agreed. Tomorrow, in her dinnertime, Lizzie would happily scour the town for a new coat. Meanwhile, there was May's discarded frock to inspect.

It turned out to be less than a year old and quite fashionable. May was a size bigger than Lizzie, especially around the bust, but with a couple of darts in the waist, some remodelling of the bodice and turning the hem up a couple of

73

inches, it would be ideal. Lizzie thanked May and the two girls took it back to show Eve. At once they had to have a fitting, so Lizzie divested herself of her working clothes and put on the new dress. Eve reached up and took her pincushion from the mantelpiece and started putting a few pins in here and there, where she needed to alter it.

'This is a beautiful frock, May,' Eve commented. 'How come you've never worn it?'

'After I'd bought it Joe said he didn't like it,' May replied.

'Our Lizzie, it'll look a treat on you.'

'Good. I can hardly wait for next Sunday to wear it.'

The dairy house, where the Clanceys lived, was a large detached house with no foregarden, but set well back from the footpath. A cobbled yard lay at the rear, accessed from the street by an entry broad enough to drive a horse and cart through with ease. On one side of the yard was a row of brick-built outbuildings, one of which was a stillroom for making butter, the rest for stabling the horses and garaging the carts. On the other side was the door to the scullery. Behind the brewhouse stood the privy, the 'miskin' where they deposited all their rubbish and a hen coop. When Jack Clancey first started up his business he kept cows in the field at the back of the house to provide the milk for his business. A picket fence and gate separated it from the yard. These days, because home-produced milk was unreliable, only the two horses grazed it now,

74

accompanied occasionally by an odd vagrant hen in search of extra food.

In the front room, standing in the square bay window looking out over Cromwell Street, was Jesse Clancey. An hour earlier he'd watched Lizzie Bishop, in all her Sunday finery, walk towards Hill Street with another girl and a young man, no doubt heading for Oakham Road and a stroll through the meadows beyond. He was hoping they would return by the same route so he could catch sight of her again. Every time he saw the girl she looked more and more bewitching. Today she wore a cream dress with pale green trimmings, narrow skirted, and high neck collar, under a cream three-quarter length coat. She looked so beautiful, her hair swept up on top of her head in the pompadour style and crowned with a fashionable cream wide-brimmed hat topped with pink roses.

If only there were some way of making Lizzie interested in him he would give up Sylvia Dando. Oh, Sylvia was a nice enough girl, and she'd make somebody a good wife, but not him. Sylvia was the same as all the others; somehow she failed, like all the others, to spark off any excitement in him, physical or mental; and for him to even consider marriage there had to be some glimmer of passion, of yearning for her, of yearning to be with her. But he did not yearn for Sylvia. He'd courted her for many months now and they'd progressed beyond canoodling, and still he didn't yearn for her. But he did yearn for this little Lizzie Bishop, Sylvia's second cousin. Perhaps it was because she was unattainable;

because she might think he was too old at twenty-six; because their respective mothers had always been at odds. At least, that was what he assumed; he did not know it for certain.

But in any case, what would her mother think if he were to suddenly start walking out with her, little more than a child at seventeen? Like everyone else, she would no doubt consider the age gap unseemly; she would accuse him of cradle-snatching. Yet all he wanted was to love her and for her to return his love. He wanted to marry her, to be the father of her children, and provide her with a decent standard of living; a standard of living befitting a girl so worthy.

Lizzie Bishop was becoming an obsession. She was the only reason he still went to church, albeit accompanied these days by Sylvia. And who would credit it? Who would believe that he could be longing for this Lizzie Bishop, whom he had watched grow up from a skinny little kid to this vision of femininity? Who would believe it, when he had a pretty girl like Sylvia on his arm, who evidently thought the world of him?

The problem was that there was never an occasion when he might meet Lizzie Bishop to tell her how he felt, or to ask her if she would like to step out with him. Even if there were, would she listen? If only he could find some way of making his feelings known before somebody else claimed her, for somebody surely would, and soon. Otherwise, how could she ever know how he felt? And, knowing, she might even respond positively...

All at once his pulse rate quickened. Lizzie

came into view again with her two companions, strolling leisurely towards the dairy house. The other girl was holding the lad's arm proprietarily. Jesse stood back a step out of the bay to avoid being seen, and watched from behind the huge aspidistra as Lizzie conversed intently with her friends, her eyes lighting up her lovely face which was vibrant with expression. He could hardly fail to notice her feminine curves contrasted against the darker lining of her open coat, the gentle swell of her breasts giving way to her rib-cage, to her flat stomach. He could hardly fail to notice her small waist; the youthful slenderness of her hips; the way she held her head; the way she walked. This yearning was turning, irrevocably turning, into an intolerable ache.

Then, the very antithesis of Lizzie appeared from the opposite direction. It was Phyllis Fat. He watched as they met and talked.

'...and the new vicar said as it'd have to be the Sunday after,' Phyllis was saying. She was telling Lizzie that she was getting married because she'd missed three months in a row.

'Who are you marrying then, Phyllis? Is it somebody we know?'

'I don't think so. It's a chap as works with me, name Hartwell Dabbs.'

'I haven't heard the banns read out in church. But yours'll be the second wedding I've heard about this week.'

'Oh. Who was the first, then?'

'Jack Hardmeat, the butcher, of all folks. He's getting married next month. Nobody knew he was even courting.'

'Jack 'Ardmate? And who'll be the third, d'you think? They say as everything comes in threes.'

Daisy cast a hopeful glance at Jimmy.

But Lizzie nodded towards the dairy house and all eyes followed. 'Jesse Clancey, for a guess. My Aunt Sarah says it won't be long before him and our Sylvia are wed.'

Chapter 5

Jesse Clancey knew enough of Lizzie Bishop's comings and goings to know that most Wednesdays she finished work at one o'clock. So, this last Wednesday of September he decided to do likewise. He'd delivered his empty milk churns, all rinsed out and clean, to the railway station for return to the farm that supplied them, and waited in the road known as Waddam's Pool, hoping to catch her as she walked home. She should be passing him in ten or fifteen minutes, assuming she stopped to gaze into a few shop windows on the way.

The day was overcast and chilly. The best of the summer had long gone. All they had to look forward to was a dubious October, with more dense fogs to herald the bleak winter. While he waited, Jesse debated with Urchin, his big, dappled grey horse, yet again, the wisdom and the folly of this ploy. He'd been preoccupied with thoughts of how best to approach Lizzie these last few days, till he was sick of thinking about it and the only way to get some relief, and some sleep, was to actually tell her how he felt. She might turn him down flat but, at least, he'd have tried. If he never tried he would never know what his chances were.

'I'm old enough to know better,' he muttered dejectedly, confiding in the horse. 'I could end up looking a proper fool – she's little more than a child.' Even if Lizzie fell over herself to accept him he could hardly expect the emotions of one so young to remain serious and constant. It was a major concern. 'If some fresh-faced, handsome, young lad came along I doubt she'd be able to resist him; and where would that leave me?'

The horse, sensing his unease, nodded as if in agreement and fidgeted, scraping his huge hooves uneasily on the cobbles. Jesse's confidence drained away as this train of thought persisted, and so did his resolve. He rested his back against the side of his milk float, loosely holding the reins, contemplating his stupidity and feeling strangely conspicuous to the world, as if the world was listening and could hear his thoughts.

There was no point to all this. He would make a move and return home.

Then, in that same moment, he saw Lizzie Bishop walking towards him with Joe Bishop's young wife. The sight of her smiling eyes immediately revived his spirits and rekindled his ardour. 'By Christ, she's here, mate.' He slapped the horse's flank affectionately. 'And looking as pretty as a picture. Damn it, let's have a go, eh?

I'll try me luck after all, what d'you say, old mate? If I end up looking a fool forever, so what? If I never try, I'll never win her.'

So he waited till the two girls reached him.

'Morning, Mrs Bishop. Morning, Lizzie,' he acknowledged nervously, touching his cap.

Lizzie returned the greeting and, anticipating no further conversation with Jesse, was about to walk on.

But May stopped to pass the time of day. 'You mean good afternoon, Mister Clancey,' she said with a hint of good humoured sarcasm. 'Mornin' passed above an hour ago.'

'You're right, you know.' He took out his fob watch and glanced at it briefly. 'You lose all track of time on this job, And I'd be obliged if you'd call me Jesse, Mrs Bishop. Everybody else does.'

'If you promise to call me May, instead of Mrs Bishop... Mr Clancey.'

He felt the tension slough off him like a skin when the girls laughed, and he smiled openly. 'Sounds fair enough to me. Look, I'm on my way home. Can I give you both a lift?'

'Yes, if you like, Jesse. Better to wear out the horse's shoes, eh, Lizzie?'

'If it's no trouble.'

'No trouble at all.' He mounted the float and took the reins. 'Seems a shame to walk when I'm passing your front doors.'

This was fine as far as it went, but Jesse had not reckoned on May Bishop's presence. It occurred to him, though, how much more difficult his task might be if she were not there. This at least was a start.

The two girls raised their skirts a little to step up onto the two wheeled float. 'Giddup!' Jesse called, and flicked the reins, causing Lizzie and May to lurch slightly as the *ensemble* pitched forward. They stood each side of him clutching the sides of the cart with one hand, their baskets with the other. He remained silent for a few seconds, looking straight ahead, desperately trying to devise some way of leaving May at her front door but keeping Lizzie on his float.

'How's our Sylvia, Jesse?' Lizzie enquired. She had put down her basket and was holding onto her hat to prevent the wind taking it.

'Sylvia? Oh, not too bad ... I suppose.'

His lack of enthusiasm prompted May to turn down the corners of her mouth as a signal of surprise to Lizzie. 'Any sign of you getting wed yet?' She hoped he might give more away.

'Huh! None at all. If I said it was serious between us I'd be telling a lie.'

'Oh, you do surprise me, Jesse. Her mother's already got you married off and no two ways. That's right, ain't it, Lizzie?'

'To hear her talk it's all cut and dried.'

Jesse shook his head. 'She shouldn't take too much for granted.'

The horse clopped on, steadily pulling the cart up the hill, its big grey head swaying rhythmically from side to side. Lizzie's thoughts turned inevitably to the Clanceys' horse that killed her father. This wasn't the same one, she knew, but there was a bizarre irony in that its replacement was now drawing her home as if that incident five and a half years ago had never

81

happened. She felt like mentioning it, but maybe it was best left unsaid.

Jesse's comments came as a shock to Lizzie. She'd always believed that Sylvia and he were devoted. 'I'm surprised as well, Jesse,' she said chattily. 'I was only saying to some of my friends the other day as I expected you to be getting wed after Jack Hardmeat.'

'You know who he's marrying?' he said.

'No. We never even knew he was courting.'

'He's marrying Annie Soap's youngest daughter, Maria. The one with the black hair.'

'The one they call the Black Maria?' Lizzie asked.

Jesse chuckled. 'That's her. I don't know if they've got to get wed, but it all seems a bit sudden.' He turned to May. 'You must be about due to start a family, hadn't you, May? You've been wed, what?... Nearly a year now, is it?'

May whooped with amusement at his candour. 'Well I reckon everybody must think it's about time, Jesse, but believe me, there's no sign yet. Anyroad, there's no rush. I'm only twenty-two, you know.'

''Course. You're only a babby yourself yet, May.'

They travelled on in silence for a while, into St John's Road. By Ivy Morris's fish and chip shop they turned into Brown Street, where most of Kates Hill's shops were. Lizzie quietly studied Jesse. He seemed more handsome each time she saw him. He was always well groomed, clean, and he always wore a clean collar and a necktie, even for work. His eyes revealed such a look of

82

sincerity in their blue grey sparkle, and she still couldn't help thinking how different things might have been. She knew she shouldn't, because of Sylvia, but she couldn't help this admiration she still had for Jesse. No, it was more than just admiration; it was a hankering. She felt a warm pleasure, a sense of awe, being in his company so unexpectedly, and was strangely gratified when she noticed him glancing at her from time to time. Yet he seemed tense, despite his easy conversation.

As they turned into Cromwell Street, they saw some activity in one of the shops. During the day it had been gutted.

'Iky's opening a fish and chip shop now,' Jesse explained. 'It'll be handy, eh?'

Iky Bottlebrush's real name was Isaac Knott, but he'd been given his nickname years ago. For years he'd owned the shop, a small grocery, but had provided plated hot dinners for the workers at the brass foundries and the other little factories in the immediate streets. Venturing into fish and chips seemed a logical progression, and everybody wished him well, since he was well liked.

Jesse called the horse to a halt outside Lizzie's home. The two girls thanked him for the lift and turned to step down. Jesse braced himself, about to suggest that Lizzie stay on the float so he could talk to her. He could say he needed her advice on what to buy Sylvia for her birthday present. He said: 'May, I wonder if you'd mind...'

'No need to mention it, Jesse,' May said, interrupting him as she and Lizzie stepped

83

down. 'I'll not breathe a word to a soul. Nor will Lizzie. Will you, Lizzie?' Lizzie shook her head. 'Give Sylvia our love, just the same. We don't see much of her these days. Not since you've been courting her, keeping her so busy. Why don't you and Sylvia come and visit us, Jesse? Bring her round for supper one of the nights. Joe would like that.'

'Eh?... Oh, I will.' He sighed with frustration. It must be God's will. He must accept that Lizzie Bishop would never be his, and perhaps be thankful for it. Fate was preventing a liaison; and fate had prevented him making a fool of himself in the nick of time. How could he reasonably expect Lizzie to have anything to do with him when he was Sylvia's sweetheart? They were a close family and no decent girl would stoop that low. In any case, any girl who would steal her own cousin's man was not the sort he wanted. It was thus an impossible situation; if this girl, whom he yearned for so much, was prepared to take him under those circumstances, he ought not to want her for having him.

'Cheerio then,' he called and flicked the reins once more. As the horse moved on, Jesse turned and waved, and the two girls stood, waving back, smiling graciously. 'There. I told you I was a bloody fool,' he muttered to the horse, who responded with a turbulent emission of wind.

May chuckled as they walked into the entry. 'That Jesse needs a dose of liquid paraffin.'

'May!' Lizzie admonished with a snigger. 'It was the horse.'

'Let's hope and pray as it was... But fancy that

84

Jesse not being interested in marrying Sylvia, eh?'

'It's a bit of shock.'

'Not half as much of a shock to us as it'll be to Sarah. God, there'll be hell to pay.'

'He might not say anything, May. He might just go along with it – for years.'

They opened the door and went in the house. Eve was sitting in her usual chair, but she was pale, her eyes were rolling, and she seemed to be fighting for breath. Lizzie was at once alarmed.

'Mother, Mother, what's up?' She went straight to her and felt her forehead.

Eve was sweating, but her skin felt cold and clammy. She looked up at her daughter. 'Thank God you'm back,' she said wearily. 'Oh, I'm that hungry, our Lizzie, but I didn't want to start me dinner till you got back.'

'Sit there nice and quiet, Mother. May and me can put the sandwiches up. Have a biscuit to keep you going.' Lizzie went to the cupboard at the side of the fire grate and took out the biscuit barrel. She opened it and put it in her mother's lap.

'The sandwiches am already done, our Lizzie,' Eve remarked. 'They'm under a cloth on the shelf at the top of the cellar steps.'

May brought them to the table.

'D'you think I ought to send for the doctor, May?'

'It'll do no harm.' May cast a glance at Eve who was tucking into her meal ravenously. 'Is she often like this?'

'Lately she says she starts to get weak just before mealtimes. She eats like a horse, yet I'm

85

certain she's losing weight. And drink? All the time she's drinking water.'

'It don't sound right, Lizzie. We'd best fetch the doctor. I'll get Joe to fetch him tonight after he's had his tea.'

'I'll go and fetch him myself when I've had my dinner.'

'No, leave it till tonight... I should... From what I can hear of Donald Clark you won't catch him at his surgery yet awhile. He'll be in "The Shoulder of Mutton" having his dinner. You know he likes a drink.'

That afternoon Eve seemed to improve, though she had little of her usual energy. The two girls blackleaded the grate as usual and, when they lit the fire, the first thing Eve requested was that the kettle be put on to boil for a pot of tea. Lizzie scrutinised her mother carefully for other signs that she was unwell. It was not till then that she noticed how often she was getting up to go to the privy.

It was at about eight o'clock that evening when Joe returned to his mother's house with young Dr. Donald Clark, who had recently taken over his father's practice. Donald was twenty-seven and a likeable young man. He wasn't especially handsome, but neither was he repulsive. He had wavy, reddish hair, a ruddy complexion and a substantial nose. There was a gap between his two front teeth, which, when he smiled, seemed to enhance his affability. As they rode together to the Bishop's house on the ancient dog cart that old Doctor Clark had always used, Joe anxiously described Eve's symptoms. Donald knew the family well, and Eve had fed him often enough when he and Ted were pals. He was thus concerned about her, and eager to help.

After the pleasantries, Donald took out his stethoscope.

Without being asked, Eve undid the top buttons of her frock. 'Should I strip off?'

'No need, Mrs Bishop,' Donald replied. 'I just want to listen to your heartbeat.' He slid the end of his stethoscope over her chest while he listened. 'Mmm ... sound as a bell... Now I want to smell your breath.' He put his nose near Eve's mouth and she breathed self-consciously into his face. 'Mmm... Tell me, Mrs Bishop, how you've been feeling ... the sort of things that have been happening recently that don't seem normal.'

Lizzie had to repeat the question for her.

'I'm feelin' tired all the while, Donald,' Eve answered. 'And every half hour I'm havin' to make water.'

'Are you having to do that in the middle of the night, too?'

'Two or three times a night. I'm sick of emptying the slops of a morning.'

'Are your bowels loose?'

'Me bones loose?'

'No, your bowels. Have you been constipated?'

'Oh ... yes ... terrible.'

'Anything else?'

'I get that weak with hunger, Donald. I tell you, I could eat a man off his hoss. And I could drink a marl hole dry, I'm that thirsty.'

He turned to Lizzie. 'Anything else, Lizzie? You

live with your mother. Have you noticed anything?'

'Only that she eats well, but I think she's losing weight.'

He rubbed his chin. 'Losing a bit of weight wouldn't do her any harm under normal circumstances, but to me it's a symptom of her illness.'

'What d'you think's up with her, then, Donald,' Joe asked.

Donald sighed and took the stethoscope from around his neck, folded it and put it in his bag. He looked at Joe, then at Lizzie. 'Her symptoms are consistent with diabetes.'

'Diabetes?' Lizzie said. 'I've heard of it.'

'All we know is that it's a disease that affects the way the body uses sugars and, to a lesser degree, fats. The problem's caused by a little thing in the belly called the pancreas gland. The disease causes certain of its cells to degenerate so that it can't cope with sugar and so the body passes the sugar out through the kidneys in the urine.'

'So what's the cure?'

'There is no cure, Lizzie.'

'No cure?'

'Having said that, if I'm right in my diagnosis, I believe we can control it so that your mother can lead a near normal life. First, I need to double check, of course. I need a sample of her water and a sample of her blood.'

Donald's words were going round and round in Lizzie's head in a jumbled whirl. They did not add up to good news. A near normal life? A disease? The pancreas gland? No cure?

'What's it mean, Doctor? Will mother be an invalid for the rest of her life?'

Donald saw the anxiety in her eyes and was concerned to put her mind at ease. 'No, it doesn't necessarily mean that, Lizzie. We've caught it just in time, I think. It's a good thing you sent for me when you did, because she would've become rapidly worse. In another week or two your mother might have slipped into a coma and that would have been a different kettle of fish. What it does mean is that your mother's got to have a very strict dietary regime. That's the only way of treating this disease in the long term. But if she sticks to it, God willing she should be able to lead a fairly normal life. That means no sugar in tea, no cakes, puddings, sweets or chocolate. This has to be done carefully though, because we still have to maintain some level of sugar in the blood.'

He paused a moment, evidently deep in thought, his fingers stroking his chin again.

'That's the standard treatment,' he went on, 'but I'd very much like to try something different. To my medical brain it seems more logical to try and starve her for a few days until her water is free of sugar, then to build up her dietary with fat and protein. I should warn you though, that this isn't the recognised way of doing it. It's never been tried officially to my knowledge, but I'm absolutely certain it would give us much quicker and more positive results. I'd like your permission to embark on that course of treatment before I do, of course.'

Joe said, 'But if it's never been tried how do you

know it'll work, Donald? You might do her more harm than good.'

'I've studied this disease as closely as anybody, Joe. I wrote a thesis at university on Diabetes Mellitus – its full name – and I've since had a paper published on it. When I was training I treated people in hospital who had the condition and, strangely, the one who fared best was a woman who couldn't take food. Only in the last ten years or so have we really begun to understand diabetes, but the more we understand it, the better our treatments get. And knowing what I know, I'd stake my doctorate that starving her for a few days would work.'

'I trust your judgement, Donald,' Joe said solemnly. 'You must know more about it than most doctors, so we have to be thankful for that. As far as I'm concerned do what you think's best. What d'you say, Lizzie?'

'You seem to know what you're talking about, Doctor. If you think it'll get Mother better quicker, I reckon you should do it.'

Donald smiled. 'Good. Now, I'm going to ask her to give me that urine sample. Then I'll explain it all to her.'

So Eve was put to bed and Lizzie took time off work to look after her. Donald Clark's diagnosis proved to be correct and his new method of treating her worked remarkably well. In consequence, the improvement, he was certain, was far more rapid than it might otherwise have been. Within a few days she was allowed to get up, and her new diet, although severely

90

restricted, stabilised her condition. It required some new thinking on Lizzie's part. She had to ask herself every time whether or not she had put sugar in her mother's tea, and usually tasted it just to make certain she had not; Eve's intake of fat was restricted and it seemed such a pity to have to deprive her of dripping, butter or fried bread; or fried anything, come to that; almost everything she enjoyed.

Donald Clark's success treating Eve's illness drew increasing esteem from everyone; always useful for a new doctor, but particularly so for him since he was being decried already because of his growing reputation for liking a drink. The whole neighbourhood soon got to know about his miraculous treatment. Only a few years earlier, patients suffering from the sugar sickness were fortunate to survive, because doctors did not understand it. Donald refused all payment for his treatment too. It was, he claimed, experimental, so how could he possibly charge for research work that was helping him as much as it was helping Eve?

In the run up to Christmas, Phyllis Fat married her Hartwell Dabbs, and Jack 'Ardmate, née Hardwick, wedded Maria Soap, née Hudson. Eve improved sufficiently for Lizzie Bishop to return to work and Lizzie regularly saw Daisy Foster thereafter. She was even introduced to the handsome, blue eyed, black-haired lad called Ben, and there was no doubt that Lizzie really fancied him. Fern, Ben's sweetheart, saw ever more reason to be jealous of Lizzie, since it was obvious that he in turn fancied Lizzie.

After their last meeting, which was at the Opera House, where they had splashed out and booked sixpenny circle seats to see Vesta Tilley, Lizzie was somewhat concerned about the effect Ben was having on her. He only had to smile at her and she would blush and feel her stomach turn over. But there was no point in dwelling on him because of Fern, who seemed a respectable girl and obviously idolised him. But as the days turned into weeks, Lizzie realised she was thinking more and more about this Ben, and even found herself talking about him to May.

Meanwhile, Eve's improvement continued apace.

Christmas came and went, bringing bitter cold and frosts. The usual procession of visitors called to see Eve. Her other daughter, Lucy, with her husband, Jimmy Sharpe came down from Stockport and stayed till Boxing Day. May and Joe invited Eve and Lizzie and Lucy and Jimmy to have their Christmas dinners with them, which they did, and they all spent the afternoon and evening pleasantly together.

On returning to work the day after Boxing Day, Lizzie was surprised to see Daisy Foster enter Trentham's shop, dressed up for the weather.

Daisy said, yes, she'd enjoyed Christmas, thank you. 'And guess what?'

'What?'

'Me and Jimmy are thinking of getting engaged.'

'No!... Honest?'

'Honest.'

'I thought you said it wasn't serious, Daisy.'

'It wasn't. But it's getting to be.' Daisy smiled contentedly.

'Lucky you! Oh, congratulations. I'm ever so pleased for you.'

'But that's not why I'm here. I'm here on a special request, nothing to do with that.'

'Oh?'

'You know Ben, Jimmy's mate? He's sent me with a message. He wants to know if you'd like to go out with him.'

Lizzie's eyes lit up, then she put her hands to her face in disbelief and delight. 'Honest, Daisy? You're not pulling my leg?'

'Honest. He asked Jimmy to ask me to ask you.'

'But what about Fern?'

'Fern? Him and Fern have fell out.'

'If they've fell out, I'd love to go out with him. When, though?'

'Well, he was talking about New Year's Eve. I think the idea was for the four of us to go to a New Year's Eve ball.'

'Then he must've finished with Fern if he wants to see me on New Year's Eve,' Lizzie reasoned.

'What shall we tell him then? We have to let him know.'

'I don't know, Daisy,' she said ruefully. 'I can't go out New Year's Eve... Damn... May and Joe are having a party. It's their wedding anniversary and they're expecting me...'

'Oh, shame.' Daisy looked genuinely disappointed.

'Hang on, though. I'll ask May if it's all right for

you and Jimmy, and Ben can come as well. D'you think that'd be all right? Would you like to come, Daisy?'

'I don't mind. I'm sure Jimmy wouldn't mind either. Nor Ben.'

'Hang on then.' Lizzie went to the back of the shop where May was sorting out a fresh stock of candles. 'May?'

May turned to Lizzie. 'What's up, my wench? You look as if you've lost a sovereign and found sixpence.'

'May, you know that chap Ben I've been telling you about?'

'Yes.

'He wants to go out with me on New Year's Eve ... but I've said I can't, 'cause of going to your party...'

'So?'

'Well he wants me to go out with him and Daisy and Jimmy as well.'

'Four of you together?'

'Yes. So, I was wondering if they could come to your party instead...'

'So's you don't miss the chance of seeing him, you mean?'

'Well ... yes.'

May smiled knowingly. ''Course they can come. The more the merrier. Just tell 'em to bring a bottle or two o' beer. It'll be nice to have some young faces among all the old fogies. Anyroad, I want to get a good look at this Ben.'

Lizzie's face lit up. 'Oh, thanks, May... Thanks... If I can do you a favour some time...'

'I daresay the time will come.'

She returned to Daisy beaming. 'May says they'd love to see you.'

Lizzie tried not to raise her hopes too high though. After all, look what happened with Stanley Dando.

Chapter 6

By New Year's Eve, a Tuesday, the weather had become settled. A clear, blue sky afforded bright sunshine during the day, but promised a hard frost that night. Eve and Lizzie visited Joe's house early to help prepare sandwiches and get everything ready for the party. May lit a fire in the front room and cursed when smoke blew back down the chimney, making her eyes run.

'I should think Father bloody Christmas is still stuck up the blasted chimney,' she complained, shoving a strand of hair from her eyes with the back of her coal-blackened hand.

'I doubt whether it's ever been swept while the Dowtys lived here,' Eve commented.

Joe had ordered a firkin of best home-brewed bitter from 'The Shoulder of Mutton' and it was standing chocked up on the scullery table with a pudding basin under the tap to catch the drips. There were four bottles of whisky, a bottle of gin and two bottles of port to offer as well, besides a gallon of lemonade.

Lizzie awaited Ben's arrival excitedly. She hardly knew him. They'd never had a conversation without somebody else being there. But the way he smiled at her, and the honesty and candour brimming in eyes that sparkled whenever he saw her, churned her stomach with longing.

He duly arrived with Daisy Foster and Jimmy Powell shortly after half past eight. Their faces were glowing from their brisk walk in the bitter cold, but they were dressed warmly in good overcoats, hats and gloves. Lizzie introduced them to Joe and he made them welcome. He took their hats and coats and offered them drinks, which Lizzie was happy to serve in the front room as they settled round the fire. Then she, Daisy, Jimmy and Ben, all sat in a group, squashed up together occupying one half of the sofa and an adjacent armchair.

'It was nice of you to invite us,' Daisy said to May and Joe equally. She shuffled to get comfortable on the armchair she was sharing with Jimmy.

'The more the merrier,' Joe quipped. 'Where've you had to come from?'

It was Ben who answered. 'Tividale. It isn't far, but it's all uphill. Here, Joe... Do you smoke?'

'Oh, thanks... How long's it took you to get here?'

Ben tapped the end of his cigarette on the packet. 'About twenty minutes. It warms you up a treat, though, on a night like this. There's a tidy frost.'

Lizzie thought Ben looked wonderful. He wore a dark grey suit with a waistcoat, a maroon and blue necktie, and a white shirt with an immaculate, starched collar. His black hair looked even blacker now it had been greased and sleekly brushed and his eyes danced with the reflected light from the oil lamps and candles. He was clean shaven with a clear complexion and his features were fine and masculine. He was possibly the most handsome man she'd ever seen, even more handsome than Stanley Dando, or Jesse Clancey. He was about six feet tall and lean, but with broad shoulders; a picture of vigorous health, and Lizzie couldn't take her eyes off him. She felt flutters in the pit of her stomach at the prospect of being alone with him. Being in the same room now, but not able to speak or act freely was immensely frustrating. She wanted to manoeuvre herself closer so she could touch him, so he could touch her, either by accident or by design. She wanted to catch the scent of him; see his eyes crease at the corners from close-to when he smiled. And she wondered if he felt the same about her.

He did. He wanted to tell her how lovely she looked in the cream dress with the pale green trimmings. He admired everything about her, not just her looks, but the easy way she seemed to have with people; and, best of all, there was no side on her – she didn't pretend to be something she wasn't. For ages he'd wanted to ask her out, but with Fern always at his side it had been impossible.

'Lizzie says it's your wedding anniversary,' Daisy was saying to May.

May linked her arm through Joe's and glanced up at him affectionately. 'Twelve months to-morrow.'

97

'And it only seems like twelve years,' Joe chipped in and took a playful slap on the arm for his trouble. He drew on his cigarette and smiled impishly. 'And afore anybody asks – no, there's ne'er a babby on the way – but it ain't for the want o' tryin'.'

May hit him again, while the men guffawed. 'You'm gettin' engaged an' all, aren't you, Daisy?' she enquired, desperate to avoid any more embarrassing comments.

Daisy nodded and looked at Jimmy admiringly. 'We'm thinking about it, eh?'

'Maybe next year,' Jimmy confirmed.

'Any plans yet to get married?'

The couple looked at each other again and grinned self-consciously. 'Not for a couple of years at least. We want to save up and get some money round us.'

'That's good sense, Jimmy,' Joe proclaimed. 'You can't argue with that. What d'you do for a living, mate?'

'I'm a moulder at a foundry in Tividale – Holcrofts.'

'I know of Holcrofts.'

'Ben works there as well. He charges the cupola.'

'The money good?'

'It's all right. We got plenty work, an' all, eh, Ben?'

'Plenty,' Ben agreed. 'But I want to come off charging. I'm keen to be a ladle man. It's hard, specially in the summer when it's hot, but the pay's better. A lot better.'

Ben was enquiring about Joe's work when they

heard a knock at the back door. It was Tom Dando and Sarah. Sarah came in complaining about the cold. Sylvia would be coming soon with Jesse, she said, when she'd spent half an hour with Ezme and Jack.

'Help yourselves to drink,' Joe invited.

Five minutes later Eliza and Ned Bradley arrived, May's mother and father. They made a fuss of Eve and asked how she was.

'By Christ, it's cold enough for a walking stick,' Ned quipped, warming his hands in front of the fire. 'It's icy already. I reckon I'll be sliding round on me arse all the way 'um.'

'Like a fairy on a gob o' lard,' May suggested.

While Eliza and Ned made themselves known to the folk they hadn't met before and supped their first drinks, Beccy and Albert Crump arrived. Joe asked what they wanted to drink.

'A glass o' port for me, please, Joe,' Beccy said, rubbing her cold hands.

'Lemonade if you've got it,' Albert requested defiantly.

'Oh, have a beer, you miserable old sod – God forgive me for me language,' Beccy said, casting her eyes upwards. 'It's New Year, Albert. Yo' can't not have a drink.'

'Give me a shandy, then, Joe. Anything to save me being nagged to death.'

Sylvia and Jesse arrived. They greeted everyone pleasantly and Jesse gave Lizzie a wink that she thought no more of, but which suggested lots to Ben. Lizzie smiled and introduced her friends. By now the house was crowded and buzzing with chatter and not all the guests had arrived yet.

Somebody called for Joe to play his new piano – his pride and joy – and he said he would in a minute.

'Jesse, fetch your mother to come and play this new piano of Joe's,' Albert Crump tactlessly called, his half pint of shandy barely touched. 'We can't wait forever for him here.'

Ezme and Jack of course had not been invited; Joe knew how much the woman antagonised his mother. Meanwhile, Daisy and Jimmy had got their heads together and Sylvia and Jesse had moved on.

Ben took a close look at the gold cross and chain Lizzie was wearing, fingering it gently. 'A Christmas present?'

'Off Joe and May.'

'I had a pair of cufflinks – off Fern. Here, look, I'm wearing them.' He pulled back the sleeve of his jacket.

'Did she give them to you before or after you fell out?'

'Before, else I wouldn't have took them, would I? I did offer them back.'

'What did you fall out about?' She'd been dying to ask.

'You wouldn't believe me if I told you.'

'Oh, go on.' Her eyes flashed with anticipation. 'Tell me.'

He emptied his glass and threw the end of his cigarette into the fire. 'It was over you.'

'Me?'

'She kept on as I fancied you and accused me of seeing you on our nights off. We had a blazing row and in the finish I said I might as well play

100

the part I'd been cast in.' He smiled at her expectantly. 'I'll get another drink, like Joe said. Shall I get you one, Lizzie?'

'Please. I'll come with you, if you like.'

To get out of the smoke-filled room through the middle door into the scullery they had to push past Tom Dando, laughing at Beccy Crump's irreverent cursing. Eve was in the scullery sitting at the table, as if guarding the beer, still wearing her white apron over her best black frock. She was talking to Sarah, with Sylvia and Jesse standing by.

''Scuse me,' Ben said, sidling into position past him to get to the beer barrel.

'Oh, Lizzie, I forgot to mention ... our Stanley's coming home in May or June,' Sylvia said casually, looking Ben up and down with evident approval.

Lizzie considered that Sylvia's comment was unnecessarily mischievous in the circumstances and she felt her colour rise. 'Well, give him my best wishes, 'cause I don't suppose I'll see him. I think he was avoiding me before he went away.'

'Oh, I don't think so, Lizzie. He's got no reason to avoid you. You two were always the best of friends.'

Lizzie was aware of Jesse's eyes burning into her, which was unsettling. She passed her glass to Ben and he filled it from the large stone bottle of lemonade, and handed it back. 'Thanks, Ben,' she said with a smile, then sipped her drink.

Sylvia said, 'Joe and May must be doing well to get the house in such fine order... And to have so many lovely things about them. Especially the new piano... And they've only been married a year, Jesse.'

'I know,' Jesse replied with indifference.

Lizzie was certain that the next thing to come from Sylvia's lips would be her own expectations of life when she married. In anticipation, Lizzie glanced at Jesse and reckoned he was thinking the same.

'With the pair of 'em workin' they can do it,' Aunt Sarah chimed. 'There's no reason why you and Jesse shouldn't do the same when you'm wed.'

'I'll wait till I'm asked, Mother,' Sylvia replied stiffly. 'And perhaps you shouldn't presume anything till I have been.' She flashed a withering look at Jesse.

Jesse coughed, shuffled his feet and ran his hand across his moustache with unease. He avoided Sylvia's glance, swigging the last drops of beer from his glass. Lizzie sensed the tension between them. This was obviously a sticking point; a matter of contention they'd touched on before, but not yet resolved.

Lizzie had no desire to witness an open argument on the subject when she already knew Jesse's feelings. Maybe it was time she made herself scarce. The last thing she wanted was to have to take sides. 'It's so smoky in here,' she exclaimed. 'I think I'll go outside for some fresh air.'

Ben put his glass of beer on the table, glad of the opportunity to accompany her.

But Jesse sensed his intention. 'Here, Ben. Fill this glass for me, will you. You're nearer the barrel than I am.'

Obligingly, Ben took the glass and began to fill it.

It bothered Jesse to witness what he believed was Lizzie's attempt to entice Ben outside. But his own hands were tied. He could do nothing with Sylvia at his side. He could do nothing without revealing his true desires and, in any case, he had more respect for Sylvia's feelings than to do so openly. But since there was this unexpected competition he ought to do something to combat Ben's apparent claim and stake his own at last, because he'd been unable to erase this slip of a girl from his thoughts. It was time to tell her how he felt. Perhaps it was even too late.

'I could do with using the privy,' Jesse remarked, in an attempt to slip his leash, and moved to follow Lizzie.

'It's the top of the yard, Jesse,' May said. 'Past Jack Hardwick's pig-sty. Take an oil-lamp with you.'

'It's all right, May, I'll find my way.' He barged past Sylvia, opened the door and went out.

'Well mind you don't mistake the pig sty for it and piddle on the pigs. It'll chap their skins vile this weather.'

He closed the door behind him. He had beaten Ben outside, but he could hear the others chuckling at May's remark. Why did she have to say anything at all? It only drew attention to him. Now he felt even more conspicuous having left at such a sensitive moment. He hoped his real intentions did not look obvious. But he'd acted on a split second impulse, less inhibited because of the alcohol, driven by this urgent need to tell Lizzie how he felt before his rival established himself, and to hell now with the consequences.

The moon was surrounded by a broad, silver halo of air frost. It shone over the back of the brewhouse, lighting the yard up more brightly than any oil-lamp could. The frost on the roofs of Grove Street beyond reflected it back through a million tiny, shimmering crystals. There was no sign of Lizzie, so he stepped down the entry and into the street. He scanned left and right and saw her slender figure silhouetted against the gas lamp opposite the brass foundry, her hands behind her back, her head down. When she heard his footsteps she turned towards him, smiling radiantly, believing it to be Ben.

'Lizzie. I've got to talk to you.'

'Jesse!'

From 'The Sailor's Return' they could already hear singing. They watched a middle-aged man, walking from the opposite direction, open the door to the pub and enter. Jesse turned and looked over his shoulder to ensure neither Sylvia nor Ben had followed.

'Look, Lizzie, I've got to talk to you.'

'To me? What about?'

'About Sylvia. I'm not in love with her.'

'You as good as said so before. Ages ago.' She turned to see if Ben was seeking her yet.

'I know I did. Trouble is, I believe she thinks a lot of me.'

'She does. And for what it's worth, I don't think you'll ever find anybody better.'

'Well that depends, Lizzie. One person's idea of

perfection ain't necessarily another's... Here, let's move away from the lamp. I feel as if the world's watching.'

They moved a few yards further on to where the terrace was staggered and the recess would conceal them from view. But Lizzie was reluctant in case Ben couldn't find her. She shivered. The bitterly cold night air seemed to penetrate through to her bones, and the gold studs in her ears were so cold that they made her lobes hurt. She wished she'd thought to put on her coat. At least she would be able to turn the collar up.

'Well it isn't really fair to let her keep thinking I'm in love with her, is it?'

'I agree. Doesn't she know yet how you really feel?'

'Well yes and no, Lizzie. We've talked about marriage, and I've told her I'm not ready for it yet. But I did tell her once as I loved her, that's the trouble. That was in the beginning, and to tell the truth I believed it myself at the time. Not now, though. It was a mistake to say it and I admit it. But how could I tell her after as it was a lie?'

'But she'll have to know sooner or later,' Lizzie said and shivered.

'I know that, Lizzie... Sooner, I reckon... You see, there's somebody else.'

'Oh, Jesse. You mean you're going with somebody besides Sylvia?'

'No, no. I mean there's somebody else I want. Somebody else I'm in love with. I'm not seeing her ... yet.'

'Oh. So are you giving Sylvia up then, for this other girl?'

'Well that's my intention. If it all works out.'

'It'll break her heart, you know, Jesse.'

Lizzie was surprised at the ease with which she was talking with him. Throughout her life till this minute she'd never spoken more than a dozen words at a time to him. The obvious differences in age and gender, and their mothers' senseless feud, had always conspired to create this unfortunate forbiddance, in her mind at any rate. But already she was engrossed in his personal life, pleased that he should consider her worldly enough to confess to. Whatever advice he asked for she would give it, impartially, and gladly. He was out of her own emotional reach now, anyway.

The sound of Joe now playing his new piano drifted out, and the accompanying singing drowned the revelry from 'The Sailor's Return'. Lizzie's teeth began to chatter.

Jesse sighed with desperation. 'Lizzie, I can't go on as I have been denying myself to spare Sylvia's feelings. I swear, you'll never believe just how hard it's been. I've got this … this longing for this girl and it's driving me mad.'

Lizzie thought how sad and intense his face looked in the half-light. She saw his eyes fill up, and his sincerity moved her. She began to understand the agony he was going through. 'Does she know, Jesse?' she asked intently. 'Does this other girl know you feel like this?'

He shook his head. 'I've never had the courage to tell her. I've always been afeared she'd turn me down.'

'Then it's time you said something. If you don't, how will you ever know whether you've got

106

a chance?... So who is she? If you want to tell me, that is.'

He bent down and picked up a stone, then immediately tossed it back into the horse road as he fought with his indecision. He had to tell Lizzie; he had to confess his love; and it had to be now, or the moment would be lost forever.

'It's you, Lizzie,' he said, turning to look into her eyes for her reaction. 'It's you. Nobody else. You're the one I want.'

Lizzie mentally gasped, not knowing what to say. Strangely she could feel the cold no more; rather, she felt hot. It was very flattering, but this was attention she could have done without. It was attention she had not sought, even though she had secretly desired it. It instantly evoked all sorts of images in her mind, some logical, some outlandish; images she would never have dreamed of two minutes ago; images of Jesse caressing her; of Sylvia heartbroken and fraught with distress; of her own mother chiding her because of the inevitable battle over who would make the best wedding dress; of Aunt Sarah chasing her with a big stick and calling her a scarlet woman.

But what could she say? If things had been different he might even now be courting her, and Ben would never even have entered the frame. But with Sylvia so in love with him it would complicate things too much; her conscience would not allow it. Even though she liked Jesse well enough.

But now there was Ben to consider. She had set her heart on Ben and she was as driven to him as the birds in the trees were driven to build nests and lay eggs. Nobody else would do. Not now.

Jesse seemed to sense her dilemma. 'Before you say anything, Lizzie, I want you to understand that I realise there's a big difference in our ages – I know you're only young. I've thought about that – but I don't think it matters much. If it doesn't matter to you, it certainly doesn't matter to me.'

Lizzie gulped. This news had come as a great shock, and Jesse had no idea how much of a shock. Already he was going too fast.

'I don't know what to say, Jesse. I'm that flattered. Really I am ... to think as you see me like that. But I couldn't be responsible for breaking our Sylvia's heart. And surely you couldn't expect me to? I could never live with myself if I had that on my conscience.'

'I think I realise that. But at least I've come out into the open with it. I had to. It's been driving me mad.'

'But I couldn't be what you want me to be without hurting our Sylvia.'

He turned away and shrugged his shoulders, and she heard his deep, heart-felt sigh. 'So what d'you reckon I should do, Lizzie? Carry on and marry her? Even though I don't love her? Should I sacrifice myself for the sake of her feelings? Should I ruin my own life so as not spoil hers?'

The biting cold seized her again. She put her hands to her shoulders, huddling herself to generate some warmth. She ought to go back indoors now – back to Ben, and all the fun – back to where all the laughter was – back to the warmth of the roaring fire. Ben would wonder what had happened to her. Any minute now he was bound to come looking. If he saw her with Jesse he would jump to the wrong conclusion, and that would be the end of that – another romance finished before it even started.

But it was not easy to turn her back on such potent admiration, when she had admired Jesse so much.

'No, I don't think you should wed Sylvia just because she expects it, Jesse. That'd be stupid. I think a couple should both want the same, otherwise there's no point in them marrying. You'll just have to tell her.'

'But what about you, Lizzie? Would you consider taking me after I'd given up Sylvia? After a respectable time, I mean. After a month or so. I can wait. Then they could lay no blame on you.'

She avoided his eyes as the magnitude of his design struck her. 'I hardly know you, Jesse. And even if I said yes, I should still know deep inside as it was me that caused our Sylvia to suffer. And what would her family think of me when they got to know that I'd taken her place?'

'Maybe you worry too much about what other folk might say, Lizzie. That's the trouble with everybody these days. It's always what everybody else might think as dictates what anybody does. Look, Lizzie, I'm in love with you... And I don't think you dislike me either...'

She didn't answer. She thought better of encouraging him; of confessing that she'd always held a sneaking desire for him. He was presentable and decent. He was devastatingly handsome, his family were prosperous and his prospects were significantly better than most men's. Of course she liked him. She had drooled over him. What girl wouldn't?

He said, 'D'you want to think about it? I imagine it's come as a bit of a surprise.'

'Oh it's come as a surprise all right, but what's the point thinking about it? I do like you, Jesse. I've always liked you. If only you knew! But Sylvia makes it impossible.'

'So if I'd asked you to start courting afore I asked Sylvia, would you have said yes?'

'Yes.' She shivered again. 'Of course I would... Gladly.'

He smiled ruefully at the wicked irony of it. 'And I wouldn't ask you 'cause I thought you were too young and your mother might not like it.'

'I suppose she'd have got used to it. But I don't think yours would have liked it. I don't think your mother's particularly fond of me, or my mother... I hear she thinks a lot of Sylvia, though.'

'What my old lady thinks is neither here nor there. I've got my own life to lead.'

'I'm sorry, Jesse. I am really. But in any case I've started seeing Ben now. It wouldn't be fair on him, would it?' It was an exaggeration of the truth, but in her desire now to extricate herself honourably, and without hurting his fragile feelings too much, she felt justified in saying it. And Jesse could not prove otherwise.

He shrugged, having to accept what she said. Yet somehow he felt better. The knowledge that he could have had her if he'd asked, and the relief of finally confessing the feelings he'd been bottling up for months, somehow lifted him. There might still be a chance.

Suddenly he reached for her, and his arms embraced her, clutching her to him. At once the heat from his body started to penetrate her own clothes, bringing warm relief from the biting cold, enough to keep her there for a second or two longer. His arms around her shoulders caused her to shiver, and she looked up at him with clear, shining eyes, half admonishing for his audacity, half grateful for those few moments of protective warmth when she needed it. But as soon as he saw her face upturned, his lips were on hers, urgently tasting her, savouring their accommodating softness, fulfilling a longing he'd harboured for so long. She allowed him to linger, not knowing whether to resist or to wring as much enjoyment from it as she could. But the immediate pleasure of his kiss outweighed her inclination to resist. She felt him growing in confidence at her unwitting responsiveness, tensing his grip around her waist with a passionate squeeze. She had often wondered how his lips, his big moustache, would feel if ever he kissed her. Now she knew. It was a rewarding experience. Her own arms went inside his jacket, to his waistcoat and around his waist, as if they had been long time lovers. It felt so warm in there and she was so cold. And his kisses were so gentle, so comfortable, so delectable.

'Say you'll be mine, Lizzie. I need you. Say you'll be mine.'

She sighed. 'Oh, I would've done, Jesse. I would've done. But how can I now? It's just impossible. You know it's impossible.'

'Nothing's impossible if you want it bad enough.'

She paused, looking into his disappointed eyes. 'I'm sorry, Jesse... I shouldn't have let you kiss me like that. It was naughty of me.'

'You didn't seem to dislike it.'

'I didn't say I disliked it,' she said quietly.

Neither spoke for long seconds. He knew without any doubt in those moments that he had failed to win her. Deep down he had always known he could never win her. She was beyond his reach; always had been.

'If you ever change your mind'

'If I ever change my mind you'll be the first to know.'

'Promise?'

'I promise.'

He hugged her again and they remained holding each other; the warmth of his body detaining Lizzie longer still; much longer than it ought.

'Do me a favour, Lizzie,' he said. 'Don't breathe a word of this to a soul, for fear of it getting back. I intend to finish with Sylvia, but I want her to hear it from me, no one else.'

'I won't breathe a word, Jesse, I promise. I'd better go back in now. I'm froze to death.'

'Go on, else you'll catch your death. I'll be back in a minute. Sylvia thinks I've gone up the yard.'

'Sylvia thought you'd gone up the yard,' a woman's voice said.

112

They both turned. There was no mistaking that tall, willowy frame even in the darkness. Sylvia's face was in shadow, the street lamp behind her, and they could not see the stony contempt in her eyes. Her tone of voice, however, was cold as frozen marble, and her diction, so prim and correct these days, lent it a colder edge, even frostier than the weather. Lizzie and Jesse instantly, guiltily let go of each other. They looked at her, then at each other. It was exactly the sort of confrontation neither wanted. They wondered how much she'd heard; but however much, she had seen them embrace, perhaps even witnessed their lingering kiss.

'So this is what's been going on behind my back, is it? This is why you only want to see me three nights a week, is it, Jesse Clancey?'

'Nothing's been going on behind your back, Sylvia.'

'It doesn't seem like it. Well, our Lizzie, you can have him and welcome, and I hope to God as I never see either of you again as long as I live.' She burst into tears and fished in the pocket of her coat for a handkerchief. 'I'm disgusted at you, Lizzie, I really am. But I shouldn't be surprised, should I? Not the way I've seen you looking at him.' She wiped her eyes. 'And to think you're leading that other poor lad on in there as well. You really ought to be ashamed of yourself. Why, you're no better than a common harlot ... and everybody thinks butter wouldn't melt in your mouth.'

Lizzie was annoyed at this slur on her innocence. Till now she'd hung her head in sheer

113

embarrassment at being caught in this compromising situation. But why should she feel guilty? She had nothing to hide. It was all innocent enough from her own point of view; yet she understood how it must have looked to Sylvia. So she tempered her pique.

Sylvia turned to go.

'Sylvia, no matter what it looked like, we were just standing here talking...'

'Yes, in each other's arms. And I heard what you were saying.' Sylvia turned to face her again with increasing scorn. 'I heard him tell you to keep it quiet in case I found out.' Although she tensed with vehement anger and frustration, her emotions were surprisingly well under control.

'For Christ's sake, Sylvia,' Jesse said. 'You've got this all wrong. You've got nothing at all to blame Lizzie for. She was trying to protect you.'

'Protect me? Holding you like that? Protect me from what? Do you think I'm completely stupid?'

'Lizzie, you'd best get back inside as you were about to. Leave me and Sylvia to sort this out between us. She might as well know the rest of it.'

'I don't want to hear anything from either of you,' Sylvia said, contemptuous of being scolded like a disobedient child. 'My eyes have never deceived me yet.'

'Well, whether you want to hear or no, you're going to listen. You can either listen here, or you can listen while I walk you back home, 'cause there's no way you're going back into Joe's house till I've told you the truth.'

Lizzie was about to wish them a happy new year as she walked away, but stopped herself;

neither the moment, nor the sentiment were appropriate.

'Lizzie!' Sylvia called icily. 'Be sure that after this I shall get my own back. If it takes the rest of my life I'll get my revenge. No woman steals my man and gets away with it.'

'Sylvia, I haven't stolen your man. I haven't even tried.'

She turned and hurried away, never more glad to be out of an awkward situation. The noise as she passed by the window drowned out any conversation Jesse and Sylvia were now having. Joe was playing 'Roll out the Barrel', and most of the guests were singing along to it. Lizzie realised that Sylvia couldn't have heard very much of what Jesse had said, from that distance at any rate. But seeing her in his arms was enough.

Back in the house Lizzie shuddered as the warm air enveloped her, displacing the cold. She headed straight for the fire and held her cold hands over it, still reeling from the encounter.

'Every time that door opens the damned cold wafts in,' Eve complained to Sarah. 'We might as well be sittin' up the yard in the privy as sittin' here. Me belly's roasted like a bit o' brisket, and me back's like ice. It serves me barbarous.'

While she stood by the fire Lizzie didn't know which experience was having the most profound effect on her: Jesse Clancey's confession; his scrumptious kisses; or Sylvia's cold hostility. None should have come as any great surprise. She recalled how Jesse always used to ogle her and smile; and Sylvia had shown signs of resentment then, come to think of it. After her

115

little outburst tonight, though, Lizzie decided she wouldn't be troubled any more at the thought of going out with Jesse. She resented Sylvia's accusations to the point where she would welcome the chance to get her own back. If her name was going to be blackened it might as well be justified. Yet she knew she would not do it, not even out of revenge. She couldn't, for she was not of a vindictive nature; and deep down she understood Sylvia's possessiveness.

'Lizzie. You're back.' It was Ben, standing at her side. She had not noticed him as she gazed into the fire immersed in her thoughts. 'I went to look for you.'

She smiled at him absently, politely, as though it were the first time she had ever caught sight of him. Then she strove to shake off the fetters of preoccupation. 'Hello, Ben,' she said, her eyes wide, happier now, relieved he hadn't spotted her with Jesse. 'I'm sorry if I've been a while.'

'Are you all right? Shall I get you a drink?'

'I should already have one somewhere. You poured me some lemonade before I went out, didn't you? I think I fancy something stronger now though. Something to warm me up a bit.'

'I'll get you a glass of port, eh?'

The piano playing and the singing stopped, and Lizzie heard Joe calling May to fetch the Hardwicks. She acknowledged him and duly disappeared through the back door. Eve and Sarah both shivered again and flashed looks of cold discontent at each other, and it was Sarah who finally suggested that they take up occupation of the front room where there was

116

only the draught under the front door to contend with; somebody would be gentleman enough to offer them a seat. So there was a temporary disruption and rustling of long skirts while they shifted. Meanwhile Joe played on. Amidst the laughing and the general chatter they heard a solitary voice rise, singing a song called, *'I Wouldn't Leave My Little Wooden Hut for You'*. It was Beccy Crump who, when she'd had a drink or two, was noted for her uninhibited renditions of it and other songs.

Lizzie, warmer now, sat down on the bottom stair next to the grate, and Ben, bearing her a glass of port and his own pint of beer, joined her. She took the port and sipped it, savouring its intensity as it slid down her throat. The back door opened and she looked up with apprehension, expecting to see Sylvia and Jesse, but it was May returned with Jack and Maria Hardwick and Jack's father and mother. May issued them drinks and they, too, disappeared into the front room, with Maria heavily pregnant, laughing, pretending to conduct the music as they went.

'When you went outside I was intending to come with you,' Ben commented when they were alone again. He lit a cigarette and exhaled a cloud of smoke. 'When I couldn't find you I came back inside.'

'Sorry,' Lizzie replied. 'I wish you had found me in time.'

'Why? What's up, Lizzie?'

'Oh, I'll tell you later, when I've stopped shivering.'

'Look, I fancy a walk outside myself. When

you've warmed up a bit shall we go out for five or ten minutes? Then you can tell me what's up.'

'It's bitter cold out there, Ben. I don't mind, though – as long as I'm wrapped up warm next time.' The idea of being alone with Ben on this cold night was starting to appeal again, not just to get away from the atmosphere that was bound to prevail if Jesse and Sylvia returned.

Beccy Crump reached the end of her song and predictably commenced singing, '*When Father Papered the Parlour*'. Lizzie turned and smiled at Ben.

'He fancies you, Lizzie – that Jesse,' Ben remarked trenchantly and drew on his cigarette.

'Oh? D'you think so?' She was hardly thrilled to be reminded of it after the trouble it had caused.

'Judging by the way he was looking at you earlier, and the way he followed you outside. D'you fancy him?'

'I suppose I do,' she said, teasing him with the truth, but absolving herself because she could not lie easily. 'I always used to, anyway.'

'Don't you think he's a bit old for you?'

'Not at all... Oh, Ben, don't let's talk about Jesse.'

'Why? Has he upset you? Tell me what's up.'

She looked around. If Jesse and Sylvia walked in now, or even just the one of them, she would want the floor to open up and swallow her.

'Let's go for that walk now and I'll tell you. Not in here where other folks can hear.'

Ben looked at the clock on the mantelpiece. It wanted twenty-five minutes to eleven.

'Don't forget your hat and coat this time, then,'

he said, reaching his own from the back of the cellar door. 'I'll wait for you outside.'

A group of people entered 'The Sailor's Return', all done up in their best clothes, and another group left. Ben could hear Joe playing his piano and it sounded as though everybody in the room was singing their hearts out. He looked up at the north sky, cloudless, clear, and drew on his cigarette. His mind was full of Lizzie. Daisy had assured him Lizzie had no romantic attachment, and whenever he'd seen her out she was never with a lad; but what was happening with this Jesse? Should he back off for fear of upsetting some other arrangement? He would be loath to do so. Before all this he thought he had a chance. Now he was confused.

Ben liked things clear cut. He liked to know where he was going long before he got there. There was no ambiguity in his own mind as to the likely outcome of a liaison with Lizzie; nor in his feelings once he was on a given course. He was straightforward and everything had to be above board. He was forthright and if he had anything to say he said it. He was not one for skirting round a problem when he could meet it head on. Neither was he one for flannelling; what he said, he meant.

He heard Lizzie's footsteps in the entry and turned to see her emerge in her pale coloured coat, her collar turned up to keep out the cold. The street lamp thirty yards away picked out her fine features and he thought she looked so beautiful, yet so preoccupied. He remembered the way Jesse had been looking at her; it was hardly surprising; how could he reasonably expect this girl to have no other admirers? They must surely be falling over each other in the rush.

'Which way should we go?' he asked.

'Uphill's best.' Lizzie clutched the collar of her coat to her neck.

'Go on, then. Tell me what's upset you.'

She made no response at first, searching for an appropriate way to begin.

'Tell me what it was, Lizzie. I like things out in the open. I'm not one for secrets and bottling things up.'

Another couple walked towards them. They said nothing more till they'd bid them season's greetings and gone past.

Then she told him the truth, exactly as it happened. She told him precisely what Jesse had said, and her response, almost word for word. She told him how utterly surprised she was to learn how he felt about her, and assured Ben that she'd never ever tried to lure him away from Sylvia. She told him how they fell unpremeditated into each others' arms. She told him how Sylvia found them thus and totally misjudged the situation, expressing her concern that such a mistake, however it looked to Sylvia, could open up a needless rift between the two families. But she did not tell him Jesse had kissed her, nor how much she'd enjoyed it.

They turned the corner at 'The Junction'. A latch squeaked and clattered, then a door banged and a man wearing a cloth cap and white muffler stumbled out onto the footpath, the worse for drink. There was raucous laughter from within, and somebody played the first few chords of *'Wait till the Sun Shines, Nellie'*, on an accordion. It seemed that the whole world was partying. Singing began as they crossed the street by Percy Collins's shop.

'Do you believe me, Ben?' Lizzie asked intently. This evening had promised so much, but so far it had yielded nothing but trouble. She prayed he would believe her.

'Yes, I believe you, Lizzie.'

'That's a blessing. Especially since I told Jesse I was already seeing you regular. That was presuming a bit, I know. Do you forgive me?'

'Forgive you? I'd like to start seeing you regular anyway, Lizzie. You're my sort of girl.'

Lizzie smiled, barely able to conceal her elation. 'I'd like that, Ben,' she said softly. 'I barely know you, though. What if we don't get on?'

'I'm willing to take a chance if you are. I'm willing to bet as we'd get on like house a-fire.' As he spoke he felt for her gloved hand at her side. It startled her when he held it. 'Would I be able to trust you, though, with that Jesse about?'

She smiled. 'Oh, Ben. If we're going to start courting, I can promise you that.'

They walked on in silence for a while, hand in hand, enjoying the moment, turning to smile at each other every few seconds, squeezing each other's fingers. Lizzie felt warm now from the glow within her, and she felt the tension of her previous encounter with Jesse drain away. Neither the bitter cold, nor the frost crunching beneath her frozen feet, could overcome the

121

warmth of this joy and relief.

'It was five and twenty to eleven when we come out,' Ben said at last. 'Perhaps we'd better get back.'

'No, not yet. Let's just walk to the top of the hill. We'll be able to see for miles from there, it's so clear. It's not far.'

Presently they reached the top of Hill Street where the road levelled out. They crossed to the other side and found themselves overlooking a steep embankment. Allotments and an array of rotting old sheds lay immediately below, and a little further away the head gear and buildings of the old Springfield Pit. Beyond that was a vast industrial plain sweeping before them to the north and north east; a landscape randomly pock-marked with quarries and slag heaps.

The light from the moon and the stars enabled them to see much more than they might on any other night; even features of the terrain. Lights twinkled as far as the eye could see, and the red glow of furnaces and ironworks in the distance, still toiling on this festive night, bloomed and faded according to their mode of activity. Products of all descriptions, from all sorts of materials, for practically every purpose under the sun, were being manufactured within sight, even tonight, for the use of mankind the world over.

From this vantage point Lizzie and Ben overlooked Tipton, West Bromwich, Oldbury and Smethwick; a massive expanse of factories. Countless red brick chimney stacks bristled up, spewing out endless columns of grey smoke that were visible even now. The dark, skeletal structures of the pit headgear of scores of collieries against the frosted landscape were no relief from the tedious acres of dismal pit banks and cheerless slate roofs, shimmering now with frost as the moonlight glinted off them. During the day the wind had cleared the dust and smoke from the atmosphere; now they could see for miles.

'It's so still up here,' Ben remarked. 'Listen. You can actually hear the sounds from the factories in the distance.'

They listened intently. It was true. Here and there they heard the sibilant clang of metal against metal as a furnace was charged, the thrum, permanently embedded in the air, of a thousand steam engines, the far-off thuds of forging hammers, intermittent and barely discernible; but it was there; all the industrial sounds ever created by man were there, like a distant abstract symphony, in the silence.

Lizzie snuggled up to Ben as if she had known him years, and he put his arms around her. But it was not the same as when Jesse had embraced her. This was easier. There was no guilt. She did not have to consider Sylvia. She did not have to consider Fern. She did not have to consider anybody, except Ben and herself. She could melt into his arms with utter contentment. No one was about to break in on them and mar their comfortable intimacy. There seemed to be such peace between them. It was such luxury.

'Look at the stars,' she whispered. 'I've never seen so many stars.'

'Lizzie?' She looked into his eyes. 'I want to ask you something?'

'What?'

'Can I kiss you? I've been dying to kiss you.'

'But Ben... What would you think of me if I let you?'

'No less than I already do. If we're gunna see each other regular then we'll end up kissing sooner or later.'

'And if I let you kiss me you won't think I'm cheap?'

'Cheap? 'Course not. I already know you're decent and respectable.'

He planted a kiss gently on her cheek, as soft as a butterfly landing on a blossom, lingering for a second. Then his lips slowly brushed across her face, moving inexorably to her mouth. She did not resist; rather she waited excitedly, her lips sensually parted; ready for him. It seemed like an age, but in a few seconds she felt his mouth on hers, soft, searching, hungry for contact. Inevitably she compared it to Jesse's kiss: it was different because Ben had no moustache, but it was no less pleasant. But with this kiss she could respond whole-heartedly; wring full pleasure from it. She felt her skin running with warmth. It was so pleasant she thought it must be utterly wicked, and broke off, panting a little, feeling guilty after all, her breath hot in the cold, night air.

'Oh, Ben,' she sighed. But she wanted to experience him more; much, much more. He made her toes curl; he sent tingles up and down her spine. Kissing him was far too pleasant to avoid.

He drew her closer. When he felt no resistance

he searched for her lips again and found them waiting for him as if she was expecting it. For the first time ever he felt her body against him, and he ran his hands down the back of her coat to better appreciate her slenderness, while his lips enjoyed the taste of her.

Lizzie's pulse raced and her mind raced with it. She sensed an unforeseen reaction deep, deep within her, ruthlessly churning up her emotions, tearing anarchically at her very soul, like nothing she had ever known before. Parts of her seemed to come alive that she never expected could, longing to be touched, longing to be caressed, and it was a revelation. Her breathing came faster, because these new, sudden sensations were exhilarating, tearing her breath away; her legs were like jelly; her head seemed to spin.

It was some minutes before she became acclimatised to all this delight. She broke off casually, reluctantly, to get her breath back and muster her thoughts. She rested her head on Ben's shoulder. Would it always be like this? Could it always be like this? Then, strangely, just for a moment, she really noticed the cold, infinitely more intense than before; foreboding; almost like a signal; penetrating through to her very bones. She shivered. He sensed it and he squeezed her affectionately, protectively, rubbing his cheek against her lush brown hair. And the awful, ominous chill seemed to disappear once more.

'I've been dying to do that for ages,' Ben whispered. 'I've often wondered what it'd be like, kissing you.'

'I've wondered the same about you, Ben, but I don't suppose you'll believe it.'

'Oh, Lizzie, I'd like to believe it. I want to believe it.'

'It's true... I swear it's true.'

He held her a while longer, savouring the emotions, savouring this other unworldly atmosphere.

'Come on,' he said at last. 'We'd better get back. They'll wonder where we've got to.'

'Oh, let 'em wonder. Come on. Let's carry on with our walk. As long as we're back before midnight so you can let the new year in for us...'

Chapter 7

January saw Ben Kite and Lizzie Bishop meeting three or four times a week when he was not working the night shift. Even when the weather was too inclement to venture out Ben would make the uphill trek from Tividale to Kates Hill and spend the evening at Cromwell Street with Lizzie, content with a lingering, goodnight kiss at the back door before he returned home. To be alone they would take a stroll, either through Oakham's quiet lanes, or into the town where they could gaze into shop windows and weave their dreams.

Eve took to Ben at once. She would have no qualms if things progressed to marriage; he was all she had hoped for in a son-in-law.

And Ben was eager to show off his lovely new sweetheart to his mother and his brothers. So one cold, crisp night, when snow was lying a couple of inches thick, he persuaded Lizzie to walk with him to Tividale to meet them. He had four brothers, but on this first visit she met only two, since the other two were married and lived elsewhere. Ben's mother, Charlotte, pale, thin and withdrawn, had sought solace in Methodism. His father was the reason.

'I can remember even when I was a babby, Lizzie, how my father used to come home blind drunk of a night,' Ben told her as they sauntered hand-in-hand past the old brick works, towards Kates Hill. 'He used to set about me and my brothers, and then our mother. Mother always had a black eye in those days. He served her barbarous. We hated the sight of him... Still do... If I thought I was going to turn out like him, I'd do away with myself. By the time he came back home of a Friday night, all his money had gone on drink and betting. Mother seldom had any money to feed us and we'd never got backsides in our trousers, nor soles on our shoes. If it hadn't been for other Methodists my mother knew, and our Cedric and David bringing some money in, we'd have starved. I got no respect for him. No respect at all.'

'It must be terrible to have no respect for your father.' Lizzie's breath hung like mist.

'It is, I agree. But, as I see it, being a father don't entitle you to respect. Respect's something you have to earn – even your own father has to earn it. Mine never earned any respect from anybody – not even his workmates – least of all from us lads. He's nothing but a pig, Lizzie.'

'Thank goodness you're nothing like him.' She put her arms around his waist and squeezed him warmly. 'If I ever see you getting like him, I'll remind you what you said.'

'There's no fear of it, Lizzie.'

'I think I know that already, Ben,' she said softly, all her love in her eyes. 'I think you're too considerate to be like your father.'

'Despite him, or because of him, I understand the difference between right and wrong – between good and bad. I can see what makes folk happy, and I can see how some folk can make others unhappy besides, as if there's a sort of sadistic pleasure to be gleaned from it. It generally all stems from drink, you know, like it does with him. Not that I'm against drink, Lizzie – I like a drink myself.'

'There's no harm in having a drink. It's when folks get proper drunk ... all the time.'

'What about your own father, Lizzie. Did he drink?'

'Like a fish. He liked a drink more than anybody, but at least he never knocked our mother about... And he always turned his money up. Mind you, I've found out, since I've been older, that he was fond of women. Rumours maybe, I don't know for sure. But even our Joe thinks he had one or two other women in his time. I loved him dearly though. He was always kind to me, and to the others, as far as I know.'

'Does your mother know he had other women?'

'She's never said as much. Not to me at any

rate. Either way, it never stopped her being a good wife.'

'It's amazing how tolerant some women can be.'

'Daft, more like. I don't think I'd be as tolerant, Ben. I'm sure I wouldn't. I'd be a suffragette.'

They walked on in silence for a few moments, the snow underfoot crisp with frost.

'What do you think of the suffragettes?' Lizzie enquired. 'D'you agree with what they're doing?'

'No, I don't. But I agree with what they stand for – the right for women to vote and all that – there's nothing wrong with that. But I don't agree with the way they're going about it. The more outrageous the things they do, the more they alienate ordinary, decent folk.'

'You'll have to talk to May about Mrs Pankhurst, Ben. May thinks Mrs Pankhurst's a saint.'

'Mrs Pankhurst's a bloody fool, Lizzie. Women would get the vote a lot sooner if she shut up. Women are denied the vote now out of defiance for the way she and her cronies carry on.'

'Well, I think she's a brave woman. May says the only reason women won't get the vote yet is because the Liberals would lose too many votes to Labour. Campbell-Bannerman would be out of office.'

'Oh, I wouldn't argue with that. It's obvious as the Liberals would lose out. Labour supports the suffragettes, and most women would vote Labour. But it'd be Lord help us if that damn fool Keir Hardie ever got to be prime minister.'

Lizzie then had a *précis* of the life of Keir Hardie. The way Ben argued it she agreed with him that somebody less radical might be the best choice for Britain.

They reached the back door of 48 Cromwell Street, and Lizzie let her mother know she was home. They stood for five minutes at the top of the entry whispering to each other and giggling, punctuating their words with kisses. But the bitter cold precipitated Ben's departure sooner than either would have preferred.

Lizzie was in love. Ben was never out of her thoughts, and seldom out of her conversation. It was like the time when she was infatuated with Stanley Dando; except that what she felt for Ben seemed many times stronger. Perhaps it was because her love was reciprocated. Perhaps it was because the memory of the heartache of that earlier unhappy time was fading. She did not have to cope with dejection, of wondering why this lad was avoiding her, for he was not; he would walk Great Britain to be with her. She had not told him yet that she loved him, but she suspected he knew. Anyway, it was up to him to tell her first. When they were together they were blissfully happy, joyful, easy with each other. Their affinity was strong, but not intense and, when they were apart, they relived over and over in their minds the moments they shared.

Jesse Clancey managed to catch sight of Lizzie one evening as she was returning from work. He'd walked to Brown Street to get his hair cut and buy a gallon of lamp oil, and as he came out of Totty Marsh's shop carrying his can Lizzie was passing on the other side of the street. He called to her, and she turned round.

'How are you, Lizzie?'

He crossed over to join her, and she replied with an open smile that she was well. She knew she must meet up with Jesse sooner or later, for she had not seen him since the fiasco of New Year's Eve; but she'd been dreading the moment.

'You look well, Lizzie. You always look a picture.'

She smiled and thanked him again.

'You're courting strong, I hear. Is it the same chap as was at Joe's on New Year's Eve?'

She nodded with a self-conscious smile as they turned the corner into Cromwell Street. They passed a woman and her daughter, poorly dressed, pushing a small handcart containing a few lumps of coal along the gutter. Jesse greeted them cheerily, then turned to Lizzie.

'I expect you've heard about Sylvia and me, eh?'

She looked up at him. 'No, nothing, Jesse. Not a thing.'

'We split up that night, you know. Well, you saw how wicked she was when she copped us together.'

'I'll never forget it, Jesse.' She blushed at the memory of Jesse's stolen kisses.

'Well, when she calmed down, I walked her back home. I told her then as I didn't love her, and there was no point in carrying on. And that was that, really. I've neither seen her, nor heard from her since.'

'I hope you told her I was innocent of everything, Jesse.'

'Oh, I did. I made that plain.'

'Well, maybe you didn't make it plain enough. There's none of the Dandos been a-nigh our house since that night. Whatever happened, there's no need for my Uncle Tom and Aunt Sarah to stop calling to see my mother. She had nothing to do with it. It wasn't her fault.'

'I'm sorry if it's caused her any trouble. I really am.'

'It's caused her no trouble in that sense, Jesse. She knows nothing about it. They haven't been to church since, either. I guessed that's what had happened, and I knew they'd blame me. I suppose Mother's all part of the conspiracy in their eyes. They're bound to avoid her. It's a shame, though, Jesse, a crying shame... So what does your mother think of it all?'

'She went mad. Mother liked Sylvia. She liked her a lot. And Sylvia liked Mother. Matter of fact, Sylvia's been up to our house since to see her – when I've been out, of course, as you might expect.'

'I bet my name's mud...'

'Does that bother you, Lizzie? You know in your own mind as you weren't to blame.'

'Your mother never speaks to me as it is. I don't see why I should appear the worse for being accused of something I haven't done.'

'I told Mother as you had nothing to do with it, Lizzie.'

Jack Hardwick was just sweeping sawdust out of his little butcher's shop as they were walking past and he hailed Jesse. Jesse paused to pass the time of day and Lizzie took advantage of the opportunity to bid him cheerio. As she went indoors the aroma of lamb stew met her. Eve was tending it on the hob, but greeted Lizzie when she entered. Lizzie took off her coat, hung it on a nail at the back of the cellar door. It was time to inform her mother that she had seen him; time to break the news that he and Sylvia were no longer courting; time to explain how it had all come about. And Eve was not so stupid that she could not put two and two together. She would soon conclude that this was the reason she had not seen Tom and Sarah.

Eve was very understanding, however. She accepted that none of the blame was Lizzie's, but explained why Sylvia would perceive it differently, since she was hardly likely to blame herself. It was in Sylvia's own interest, Eve said, to remain the injured party.

On 4th of March, a Wednesday, Lizzie overheard two men who'd stepped off the West Bromwich tram talking about two dozen miners that were said to be trapped underground at the Hamstead Colliery at Great Barr. The thought of such a catastrophe, if it was true, horrified her. Ben was certain to know about it but, as he was working the night shift, she was unlikely to see him; unless he called for her at dinnertime, as he sometimes did if he rose early from his bed.

Next day she gleaned other snippets from customers and there was no doubt that what she'd heard was true. But, again, Ben failed to meet her at dinnertime to verify it. So she went out to buy a newspaper to try and find out more.

133

It turned out that a fire was raging underground at the colliery, and rescuers were doing all they could to get twenty-eight missing men out.

It was the first Friday in March 1908, that Tom Dando decided that much of what he'd been hearing about Jesse Clancey and Lizzie Bishop was supposition. On his way home from work he would call in to see Eve, to try and discover the truth. He was wound up with guilt at not having seen his old friend since New Year. And all because of what Sylvia had told her mother. But what Sylvia had told Sarah did not ring true.

As he trudged through the dark, dilapidated streets of Dudley, he realised that it was almost six years since Isaac Bishop had been killed. He recalled how they used to walk home together chatting like two old biddies. Isaac would talk about whatever came into his head. But Tom was different; he was more reserved and could not make small talk that readily so, even though he did not altogether admire Isaac, Isaac was easy company because he did most of the talking. And Isaac, Tom was sure, was not aware of the contempt he held for him; he was oblivious to it.

Tom could picture Isaac now, in his baggy cord trousers and the oil-stained jacket to his old suit that was elbowless and rumpled. Round his neck he always wore a grubby muffler that used to be white before it was relegated to working attire, and an old bowler hat that many a time was irreverently used as a bucket to fetch coal from the cellar, when his back was turned. The family, including Tom, often laughed about that.

Six years. Lord, how the time had fled. That fateful day Isaac was killed had been like any other Saturday. Except for the wind. That damned, biting wind had been howling through the narrow streets, snatching the very breath from their mouths as they speculated on Kitchener's endeavours, and how soon it would be before the Boers finally surrendered. The howling of the wind had prevented Isaac hearing Jack Clancey's runaway horse and float careering fatally towards him along Brown Street.

Isaac had had other women, but how many, and who they were Tom might never know. Who was to know? Isaac would never admit to anything. Rumours surfaced with the persistence of a cork bobbing up and down in a flooded stream. But Isaac would never divulge what he wanted no one else to know. He never talked about his indiscretions. Of course there had been other women; there must have been. Just as long as Sarah had not fallen prey. That possibility had plagued Tom for a good many years. Sarah, though, was never noted for her beauty; she was plain and on the skinny side; whereas Isaac liked his women well-fleshed and handsome; and the way they used to be attracted to him he could pick and choose. Isaac had loved Eve in his way, but could never remain faithful while other women were prepared to risk his attentions. Women were like a drug. One was never enough; twenty never too many.

Eve had deserved better. She'd always been a fine-looking woman. She was getting old now

135

and deaf as a post since Lizzie was born. Even in her forties, after all those children, she was a handsome-fleshed woman but, as a young woman, she really had been the pick of the bunch.

Tom had always carried a torch for her, yet it was Isaac who'd won her.

When Tom reached the house in Cromwell Street he ceased his daydreaming and walked straight in.

'Tom!' she exclaimed, putting her hand to her breast. 'You frightened me to death.'

'Sorry, my darlin'.' He bent down and kissed her on the cheek like a long lost brother.

'Where's our Lizzie?'

'Not back from work yet. I'm waiting for her to come before I start boiling these two pieces of cod I've bought... Sit you down, Tom, and I'll make you a cup o' tea.' She got up from her chair slowly. Her diabetes, though stabilised, was the cause of her feeling tired much of the time. She no longer had the energy she used to have, and moving required effort. 'Where've you been hiding all this time? It's been weeks since I last clapped eyes on you.' She nestled the kettle on to the coals and reached for the japanned tea-caddy on the mantel shelf, where it stood next to a vignetted photograph of Isaac aged forty-two, posing formally, wearing a stand-up starched collar and his usual arrogant expression.

Tom did not sit down. 'Here, I can do that, my flower.' He reached the caddy for her. 'Just you tek it easy. How've you been keeping?'

'Oh, well enough.'

'An' our Lizzie?'

'Lizzie's happy. She's courting now, Tom. But I suppose you didn't know.'

'Who's she courtin'? Jesse Clancey?'

She put her hand to her ear.

'I said, is she courtin' Jesse?'

Eve calmly spooned tea into the brown, enamelled teapot, then set it down on the hob to warm. 'That's what I thought you said.' Their eyes met. 'What makes you think as she's a-courting that Jesse? He ain't the only fish in the sea you know. No, she's courting a lovely lad from Tividale. A chap called Ben Kite.'

'Oh? Am yer sure?'

'Sure? 'Course I'm sure. He's been here often enough. He was at our Joe's with her on New Year's Eve. You must've seen him.'

'No, I don't remember.'

'Why? Who says different?' She put her hand to her ear in anticipation of his reply.

'Jesse called it off with our Sylvia. You must've heard. Sarah thinks it's Lizzie's fault.'

'Well tell Sarah from me as it ain't Lizzie's fault. Whatever cock'n'bull story Sylvia's told her, it ain't Lizzie's fault, take it from me. I suppose that's why you ain't been a-nigh?'

He nodded glumly.

'Then you ought to be ashamed – especially you, Tom – judging our Lizzie like that. You know very well she wouldn't do a thing like that – pinching another woman's chap. Especially somebody she's close to, like our Sylvia.'

'It's as I thought, Eve. Sarah's got the wrong end o' the stick, then ... but it's only what our

Sylvia's told her. Don't fret. I'll sort it out.'

'Whether or no, the damage is done.'

'Well they've both always been jealous of Lizzie, you know that as well as I do. It don't surprise me as either of 'em should grab the first chance to show her up in a bad light.'

'I know all about that, Tom. But afore they spread wicked gossip they ought to get their story right.'

He put his hand in the pocket of his cord, working trousers and fished out a half sovereign. 'Here, I've got a bit o' widow's pension I've been savin' up.' He pressed it on her.

Eve gave it back. 'I don't want it. You won't get round me like that... And you can stop your laughing.'

'I ain't trying to get round you, yer saft madam. After everything we've been to each other I hardly feel as I have to get round yer. I'm trying to help.'

'If you'm determined to give it away, then give it our Lizzie this time.'

Tom picked up the oven glove from the table and lifted the boiling kettle from the fire, then filled the teapot.

'Well, I'll leave it for our Lizzie, then, Eve.'

On the Saturday evening when Lizzie left work Ben was waiting for her. She was so glad to see him. It was the first time she'd seen him for nearly a week.

'Hello, stranger,' she said. 'I thought you'd forgotten me.'

He took her hand and they started to walk

138

down High Street towards the Market Place. 'No fear of that, my flower. I've been thinking about you all the while.'

'Flannel!'

He laughed. 'I never flannel, Lizzie.'

'Except when you think I'm vexed at you.'

'And are you vexed at me?'

She shook her head and smiled.

'Good. Thinking about you has been the only pleasure I've had this week. Have you heard about the fire at the Hamstead Colliery?'

She said of course she had.

'That bastard of a father of mine is one of the missing men.'

She gasped. 'Oh, no, Ben. Oh, I'm ever so sorry.'

'I'm not. That's why I haven't been to see you sooner. Looking after Mother and that.'

'You know, I feared as much. Something told me your father was one of those poor souls trapped, and I didn't even know what pit he worked at. Your poor mother! How's she taking it?'

'Oh, I'd love to know what's going on inside her head. She's worried to death – bound to be. But she's shed ne'er a tear yet.'

'D'you expect her to?'

'Maybe not. Not after he's been such an evil swine. But he is her husband and the father of her sons. But knowing Mother, if she sheds no tears over him she'll shed 'em all the more over the other poor devils stuck down there. If none survive, just think of all the heartache it'll cause.'

'I know. I could cry. Everybody you talk to

feels the same.'

High Street was busy with people rushing home. A tram crammed with folk whined towards Top Church, ringing its bell to warn stragglers walking in the horse road to make way. Lizzie and Ben turned into Union Street away from the mainstream, thus avoiding the Market Place and the crowds.

'It's ironic, Lizzie. We all hate our father's guts, and more than once I admit I've wished him dead, but we all want him to come up from this alive. Not for himself, though. But if he survives we know as all the others should survive as well.'

At Hamstead Colliery another rescue party from Barnsley in Yorkshire had arrived to help, but hope of finding the men alive was diminishing. Everyone waited anxiously for news. Prayers were said in churches the length and breadth of the nation for their safe deliverance. So far, however, the rescuers had only recovered the cat, and it didn't survive long afterwards. As if to underline the hopelessness one of the rescuers was overcome by poisonous fumes, and he died as a result.

The lack of success so far did not augur well, but rescue work continued tirelessly, inspiring hope among wives and mothers who wept and waited at the pit head. There was a feeling that all this heroic effort and self sacrifice must surely bring good fortune. Nobody yet dared contemplate failure. Every night and every day, for nine days, the cage of the small shaft wound up and down, discharging exhausted rescuers, then slowly descended eighteen hundred feet below ground again with fresh gangs to continue the search. The process was pitifully slow, but so methodical was its organisation, and so strong the will to succeed, that everyone was lulled into a sense of expectant optimism; and those families who waited, though fraught with worry, remained remarkably patient.

On the 12th, a Thursday, a large rescue party descended in the morning, but it was not until three o'clock in the afternoon that onlookers watched in apprehensive silence when they saw the shaft wheels begin to revolve bringing them back up. Eventually, the bell rang and the cage came to a standstill at the mouth of the shaft. Only two men stepped out, blackened and weary, their breathing apparatus still strapped to their backs.

They broke the tragic news that the first thirteen bodies had been found.

Another tragedy befell that March. When Phyllis Fat was about to give birth, her husband, Hartwell, duly fetched Annie Soap to attend her. Annie came at once, complete with the pipe she was always smoking, and, began to organise everything to her liking, while Phyllis's contractions became more frequent. The child, however, was in the breeched position, and while Annie had successfully delivered a woman of a breeched baby before, this time she was not so fortunate. The whole process was taking too long, the umbilical cord had become compressed and the baby was asphyxiated.

Chapter 8

Lizzie Bishop celebrated her eighteenth birthday that March, and she and Ben Kite welcomed the warmer weather, especially at weekends, when they would invariably take a tram ride on a Sunday afternoon to somewhere exotic, like the Birmingham Botanical Gardens, to Cannon Hill Park, or to the picturesque village of Kinver in South Staffordshire.

It was during one such excursion to the Clent Hills in June, that Ben confessed he was in love with her, and expressed the hope that someday they might marry. It was news Lizzie had been longing to hear.

'When I get this job as ladle man I'll be earning more money,' he said, looking across to the distant hills of Dudley. 'That'll help our savings.'

'But when d'you think you'll get it?' Lizzie was industriously threading daisies into a chain.

'Soon, I reckon. Old Amos, who does the job now, is past it. Charlie Lightwood, the foreman's as good as promised it me. The only trouble is, I don't know when exactly.'

'But if you never got the job it wouldn't stop us getting married, would it?'

'No, it wouldn't stop us. But the more I earn, the better house we can afford.'

'Then it makes no difference at all, Ben. None at all. Wherever we live, Mother would have to live with us. So we might as well live at our house. That way we'd save money as well.'

He laughed, put his arm around her shoulder and kissed her on the cheek. 'I half expected as much. Oh, I think I can stand your mother round me. I like her. She's a decent sort. And besides, she won't be able to hear what we do when we're abed.'

Lizzie gasped theatrically. 'Ben, that's a terrible thing to say. It sounds to me as if *that's* the only reason you want to get married.'

'Oh, no, Lizzie. Don't think that. I want to marry you 'cause I want to spend the rest of me life with you. I know we shouldn't get married yet, though. You're a bit too young yet. So am I, for that matter. But maybe in a couple of years – when you're twenty. Mind, I hope I needn't wait that long afore we have it for the first time.'

She looked up at him, feigning shock and indignation. 'Well fancy that. Then if you got me into trouble we should have to get married before I'm twenty. No, Ben, you'll have to wait till we're married for that sort of thing.'

'What's the point in waiting, Lizzie? You want to as much as me.'

'Then you know more than I do. How could you possibly know? You don't know what I'm thinking.'

'I can tell when you kiss me. When we have a real good session in the entry, I can tell as you want to. Anyway, you wouldn't be normal if you didn't. All women have them feelings – same as men – if only they could admit it.'

'Well! I didn't know you knew all about

143

women. Anyway, whether I want to or not, I'm not going to.' Her tone, half haughty, half kittenish, appealed to him. 'Such things should wait. Anyway, a lot of women say it's horrible and messy. So I'm quite content to put it off till then, if it's that bad.'

'Admit it,' he persisted. 'Admit that you do want to?'

She looked at her daisy chain and smiled acquiescently, blushing a deep pink. Oh, yes, she wanted to all right; and he had no idea just how much. Some nights, when they became really engrossed in their kissing he could take her easily, if only he knew it; if only they were somewhere comfortable where they might not be disturbed. She tingled in all her secret places, but he never went further than fondling her breasts and, even then, never inside her blouse. When they'd enjoyed their last peck and said goodnight her lips still tingled, as if tiny sparks were dancing on them. She always felt unfulfilled at those times and just a little light headed. When she was married it certainly would not be a question of having to put up with it. Even now it was more a question of how to refrain.

'Go on, admit it, Lizzie,' he pressed again.

She put the daisy chain she'd made around his neck, stood up, kissed him briefly, and laughed. 'Come on,' she said. 'Let's see if we can see that ice-cream man on his tricycle. I just fancy an ice-cream. Then we'd better get back if we're going to church.'

Lizzie's own meals were influenced by Eve's

dietary regime, and she lost a few pounds in weight herself as a result, becoming ever more slender, her figure becoming more clearly defined, and ever more appealing to Ben. Her simple clothes only served to enhance her natural beauty and she looked good in anything.

Eve remained well, due in part to Lizzie's diligence. Dr. Donald Clark was still a regular visitor, frequently checking her condition and advising this, that, or the other modification to fine-tune her diet. He maintained now that the occasional nip of whisky, or glass of stout, would do no harm. Accordingly, Tom and Sarah began calling for her on Saturday evenings to take her to 'The Shoulder of Mutton'. It was company for her, especially now that Lizzie was out courting so often, and it went some way to easing Sarah's conscience. Sarah had at last realised that Jesse's jilting Sylvia could not be blamed on Lizzie, and she and Eve had consequently become reconciled after Sarah had apologised.

It seemed that Sylvia Dando had recovered from Jesse Clancey quicker than anyone would have predicted, since she was already stepping out with a young man nearer her own age at twenty-three. He was articled to an architect in Dudley, and had a bright future ahead of him, but it would be some years before he started earning good money. So she did not set her sights on an early marriage this time. It was too soon yet to know whether he was the right man for her. She was intent on letting this romance go its own way. If the chance of marriage came and she felt like accepting it, all well and good; if it did not – then so be it.

But James Atkinson was just a plaster for Sylvia's sore. He took her mind off her real love and so dulled the pain. But although she did not love James in the way she loved Jesse, she couldn't help admiring him, and so allowed his aspiring attention. He had great potential, after all.

Sylvia still clung to her belief that Lizzie Bishop was behind her break-up with Jesse. She was convinced that the girl had tried to emotionally trap him at some time. They lived so close to each other, how could Sylvia possibly know what had gone on in Cromwell Street over the months when she wasn't there to witness it? The subsequent reasoning of her father and her mother, after the real truth had come to light, made no impression on Sylvia at all. She loathed Lizzie for what she believed she'd done, and reaffirmed her vow that if ever the opportunity arose to hurt her, she would grasp it with both hands.

Jesse Clancey, however, had met no-one. He still yearned for Lizzie Bishop and watched her comings and goings with Ben Kite, wishing, as they walked past the dairy house, that he was the one holding her hand. He accepted now that any chance there might have been was gone for good. The way those two were when they were together was plain for all to see, and he predicted that she and Ben would wed sooner or later. Yet it was not in Jesse's nature to harbour any ill will towards his rival; his own stupid procrastination had cost him his best chance. What he saw and knew of

Ben he did not dislike; the lad was always pleasant, ready to wave or call a greeting, and would no doubt be quick enough to buy him a pint if he saw him in a public house.

As spring turned into summer Herbert Henry Asquith was appointed Prime Minister, following the resignation of Sir Henry Campbell-Bannerman through ill health; Jack Hardwick and his young bride Maria of six months, became the proud parents of a bonny, little daughter, christened Marjorie; and Stanley Dando came home on leave for two weeks in June.

Stanley did not visit the Bishops, but Lizzie knew when he was due home, and that he was likely to be at church on Sunday with his mother and father. She was apprehensive about seeing him, because their all too brief romantic adventure had remained unspoken and unresolved for nearly two years, and she had not cast eyes on him since. Stanley was nearly twenty-one, and Lizzie wondered whether he still had his cheeky, girlish good looks; whether she would be able to look at him without feeling something. Would she be able to talk to him without blushing to her roots?

The day came when all these questions were answered. As usual the two families, with the exception of Sylvia, who had defected to St. Thomas's – Top Church – these days, met at St. John's lych gate to catch up on gossip before the service. Ben, smart in a new navy blue suit, starched collar and necktie, stood territorially at Lizzie's side.

Stanley seemed taller, and broader in the shoulders as he stood, with military bearing, in his uniform. His face and his hands were bronzed and he looked an icon of lean, soldierly fitness. He was no longer the baby-faced, drowsy-eyed youth she used to know, but more masculine, rugged and, somehow, more worldly. There was a bright gleam in his eyes, an alertness that was never there before, and he exuded an air of quiet confidence and authority. Whereas he used to be casual and unconcerned, now he was as alert as a cat on the prowl; two years of army life, living on his wits, had made him as taut as a trip-wire. His hair was cropped short and gave him a muscular, flinty look. Oh, he was the same handsome Stanley, but so unbelievably different.

And a hundred times more heart-stirring.

He greeted Lizzie warmly when he saw her, with a brotherly kiss on the cheek, almost as if he'd never been away; almost as if there'd been nothing untoward about the way they parted. Lizzie felt herself tremble and, of course, she blushed vividly, which made her angry with herself, especially as Ben was watching. With her colour still high, she introduced them.

'So this is your new chap, eh, Lizzie?' Stanley chirped, confidently shaking Ben's hand. 'Somehow I never expected her to wait for me, you know, Ben. Just look at her. She's too fine looking a madam to leave behind and that's the truth.' He even sounded different.

She wasn't sure whether this comment was sincere or just bravado. 'You never let me know whether I was supposed to wait or not, Stanley.'

Stanley smiled; one of his devastating smiles. 'Would it have made any difference?'

She turned to Ben to avoid a direct answer. All this talk of past familiarity warranted an explanation. 'That's how close we were, Ben. We've known each other all our lives, Stanley and I, and we had one night flirting with each other. Full of promise, it was... I didn't see him again after that.'

'Oh, I was always sweet on Lizzie, Ben, but the minute I made a play for her me father told me it was time I joined the army.' He guffawed aloud. 'I've never forgiven him, the rotten old sod.'

'I suppose your loss is my gain, Stanley,' Ben said pleasantly.

'And if you've got any sense, Ben, you'll snap her up pretty damn quick.'

'Oh, I intend to. I certainly intend to... Anyway, what's it like in the army? I've often fancied it.'

'Oh, it's a good life – in peacetime at any rate. It ain't so bloody good when there's a war on, though.'

'I bet. So where are you stationed?'

'I've been in Calcutta these past eighteen months. I've finished me tour there now, though. I'm due to stop in this country a few months, then I'll try for a posting to the Cape. I fancy the Cape.'

'Didn't you meet any nice, rich, colonial girls in India, Stanley?' Lizzie asked, bursting with curiosity.

Stanley shook his head. 'Oh, there are some beautiful girls in India and no mistake. Not necessarily colonials either. Some of those Indian women are all right, I can tell you... None to compare with you, though, Lizzie. Not one.'

Tom Dando ambled over. 'I see as you've met our Lizzie's chap, Stanley. Don't try and entice him into the army, either. I've got great hopes as these two'll mek it to the altar one day. Come on, then, eh? It's about time we went in, else we'll have the bloody vicar glaring at us. He's a stickler for time, you know.'

They walked through the lych gate towards the main door of the church, and Lizzie took Ben's hand. The bells had stopped pealing, giving way to the sounds of the birds in the treetops, the pigeons cooing in the bell-tower and Ivor Danks's pre-service musical endeavours on the organ filtering outside. Inside, they filed into a pew and, as she knelt on the hassock at her feet to mentally recite The Lord's Prayer, Lizzie pondered Stanley. She'd been dreading this meeting but, finally, the ice had been broken and it hadn't been too uncomfortable. But the sight of him still churned up her insides. This surprised and alarmed her. She was devoted to Ben, but just seeing Stanley made her feel all limp. While she was in no doubt that she was in love with Ben, and not still in love with Stanley, she could not deny she still fancied him. There was something about him that dangerously unbalanced her. Something entirely physical. His lips were still as alluring as ever – but she'd never kissed them properly. She still wondered how they would feel on hers, how his body, firm and muscular would feel pressed against her in an ardent embrace. While she whispered her prayer, her face hidden, she tried to imagine it, feeling a pang of guilt that this wanton desire remained when the man she truly loved was kneeling by her side. She should be ashamed of herself. But she could not help it.

As summer rolled on, typically mixed in its weather, Lizzie paid considerable thought to the depth of her involvement with Ben. Seeing Stanley again had profoundly shaken her, and consequently aroused her guilt. She had to compensate. Ben was her sweetheart and, whilst she felt close to him spiritually, she felt that her commitment ought to be even stronger. There was one final element that she believed had the potential to bind them together irrevocably, spiritually and physically; that one final element which would ensure that Stanley Dando was forever shut out of her thoughts. And although Ben referred to it often enough he never actually pressured her into feeling that sex must be a part of their relationship at all costs.

Any reluctance had been on her part. Yet it was not a reluctance in the sense that she was unwilling. Oh, she would be willing enough, but such activities prior to marriage went against all the established principles of respectability, propriety and common decency; virtues with which she'd been indoctrinated, and so naturally sought to uphold. Sex was reserved exclusively for marriage, within marriage, and according to some, was nothing to shout about anyway. She debated with herself long, and with some intensity, everything there was to consider: the risks; the shame and the finger wagging if she became pregnant; the subsequent worry it would most certainly cause her mother, who had worried enough in the past. She'd anticipated the guilt that would inevitably follow the doing of something she knew she should not do.

But she realised she was judging herself by society's standards. What she and Ben felt and did was between the two of them and nothing to do with society; and God willing, society would never know. However she behaved, she would be doing it out of sheer love and respect for Ben; to better their relationship; to add a deeper, more understanding dimension to it. So society and all its hypocritical conventions could go and hang.

Naturally she had no idea of what to expect physically from full-blown lovemaking. Often she heard her friends talk about it – single girls who actually did it regularly – and their comments, whether sincere or merely driven by bravado, led her to believe that it must bring some sort of exotic, addictive pleasure to their lives, intense enough to negate entirely all concern for the attendant risks, whatever some might say.

Lizzie recognised that she might be deemed young for that sort of thing, especially as she was considered too young to sensibly think of marriage. It was strange, though. If she were already married the question of her age would not be a concern. Legally she could be wed at sixteen; so, why was eighteen too young? She was old enough to bear children, so why should she be considered too young to indulge in the act that could conceive a child? She knew of girls who'd had babies at sixteen. It hadn't occurred to her before, but it was possible they'd been indulging in sex even before the legal age of consent. All right, instances such as those might be frowned on, but at eighteen?

She thought about discussing it with Ben, but dismissed that idea. It would hardly be conducive to a rational exchange. How rational could even Ben be when his opinion was so one sided? It would be like asking a starving man whether or not they should dine together. In any case, there was nothing he could say that might significantly alter her opinion. The more she considered it the clearer it became: it was time to break with convention and long-held principles, and allow Ben to make love to her, body and soul.

The 12th of September provided an ideal opportunity: May and Joe held a party to celebrate Eve's sixtieth birthday. The usual friends and neighbours were invited and drink was once again readily available at Joe's expense. During the celebrations, Lizzie whispered to Ben that it might be a nice idea to step out into the fresh air. He was more than ready to comply, not least because Albert Crump had been extolling the virtues of temperance to him for a solid half hour, when he was already aware of the vices of excessive drink as exemplified by his late, unlamented father. So they made their excuses, saying they were going for a walk. They walked down the entry to the street and Lizzie took Ben's hand. They turned right, as if heading for 'The Junction', but Ben was surprised when Lizzie tugged him gently into the next entry.

153

'I thought we were out for a walk,' he said.

'That was your walk.' Her resolute smile masked her nervousness. She took the key out of her handbag, unlocked the back door and opened it. As they entered the house she turned and smiled at Ben self-consciously, feeling her colour come up. She wondered whether he realised what she was up to and a wave of reticence washed over her. But she had come this far, and how peculiar it would look if she suddenly changed direction. So when Ben shut the door she put the key in the lock and turned it.

It wasn't yet dark and the greying dusk infiltrated the house, rendering colours dim and indistinguishable. Lizzie leaned submissively against the back door, and Ben, hearing the key turned in the lock, swivelled round to face her. It was light enough yet for him to see the tantalising, compliant look in her beautiful eyes; a look he'd never seen before, but which he instantly recognised. So this was the moment he'd longed for. He stepped forward and put his hands to her slender waist. Her skin felt warm and smooth beneath her cotton blouse, and his heart started drumming in his ears. As he kissed her hungrily, he could smell the sweet softness of her perfume.

She trembled with anticipation, and sighed, breaking off their caress for just a second. Then, she put her hands to his head to draw his mouth hard on hers. Her desire was fuelled as much by the forbidden nature of what she envisaged, as by the sensuality of Ben's lips. Her heart seemed to be leaping out of her body at the prospect of tasting real physical love; and the expectation fed her lust.

Ben undid the buttons at the front of her blouse with a new confidence and, experiencing no resistance, in itself unique, allowed his hand to wander inside. For the very first time he savoured the silky, smooth skin of her breasts.

Her breath was faltering and her parted lips found his again for a few more delectable seconds. 'Oh, I want you. I do want you... Do you want me, Ben?'

'Mmm,' he uttered inadequately.

'Undress me, then. Take me.'

He looked behind him unsurely. The fire, banked up with slack and potato peelings, was burning slowly in the grate. Around the scrubbed, wooden table were three chairs and, next to them, Eve's high-backed chair about two feet from the brass fender. Almost touching was the horsehair sofa, and little space between the back of that, the bottom stair and the middle door to its left.

'What, here?' He was afraid of losing the moment and almost panicked. 'There's no room.'

'No, you fool. Upstairs.' She was unwavering now in her resolve.

They climbed hurriedly up the narrow, winding staircase, and Ben was careful to shut the stairs door behind him. The light was even dimmer in the stair-well, but he saw her hand extended down, and he took it, stumbling at the bend where the stairs were at their narrowest. Lizzie gripped his hand tightly, momentarily, and they both laughed at his awkwardness, releasing some of the tension.

Once in her bedroom, Lizzie turned to face him, her blouse unfastened, half in, half out of her skirt. Ben gently slid it off her shoulders so that it hung around her waist, held only by her cuffs. He kissed her neck and his teeth scratched her flesh slightly, sending shudders down her spine, making her whole body tingle. She unfastened the cuffs and her blouse fell to the floor, then she undid her skirt before her arms went round his waist and her hands roamed over his buttocks. She wriggled, and her skirt slipped over her petticoat to the floor. The pace was quickening inexorably and, to assist him, she took off her petticoat herself. Ben's hands ventured inside the waistband of her drawers and slid them down, thankful that she had no need of stays. He lifted her chemise and felt the firm, warm flesh of her backside.

'Come on, then, take your clothes off,' she whispered, aware that she sounded thoroughly brazen, but trembling inside all the same, for this was deadly serious. 'I'm getting into bed.'

Ben fumbled with his jacket, then his trouser buttons, anxious to divest himself of all his clothes before Lizzie changed her mind. She, meanwhile, removed her stockings and pulled her chemise over her head, and he had the first glimpse of her slender, naked body, pale as porcelain in the half light. Hurriedly he pulled off his shoes and his trousers, but left his socks on to save time. He struggled frustratingly with his

156

necktie, clumsily removed the stud from the front of his collar. He shed his shirt, then his vest, and then his long johns. They jumped into bed simultaneously and, at once, Lizzie grabbed him for warmth, for reassurance, and for the new sensation of feeling his actual flesh, smooth, firm, and sensuous against her own. She had never imagined it might feel this good.

They kissed frenetically, hands urgently exploring yet unfamiliar hills and valleys, lingering here and there to savour some fascinating mound or crevice. Ben eased himself onto her, feeling her breasts yield sensually against his own bare chest. She parted her legs, and he attempted unsuccessfully to enter her. Aware that he needed as much help as herself, she took him and guided him to her, her breath coming in thrilled, short gasps. The pain made her gasp, and he withdrew, anxious not to hurt her, but she coaxed him back immediately, more slowly, deliberately, determined to withstand any discomfort. And soon, they were rocking gently with soft vocal sighs and words of undying love... The pain was gone, drowned in the rising tide of emotion.

Chapter 9

In August, Joe and May Bishop called at the surgery of Donald Clark, at May's insistence, to discuss with him the possible causes for her failing to get pregnant. Donald was intrigued, but very attentive in response to this unusual type of consultation.

'So how long have you been married now?' he asked, dipping his pen into his inkwell, ready to jot down a few notes.

'Over two and a half years, Donald,' May answered.

He scratched it down. 'Mmm... Well, that's not an excessively long time, I don't think,' he counselled, looking up at them again. 'Many couples go much longer than that before the wife conceives. I shouldn't worry yet, if I were you.'

'Well, we ain't worried exactly,' Joe chipped in. 'Just a bit surprised as May ain't caught yet. We want kids, see. We just wondered if there might be something wrong.'

'Certainly we can't rule out the possibility.' Donald put down his pen and sat back in his leather chair. 'But, at this stage, I wouldn't be looking for anything wrong.'

'It does seem funny, though,' May said. 'We are fairly ... you know ... regular ... in bed, like.'

'You have to give it time, May. Human beings are not like rabbits.'

'Yes, but how much time?'

'Another couple of years wouldn't be amiss. You're both still young.'

'Well, we don't want to have to wait till we'm old,' Joe quipped.

'Well, of course, Joe, I understand that.'

'But could there be a problem, Donald?' It was May who asked.

'There could be. And any problem, such as there might be, could lie with either of you. In

158

you, May, obstruction could be the cause – an unruptured hymen, perhaps.'

Joe scoffed. 'Well there ain't much fear of that, Donald. Christ!'

'Is your monthly visitor regular, May?'

'Like clockwork.'

'Hmm... I'm not suggesting for a minute that this is the case, but an abnormality of the cervix could obstruct the passage of sperm – or it could be the fallopian tubes. The fallopian tubes are thin tubes on each side of the uterus through which May's eggs travel from her ovaries, Joe,' Donald explained. 'They might possibly be occluded.'

'May's eggs?'

'Yes, Joe. May's eggs.'

'May don't lay eggs. She ain't a blasted fowl.'

Donald smiled patiently. 'Not in the sense that a hen lays eggs, Joe, but her reproductive system manufactures them just the same – tiny ones. Those eggs have to be fertilised by your sperm before a baby can be conceived. Other uterine anomalies may play a role in infertility, besides. An internal examination might reveal something ... if I deem it necessary.'

Joe looked around the surgery. The sight of rubber tubes, forceps, tweezers, pliers, funnels, sample bottles, syringes and sundry appliances for purposes unimaginable, was intimidating; and the picture invading his mind of it all being used upon, or inserted into, his poor May made him feel queasy. He imagined them being probed here and there, like skewers into pork, and May shrieking with pain. And Donald's words all sounded so surgical, a million miles away from the sensuous, loving performing of the sex act. Joe suddenly felt nauseous, and ran his finger round the inside of his collar.

'Have you ever had mumps, Joe?'

'Mumps? Not to me knowledge. Mother would've said.'

Donald was beginning to enjoy this. He was surprised to detect some squeamishness in Joe, who was normally full of bluster. 'An obstruction in the sperm passageways can account for infertility in men, you know, Joe.'

'Oh?'

'Yes... Perhaps a congenital defect. This can usually be rectified by surgery, though.'

'Surgery? What's involved with that, then?' Joe was noticeably paler. He inhaled deeply. It felt so hot in this surgery.

'It means making an incision or two in your scrotum, snipping a tube here and there and relieving any blockage. Then we'd stitch it all back together again. It would all heal up as pretty as a picture in two or three weeks. Four at most ... with minimal pain, and minimal discomfort.'

Joe shuddered and pulled a face. 'Oh, God ... I don't fancy that, Donald.'

'In all probability it wouldn't be necessary. Don't dwell on it.' He turned to May. 'Now, May – I suggest that...'

There was a dull thud on the floor. May looked to her left from whence the sound had originated, to see Joe lying in a heap on the worn linoleum. She looked with alarm at the doctor.

Donald laughed mischievously. 'I think he's

passed out, May. Sorry, I didn't know he was tickle-stomached.'

Love-making was now a part of Lizzie's and Ben's staple diet. It usually took place in the front room, on the hearth, or half on and half off the settee, after Eve had gone to bed. To Lizzie's surprise, she experienced no guilty feelings. On the contrary, the forbidden nature of performing this increasingly gratifying act before marriage made it all the more exciting. Not that they were likely to be caught: Eve was never quiet when she retired, and getting out of bed again was itself always accompanied by many early warning creaks and bumps, before ever she might have begun descending the stairs. On Saturday evenings, when Eve went out with Tom and Sarah, they enjoyed the safe, comparative luxury of her bedroom. Lizzie would have to be pregnant for anybody to know what they were doing, and have a belly big enough to show that she was. And Ben was as noble as his passion would allow him to be when it came to taking care that Lizzie didn't get pregnant. Over the ensuing months, though, their passion did overwhelm them on occasions and she had several worrying weeks; but they amounted to nothing, and she put the delay in her monthly bleeding down to simply worrying about it, and duly counted her blessings.

So, as their relationship was hoisted to new heights of involvement, Lizzie and Ben told their respective families in September that they were engaged to be married and, subject to Eve's consent, the wedding was to be in six months time on Lizzie's twentieth birthday. It had been largely precipitated by Ben's having been given the job he'd wanted for so long – that of ladle man at Holcroft's Foundry. Both families were delighted and straight away started planning what they were going to wear, and the party afterwards. Jimmy Powell was to be best man, Daisy Foster was to be bridesmaid, and they were the only two people outside the two families to be invited. Eve was beside herself with joy, only too pleased to give her consent.

'Mother says I'm to have a white satin wedding dress,' Lizzie told Ben.

'White?' he chuckled. 'If only she knew!'

As autumn turned into winter, so the pace of the arrangements quickened. Christmas came and went and would have been uneventful, except for May, who was upended in their entry on the Sunday morning before by one of Jack 'Ardmate's terrified pigs trying to escape slaughter. She suddenly found herself on her backside, her best Sunday hat over her eyes and dirt over her best coat. The bruises on her backside might have been tolerable but, prior to it, May had been clinging to the hope that she was at last pregnant, having missed a month. Before New Year arrived, she was back where she started.

Towards the end of January the banns were read out for the first time in St. John's, Kates Hill and St. Michael's, Tividale, alerting those, who didn't already know, of the forthcoming wedding. Lizzie remained calm throughout, allowing everyone else around her the privilege of panicking. She was more concerned with her relationship with Ben than with the material trimmings of the marriage ceremony; not that she needed to be anxious; Ben loved her deeply, and that mattered more than anything else. She was ultimately feminine and her eagerness to use her femininity for pure love, rather than sheer permissiveness for its own sake, had already given her a clear insight into the physical side of marriage.

For Ben, the prospect of marriage was the culmination of a dream rooted in the moment he first set eyes on Lizzie, and it couldn't come quick enough. He'd worked diligently to get the well-paid job he felt he deserved. Never would it have crossed his mind to take on the responsibility of marriage without the capability to support not just a wife, but a family as well.

While he waited he concerned himself with the General Election. Its outcome was not greatly to his satisfaction; a dead heat between Tories and Liberals. Herbert Asquith, whom he did not greatly admire because he was too compliant with the demands of trade unions, held on to government with the support of Labour, whom he also deeply distrusted.

Eventually, however, the big day arrived and, at twelve noon, after the Service of Holy Communion, Lizzie Bishop was married to Ben Kite. The Reverend Mr John Mainwaring, reeking of Communion wine, performed the ceremony. It all took place quietly and unpretentiously in the presence of a few of their immediate families.

Eve couldn't help shedding a few tears, while Charlotte Kite, Ben's mother, dressed up like a shilling dinner, May said, smiled proudly. Ben thought Lizzie looked incomparable in her wedding dress with short, ruched sleeves. Her rich, brown hair, elegantly swept up beneath her headdress, shone.

Lizzie, for once, was the more composed of the two. She smiled happily as she recited her responses, while Ben was more nervous and stumbled once or twice over his words. After the photographs and the showering of the happy couple with rice – confetti was banned outside the church because of the litter it made – the wedding party walked conspicuously back to 48 Cromwell Street. The bride and groom cheerfully accepted the congratulations of everyone they met on the way. Fortunately, the weather was mild for early March, and occasionally the clouds parted sufficiently to allow patches of yellow sunshine to add fleeting colour to the grey landscape.

Lack of accommodation at home had limited the number of guests, but there were twenty-two in all, including five assorted children. The unfailing ability of May and Joe to amuse everybody with their self-deprecating humour got the party off to a good start.

Iky Bottlebrush's wife had done the catering. Ben had provided a firkin of strong ale, some bottles of spirits, with lemonade and American ice cream soda for the children. May and Joe, and Beccy and Albert Crump had lent extra chairs.

At about two o'clock, Mrs Bottlebrush served

the roast beef. The adults were all packed tightly around the two tables – one in the back room, the other in the front, whereas the children, nieces and nephews, sat in tiers up the staircase, their dinners on their laps, the youngest at the bottom, the oldest nearer the top.

After the meal, Jimmy Powell had a few words to say. He told how Ben, whom he used to go to school with, once had a trial with Aston Villa Football Club after their scouts watched him play for the works' team. But he refused an offer to join them because he felt he might get a similar offer from West Bromwich Albion, his favourite club. Of course, no such approaches came, but Jimmy assured them that Ben did not regret it one little bit, since he might never have met Lizzie.

Later, while Joe was playing his father's old piano, and everyone was singing and generally having a good time, Eve approached Ben just as he reached the back door, having been up the yard.

'Ben,' she began, 'I don't know how much all this has cost, but I expect it's a tidy penny. Well, I've got some money saved up, just for this very day, and I want you to have it.' She tried to press a small bag of sovereigns into his hand.

'No, Mother,' he answered firmly, shaking his head.

It was no more than Eve expected. 'Please, my son. It'd make me ever so happy if you was to take it. I reckon you'll be as good a son-in-law as any mother could wish for, and if her father had been alive he'd have paid for everything. Well, I

165

see it as my duty now. Here, take the money.'

Ben held Eve's left hand, and closed it around the bag, keeping his own hand over hers. He leaned forward to speak into her ear.

'Mother, it's kind of you, but I won't hear of it. You're too soft with your money. I've been saving up myself for this. Anyway, I asked Lizzie to marry me, so it's up to me to pay. Spend the money on yourself.'

'What do I need with money at my time of life? You'm still young. It'll do you more good than me.'

'Buy yourself a new frock, a new coat, a new fancy hat, a new pair of shoes. Treat yourself, Mother. You deserve it.' He nodded, affirming his resolve, and Eve shook her head admitting defeat.

She knew it would be like this, but she wanted to make the offer. 'Ah, well,' she sighed, 'I could do with some new bloomers ... and some new stays. These I've got on am a-crippling me. I've had 'em donkey's years.'

Marriage heralded a number of changes. Apart from the obvious ones, it was incumbent on Lizzie to look after Ben in the way any wife would look after her husband. Right up to the wedding day Eve had taken care of Lizzie and worried about her as if all along she was a vulnerable child; and it would have been so easy to draw Ben under the same maternal mantle. But Lizzie knew her mother and foresaw the potential pitfalls, so she and Ben devised a new set of house rules. The first was that Ben would

166

pay the rent, even though Eve's name remained in the rent book. The second was to pay Eve's keep.

Eve recognised it all as the passing of an epoch; of old age inexorably creeping on. But she also saw this release from the responsibilities of parenthood as a blessing. The arduous burden of juggling housekeeping money, meagre since Joe married, of robbing one tin to pay another, was at once eliminated. She had always been thrifty, her prudence proportionate to the funds available, but since Isaac's death they'd had damnably little, and every penny had to be allocated thoughtfully to avoid debt. But with wisdom and abstemiousness she managed, without having to pawn the best tablecloth every Monday morning, or Lizzie's best shoes, and without having to approach either the vicar or the doctor for poor relief vouchers. Now Ben, bless him, insisted he meet all household bills.

Because Lizzie's own domestic obligations suddenly increased, she found that getting back from work after six o'clock every evening didn't allow her to perform some of the more mundane, housewifely duties. Conscientious about doing as much as she could herself, it bothered her. Eve didn't mind cooking an evening meal for them and even laundered their dirty linen on a Monday; rather it kept her occupied, even though, increasingly, she did not feel up to doing much. But Lizzie had already made up her mind that some things were not Eve's responsibility – such things as making or changing their bed, emptying the chamber pot that lurked under it.

Such things she must undertake to do herself.

Lizzie decided, therefore, that it would behove her to change to part-time work, or even give it up altogether, like most girls when they married. But since the arrival of a family would preclude her working soon enough, she decided to continue a while and see something of the outside world.

It was on the first Monday evening of May that a neighbour from Grove Street called to see Lizzie. Maggie Growcott was a married girl, a year older, whom Lizzie had spoken to a couple of weeks earlier about her desire to find a part-time job. Maggie was one of Annie Hudson's daughters and, although she'd now shed that family name, the girl was still known as Maggie Soap.

'I just thought yo' might be interested in a little job at the bottlin' stores down Caroline Street,' Maggie said, stepping inside at Lizzie's invitation. Ben came in from the brewhouse at the same time, stripped to the waist, towelling himself dry after his thorough wash down. 'Ooh, I'm sorry. Shall I come back after?'

Ben laughed. 'Come in, Maggie, and take no notice. I'm off upstairs now to put a clean shirt on.' He tossed his towel to Lizzie and disappeared behind the stairs door.

'How's married life suit you, Lizzie?' Maggie asked, blushing at seeing Ben half naked.

'It suits me well...' She draped the towel over the back of a chair to dry, and rolled her eyes in mock frustration, '...so far.' Lizzie swung the kettle over the fire to boil, already half full of water, and spooned tea into the enamelled teapot. 'So what's this job, Maggie?'

'Stickin' labels on pop bottles. It's on'y mornin's – eight till one. I thought it might suit you after what you said.'

Lizzie rubbed the palms of her hands on her apron and sat down on her mother's chair. 'Sounds interesting. What's the money like?'

'Threepence an hour. That's what Edie Rollason was on. 'Er's finishin' this wik. 'Er's due to have a babby–'

'Threepence an hour? Why that'd bring in over six shillings a week, Maggie. I only get seven and six now and I have to work Saturdays as well. Who would I have to see?'

'Ask for Cephas Vanes. I already told 'im as I knew somebody who might be interested. When can yer goo?'

'Wednesday afternoon, about half past two. Threepence an hour, eh?'

That Wednesday in May 1910, Ben left work early. There was an allotment in Hill Street to rent and he'd gone to the council offices to see if they would let him have it. He knew nothing about horticulture but, all day, he'd been turning over in his mind what vegetables he could grow; and if he grew enough he could sell them and earn another copper or two. It might be a bit late in the season now to start growing, but there must be some varieties that could be sown for harvesting in the late summer or autumn. In any case, if the allotment had been overlooked it would need to be cleared first, so it was already too late for summer produce.

Since nobody else had their name down for an allotment in Hill Street, Ben was successful. On his way home, reflecting on his good fortune, he made a detour. For some time he had pondered the benefits a bicycle would give, so he took advantage of the occasion to visit the bicycle shop in King Street. A black, second-hand Elswick machine standing on the pavement outside caught his eye. After inspecting it thoroughly he left a shilling deposit on it, promising to return for it and pay the balance on Friday. As he headed for home the newspaper placards bore information that saddened him, so he bought an evening newspaper.

'You look bothered,' Lizzie commented when he arrived. 'What's up?'

'I've just read this... The King's very poorly. Pneumonia. It don't look very promising.' He sat down and shoved the newspaper across the table towards her.

Lizzie read it and shook her head. 'Poor soul. It doesn't sound very promising, does it?... I've got some good news, though...' Her frown changing to a smile. 'I start at the bottling stores a week on Monday.'

'You got on all right, then?'

'Oh, it'll be much better, Ben. No more working Saturdays. Every afternoon off. We shall be able to go out together of a Saturday.'

'When I ain't working on the allotment, that is. Oh, and I've bought a bike to go to work on. That'll give me an extra ten minutes in bed with you of a morning.'

Two days afterwards Lizzie gave notice that she wished to terminate her employment at Trentham's. Later, she and May set off home and May talked about how it was time she got out of the shop too, because she'd worked there since leaving school, and was convinced they thought she was a fixture.

'But they're better than some shops, to work for I mean, May. At least we get an afternoon off in the week. Some shop girls don't get that.'

May shrugged indifferently. 'Maybe. But I still reckon I've had enough.'

It started to rain again and May put up her brolly, cursing the rotten weather. It had been so bad lately that many were blaming Halley's Comet, which was known to be approaching. They headed towards the Market Place, huddling close under the umbrella, Lizzie holding May's arm.

'If I was having a child you wouldn't see my behind for dust getting away from this place,' May assured her. 'Are you planning any babbies yet, Lizzie?'

'Not particularly. But if any come along we shan't mind.'

'Shan't mind? Take a tip from me, Lizzie, and never try an prevent 'em. Just imagine if you and Ben was to turn out like Joe and me, and don't have none. You'd wish then as you hadn't bothered with all this birth control saftness you keep hearing about. I'd give my eyeteeth for a child, God knows I would.'

'Oh, I know you would, May. But Ben and me

are in no rush. We want to delay it if we can, so I daresay you'll get pregnant well before me.'

'Oh, I can get pregnant, Lizzie. I've been pregnant, I'm certain. More than once. I can't carry 'em though. I seem to lose 'em after about three months.'

'Oh, May! I'm that sorry. You never said.'

'Well, I'd never dream of saying anything till I'm sure. I'm superstitious, Lizzie, and I don't want to say nothing for fear of tempting Providence.'

King Edward VII sadly passed away, and was duly buried on May 21st 1910 in the family vault at St George's Chapel Windsor. All the pomp, splendour, sadness and homage befitting the monarch of the greatest empire the world had ever seen, attended him. But beyond all the pageantry, all the refinement and superiority which Britain manifested to the rest of a subordinate world; beyond the noble quests for the South Pole; beyond well-intentioned prison reforms; beyond the ideology of reforms to the House of Lords; beyond the high drama of ritual ceremony, there were dark rumblings of discontent throughout the land at every level. Miners in Northumberland and Durham had been striking for an eight hour day and riots had broken out. Lloyd George claimed in a speech that the question of women's suffrage must be shelved since reform of the Lords must take priority. Wild cat strikes by dockers prompted employers to lock out a hundred thousand men in an effort to eliminate the problem conclusively

172

and, immediately, ten thousand Welsh miners came out in sympathy. Another general election resulted in yet another dead heat and Herbert Asquith once more held on to power.

But Britain was not the only place where unrest and upheaval was growing. The whole world seemed to be on the brink of chaos. In Spain there was rioting as miners in Bilbao went on strike. Berlin witnessed an anti-government demonstration by a quarter of a million socialists after suffrage supporters in an earlier demonstration were either shot or cut down. Rioters in China burned property owned by foreigners. Cholera raged through Russia, claiming sixty thousand lives, and then broke out in Naples resulting in the fleeing of a hundred thousand frightened people. Japan formally annexed Korea and prepared for an uprising. A revolution ousted the Portuguese monarchy and, significantly, the Reichstag voted to increase the strength of the German army by half a million men.

Yet, despite all this ferment, ordinary people still lived and breathed, ate, slept and went about their daily lives as normal, hoping that none of this mania would touch them or their families. There was still work to be done, there were wages to be earned; life had to go on. The coronation of King George V on June 23rd 1911 brought some respite for the population of Britain, since it was declared a public holiday. To most the pomp and glory of that monumental event was overtly reassuring; nothing could undermine a nation whose society was rooted in such an unshakeable system of hierarchy, where everybody unquestioningly knew their place.

Dudley was a riot of celebrations that day, teeming with folk. The weather was warm, though mostly overcast but, at least, it remained dry – a blessing, since many streets were due to hold their own outdoor parties in the afternoon and evening. During the morning Lizzie and Ben Kite walked to the town to see the flags and bunting flapping like strings of live, tethered gulls across High Street. They watched the side shows around the crowded Market Place; Find the Lady; jugglers, a barber-shop quartet harmonising cleverly to appreciative applause; a street entertainer riding on a huge ball that he controlled with his feet; folk joining hands and dancing to the mechanical music of a hurdy-gurdy, breaking into spontaneous laughter, before the player passed round the monkey, which was holding a little tin cup to collect pennies. The couple threw more coins to a man playing a concertina and to two men dancing with bells on their feet. Arm in arm they sauntered along through the crowds, enjoying the friendly, festive atmosphere.

At about half past twelve Ben decided to take Lizzie for a drink in one of the pubs. He really fancied a pint, and it would be an experience for her, he said. It was. Her appearance, in her new cream blouse with soft, flowing sleeves and waterfall style skirt, tight at the hips, raised a few eyebrows and more than a few admiring glances in 'The Woolpack'. Ben called for a pint of bitter for himself and a half for Lizzie. But she couldn't wait to get out. It was smoky, and the stench of stale beer and of sawdust on the floors held little appeal. Men grunted and coughed up phlegm, which they spat into spittoons, making her feel sick, and their colourful language was hardly tempered for her benefit. But Ben smiled and passed the time of day with the regulars, who were affable enough despite their roughness. Soon after, they returned home for a dinner of cold chitterlings with salt and vinegar and bread and butter, before their own street party began at four o'clock.

Scullery tables, scrubbed extra clean for this special day, were put out and laid end to end, and covered with best tablecloths, for nobody wanted to be outdone by their neighbour. There were sandwiches, enough to feed an army, of hot pork and stuffing with the bread dipped in gravy. There was cold ham, beef, cheese, pork pies, salads and pickles. There were apple pies, custard, cream, bread pudding, jelly, and even ice-cream. Huge teapots and urns appeared as if by magic, to provide some liquid refreshment for the hard-working ladies.

It went on into the night and Ben appeared to be drinking more than Lizzie had seen him drink before. But it only seemed to enhance his good humour. The landlords of 'The Dog and Partridge' and 'The Sailor's Return' donated a barrel of beer between them, so it was no surprise to note that most of the men and, indeed, some of the women, were already heady from the effects of it. Lizzie realised, of course, that it would be ridiculous to try and keep up with Ben, drink for drink but, as she emptied her glass, so it was filled again when her back was turned. The cumulative effect of all her drinking was having a remarkably relaxing effect.

Six strong men had carried Ezme Clancey's prized pianola outside, and it stood on the footpath with a couple of broken slates under one corner to keep it level. She played some of her favourite tunes, while Jesse accompanied her on his mouth organ and others sang. Lizzie giggled when she saw that every time Jesse put the mouth organ to his lips and blew, the black and white mongrel, belonging to another neighbour, howled tunelessly along with the music.

Children were everywhere, running riot up and down entries, under tables and chairs, exploiting the freedom they acquired while their parents and grandparents applied themselves single-mindedly to the serious business of drinking. Laughter rang through the street as one amusing comment was topped by another, and both Lizzie and Ben found the mirth infectious.

At a quarter to ten it was not yet dark, but word reached them that a huge bonfire had been lit on the top of Cawney Hill, so they decided, along with Joe and May, to take a look. When they arrived, panting from the steep climb, they were plied with more drink by Neddie Growcott, Maggie Soap's husband. They fell into conversation with him and Alf Collins, and a pretty young girl Alf was trying vainly to impress.

But the conversation was going over Ben's head. Lizzie was by his side and he kept glancing at her, mentally undressing her, thinking about her smooth, firm body, nubile, vibrant beneath her best clothes. He never grew tired of making love to her. While he was at work he would think about the way she held him, the way she kissed him, the way she responded with enthusiasm to his touch. He was entirely besotted. And the alcohol was rendering him lustier than ever.

He drained his glass. 'Come on, Lizzie,' he said, 'it's time we went. It's past our bedtime.'

'Aha!' Alf exclaimed. 'It's your lucky night by the sound of it, Lizzie.'

'Well, I don't think it'll be his,' Lizzie laughed. 'With what he's had to drink he'll be falling asleep before his head touches the pillow.'

'Just gi' me a shout, then, eh?' Alf suggested, all beer and bravado.

Ben grinned and took Lizzie's hand, leaving Joe and May to make their own way back in their own time. When they returned to Cromwell Street the party was still in full swing. They saw Eve chuckling at something Beccy Crump was telling her, and Albert looking on with a superior expression, a picture of upright sobriety compared with everyone else. Jesse Clancey saw them return and straight away handed them fresh glasses of beer.

'Cheers, Jesse,' Ben said, and raised his glass. 'It'll be a wonder if I don't drown, the beer I've drunk today. This'll see me off.'

'Enjoy it, Ben. There's ne'er a coronation every day. What d'you say, Lizzie?'

'I say enjoy it, Jesse. But I'm tired now and Ben's got to be up early for work. He's on at six.'

'Then let him go to bed. You stop here and have a good time with us.'

'I don't think he'd let me do that, would you, Ben?'

He shook his head. 'Not on your nellie. You're coming to bed with me. Tell your mother we're going up.'

'See?' she said, and shrugged as she waltzed over to her mother.

Lizzie caught up with Ben half-way up the entry. As soon as they entered by the back door he stopped and pressed her against the wall. His mouth urgently sought hers. The feel of him, thrust hard against her, lit her up, and he recognised the signs.

'Come on to bed afore your mother comes up.'

She assented wordlessly, following him upstairs in darkness. In their bedroom Ben lit a candle and placed it on top of the tallboy, then began to undress.

'Damn it,' he said. 'I'd best go up the yard afore I get into bed. I should've gone before we came up.' He disappeared down the stairs again.

When he returned, three minutes later, Lizzie was as naked as the day she was born, her hair let down. She was erotically performing a belly dance by the light of the candle, in time to the sounds of a march being played mechanically through the pianola outside. She wafted a square of satin, sensually passing it over her breasts and stomach.

'You brazen trollop,' Ben breathed, incredulous. He watched her for a few minutes, mesmerised. Her lithe movements tantalised him, stoking his already rampant desire. The spittle thickened in his mouth. He pulled her to

178

him and, as she fell onto the bed, laughing, wriggling, enjoying her wantonness, he at last felt her firm, satin flesh yielding to him once again. She helped him off with his clothes, making a game of it, and they lay naked, quiet for a few moments, laughing, panting, savouring each other's damp, perspiring skin, which was causing their bodies to cleave.

'Have I got to dance to get you going again?'

She went to get off the bed, but he pulled her back. 'Stay here. Kiss me, Lizzie. For Christ's sake come here.'

She kissed him, hungrily, her head swimming with alcohol. But it was with a little gasp of pleasure that she felt him slide into her. Her tongue probed his mouth and she kissed him with passion. She raised her hips and sighed as he probed her even more deeply. Their bodies quickly found their natural rhythm and they were caught irrevocably in the intense, seductive power of the moment. Next morning, when she recalled it, she realised that she'd never experienced such abandonment from Ben.

Chapter 10

The beginning of October in 1911 provided two significant events in Cromwell Street. First, gas was laid to the remainder of the houses that didn't already have it, which included number 48. Workmen dug up the pavements and ran

179

pipes to the houses, while others installed piping runs in the downstairs rooms. Unfortunately, the landlord made no provision for extending the luxury to the upstairs rooms, but for the first time, the family could enjoy evenings brightly lit in the scullery and in the front room. Eve was able to read and sew easily, without her usual squinting.

The second event directly involved Lizzie. Ben was working shifts, which this particular week meant starting at two o'clock in the afternoon. She'd said nothing to him yet, but she was certain she was pregnant, having missed three months. So after a hurried meal at teatime on the Thursday she got ready to visit Dr. Donald Clark. As she emerged from the bottom of the entry, Joe was just about to enter it.

'What-ho, our Lizzie. Where'm you off all decked up in your hat and coat?'

'I, er ... I was just on my way to the doctor's, Joe.'

At once he looked concerned. 'Why, what's up? Is Mother bad again?'

'Mother's all right. It's me this time.'

'Am you bad, then?'

'No, not bad exactly.' She looked at him, half smiling, half serious; a knowing look, which he picked up at once.

'You mean you'm pregnant?'

'Shh! Keep your voice down. I'm not certain yet, that's why I'm on my way to see Donald. Ben doesn't even know yet. Now I suppose you'll go and blab it all round the parish before I have a chance to tell him myself.'

'Hey, I can keep a secret, Lizzie. But congratulations.'

'Congratulate me when I know for sure... I'd better go.'

'It'll be dark soon. Look at the sky. I'd feel easier if you let me walk you there and back. I know you – you'm ever likely to walk down Pitfield Street by yourself, when two bobbies together would think twice about it.'

'Come with me then, if you want.'

'I think I'd better. I'll just tell May, and get me jacket.'

He was back with her almost at once, and she heard May call 'ta-ra' to him. On the way they talked exclusively about the new gas lighting and agreed what a boon it was. Joe said that May was already planning to have one of those new gas ovens in the scullery, and he agreed it made sense, since they needn't light a fire every day in the summer for cooking and boiling kettles. They would save a fortune on coal – and the supply of coal was unreliable anyway.

Donald Clark held his evening surgery in a front room of his elegant house on Dixons Green Road, while patients waited in another room on the opposite side of the hall. When they arrived only one other person was waiting, a familiar old lady dressed entirely in black. She had a whiskery chin and kept chewing her gums and humming. Lizzie and Joe both nodded to her and sat down. Within a few minutes, a bell rang, and the old lady rose to her feet painfully and shuffled across the hall into the room opposite.

'Why haven't you told Ben you think you'm

pregnant, our Lizzie? Don't he want kids?'

"Course he wants kids, Joe. It was just something May said a long time ago...That she'd never tell anybody she was pregnant till she was sure. Tempting Providence, she reckoned.'

'By Christ, we've been close though. A couple or three times we've known she's been pregnant ... but she's lost 'em at three or four months. She's pining for a child now. It's pitiful to see. I dread it every month when she's due.'

'What's Donald say?'

'Donald reckons there's nothing amiss necessarily. Just keep trying, he says. I'll be honest, our Lizzie, I used to enjoy sex when we did it for pleasure but, nowadays, doing it as if it's a perishing duty – like a job of work – I ain't so bloody keen. I'd just as soon have a piece of bread and dripping... It ain't funny, you know.'

'You are hard done by,' she chuckled.

They heard the elderly woman go out, and Donald rang the bell, calling his next patient.

'Wish me luck, then,' Lizzie said and got up to go in.

Joe winked. 'I wish you all the luck in the world, Lizzie.'

Lizzie reappeared about ten minutes later with a smile on her face, her cheeks glowing. Donald was behind her and he greeted Joe affably. No other patients had followed them into the waiting room.

'If you were Ben, Joe, I'd be congratulating you now,' he said. 'But your time'll come.'

'Is it right, then? Is our Lizzie pregnant?'

There was contentment in Lizzie's eyes.

182

'Donald says there's no doubt. He's even given me a date.'

'Go on, then. When's it due?'

'Twenty-eighth of March. And he'll attend me when I'm confined. I don't want Annie Soap.'

'Oh, Annie's all right if there are no complications. If you can stand the smell of her pipe,' Donald said. 'But I'll be happy to oblige, seeing as it's you, Lizzie.'

'Well if Ben's on shifts and I have to come and fetch you, you'd best be ready, Donald. And you'd best be sober.'

Donald's eyes creased, showing his amusement. 'Are you trying to insinuate that I get drunk, Joe?'

'Well, if you don't, it's only 'cause you spill most of it.'

'Well, at least I shan't faint when presented with childbirth, Joe. Drunk, or sober.'

Lizzie stood on tiptoe, stretching up as high as she could, yet the broken gas mantle remained obstinately out of reach. Warily, because of her condition, she took a chair from the table and dragged it over the rag rug, struggling to position it beneath the gaslight. She expected another torturous pain at any moment.

By the scant illumination from the coal fire Eve looked on, lips tightened with apprehension. 'Be careful, our Lizzie. You'll start yourself lifting that heavy seat. Why didn't you get Ben to mend it afore he went on his night turn?'

''Cause he'd gone before I could ask him,' Lizzie murmured to herself.

She lifted her skirt, revealing her neat ankles, but it was with little elegance and a womanly grunt that she heaved herself up onto the chair. Any graceful motion was clearly impeded by her nine month belly. Once on the chair, however, she reached up comfortably, detached the flimsy broken mantle and carefully fitted the new one. Eve folded a strip of newspaper into a spill, kindled it in the fire, and handed it to Lizzie. She lit the gaslight and gently pulled the chain on the tap to increase the brightness. The moment it glowed she felt another agonising pain deep inside her. There could be no doubt that her child was on its way.

She'd known, almost from the morning after the coronation that she was pregnant. Not because she felt ill; she just felt different. It might have been her imagination, but somehow her belly felt more sensitive, more aware of something new and important going on within. Maybe she simply fancied she was carrying a child in those early days, but those fancies turned out to be fact. All the way through she'd kept well. Morning sickness was minimal and lasted but a week or two, and she'd put on little extra weight, though she'd eaten well. Indeed, Ben urged her to eat more, but she ate only what she felt she needed and was content. Her only craving was for sardines.

Ben was delighted when she first told him he was to become a father. No man could have been more pleased. Whilst they were courting he'd often wondered, since he was obviously aware that they were at risk, what a child of theirs might look like. So the idea of being a father at last, at the advanced age of twenty-four, appealed, and he was as anxious as Lizzie to meet his child. He had no preference for a boy or a girl – either would be loved – just so long as the child was normal and healthy, and so long as Lizzie came through it all well; for he worried about her.

Later that night Lizzie sat at the hearth deep in thought, her hazel eyes fixed by images of bizarre faces in the fire's glimmering flames. As the contractions came and went, doubling her up with agony for long, hard seconds, she pondered the events that had brought this all about nine months earlier: that night of the coronation; shamelessly dancing before Ben by the light of the candle, naked, wickedly tantalising him. God alone knew where she'd picked up the idea. Perhaps she'd read about those mysterious belly dancers somewhere; perhaps it was from some of those saucy old photographs of semi-clad girls – from that era twenty-odd years ago flippantly referred to now as the 'naughty nineties'. She and her mother had found such photographs among her father's things after his death. Or was it because she was just naturally, sexually creative? If ever her mother knew what she was really like she would disown her. Lizzie knew she should have been thoroughly ashamed of herself but, on that memorable night, she saw with excitement the effect she was having on Ben and remorselessly teased him the more, no less driven by lust than he. Any thoughts of being careful were far distant from Ben's mind. And Lizzie recognised then that she wasn't just heady with the effects of her wantonness; she was also too tipsy to care.

Now she was about to have his child. But, at least, she was married. At least she and her baby would have a home. At least the child would have a father. When she looked back at the days when she and Ben were courting she realised how much at risk she used to be. It was a wonder she never became pregnant then. What if she'd found herself carrying a child and Ben had scarpered, never to be seen again, disclaiming all responsibility? She and her mother could never have afforded to keep themselves, let alone a child as well. It would have meant the workhouse, branded as feeble-minded, shut away for her own good never to emerge again. She knew well enough though, even then, that Ben was an honourable man; that she was safe from that.

She'd mentioned nothing yet to her mother about the recurring pains, but now they were coming more frequently. A new one gripped her and she winced. She looked up at the black, marble clock squatting in the middle of the crowded mantelpiece, its peaceful tick as gentle and as regular as the heartbeat of her unborn child. It had stood there all her life, announcing the hours and the half-hours for many more years than she had known. They'd lived together, Lizzie and the clock, through her childhood, through illness, through grief, through unbounded joy, sharing both the monotony and the gaiety of life. Through her nightmares and through her daydreams the clock had remained indifferent, constant, reliable, unaffected by the emotions that affected her.

It chimed half past ten.

As the pains temporarily receded, Lizzie's eyes scanned the room. Everything in it was as familiar to her as her own body; every run of brown paint on the doors, every knot and dent in the woodwork, every mark cast into the shining black Coalbrookdale fire grate, every tuft of material in the worn rag rug at her feet, every bubble in each imperfect window pane. And through that window she'd looked out onto the unchanging backyard with the changing eyes of childhood, of youth and of womanhood. She'd seen frost etch its intricate, grey patterns on the panes, raindrops roll down them like tears, the southern sun radiate its summer warmth onto the scrubbed, white table and the cracked linoleum of the floor.

At the other side of the hearth Eve sat reading a newspaper in her high backed chair, tonelessly whispering every word slowly to herself, as she always did. Lizzie glanced at her, then took the poker to prod the coals into life. A flurry of gold sparks flitted up the chimney in a lick of smoke, then settled back into a hypnotic flickering. Eve peered over her spectacles and their eyes met.

'I've started,' Lizzie mouthed, soundlessly.

Eve cupped her right hand alongside her ear and leaned towards Lizzie with an apprehensive look.

'I've started.' She gave a visual sign by gently prodding her belly, grimacing and nodding.

Eve understood perfectly. 'Has your water

broke?' she croaked, folding her newspaper. She'd been anticipating this moment for days.

Lizzie shook her head.

'Get yourself to bed, my flower.' Eve eased her own unsteady bulk out of the creaky chair, unflustered. 'I'll just pop to our Joe's and ask him to fetch Ben and Annie Soap.'

Lizzie leaned forward and flicked a speck of ash off the polished, brass fender with her apron, then stood. She turned and shook her head emphatically, and Eve cupped her hand to her ear again.

'Annie Soap's coming nowhere near me and my child, Mother. Remember Phyllis Fat? I'm having Donald. I want my child to live through this after I've carried it all this while. Our Joe'll fetch him.'

Lizzie believed that breaking with convention and having a man supervise the birth, albeit the doctor and long-time friend of the family, would not sit well with her mother, and it was the reason she had not mentioned it before. There would have been unending dissension. But Eve nodded her consent, even though the ritual of childbirth had conditioned her to believe it was women's business. Women could cope well enough. Men should not intervene; not even the doctor, except in a dire emergency. In any case, she thought, it was too degrading to have a young man who was not your husband seeing everything. But if that's what Lizzie wanted she had no intention of trying to persuade her otherwise, especially at the eleventh hour.

Lizzie lifted the stairs door latch, and apprehensively went upstairs. The stories she'd heard about the horrors of giving birth made her more than nervous. So far she'd only imagined what it might be like, though the contractions were giving broad hints. Now she was about to find out.

Meanwhile, Eve lit the candle which she kept in a jar in the cupboard to light her way outside in the darkness. It had a length of string tied round the neck forming a long handle and she hung it around her neck like a pendant. She filled the kettle and put it to boil over the fire before she tottered down the entry to the dimly lit street. It was windy, wet, and the cobbles and puddles of Cromwell Street reflected the lights from the terraced houses. Suddenly, before her, the inky sky, heavy with low, racing clouds, took on a phosphorescent glow – another twenty tons of white hot slag were being tipped at the Round Oak ironworks in Brierley Hill. Its intense bloom silhouetted the rows of chimneys, and the writhing smoke from household fires made from anything that would burn. Eve slowly made her way up the next entry, clutching her shawl to her throat with her left hand, feeling her way along the wall with her right. Before she even reached the end Joe was there to meet her.

'I thought I heard you coming up the entry, Mother,' he said loudly as Eve put her hand to her ear. 'You'm out late. What's up? Been courting?'

'Our Lizzie's started, Joe,' she answered as though she'd caught every word. 'Will you fetch Ben from the foundry, and let the doctor know?

She says the doctor's got to come and see to her. She don't want Annie Soap.'

'I know all about it. Get back home, Mother, and I'll fetch 'em both. May'll be round quicker than you can change your bloomers when she knows our Lizzie's started.'

Eve turned for home. She lifted her skirt a little to prevent the hem dragging on the wet stones, and the prospect of a newborn baby in the family brought a lump to her throat. She offered a silent prayer that her daughter and the child would enjoy a safe delivery, recalling the daughter she'd lost to childbirth a few years earlier.

As she entered the tiny, back room Eve stirred the coals again. The brown, enamelled kettle swung slightly on its gale hook and gasped like an old biddy as the hot water inside lapped against the sides. Coal was scarce due to another miners' strike, but she reached into the coal-scuttle and lifted out two lumps, broke them into smaller pieces with the hammer, and placed them on the fire. Smoke billowed back into the room from a down draught, and its smell filled her nostrils making her eyes run. She tried to ignore it, but it always vexed her, even though she was used to it. She went to the cellar and fetched more coal to light a fire under the copper in the brewhouse. That done she filled the boiler with water. Before she went upstairs to settle Lizzie, now abed, she took a clean apron from the chest of drawers that stood against the entry wall, and put it on.

Joe Bishop strode hurriedly through the streets of

red brick terraced houses, his collar up to keep out the blustery March wind. In no time he was tugging the bell-pull at Hawthorn Villa on Dixons Green. The door opened tentatively and a maid put her head nervously round the jamb to peer out into the darkness.

'I've come for the doctor, my flower,' Joe panted.

'You'd better come in.' The maid opened the door wide. 'He's asleep, though.'

Joe doffed his cap. 'A-bed, drunk, or what?'

She shrugged non-committally. 'Well he ain't a-bed.'

Joe smiled knowingly. The maid led him across the quarry tiled floor of the hallway and into a well-furnished drawing room at the rear of the house. Donald was snoring in a comfortable armchair, unresponsive to the respectful tapping of the young girl.

'You'll never wake him like that, my flower.'

He tossed his cap on to the polished table and shook the doctor vigorously, but without effect. Again he tried, but still Donald did not stir. Joe's eyes scanned the room. On a narrow whatnot he spied a heavy cut-glass vase containing a neat arrangement of daffodils. He picked it up and tipped the contents unceremoniously over Donald's head. Donald screwed his face up, licked his lips wearily and opened his eyes, grunting with irritation. As he sat upright, the maid stifled a chuckle.

'Doctor Clark, this man's called to see you.' The incredulous maid was finding it difficult to muffle her amusement.

191

The doctor looked up at Joe, then flopped back down in his armchair again as if greatly relieved. 'Oh, it's you. It's all right, Florrie. It's Joe Bishop. Get me a towel, please.'

'Our Lizzie's started, Donald. I'm off now to fetch her husband. He's on the night turn. Mother's looking after Lizzie till you get there.'

'Lizzie? Right. I'll be on my way in a minute or two.' He stood up and turned to the maid who handed him a towel to dry his face. 'Make certain my father's all right before you turn in, Florrie. And don't wait up for me.'

Joe left the doctor to rally himself and make his own way, then hurried on, smiling that he'd drenched Donald. At the bottom of the hill past St. John's church he climbed over a stile and picked his way down the muddy footpath through the fields. In a few minutes he reached the main road from Dudley to Birmingham. It was deserted, but for a distant tram he could hear. Joe turned to look. The rails of the tramway, picked out by the gas streetlights, glistened like burnished needles against the dull sheen of the damp cobbles. The tram was coming his way. He ran to the stop.

'We'm on'y gooin' as far as the Tividale sheds,' the conductor called as he reached his passenger. 'We'm finished then for the night. Any good to yer, my mon?'

'God bless yer.'

There were no other passengers on board. The driver turned off the brake and pulled the control lever towards him while Joe watched the routine. The tram gathered pace, then drew to a halt again for the conductor to get off and change the points.

'It's a stroke of luck you coming when you did,' Joe said when the man resumed his place by the driver. 'I only want to go as far as Holcrofts.'

'Late startin' your shift, eh? They'n bin at it hours a'ready. I bet they'm tryin' to mek as much pig-iron as they can afore the coke runs out.' The conductor laughed at his own weak joke. 'Bloody miners. Wha'n yo' say, 'Orice?'

'Bloody right. Bloody miners,' Horace concurred.

Joe felt in his pocket. 'What's the fare, mate?'

'Aw, nothin'. We've finished the reckonin' up for the night.'

When the tram eventually drew to a halt Joe stepped down and gave a grateful wave as he caught his first familiar whiff of scorching sand and acrid foundry fumes. As he turned into the gate the night watchman challenged him. He explained that he wanted Ben Kite.

'All right. Watch the gate for me a minute while I fetch him.'

Joe lit a Wild Woodbine while he waited, and savoured the smoke as it filled his lungs. He envied Ben; married not two years yet and already about to become a father. What the hell was wrong that May hadn't carried after five years? Or was it six? Two minutes later he saw the silhouetted figure of Ben, tall and lean, pulling his jacket on as he walked towards him, accompanied by the watchman. They disappeared into the time office, then Ben came out alone, fetched his bicycle from the shed and wheeled it towards Joe with a nervous grin on his handsome face.

'What time did she start?'

'I don't know for sure. Mother fetched me about half past ten. I've let Donald know. He should be there by now. Drunk as a lord, he was, though... Here, have a fag.'

They had reached the main road, and Ben shifted the bicycle to his other side so that he could wheel it along the gutter. He stopped, took the cigarette, and lit it off Joe's. 'I hope she'll be all right, Joe. First child and all that. And Donald three sheets to the wind. God! Trust *him*.'

'Lizzie'll be all right, Ben.' He realised he'd alarmed Ben unnecessarily. 'There'll be Mother and May looking after her besides. They know what to do. Anyway, Donald wasn't really that bad. I've known him a sight worse. At least he could stand. Come on, let's get a move on. It's a tidy walk. If only that bike of yours could whisk us up these hills without pedalling, eh?'

They walked briskly but, by the time they reached 48 Cromwell Street, it was practically all over. As soon as they walked in the back door they heard the muted cry of a new born baby, and several sympathetic oohs and admiring ahs from May and from Eve. Ben looked at Joe, his work-dirty face alight with anticipation.

'Jesus! Already?' His first instinct was to run upstairs, but it occurred to him that maybe the child had only been delivered at that very moment. Maybe they didn't want him yet. So he called up the stairs. 'It's me ... Ben. Can I come up?'

'No. Not yet, Ben.' It was May. 'There's still a bit to do.'

'But I can hear the baby crying. Is everything all right?'

Donald answered. 'Everything's fine, Ben. We'll give you a shout. Give us five minutes.'

'Is Lizzie all right?'

There was laughter. 'Lizzie's fine, Ben.'

He lit another cigarette, made some comment to Joe and instantly lost all recollection of it in his preoccupation. He poked the fire, then decided it needed making up, so went to the cellar to fetch a bucketful of coal. There was about a hundredweight left and little prospect of any more till the miners had been back at work a while. He broke a lump into smaller pieces with the coal hammer, took it up the brick steps in a bucket. As he banked the fire up, May came downstairs carrying a parcel wrapped in newspaper, and an enamelled bowl. She went outside. Ben followed her to the brewhouse and washed his hands. As he dried them, May threw the parcel into the glowing coals under the copper and began swilling out the bowl.

'Is Lizzie all right, May?' This was the longest five minutes of his life.

May smiled. 'Lizzie's fine, Ben, my lad. Stop werriting.' She turned off the tap, and drained the bowl before wiping it. 'If ever I'm blessed with babbies I hope and pray as I have as good a time as Lizzie.' She half filled the bowl with cold water and went indoors again, then topped it up with hot water from the kettle and checked the temperature with her elbow. She smiled again at

Ben and climbed the stairs. 'Only a few more minutes,' she called over her shoulder.

Ben handed Joe a cigarette and lit one himself. Joe sat convincing him that everything was fine. Then he heard Lizzie call him. At once he sprang up the steep, bent staircase. May had just finished cleaning up his child and, as she sat on the bed she was gently patting it dry with a towel. Lizzie peered contentedly over the bedclothes from her pillow, smiling at Ben, a gleam in her eyes. He could see for himself now that all was well.

'God bless you, Lizzie. What is it? What've we had?'

They all looked at Lizzie, waiting for her to tell him.

'A daughter. And she's a beauty. Look at her hair, Ben. There's lots of it, and see how dark it is. Just like yours. She's got beautiful, blue eyes as well, just like you.'

Ben peered at the child again, then leaned over and kissed his young wife. 'God bless you, my darling,' he said softly, tears welling up in his eyes. 'God bless you... and thank you. Are you all right yourself?'

'I am now. But I'm glad it took no longer than it did.'

They all laughed with her. Eve sat on the new ottoman and looked on with a proud smile, relieved it was all over, relieved it had been so easy for her daughter.

Donald offered his hand. 'Congratulations, Ben lad. They're both fine and dandy. You've got a beautiful daughter. And Lizzie was superb.'

They shook hands. Ben leaned over to inspect his new daughter, still in May's arms, and to rub the back of his forefinger over her soft cheek.

'You know, Ben, Lizzie had been in labour quite a while before she told anybody. I've told her off for that. It was an easy birth, though. Just the way I like 'em.'

'I'm that relieved,' Ben exclaimed. 'Lizzie, have you thought what to call her?'

'Henzey – after my grandmother. I think it's a lovely name.'

Chapter 11

Although Annie Soap did not attend the birth of little Henzey, Ben engaged her for ten days afterwards to tend to Lizzie. The seven and six she charged, he considered well worth it. Annie was noted for her discipline and was particularly strict with Lizzie; perhaps vindictive for not being called in to supervise this birth which, she discovered, had been straightforward enough. Annie strapped a breadboard to Lizzie's stomach to flatten it, using swathes of old sheets, and told her to keep it in place for the whole ten days. After that she could do as she pleased. But Lizzie deemed it all a waste of time and ridiculously uncomfortable. So whenever Annie left she took off the strips and removed the breadboard, wallowing in unrestrained freedom. Eve laughed when Lizzie asked her to replace the whole device just before Annie was due to call again. This went on for about four days, till Lizzie saw no point in keeping up the pretence and told Annie bluntly that she was not prepared to be subjected to such archaic practices. When Donald Clark visited he agreed, and laughed.

From the outset it was evident that Henzey would be an easy child. She took her feeds well, when they were due, and slept. Eve claimed she'd never known such a contented baby. Ben watched in wonder and admiration as Lizzie fed her. Those first few days were the beginning of another wholly different routine, another completely different way of life, and he'd never been so happy. That this child was his, the fruit of his loins, had still hardly registered.

Besides rejecting Annie Soap's stomach-flattening treatment, Lizzie also refused to remain in bed for the requisite ten days. She felt fine, and because she could get up to answer nature's calls, she saw no reason to go back to bed.

On the morning of the first Sunday in April she and Ben took Henzey to Matins at St. John's so that she could be churched. After the service, the three of them stayed in their pew till everyone else had left, Henzey asleep in Lizzie's arms. Ben fell on his knees and prayed quietly in his own words, giving his heartfelt thanks to the Almighty for this gift of a child, and for His watchfulness over Lizzie. As he resumed sitting, Lizzie looked at him, and the sight of tears streaming down his face moved her to weep too.

Neither felt the need to speak. Their tears

abated in their own time and, when Ben wiped his eyes, he looked at Lizzie and smiled, and she smiled back lovingly. Then he stroked Henzey's round cheek gently with the back of his forefinger.

'Only God knows how much I love you, Lizzie Bishop, and this little child of ours.'

Tears welled up in her hazel eyes again and trickled down her cheeks. She wanted to thank him for his love and devotion, but she knew it was unnecessary. Thanks were hardly appropriate.

He put his handkerchief to her face, and caught her tears, tenderly dabbing her cheeks dry. 'I can scarcely believe as I should be this lucky,' he said, almost choking on his emotion. 'I can scarcely believe I should be lucky enough to have you, Lizzie, and this lovely child.'

These were moments to savour, Lizzie knew. Moments they would remember always. Brief moments, insignificant to an onlooker, but monumental in their lives. Whatever else befell them, good or bad, they would be able to recall this time and draw strength from it; for it was uncontrived, spontaneous, pure in sincerity.

Lizzie took to motherhood like woodland takes to bluebells. She had plenty of help and advice from her mother, and sometimes some interference, but it all came naturally anyway. She felt everything that a first time mother should feel for her child and, when she fed Henzey, she savoured a delightful ache inside her breast, followed by a great feeling of satisfaction as the baby settled to a steady, rhythmic sucking. The days and weeks seemed to fly, and Lizzie's joy was undiminished as she gave the child every attention. Her whole life was transformed. Little Henzey generated feelings and emotions she'd never experienced before as she looked into her deep, clear blue eyes. It was all so new, a million miles from anything she'd ever known, and it gave her the utmost contentment. She loved Ben no less, but her love for her child was different: it was fierce, obsessive; and yet it was tender, caring, and utterly selfless. At first she worried ceaselessly, going out of her way to make sure her baby was breathing while she slept. During the night, Henzey only had to sigh and Lizzie would be wide awake, ready to get up and do whatever was necessary to make her comfortable.

As the days grew longer, bringing fine spring weather, Ben Kite enjoyed the quiet, strenuous hours he spent growing vegetables in his allotment. It was still a novelty, since he'd only just begun learning about vegetables. He received plenty of advice from other allotment holders, and welcomed it. Now it was all starting to take shape, and already he was contemplating growing more produce than he needed, with the intention of selling the surplus to workmates. Working there in his spare hours gave him time to think; to mull things over. While he turned over the black earth, pondering his wife, his child and his own good fortune, he also pondered the state of the world around him. And the world around him was a constant worry. Only two weeks ago he was appalled at the loss of the Titanic and some fifteen hundred of her passengers. He still could not erase the horror from his mind. To make matters worse Barnsley had beaten his beloved West Bromwich Albion in the Cup Final replay.

Ben was just about to thrust his spade into the ground when Alf Collins called him from outside his father's shop at the bottom of the hill. Ben waved. Alf had been pushing a handcart, evidently full of coal. He left it at the gutter, walked up to the allotment and opened the gate.

'What yer plantin', Ben?'

'Coal.'

'Christ, and we could do with it.'

'I'm planting a bit of everything, Alf. I want to grow enough to sell. The way things are going we'll need it.'

'Take some round to me father when it's ready. He'll buy some.'

Ben leaned on his shovel. 'Think he would?'

'If the price is right. It's a pity you can't grow coal, though, eh? That's what we need most of. We've bin laid off over a month now at the Coneygree. There's no more coke to fire the cupolas and, even if there was, they can't get no more pig iron.'

'Well we're back at work now, Alf. The coke's starting to come through now the miners are back. But what a mess. Now the blasted dockers are on about striking again. It's always the same. The miners, the dockers, the railway workers. They always go on strike together. The country's gone soft. It's all these unions, and that barmy Labour lot.' He felt in his jacket pocket and pulled out a packet of Woodbines. He offered one to Alf.

'Ta, Ben. Am yo' in a union yet?'

Ben struck a match and offered a light to his companion. 'What for? So they can stop me working? So they can tell me I've got to go out on strike all the while? Where's the sense in that, Alf? I tell you, I've seen enough of strikes. I wonder how much money they've each lost being out on strike? I know I've lost four week's money through 'em.' He lit his own cigarette, waved the match out and tossed it away as he inhaled the smoke deeply.

'It don't matter how much money they'n lost not workin', Ben. Yo' should be in a union to protect your own interests.' Alf regarded him earnestly. 'Unless everybody's together and stands firm the gaffers'll walk all over yer.'

'Is that right?'

'It is right, Ben.'

'That's what they want you to believe, Alf. I've heard it all before till I'm sick of hearing it. But it's all lies. Believe me, there's a sight more to fear from the unions than from any of the gaffers. Look at all the trouble they're causing. There's ne'er a union interested in the likes of you and me. All they're interested in is using us for their politics. We're just political fodder – pawns in a big game of politics.'

'Doh talk saft. Look at them poor sods in the cotton mills in Lancashire, locked out by the gaffers. Where would they be without a union?'

'At work, I expect,' Ben said cynically. 'The gaffers shut the mills because they didn't want a union telling 'em that all their workers should be

202

members. I don't blame 'em, either. If folks don't want to be in a union they shouldn't have to be. It ain't democratic.'

'But, on the other hand, Ben, if they want to be, then let 'em. All the while the unions am strivin' for better conditions for the likes of yo' and me – for better pay.'

'Alf, the only thing the unions are striving for is trouble. Striving to bring even more bloody poverty to everybody. Striving to bring the country to its knees by spreading discontent, so as the Marxists can take over the government.'

Alf inhaled the smoke from his cigarette, savouring it. 'Well, I'm in the union, Ben.'

'That's up to you, Alf, but you're laid off all the same. And d'you know why? Because your soft *brothers*, the miners, have been out on strike. That's why you're having to suffer. That's why we're all having to suffer. That don't strike me as being very brotherly, eh? When they went out on strike did you honestly believe as they considered the likes of you and me – other workers who depend on coal for our work? D'you honestly think they considered our wives and children, who depend on coal to keep warm through the winter?'

'I hadn't thought about it.'

'No. Not enough folk do. So where's the sense in it?'

'We'm all brothers, Ben. We'm workin' class. Don't yer see? We gorra stick together. As long as they get what they want I doh mind bein' laid off. It'll be for the best in the long run. We gorra show the gaffers who's boss.'

'Listen, Alf, you're single. You've got no wife and no kids to provide for. A good many have, and some are starving. Not only that, I see you're wheeling a cartload of coal home. Where did you find that?'

'Never mind where I found it,' Alf protested, 'but I paid over the odds for it.'

'You damned hypocrite. You're like all union men – grab, grab, grab. It don't matter who has to suffer, just grab what you can off anybody – off everybody. If you were true to your cause you'd do without.'

'Oh, I could do without all right, Ben, don't get me wrong. It's me mother and father I have to think about. They'm gettin' no younger.'

Ben tutted and shook his head in despair. 'Alf, you're softer than the bloody miners. And I should know. My own father was one.'

Poor Alf always had the feeling he was being savaged whenever he and Ben discussed politics. It wasn't so much that he believed Ben was right – far from it; he had his own beliefs – but Ben had a way of expressing himself simply and directly. Alf dearly wished he possessed the same talent.

'There's trouble brewing in the Dardanelles with them bloody Italians and Turks,' Alf remarked, changing the subject.

'There is, and let's hope we don't get dragged into it.' Ben stooped to pick out a stray weed. 'At least Winston Churchill's got it right. We've got to make sure we've got the best navy. We've got to build more warships. The Kaiser's got plenty now with his new dreadnoughts, and he's building

204

more. We'll have to watch them blasted Huns. We don't want them invading this country. They ain't like us, Alf.'

'I agree wi' yer there, Ben. They'd bugger things up for us good and proper.'

'And one thing we don't need is Huns here to bugger things up. We can do a great job all on our own,' Ben absently kicked a stone into the next allotment and flicked ash from the end of his cigarette. 'What d'you think about all these suffragettes, eh, Alf? I didn't mind them tying themselves to the railings and starving them- selves to death. That's up to them. But now they're smashing windows in the shops in London I think that's taking it a bit too far. It'll be Brummagem next, you'll see. And they think that sort of behaviour should entitle them to the vote? They'm softer than bellyache shit.'

'But we'm the saftest for standin' for it, Ben. I'm sick to death o' readin' about 'em in the paper. Would you let your missis do anythin' as saft?'

'Lizzie's got more sense.'

'Yes, I reckon so. How is Lizzie, anyroad, and the babby?'

'Lovely. Our Henzey's golden. We hardly know we've got a child.'

'Listen, I'm off for a pint in "The Junction" when I've tipped the coal in the cellar, Ben. Fancy one wi' me?'

Ben took a last drag on his cigarette and threw the end away. 'Go on, then. I'll just put me fork and shovel in the shed. There's a horse running at Chester that I fancy having a flutter on. I should be able to get a bet on in "The Junction" with Colonel Bradley.'

August 25th 1912 was the day Henzey was baptised. Daisy Foster, still unmarried, and May, were both godmothers, and Joe was godfather. The day after, the heaviest August rainfall in living memory fell, bringing widespread flooding. In early September Albert Crump died suddenly after a coronary thrombosis, and was buried on the 12th. He was sixty-six. As if in sympathy old Jack Clancey fell ill after the funeral, took to his bed and never got out of it again, save for using the commode they'd had in the family for years. He passed away at mid-day on the first Saturday in October, leaving Jesse to run the dairy business alone.

It had been nearly four years since Sylvia Dando and Jesse Clancey had split up. In that time she had not set eyes on Lizzie Kite, nor did she want to, but she was kept up to date on her life by her mother and father. Sylvia received a shock one Saturday morning when she answered the door to the milkman to find Jesse himself standing there waiting to fill their jugs. Prior to his death, Jack Clancey had always serviced the area where the Dandos lived. Seeing Jesse again set her heart fluttering. Time had healed her broken heart, but the scar that remained was tender and fragile; fragile enough to be ruptured by his friendly, easy conversation now.

'It's lovely to see you again, Jesse,' she said, 'and I was so sorry to learn of your father's death. Please give your mother my condolences.'

'Thanks, I will. So how are your own family, Sylvia?'

'Mother and Father are well, thank you.'

'And Stanley?'

'Well, as far as I know. He's still in South Africa, you know, but we expect him home within the next few months.'

'If we get embroiled in this trouble in the Balkans, I bet he's ever likely to be drafted there,' Jesse suggested.

They talked for a quarter of an hour, the quarrel that finally split them no longer relevant. Sylvia avoided telling Jesse that she was due to be married in November. Indeed, if he asked her out again she would accept and cancel her wedding if need be. Seeing Jesse made her realise that her love for James Atkinson, which she believed had flourished, was nowhere near as strong as it ought to be. But Jesse did not ask to see her. So Sylvia resigned herself to her forthcoming union with James, whom she still greatly admired, nonetheless.

When the day arrived that she was to be joined in Holy Matrimony, she smiled her lovely, even smile bravely, but complete contentment evaded her. The wedding took place on Sunday 10th November at St. Thomas's church at the top of the town. To Sylvia's profound disappointment the day yielded the densest fog for two years and it was bitterly cold. They'd booked a photographer, but the fog rendered his presence futile. When he was far enough away to get everybody in the frame of his plate camera and viewed the ground glass screen under his black cloth, he could see nobody. Experience told him that clients were seldom pleased to receive pictures of grey fog with the bride and groom hidden somewhere unseen in its murky depths. So he abandoned the photography and scheduled another day when they could all dress up again, and visit his studio.

At Christmas Ben was delighted when Lizzie informed him she was pregnant again. He reckoned it was the finest Christmas box he'd ever had. Henzey was in her shorter clothes by this time, and Lizzie began planning what extra things she would need for the new child, and what cast-offs she could utilise. She knew it would be hard work with two babies still in napkins but, for her, there was something about a new-born child that was hard to resist. Lizzie was unsure whether it was its total dependence, its smooth skin, or even its sweet, milky smell. It might have been all these things; and more. Whatever it was, Lizzie looked forward to her new child.

This time Lizzie gave Ben plenty of notice that she was having birth pains. On the Saturday night of Whit weekend everyone went out into the street to watch the fireworks display taking place in the castle grounds. The occasion was the Dudley Fete, held every Whitsuntide to raise funds for local charities. There seemed little sense in going and paying to watch when they could see it all across the valley. There was a great party atmosphere. Ben fetched two large jugs of bitter from 'The Sailor's Return' and placed them on the window sill while his mother-in-law gossiped with her life-long friend, Beccy Crump. While Lizzie sipped her drink leisurely, Beccy's cat stole under her skirt and sensually rubbed its soft, warm body against her shins. While she was secretly enjoying the sensation she felt a familiar twinge deep in her belly.

By bedtime, however, the pains seemed to have stopped. Therefore, she saw no reason to wake Ben during the night. But when he arose at seven next morning, urgently seeking the chamber pot, she announced that she'd been having pains again for more than three hours. He dressed at once, alerted Eve, and ran like a hare for Donald Clark, who should be sober at this time of day.

By this time Henzey was a bonny fifteen month baby, and had been walking for some weeks. May and Joe took her to the castle grounds in her wicker baby carriage while Lizzie rested with the new baby. Henzey sat up and smiled, gurgling with delight and flapping her arms excitedly at the hundreds of people she saw at the fete. Her blue eyes widened with wonder as Joe picked her up and, together, they watched a huge, hot air balloon rise gently from its mooring in the courtyard and float magically above the white castle keep in the warm sunshine.

To May it seemed painfully ironic that, as Joe carried Henzey in his arms, she should be pushing an empty baby carriage. She'd yearned for a child for so long that she despaired of ever realising her dream. They'd been married six years, she was twenty-eight, and still childless.

But Joe was philosophical. If God wanted her to have a child He would send her one, he said. It was little consolation, and she was sorry the baby Joe was holding so affectionately was not his own. He would make such a loving father.

Ben Kite was thoroughly proud of his new son, whom they christened Herbert, after Herbert Asquith. He adored his daughter, but a son was special. He thanked Lizzie and kissed her as he lay on the bed with her the day after the birth.

'When he grows up I'll teach him to play tip-cat and football,' he said fancifully, his hands behind his head. 'I'd love to see a son of mine playing for the Baggies. Then I'll teach him to make a catapult from the branch of a tree, like we used to when we were kids. I'll teach him how to swing a fire can...'

Lizzie turned to him. 'What? So's he can put stones through folks's windows and set himself on fire? There's nothing clever in kicking a bladder of wind about either.'

But he saw the humour in her eyes. 'Listen, Lizzie, we're talking about a lad here. Not one of them hooligan suffragettes.'

'Well, don't forget who'll have to rear him first ... me.'

'And you'll do a good job, Lizzie... Look at our Henzey'

Lizzie held Herbert in her arms contentedly while she and Ben continued to talk of the future. Their family was growing, and they had a great deal to look forward to.

The custom on most Saturday nights was for the

Kites and the Bishops to go either to 'The Junction', or to 'The Shoulder of Mutton', for a drink and a sing-song. Joe usually ended up playing the piano in the smoke room. Alcohol always loosened tongues, so the more they drank the more the gossip punctuated the singing. It was also a night when Lizzie put on her best frock and Ben dressed up in his three piece suit and stiff collar. Eve usually stayed at home these days with a bottle of stout, which she would pour into a glass and mull for a few seconds by immersing a red hot poker in it. She was content to stay indoors reading the newspaper and keeping an eye on the sleeping children.

One Saturday in May 1914, smoke hung like fog in 'The Junction' as Joe played *'Lily of Laguna'* specially requested by Jack Clayton, the landlord. Jack pulled him a foaming pint of bitter and placed it on top of the piano for Joe. Joe nodded his thanks with a smile, but kept on singing, and Tom the Tatter, the local rag and bone man, went up to replenish his glass.

Lizzie gossiped about a woman they knew from Brown Street who had run off with another man and all the money from her didlem club. It was scandalous, she said. She was glad she'd never joined her club. But May just tutted absently. She seemed preoccupied. Although she commented in the right places it seemed she was hardly listening properly to what Lizzie was saying. Joe, on the other hand, appeared full of vitality, and Lizzie watched him, throwing his head back in abandon as he played and sang; he was in his element.

'Our Joe's on form tonight, May. I haven't seen him like this for ages. Has he picked a winner today or something?'

'Not to me knowledge.'

'What are you feeding him on, then? He's really on form.'

May hesitated to answer, then smiled; a smile that spanned anxiety and contentment. She picked up her glass of beer, sipped it, then put it down again.

'What's the matter, May? You're fidgeting.'

'Oh, nothing's the matter, Lizzie. It's just that... Well, I didn't intend telling you yet, but I don't think as I can keep it to meself any longer.'

'What is it?' Lizzie picked up her own half pint glass and took a sip.

'I'm five months, Lizzie. I've never gone five months before.'

Lizzie put her glass down at once lest she spill any beer. She flung her arm round May's shoulders and gave her a hug. 'Oh, May, that's the best news I've heard for ages. When are you due?'

'End of September. Ooh, I'm that pleased. But I'm that frit as well. I just hope to God as nothing goes wrong this time.'

'I'll pray for you, May... Oh, wait till Mother knows. Have you told our Joe yet?'

'He knows all right. He's proud as Punch. That's why he's playing like Paderewski tonight, bless him. Hark at him.'

Lizzie laughed. She was heavily pregnant herself, yet again, expecting her third child in little over a month. They had not intended this one and, at first, she was not pleased about it. Herbert would be barely a year old when this next child was born. Her body was getting no respite; bearing children and giving succour to them was wearing. Ben was more enthusiastic, though, and said he hoped they'd have ten; somebody to look after them in their old age. Yes, she'd replied, it was all right for him; he didn't have to carry them for nine months; he didn't have to get up in the middle of the night to feed them; he didn't have to wash their dirty napkins. Yet soon enough Lizzie accepted it willingly, and quite fancied the idea of another son.

Now she was happy for May. She knew just how much her sister-in-law had longed for a child, and how anxious Joe was that they'd met with no success. They must be ecstatic.

'D'you want to keep it secret, May?'

'Keep it secret? Why, I'm like a dog with two bones. I want to bawl it from the top of Cawney Hill.'

'Well there's no need. Phyllis Fat's over there. She's got a mouth bigger than a parish oven. Tell her tonight and the world'll know tomorrow. But let me tell everybody in here, eh?' She took a sip of her beer. 'Here's to you, May.'

When Joe finished playing and was ready for his next tune, Lizzie stood up and called to him. Joe turned round.

'Everybody, there's something you should all know.' She gained attention straight away. 'Our Joe's going to be a father in September, and it's the best news I've heard in a long time.' She took up her glass again, raising it into the air. 'Here's to you both – to the three of you.'

Everybody cheered, raised their glasses, and drank. May blushed vividly as she received everybody's congratulations.

'How about a round of drinks, Joe?' called Colonel Bradley, who was really a woman. She wore men's clothes, had a military bearing, but drank and swore like a collier.

Ben got up from his stool and went to the bar. He placed a half sovereign on the counter and asked Jack to fill everybody's glass.

'It'll be worth it, just so's I don't have to hear 'em going on all the time about how they wish they could have a child,' Ben remarked to Jack Clayton. 'Jesus, I only have to throw me trousers over the bed rail and our Lizzie's caught again.'

Chapter 12

In June 1914 two million people, including Ben Kite, were laid off work as a result of strikes by railwaymen, miners and building workers. Ben was incensed that his earnings should be cut for causes with which he had utterly no sympathy. It affected him the more since Lizzie presented him with their third child, born on the 21st; another daughter, to be christened Alice.

So besides a wife and a mother-in-law to support he was now father to three young children. His only source of income while he was laid off work was from produce he could sell from his allotment. It didn't amount to much, but the allotment also yielded some free food for their table. Meat of course, was not free, and they had to do without, until Beccy Crump donated one of her hens, which Lizzie plucked and drew and roasted one Sunday.

Besides all the industrial strife that seemed never ending, the suffragettes had been misbehaving again, setting fire to churches this time. Ben swore he would set fire to that damned Mrs Pankhurst and oblige the rest of civilised society, if ever he came across her.

When she could finally sit down in an evening, Lizzie read the newspapers Ben brought home; and what she read did not charge her with complacency for the future. It had become clear that war in Europe was inevitable. She didn't understand the issues as Ben did, but she was afraid that Great Britain could never stay out of it. She feared for other women; women like herself who might lose husbands or sons. She recalled the heartache she felt when her own father was killed so needlessly by Jack Clancey's runaway horse and cart, and tried to imagine how she would feel if she lost Ben, just as needlessly, on the battlefield. The thought sent a shudder down her spine. How would her children turn out, deprived of a father? How would she and her mother cope having three children to feed? Would she ever get over the heartbreak? It was a monstrously depressing thought.

But she knew she needn't concern herself. Thank God, they would be safe from such traumas, because Ben was in an essential job, ladling the pig iron that the local foundries needed to produce engine blocks and pistons, gearbox casings, arms and munitions, parts for machine tools, for locomotives, and for anything that was produced from cast iron – when he was not laid off. He would never have to go and fight, and she was eternally thankful. At least he would stay at home, safe. They would remain a complete family.

Ben arrived home sweating and grubby from his allotment on the first Monday in August. It was a Bank Holiday and the weather was hot and humid. Lizzie, breast feeding Alice when he came in, noticed his worried expression. Herbert was in his high chair, his face smeared in home-made damson jam, and he was busily rubbing a crust of bread into his fair hair. Henzey sat at the table, her pretty face just peering above it, drinking a cup of milk.

'Have you heard the news, our Lizzie?'

Lizzie's face dropped at the gravity in his voice. 'No. What is it, Ben?'

He took off his jacket and hung it behind the cellar door, then peered at himself in the mirror over the mantelpiece inspecting the stubble on his chin.

'The damned Kaiser's declared war on France. To get there he'll invade Belgium. You know what that means?' He turned from the mirror and sat beside her on the brown leatherette couch. 'We could be at war tomorrow, our Lizzie. Asquith's already told the Germans we shall stand by the

Treaty of London.'

'What's the Treaty of London mean?'

'Well it guarantees Belgian neutrality. It means we're obliged to defend 'em.'

'Oh, God, no. So when did you hear this?'

'There's a special edition of the paper tonight. I've just met Alf Collins in Brown Street. He let me read his. I've tried to buy one, but everywhere's sold out.'

For months Ben had seen the threat growing with the massive build up of arms in the whole of Europe; Germany vying for naval supremacy with new submarines and warships, Russia quadrupling her army. The assassination of the Habsburg heir, Archduke Franz Ferdinand, at Sarajevo in Bosnia, a province that Austria had seized in 1908, had precipitated their invasion of Serbia, so drawing in the Russians, who supported Serbia. Thus, the Triple Alliance with the Austro-Hungarian Empire bound the Kaiser to declare war on the Czar. The signing of the Triple Entente in 1893, initiated by their mutual fear of invasion by Germany, meant that France was Russia's ally. And in order to attack France, German forces would march through Belgium, embroiling the British.

'What's for tea, Lizzie?'

'Rabbit pie, love. Mother'll serve it up in a minute. She's in the brewhouse. Why don't you go out and have your wash, and tell her you're back?... What are you smiling at?'

'Well, if I go to the brewhouse for a wash she'll see I'm back. I won't need to tell her.'

Lizzie tutted, incredulous that at such a time he

217

should find something that trivial so amusing. The child she was suckling momentarily lost her nipple, and she guided it back to her searching mouth.

Ben looked at his son, covered in jam, and he smiled again. He put his hand on Henzey's head and felt her soft hair. 'All right, my little sweetheart?' he asked, almost in a whisper. She nodded, grinning with a mouthful of bread, and he bent down to plant a kiss on her grubby cheek. Ben prayed silently, as he stripped off his shirt and vest, that God might spare him to see his children grow up.

Next day, August 4th, Britain declared war on Germany.

That month the heat was sweltering. Suddenly, the whole country was on the move. Families who could afford a holiday decided to return home early. Consequently, trains were delayed and overcrowded. In Dudley, as in every other town and village, men flocked to recruiting stations that had been hastily set up, and queued to enlist in the army. Normal daily life was suspended, and nobody knew for how long. Panic buying caused a sharp rise in prices, and some shops opened only three days a week afterwards because they had nothing left to sell. In the town several shops soon had no staff due to army recruitment and, to make matters worse, there was a critical disruption of all deliveries. Territorials left their idyllic summer camps to be equipped for active service. Army officers scoured the country to requisition horses for the cavalry, for the artillery and for general transportation, while women began assuming men's jobs.

In mid September, Ben, no longer laid off work, read the heartening news that the Allies had driven the Germans back to the Aisne. The threat to Paris had been removed and the war would soon be won. It would all be over by Christmas.

War meant that every last drop of effort was required from a work force no longer concerned with bickering over conditions of employment, wages and other such issues. Survival against an enemy who had been spoiling for a fight for years was uppermost in everyone's mind. All at once industry was at full stretch, trying to satisfy the demands the situation imposed on it. Holcroft's, like any other foundry, struggled to meet orders, and they worked twenty-four hours a day.

Ben Kite preferred the night shift in the summer; it was cooler. In the sweltering heat of an August daytime, working over a pig-bed – row upon row of open sand moulds filled with white-hot, molten iron, which had to remain where it was till it solidified and cooled to five or six hundred degrees – was barely tolerable. Besides having the pig-bed to contend with, when his ladle needed refilling Ben had to push it to within a few feet of the searing heat of the blast-furnace in order to 'tap out' from the hearth. Then the iron flowed along a channel, lined with refractories, from the tap hole, and filled his ladle. It was no wonder he was so lean.

The ladle was a device for transferring the

molten iron to open sand moulds lined up on an uneven floor, strewn with used sand and solidified slag. It hung suspended from a track akin to an overhead railway line, and its whole weight, massive when laden, had to be pushed and pulled into position manually, and swivelled when about to be poured. To help him, Ben had a workmate, Toby Bott, a small man twenty years his senior, who generally did the tapping out and some of the shoving.

'Ready to slag off, Toby?' Ben was barely audible above the roar of the blast furnace, but Toby, attuned to the call, acknowledged it. Ben pointed to the slag hole as he began to haul the ladle back, wiping sweat from his brow with the back of a well-worn leather gauntlet.

Toby first tapped off the slag, a mixture of molten limestone and coke ash, from the other side of the furnace into a truck that ran on rails along the floor. At the same time Ben positioned his ladle, ready to receive the relatively pure iron from the other tap hole. He never ceased to marvel at the material. It seemed to flow and splash like water at this temperature, but solidified while still glowing red. He treated it with the utmost respect; too often he had received minor burns from splashes, and they hurt. He had no wish to invite a major accident by careless handling. So he wore a ganzie – a rough protective garment akin to a heavy pullover; a leather apron, moleskin trousers, and high boots; all to protect him from burns; and all this despite the heat.

Toby plugged the slag hole and shoved the

freshly filled truck along its track, where another man, Sol Bennett, shoved it away it to tip it on the slag heap beyond the charging bay. He then walked round to where Ben was waiting, and tapped off the pure iron. Conversation was limited because of the deafening noise and, while Ben watched this white hot metal flow, his head was filled with thoughts about the war; thoughts he couldn't yet reveal to Lizzie, although they'd been crowding his mind for months. Nobody wanted war. The sooner it was over, the sooner everybody could breathe again; the sooner life could continue normally. Ben was beginning to believe that the quickest way to end this war was to deal a crushing blow to the enemy; and such a crushing blow could only be dealt if there was an army big enough, and sufficiently well trained and equipped. The strategists had to do their bit, but the army needed every man who could be spared.

'Have you thought about volunteering for the army, Toby?' Ben shouted.

'Me? The army?' Toby was yelling at the top of his voice. 'Why the bloody 'ell should I want to join the army? This job's bloody 'ard enough. It needs to be done by men. Do yo' know e'er a woman as could do it? That's why it's a reserved occupation, mate. Kitchener can kiss my arse.'

Those words 'reserved occupation' were creeping into everyday language lately. All right, so they were in a reserved occupation, like miners, like policemen, like farmers; they were doing their bit for their country.

The ladle was full, and Ben turned, putting his

221

weight against the wheel, about to pour. Toby plugged the tap hole and joined him. In the acrid, smoky atmosphere Ben could see men dragging solidified ingots away with huge steel tongues, shaking the scorched sand off them. Other men placed new moulds in the space made available, ready to be cast. Toby thrust the ladle forward.

'I wouldn't fight in this war if they was to crown me wi' gold,' Toby said. 'There'll be some blood an' snot flyin' yet, yo' mark my words. The Germans have bin dyin' to have a goo at we for donkey's years, mate. They wo' gi' up that easy. They'm like we – bloody 'ardened bastards.'

They reached the first of the new moulds, and stood back from the ladle. Ben wiped his brow again, and the sweat out of his eyes with the sleeve of his ganzie. He put his hand on the wheel and began turning it. The ladle tilted and iron began to pour out, right on target.

'They ain't so hard as they can't be beat, Toby,' he said. 'I wouldn't mind a crack at 'em.'

'Yo'm best off 'ere, mate, tek it from me. Anyroad, what would your missis say now yo've got three babbies to consider?'

'That's exactly who I am considering, Toby. It's their future I'm concerned about.'

As soon as Lizzie went downstairs next morning she knew Ben had not intended to go to work. He'd taken his bike and gone out as usual, but he seemed in no hurry. He'd said nothing, but she knew him well enough to know what was on his mind these last few weeks. He was not an adventurer, but his honest principles and his conscience drove him, and they would drive him to war just as sure as death. Her only hope now was that this same conscience would drive him to stay with his family. Oh, others equally conscientious had been quick enough and brave enough to volunteer, she knew; but not Ben. Please, God, not Ben.

All day she was preoccupied, worrying about the future; and the children had got on her nerves. Lizzie wanted them all to be together always. Nothing else really mattered. The thought of war, and losing him to it, scared her to death. She was certain that war would part them for ever.

Ben arrived home early. As soon as he walked through the door she challenged him, her face stony but her eyes filling with tears.

'Where've you been, Ben? I know you haven't been to work.'

Guiltily he looked into the fire. 'I have, my flower, but I went to volunteer first. I'm due to report to Brummagem New Street in the morning. I got a travel warrant.'

Lizzie said nothing. She sat down on the couch and ran her fingers anxiously through her dark hair. Her thoughts turned to the reports she'd read in the newspapers of thousands dead and wounded, of the German army's relentless advance now through Europe. She imagined the destruction and the carnage, and her husband caught up in it. Anger welled up inside her that he should even contemplate such recklessness, risking his life when there was no need. There

223

would be nothing but uncertainty, strife and darkness ahead; perhaps years of not knowing where or how he was; whether he was fit, or wounded; among the quick, or the dead.

At that moment little Henzey ran up the entry with Marge 'Ardmate, and Lizzie heard her chuckling in the back yard as she played, oblivious to the trials besetting her mother and father. Eve sat on her high-backed chair bouncing Herbert on her knee, sensing a crisis from the tense atmosphere.

'I'm sorry, my flower.' Ben sat beside Lizzie and put his arm around her. 'I had to do it. My conscience would never let me rest if I didn't go and do my bit. The country needs men like me to fight and, unless we do, we shall lose the war. Nobody wants to be ruled by the damned Kaiser. D'you want our kids ruled by him?'

Still she said nothing.

'We've all got to stand up and be counted. We've got to fight for what we believe in.'

Though she tried, Lizzie could not stop her tears. They trembled for a second or two on her eyelids before rolling down her face, making her cheeks wet as if she were out in a rainstorm. But her anger was dissipating.

'I knew you'd go and do it, Ben. I just knew.' She pulled a handkerchief from her sleeve and wiped her eyes. 'You're too good – too decent. You'll go and get yourself shot or something for what you believe in. How d'you think I'll feel if that happens? How d'you think the children will grow up without a father? What shall we live on? Have you thought about that? I'll be a widow for the rest of my life and I'm only twenty-four now. Have you thought about that?'

He hugged her tight, and Eve looked on with concern. Though she could not hear, she knew exactly what the fuss was about; she'd seen it all before.

'But you're talking as if I'm already dead, Lizzie. I've no intention of getting myself killed. We're doing well in this war and it'll be over in no time – by Christmas they reckon. That's all I shall be away – a few months... Then I'll be back, and things'll settle down to normal, and you'll be as proud as Punch that I went.'

'But you don't have to go, Ben. You can still be here with me and the children, while you're doing your bit for the country making pig-iron. Why d'you want to go? I don't understand you. Let the single men go.'

'You don't understand what it means to me, my flower.'

'And you don't understand what you mean to me, Ben. I'll never understand why you want to go and leave us.'

'Oh, please don't cry, Lizzie. Here, let me dry your tears.'

'Leave me alone. I can dry my own tears.' It was hopeless. Why was he so stupid, so inconsiderate? Why did he want to make a hero of himself? She did not want a hero for a husband. She just wanted him safe, with her. She began thumping his chest in frustration. 'I love you with all my heart, you big soft fool,' she blubbered. 'The children love you, you must know that. What about if you do get killed? I couldn't live without

225

you, Ben... I'd die without you. Oh, Ben! How can you leave your kids, knowing you might never come back?'

Eve looked on and tears welled up in her eyes too, though she tried to suppress them. She eased herself onto her feet and hobbled over to Ben, the child in her arms.

'What's up? Have you joined up, or something?' Both Ben and Lizzie looked up at her, and Ben nodded solemnly. 'I thought as much. You won't be the last to go, either, I don't suppose. God be with you, my son.'

Little Henzey, two and a half years old, saw her mother weeping at the dinner table. Her father, looking aggrieved, said little, and the lack of conversation induced deep anxiety in her. She did not understand the sudden, silent drama being enacted before her, but her alert mind perceived that all was not well. Her limited experience suggested that only little girls and little boys cried. To see her mother crying was perturbing.

Ben put the two children to bed in the box room where they slept a little earlier than usual that night. First, he tucked in Herbert and kissed him on his forehead.

'Goodnight, my son,' he whispered, and touched the top of his head lovingly.

'Why's Mommy crying?' Henzey asked as she snuggled down in the same bed and tugged the blankets up around her neck.

Her hair cascaded onto the pillow like ten thousand strands of dark brown silk. Ben sat on the bed beside her and leaned over her. Tears stung in his eyes as he looked at her pretty face, but he fought them back. God alone knew how much he would miss his children. God alone knew how long it would be before he saw them again – if he ever did. It grieved him to think he might miss the best years of their growing up if this war was prolonged. He began to feel guilty.

'Mommy was crying because Daddy's got to go away for a long time, my little precious, and Mommy doesn't want Daddy to go.'

'Oh. Am you goin' to join the army?'

He nodded, smiling into her trusting, blue eyes. 'Shall y'ave a gun?'

'Yes, I'll have a big gun. And I'll shoot all the Germans.'

Henzey grinned. 'Will it be a pop-gun?'

'No, my flower, it won't be a pop-gun. It'll be a real gun. Now listen, sweetheart – when I'm gone I want you to be a big girl and look after your Mommy for me. Will you do that? I want you to promise me that you'll be good and help her all you can looking after Herbert and little Alice... Promise?' She nodded. It was a solemn, binding pledge. 'When you wake up in the morning I'll already be gone.'

He pressed his cheek against hers and she felt the hard stubble of his face. Then she felt his lips, soft and warm, brush her cheek and linger for a second as he kissed her. The contrasting textures of his face seemed to amplify the two sides of him that she already took for granted: his roughness and his gentleness, though she instinctively preferred the gentler side. She wrapped her little

227

arms around his head and felt a tear from his eye smudge across her cheek. Her anxiety returned. She had no comprehension of why her father had to go, but she accepted it with trust enough. It was not so easy for her mother to accept, that was obvious. Ben turned and blew her a kiss as he lingered for a second by the door. Then he pulled it to, and she heard him trudge downstairs.

Next morning, Lizzie got up with Ben at half past five, full of foreboding. It was still dark. He lit the gaslight and raked out the fire that had been left in overnight. Flames danced into life, and she cooked bacon and eggs in the Dutch oven that sat on the strides in front of the fire. Ben boiled up the kettle, brewed a pot of tea, and shaved in the mirror over the mantelpiece. That done, he cleaned his teeth and swilled his face. At twenty five minutes past six Lizzie was holding him in her arms on the back doorstep. They had said most of what they wanted to say as they lay in bed last night. Lizzie wanted those precious moments to last forever, even though she silently cried the whole time they were making love. It might have been the very last time they did it together. She would have given anything for time to have stood still, before it could finally rob her of the husband she loved so much. A shiver ran cold down her spine. Now it was time to say their last good-byes for heaven knew how long.

'I love you, Ben. Take good care. And write every day.'

He stroked her loose hair. 'Try not to fret, our Lizzie. I'll be all right, I promise. Just take good

228

care of yourself, and the kids. Give them a kiss for me every night when they go to bed, and don't let them forget me. For Christ's sake don't let them forget me. And say cheerio to your mother for me.'

'Oh, God bless you, Ben, and keep you safe.'

He hugged her a last time. 'You look so beautiful when you cry, Lizzie,' he said softly, and let go of her. He picked up his grubby, brown suitcase and walked down the entry.

She did not follow. She couldn't bear to see him walk away. It might be the last time she ever caught sight of him. So she wanted this treasured memory to be of him holding her in his arms, not watching him disappear down Cromwell Street, forlorn, heedlessly walking to his death carrying a suitcase.

She turned and went indoors. In the tiny back room she poked the coals into life again and sat on the chair he always sat in. A tear rolled down her cheek and she took a handkerchief from her apron pocket and wiped it away. Never before had she felt so wretched. She gazed blankly into the coals and felt an intolerable ache in her heart. The wedding ring she'd worn for the last four years she turned around on her finger absently, and she thought she was going to choke on the lump that came to her throat. Why must there be wars to create all this unbearable heartache? Another tear wet her cheek and she felt it trace its way to her chin. She whispered his name, over and over, and for every time she spoke it another tear fell. Her heart was stone cold with grief for the only man she had ever truly loved. He might as well be dead already. A whimper escaped her throat, and then tears flowed in a torrent. 'You look so beautiful when you cry,' he'd said. The whimpers turned to sobs, and the tiny handkerchief she held to her eyes was soon saturated. After some minutes of uncontrollable sobbing she felt a gentle touch on her shoulder. Her heart thumped and she looked up, expecting him back.

'Has he gone already?' Eve asked.

Lizzie nodded and blew her nose, her eyes puffy from all this useless crying.

'Come back up to bed, then, my wench. Maybe you'll cry yourself back to sleep.'

'I doubt if I'll ever sleep again, Mother.'

Chapter 13

May Bishop squirmed agonisingly in her bed, her contractions more frequent now. She was wide awake and apprehensive and, to take her mind off the searing pains in her belly as her unborn child began to make its way into the world, she tried to imagine what it might look like, whether it would be a boy or a girl. Her eyes were wide, alert, but in the darkness she could see nothing. No moonlight infiltrated the room through the heavy, velvet curtains that hung at the window. Joe was beside her, his back towards her, snoring like a pig in a stupor, but through his hideous grunts she could hear the rumble of the night soil men's wheelbarrow in the entry. Another pain gripped her. She'd better wake him before her water broke.

'What's up?' he croaked.

'You'd better fetch Annie Soap, Joe.'

He rolled out of bed at once, stood up, and fumbled round on the mantelpiece where he knew a box of matches should be. In the charcoal dimness he found them and lit a candle. Shielding his eyes from the brightness he squinted at the clock: ten minutes past one. He'd been in bed two hours. He picked up his long johns and pulled them on, then his vest, his shirt and his trousers.

'The night soilers have just come,' May said. 'Mind you don't fall over the barrow.'

'Mind I don't fall *in* it might be better advice.' He put on his socks and shoes, pulled his jacket from the back of a chair, donned his cap, and yawned. 'Now you'm sure you'm well on the way? I don't want to fetch Annie if you've got another day to go. She costs enough as it is.'

'Fetch her, Joe. If I'm not ready yet she can always go back home to wait. But the pains are coming regular now. It's a sure sign.'

'Well at least it ain't so far as fetching Donald Clark.'

'Donald Clark. Pooh! He's about as much use as a glass eye. He's never sober when you want him. Anyroad, I don't agree with having men to do a midwife's work, doctor or no. And I didn't agree with Lizzie having him. Still, that's her business, not mine.'

Joe had no wish to discuss the vices and virtues

231

of the doctor and the midwife, especially if it meant being critical of his own sister's preferences. He was content that May wanted Annie Soap to attend her, and Annie would come gladly – she would be glad of the money. So he said he wouldn't be long, and left.

The night soil men were emptying the communal privies of Cromwell Street. They dumped the awesome contents of their wheelbarrows into six foot rings of lime, laid at the side of the road, ready to be mixed and shovelled onto the muck cart following behind. They worked quickly and quietly, their only light a lantern. Joe held his breath as he hurried past a reeking pile dumped outside Beccy Crump's front door. A man was mixing the lime into it with his shovel to make it drier and easier to handle. Joe bid him goodnight and silently thanked God that he was a ships' chainmaker and did not have to shovel that stuff for a living. Working in a forge was hot, noisy, and the air was laden with dust, scale, and oil fumes, but it had its compensations. He headed up Watson Street, heading for Annie Soap's house on Cawney Hill in the black, moonless night. No gas had been laid on there, so there were no street lamps. Another night soiler was hanging on to his wheelbarrow and its unpleasant cargo as it tried to run away with him down the hill. Even the muck cart couldn't get up there, and the stuff had to be brought down in wheelbarrows. As they passed, the two men wished each other good morning, and the man's lantern afforded Joe light enough to see the entry he was seeking. Cautiously, he walked through it and into the back yard. Annie's was the end house on the right. He rapped loudly on the back door. Within seconds a croaky, female voice called through an open upstairs window, and Joe identified himself. He told her that May Bishop's time had come.

'Babbies! Why dun they always drop when I'm tryin' to get some shuteye?' Annie squawked. 'Never mind. Put plenty wairter on th'ob to bile, my mon. I shall need some twine, a pair o' scissors, and plenty towels an' all. I'll be round as soon as I've fastened me stays.'

May had lived in the hope that she would have as easy a time of childbirth as Lizzie. But she was nervous and tense because of her previous disappointments. She did not want to lose this child. By the light of a candle Annie tried to coax her gently, kindly, to relax her, but May started yelling with pain and with fear. Never in her life before had she experienced anything so unpleasant. Then her water broke, at last. The contractions came hard and powerful. She tried to relax. She pushed. She strained. The contractions came again and she screamed, clinging to the brass bedrail so tightly for comfort in her anguish that her knuckles were white. She twisted and turned endlessly, seeking relief, her contorted face wet with perspiration. For half the night hideous pains gripped her like some wild animal with its teeth in her belly. For half the night she pushed. For half the night she sweated like a furnaceman, biting her bottom lip till it was raw. Was it hurting her child as much? But the child could not cry stuck inside her.

Then the baby's head appeared. Thank God it would soon be over. She couldn't stand much more of this gruesome pain. She pushed again... And again. It was sheer bloody torture. She was so hot, so tired already, but worst of all she was making no headway. The child didn't want to come any further. It wasn't like this for Lizzie. She heard her own cries becoming weaker, desperate, like a cat caught in a trap. Perhaps she was going to die. It was easy now to understand how women died in childbirth.

Now Annie fretted. May emitted a series of piercing screams. Why wouldn't the poor little soul come further? She pushed, yelled some more, but she was utterly exhausted. And Annie Soap cursed like a pit bank wench as the forceps failed to urge the child out into the world.

Joe sat downstairs at the table, his head in his hands. With all the commotion he thought his wife was being murdered. Time dragged while he waited tensely for news. He started feeling faint, so sought his bottle of whisky and poured himself a large one. Long since, the night soilers had departed. At five o' clock he'd heard the clatter of hoofs and wheels outside, as Jesse Clancey drove his cart over the cobbles on his way to the station to collect his churns of milk. With all the anxiety waiting brought, and poor May's physical suffering, Joe made up his mind there'd definitely be no more children. He wished he could sleep, oblivious to the wailings, but he knew he could not. Each time he heard May screaming he wanted to scream himself. He parted the curtains in the scullery and saw that day was breaking.

How much longer could this go on? Then, at last, he heard Annie's cumbersome footsteps slowly trudging down the wooden stairs. He looked up apprehensively.

'Is it all over?'

Annie shook her head. 'Yo'd better fetch the doctor, Joe. And yo'd better be quick. The babby's stuck. Quick as yer can. Goo on, my mon! Run... Run!'

Joe grabbed his cap and ran like a frenzied terrier to Donald Clark's house. He didn't understand the implications of his child being stuck, but it sounded ominous. It was light now and the early morning haze hung over the trees in Dixons Green like a fine lace mantle. Urgently, he tugged the bell-pull at Hawthorn Villa and waited for what seemed like hours. The maid appeared, still fastening her dressing gown. She adjusted her cap and said she remembered him. But this time there was no mischievous gleam in his eye. This time he had no inclination to stop and jest. Joe explained that his wife needed the doctor quick. So the maid ran upstairs to wake Donald.

Donald came down trying to smooth his tousled hair.

'What is it, Joe?' he asked kindly.

'It's May. She's in labour, but the babby's stuck. Annie's sent me to fetch you.'

'Is it breeched?'

Joe tried to read the doctor's concerned expression. 'God only knows. All I know is that May's been squealing like a scalded cat all night. Can you come?'

'Of course. Give me a minute to get dressed.'

In ten minutes Donald Clark was at May's bedside. He worked quickly and efficiently, reassuring May that it would soon be over. Unfortunately he was unable to prevent the very thing he dreaded most: whilst May and Joe's daughter was alive she had been starved of oxygen for too long, and he feared she would be brain-damaged.

As he promised he would, Ben Kite wrote every day to Lizzie. His letters were a joy when he told her of the amusing incidents that peppered his training. He'd ultimately been posted to France, and his tone suggested it was a relief to go. Thereafter, Lizzie deliberately avoided looking at newspapers, and tried to shut her ears to the cries of the street vendors who shouted the latest disturbing news. It was clear now that the war would be long and drawn out. David Lloyd George doubled income tax to pay for it, raising it to a shilling and sixpence in the pound. Yet despite trying to cut herself off from the news, the hearsay, and the prophets of doom, she still heard about the German warships callously shelling north east coastal towns just a few days ago, killing hundreds of innocent citizens. She was thankful she lived where she did in the middle of England, where German shells couldn't reach.

That December, Lizzie walked up Cromwell Street's gentle incline holding Henzey's hand. The thought of the roaring fire in the shiny, black grate waiting to warm her and welcome her, made her eager to get home. She'd been to the Post Office to get her allowance, and queued at Totty Marsh's in Brown Street for Sunlight soap and Reckitt's Blue for washing day. From the fishmonger, who came round with a cart, she bought 'cockeyed salmon' for tea, which was actually bream, but so called because of the pink flesh. She bought firewood and vegetables, and then called at Sammy Giles's sweet shop in George Street, where she was paying a penny a week for the children to have some sweets at Christmas. Henzey charmed Sammy with a rendering of *'Here we go round the mulberry bush'*, as she sat on the counter. Her reward was two ounces of dolly-mixtures.

They reached home and the warmth. Lizzie took off Henzey's winter coat, then her own, and rubbed her hands together in front of the blazing fire.

'Kettle's just come to the boil,' Eve said. 'I'll make a cup of tea. Oh, there's a letter for you in the second post, our Lizzie.'

Lizzie took it and smiled. She read it avidly, and breathed a sigh of relief. Ben was all right.

Eve made the pot of tea, which she placed on the hob to steep. She turned to her granddaughter who'd just handed Herbert two dolly mixtures as he sat playing in a creaking wicker clothes basket with some clothes pegs.

'Come and sit with me at the table, Henzey, and we'll make some paper chains to hang up for Christmas,' Eve said. The child jumped up and down excitedly and took her place at the table. Grandmother took a cracked cup from the

237

cupboard at the side of the grate and made some paste with flour and water. Then she went into the front room and came out with some brightly coloured paper and a pencil. 'Here. Here's a blacklead to draw with.'

'Draw me an 'orse again, Gran, please,' Henzey said.

'Oh, I wish I could draw like your daddy.'

Somehow the horse Eve sketched so unsophisticatedly always had a smile on its face. The few simple lines fascinated the child. Henzey saw a magic in being able to represent objects this way. Thus, she spent hours quietly occupying herself, drawing and crayoning animals. She drew odd characters she claimed were her grandmother, her mother, her father, and Marge Hardwick. Sometimes she crudely tried to copy pictures she saw in newspapers and, when she finished them, she proudly showed them off, usually to her grandmother, who praised her and encouraged her.

That afternoon they sat for an hour, when Eve produced several yards of paper chain, and little Henzey several strange looking horses on the scraps left over. Lizzie hung the crude decorations across the room along with some silver balls that were given an airing every Christmas. When she finished she heard Alice, now six months old, crying upstairs. As she climbed the narrow staircase she considered what she would say in her next letter to Ben. She had something special to tell him: she was pregnant again.

Four children in as many years was too many. It crossed her mind that the war might be a blessing in disguise as far as her body was concerned. Much as she loved her husband, the longer war continued the longer she might keep her belly vacant. She picked Alice from her crib and cuddled her, cooing soft words of love and comfort to the child.

And she thought about Ben, languishing, wet through, chilled to the heart, and probably louse bound in some squalid, muddy trench. She wished with all her heart that he was with her instead. She missed him dreadfully; especially at night. God, how she missed him at night. To even think about war detaining him just for the sake of her own stupid vanity was not only selfish, it was also tempting Providence.

In May 1915 Lizzie gave birth to another daughter. She decided to call the child Maxine, simply because she liked the name. It was another easy birth, conducted entirely by Eve and May. As with all her children, there was an immediate bond, a grateful acceptance of the child, and an instant love. Lizzie's only regret was that Ben was not there to share her joy.

The easy time Lizzie had giving birth galled May Bishop. May was bitter that her own daughter, christened Emmeline after the suffragette, Emmeline Pankhurst, was so obviously mentally retarded. The knowledge that her baby would never be like other children was almost impossible to accept. Poor Joe had been reduced to tears, and he wondered what wicked deed he'd perpetrated to be thus punished. He was devoted to his child, however, and swore to do all he could that she might enjoy as near normal a life as possible.

May's frustration was the cause of her acting spitefully towards little Henzey. While Joe or Lizzie were with her she would show only affection and kindness. Yet once, when their backs were turned, she vindictively shoved Henzey over some coping stones and into a small flower bed that Ben had made in the shared back yard. The backs of her legs were grazed and bleeding and she cried copious tears. But the real hurt she felt was that her Aunty May had deliberately tried to hurt her, and she didn't know why. She'd done nothing wrong. She hadn't been naughty at all. Aunty May came past her and just seemed to push her backwards. Then, to add to her confusion, she said how sorry she was for being so clumsy, and carried her to the brewhouse where she bathed the wounds and tried to calm her down with a boiled sweet and lots of kisses. There were some things about grown-ups that Henzey could not quite fathom out.

Coincidentally, in October that year, Eve Bishop fell over the same coping stones and into the same flower bed. She broke her wrist, dislocated her shoulder and twisted her ankle. Lizzie immediately sent for Donald Clark. He set her wrist in plaster and tried to manipulate her shoulder, but the pain was excruciating. Eve took to her bed, and Lizzie sent word to Ted and Grenville, and to Lucy. In turn, and in time, they all called to see how she was.

Ted brought with him two pounds of bacon, a pound of butter, half a pound of Typhoo tea and a bottle of Camp coffee from his corner shop in West Bromwich, all of which were in short supply and expensive because of the war. Grenville, however, lived in Whitmore Reans in Wolverhampton and, since it was half a day out to get to Dudley and back, he rarely saw his mother, or any one else in the family, but to show willing he brought her a bottle of Stothert's head and stomach pills. Lucy made the journey from Manchester and stayed a couple of nights. However, she was not a lover of children and, even though Lizzie's behaved well, they irritated her.

Despite the best endeavours of Donald Clark, Eve Bishop's condition deteriorated. She lost her appetite and couldn't face food, so her dietary regime went awry. Her general condition went awry with it. Pneumonia set in, which Donald feared might happen, and Lizzie watched anxiously as her mother's health rapidly deteriorated. Lizzie did all she could, tending her mother with care and devotion; but with four little children to look after as well, and Maxine still being breast-fed, she felt totally exhausted.

Lizzie felt that her world was caving in on her. How come the contentment and happiness she took so much for granted a year or so ago had suddenly vanished? Her safe little world had been turned upside down. What had she done to deserve it? She was so lonely, her husband half a continent away, a target for those damned German guns. She'd had another child that she could have better done without and, now, her mother, her mentor, her best friend, was gravely ill. She had only May and Joe to turn to for help and, whilst they did all they could, and willingly, their own child needed constant attention too. Lizzie was tired; too tired to be angry, and her exhaustion was matched only by her profound depression.

On the evening of the tenth day of the pneumonia, Donald Clark made his second visit of the day. It was Eve's critical day, he said; today would tell whether she was going to recover. So he went upstairs alone to examine Eve, while Lizzie stayed downstairs and got her children ready for bed. Alice was standing on the table and Lizzie was undressing her when Donald opened the stairs door and re-emerged. She turned and looked at him apprehensively.

Donald smiled, a sad smile, acknowledging her evident concern. 'I see no improvement, Lizzie,' he admitted.

Lizzie took Alice in her arms, lifting her from the table, 'I know, Donald. If anything I'd say she's worse. So what are her chances?'

'Remote.' He put his bag down on the chair Eve always sat on, and sighed. 'But let's see what tomorrow brings. Let's see how she is tomorrow. It's just possible I've misread the early signs by a day. She's comfortable now, so let her sleep. I'll call in the morning straight after my morning surgery.'

'Thank you, Donald, for all you've done. You've been so kind. I only wish to God that I could afford to pay you straight away for

242

everything. But we will, I promise. When Ben's back home and back at work. I'll pay you everything I owe.'

'Lizzie, don't even think about it.' Donald placed a hand on her arm reassuringly. 'Your mother's own generosity and kindness to me over the years more than pays for my meagre services. She never asked me to pay if she fed me when I used to come and play with Ted.' He smiled wistfully. 'She used to mend my trousers, you know, and sew buttons on my shirts. They often got ripped off horsing around. She never suggested I should pay for that, Lizzie.' A smile of nostalgia lit up his face. '...Once I fell in the night soilers' lagoon – I stunk to high heaven, I can tell you – but she never asked me to pay when she bathed me and washed my awful smelly clothes ... nor when she lent me some of Ted's to go home in. No, Lizzie. Please don't ever think about payment. I've had payment enough. I desire no more.'

Lizzie's eyes filled with tears. 'Donald, you're so kind.'

He picked up his bag. 'Think no more of it. I'll see you in the morning. If you need me in the meantime you know where I am.'

It was three weeks before Christmas that Eve Bishop passed away, aged sixty-seven. Lizzie felt her loss acutely. She felt the desperate need to be comforted by Ben, for him to hold her tight in her grief, so she could cry and cry and cry. But Ben was still away, still at war in France. It would be her first Christmas ever without her mother

243

and, to make matters worse, her second without her husband. She did not look forward to it; rather, she dreaded it.

It was difficult to accept that Eve was dead. And during those last days of her illness Lizzie had had no time to write to Ben. He didn't even know Eve was so ill. Other people got to know, of course, and they all offered their condolences. But how many really cared? How many people had the time to worry about Lizzie Kite and her problems when they had so many problems of their own? More and more young women she saw in the streets were wearing black, their husbands killed in this damned war. At least she was not a widow – well not yet at any rate. Fewer and fewer families were free of grief in these accursed days. Why should they concern themselves with her?

Over the next few days May, Joe and Lizzie sorted out what meagre chattels their mother had bequeathed them. They found money she'd put aside for her burial, which Joe took charge of, along with all the arrangements. He engaged Charlie Sixfoot, the undertaker from Peel Street, and Eve was buried on a bitterly cold, grey day with the hoarfrost sticking to the bare trees like fleece. They huddled round the oblong hole in the rock hard ground while she was lowered in to rejoin Isaac, their father.

The Reverend Mr John Mainwaring tossed cold, black earth onto the top of the coffin, and Lizzie shivered, unable to look. At least they are together again, Lizzie thought. It was a poignant reminder of how much she missed Ben.

When it was all over Lizzie lingered like one of the rimy trees as the gravediggers began to fill the hole. She shuddered with emotion and with cold in the bitter gloom and wept, her face racked with anguish. The church loomed grey in the icy mist; and the other mourners, Tom Dando among them, stood, sombre, black, watching her, awaiting her on the path at the top. As she wiped the tears away with a dainty, lace handkerchief Eve had made, Joe came back for her and put his arm round her waist to lead her away.

'Perhaps it would've been better if you hadn't come, our Lizzie,' he said softly.

'I had to come, Joe,' she sobbed. 'I wanted to come. I wanted to see her off safely.'

Lizzie had reached her nadir. Things could surely get no worse. With Joe's arm around her the tears flowed more profusely. Her mind wandered feebly here and there, feeling wretched and forsaken, left alone to cope with life's immense disappointments. Joe's murmured words of comfort were of little help. Her heart was stone cold with suffering, and she was tortured with the pangs of emptiness, and longing, and loneliness; and a lack of love.

Beccy Crump, Eve's friend and *confidante* of more than forty years, had agreed to look after Lizzie's children during the funeral and when the mourners came back to the house afterwards. Meanwhile, May had prepared sandwiches and brewed tea.

Sarah Dando helped too, while Tom paid his last respects to the woman he'd loved and lost. If he could have had the choice he would have

245

married Eve. Eve should have been his wife; and if she had been, who knows, she might even still be alive. Certainly he would have looked after her with devotion through her illnesses.

During this time of sadness Tom Dando could not condone Sylvia's avoidance of Lizzie and Eve over the years – especially Eve – especially now, at Eve's funeral. It was as if the events all those years ago concerning Lizzie and Jesse Clancey had prejudiced her irrevocably against them. Even since her marriage to James Atkinson nothing had changed; the same futile hostility remained.

As Christmas approached so Lizzie's grief grew more intense, heightened by Ben's continued absence. It seemed that she would never know happiness again. Happiness, she was sure, would avoid her for the rest of her life. She had her children, each a part of Ben, and she was thankful for that. She loved them with all her heart, but they were no substitute for her husband. The love she felt for him was different. It was earthy, lusty, sensuous; but profound and utterly respectful. They were soul-mates after all.

Lizzie and her children spent Christmas day with May and Joe and Emmie. It would have been a depressing time, indeed she expected it to be, but the children turned it into an amusing and pleasant day; they, at least, were not burdened with grief, and it brought some respite; a waft of warmth in the bleakness. By nine o'clock, however, Alice, eighteen months old, had fallen asleep on the floor where she had been playing, Maxine was sleeping in Emmie's crib having been fed an hour earlier, and both Herbert and Henzey were miserable with fatigue. It was time she put them to bed. So while Joe carried Alice back next door, Lizzie took Maxine in her arms, and the other two stumbled down one entry and up the other, grizzling irritably. None of them saw a soldier lingering in the shadows of 'The Sailor's Return', watching.

Joe left soon after he'd poked the fire into life and stacked some lumps of coal on for her. At once Lizzie put the children to bed, looking forward to an hour or so of peace and quiet. She returned downstairs quietly and opened the letter she'd received from Ben on Christmas Eve. She sat down and read it again. Just as she was about to read it once more a knock at the back door surprised her. She returned Ben's letter to the envelope and the mantel shelf. When she answered the door a tall, lean, young man wearing a military uniform stood before her, and her heart danced with joy. God bless him, he could not have timed it better. He was home, at last; home to the wife who so hopelessly craved him. He carried a large leather bag and, in the shadow cast by the back door, she could just make out his smile as he looked at her expectantly.

'Merry Christmas, Lizzie,' he said. 'Aren't you going to ask me in?'

He removed his peaked hat, leaned forward and kissed her, putting his free hand to her waist. Just in time she stopped herself flinging her arms around him.

'Stanley! Oh! Come in, Stanley. This is such a surprise. It's lovely to see you.'

He took off his gloves and placed them on the table. 'I bet I'm the last person in the world you expected to see.'

She fluffed up a cushion for him, inviting him to sit down. 'What brings you here? I didn't even know you were due on leave.'

'Well, I was sorry to hear about your mother, Lizzie, and I thought, what with Ben still away, maybe you wouldn't mind some company for half an hour or so. I've brought some things for your kiddies – for Christmas. Sorry it's a bit late... The bag's for you, by the way. What's inside is for the children – just a few clothes, sweets, and things.'

'Oh, Stanley, you shouldn't have. It's ever so kind of you. Thanks ever so much... And this is a beautiful bag. I've never seen one like it before.'

'It's not quite new, Lizzie. I picked it up in Italy before the war. For some reason, the moment I saw it I thought of you. I've carried it with me everywhere since, with the intention of giving it to you some time.'

'You shouldn't have.' She felt herself blushing and, to conceal it, she bent down to look inside the bag. Why was it that Stanley always had this effect on her, as if she were a shy schoolgirl? 'Well whatever it is you've brought the kids, you've wrapped them up nicely. I'll let them undo the parcels themselves in the morning. They'll love that.' She stood up. 'I'll boil the kettle for some tea, Stanley. Sorry I've got nothing stronger to offer.'

'Tea'll be fine, Lizzie... You're looking a treat, you know, considering the loss of Aunt Eve. You've barely changed since the last time I saw you. You're still as beautiful as ever. But you always were a bobbydazzler.'

She lifted the kettle onto the biggest gale. 'It's nice of you to say so, but I don't feel it. I've lost weight. Worry, I expect. And because food's scarce.'

'You look as beautiful as ever. No different to when you were sixteen. Believe me.'

Her colour came up again and she sat down beside him. 'Oh, tell me more, Stanley. I could do with cheering up, God knows – what with one thing and another. Where've you been hiding anyway? I haven't seen you for what? Six or seven years?'

'Has it been that long? The last posting I had was Togoland, when we shunted the Hun out at the start of the war. I've been back home a few days that's all. The day after tomorrow I have to report back to my regiment. Then God knows where they'll send us. I'm a captain now, you know.'

'A captain? Congratulations. I always knew you'd do well in the army. I always knew you'd get on.'

'And how's Ben doing? D'you hear from him regular?'

'Oh, I get a letter most days, thank God. Some days two, even. Other days none at all.'

'Where is he, Lizzie? Do you know?'

She leaned forward to poke the fire. 'In Northern France somewhere. In the thick of it, though he doesn't say much. He's a gunner. Fourteenth Battalion Machine Gun Corps. I don't suppose you've come across him?'

'I've not been to Northern France, thankfully. To be honest, I don't envy him. Chances are I'll end up there soon enough. My regiment was due to go to Gallipoli, but that expedition's been scrubbed in the last day or two, I hear. Trouble is, this damned war's being fought on too many fronts. We've lost half a million men already. Half a million!'

'I haven't seen your mother and father since Mother's funeral. Are they all right?'

'Oh, Mother seems fit enough. Father's not too well, though. He took your mother's death badly.'

There was a silence for a few moments. Lizzie stood up again, reached for the tea caddy and spooned tea leaves into the teapot.

'I thought you were Ben standing at the door, you know. You gave me quite a turn.' She replaced the caddy and faced him, leaning against the brass fireguard.

'You miss him, don't you, Lizzie?'

Lizzie nodded, and smiled. 'Words can't tell,' she answered quietly, and felt her eyes fill with tears of self-pity. She bit her bottom lip so she wouldn't weep, and turned away. But she was so depressed with grief, so deprived of love, and so sensitive to the loneliness that had befallen her, she couldn't help but respond with tears at such a question, so touchingly phrased. At once she took her handkerchief from her sleeve and dabbed her eyes, but she felt such relief shedding these tears, that she let them flow.

She felt Stanley's arms about her, surprising her. But she turned to him, allowing him to press her head to his chest and run his fingers comfortingly through her hair, like Ben would. He hugged her, and she savoured the sensation of physical affection, yielding to it, exploiting it to coax more tears, which were bringing so much relief.

'That's the way, Lizzie,' he breathed. 'Let it all come out. You'll feel better after.'

She closed her wet eyes. It could have been Ben speaking; the one clear voice of sanctity and sanity in a world riven with tragedy and sorrow. She huddled up to him and put her hand to his chest, feeling the texture of his uniform. It could have been Ben standing there, holding her so lovingly; he must have a uniform like this; like this one she was fingering now, tentatively, fancifully. 'Ben... Oh, Ben...' she mouthed to herself, silently willing him back to her in her absolute heartache. She turned her face to his neck and, with every indrawn breath, she could smell the clean, sensual smell of his skin, of his uniform, and a deeper, sweeter manly smell. It could so easily have been Ben. She looked up into his face. It could so easily be Ben's face she could see through the indistinct haze of tears.

'You look so beautiful when you cry,' Stanley whispered.

It *was* Ben.

At once she was swept back to that early morning fifteen months ago when he left her. 'You look so beautiful when you cry.' Those very words had been his last to her. How could she

251

ever forget them? Now she felt his lips on hers, at last, cool, probing, sensual, like a soothing balm bringing succour to a stinging wound, wringing every last drop of bliss and sensation out of this one kiss. Eagerly she responded; as she had always responded, and it went on and on, intoxicating her with pleasure. He urged her to one side and she felt herself gently pressed against the cupboard at the side of the grate. The length of his warm body was pressed against her, as lean and as firm as ever it had been. Now, eyes closed, she held him tight, savouring the moment, and they kissed again. This time she was not going to let him go off to war. He scooped her up into his arms as if she were a child, and lifted her, and laid her down gently on the hearth-rug. He lay beside her and kissed her wet, closed eyelids, but her mouth searched again hungrily for his; such an alluring mouth. God, it had been so long. She touched his face tenderly with her fingers and felt his smooth forehead, moist with perspiration, and his dark, close cropped hair. She felt him unbuttoning her dress at the back, and raised her shoulders off the floor to make it easier.

'Ben ... oh, Ben,' she whimpered, 'never ever leave me again ... please ... never, ever...' She felt him take a handful of material at the hem of her dress and pull it up above her waist.

Above the sound of her own expectant sighs she could just about hear the voices of a group of carol singers outside, somewhere in Cromwell Street, singing *'The First Noel'*. Inside, the kettle started to boil and she heard the lid bobbling, the rush of steam and hissing as it spat boiling water into the hot, eager fire through the spout.

It was well after midnight when Stanley left Lizzie that Christmas night. He would not see her again, he said, since he had to rejoin his regiment so soon. She told him it didn't matter, but wished him well and said good-bye. As she climbed the stairs to bed, naked, she carried her clothes in a bundle under one arm and an oil lamp in her other hand. She dumped the garments onto the ottoman and placed the lamp on the tallboy, then took her night-dress and pulled it over her head. She brushed her tousled hair before she took a last peek at Maxine sleeping soundly in her crib in the same room. Then she dropped on the bed, utterly exhausted, but wonderfully content.

But she could not sleep. She relived the past three hours over and over in her mind. The intense emotions she experienced surprised her, but the welcome relief, the fantasy, the sheer sensual pleasure, were like a healing elixir to a tortured soul. There was a sort of twisted irony in what had occurred with Stanley after all this time, in the shameless lust that had driven her; that she knew had always driven her. In the past they were like brother and sister. Years ago, as their sexual awareness increased, she'd tried to imagine what it would be like making love with Stanley yet, as time passed, she realised she would never know; and the desire to know had diminished with her changing circumstances. Now, paradoxically, she did know, when she was a supposedly respectable, married woman with four children.

Lizzie was tortured with mixed feelings. Guilt she certainly felt, but not regret. How could she regret such unexpected pleasure after such abject deprivation? There was no doubt that the one was heightened by the absence of the other. She wanted so much for it to have been Ben that she made believe it was Ben, and lived out the fantasy. And this pretence justified her allowing herself to be seduced, suppressing some of the guilt. She relived Stanley's kissing her throat, then suckling her breasts, robbing Maxine of her precious feed. She was sprawled out, paralysed and astounded, giving little cries of pleasure and shock as he kissed her belly, then unbelievably, between her thighs. She remembered calling Ben's name again and again when his body finally, thankfully, entered hers with such piercing sweetness.

It did not matter that Stanley couldn't see her again after this. Indeed, she had no wish to see him; not for a long time. She was thankful he was going away so soon. To meet again would be an enormous embarrassment. What had happened would never be repeated. She was not in love with Stanley, she merely exploited his unexpected appearance; used him like a poultice on inflamed skin for the relief he could bring. No doubt in a similar way he'd used her.

Of course it crossed her mind that she might be pregnant. But with everything else to worry about she was not going to dwell on that. If she were, somehow she would get rid of it. She would

254

have to get rid of it.

At last, having weighed up the sinfulness against the pleasure, on balance she felt better for her unforeseen adventure. With Ben away, she knew, the guilty feelings would wane and she would be able to face him normally when he returned. But it had released many of the tensions stifled inside her for so long and, already she could see her way ahead, still alone except for her children perhaps, but with a clarity of mind now and a ready acceptance of her situation. At least Stanley had still found her desirable after all this time. That in itself was gratifying. So she turned over in her bed and even allowed herself a smile, before she drifted off into a deep sleep filled with pleasant dreams.

Chapter 14

In January 1916 Parliament voted overwhelmingly for the introduction of conscription. There were, it was reported, half a million single men fit for service who so far had not volunteered, and about the same number of married men waiting, willing to do so. Miners' unions, however, voted against it, and so did the Labour Party Conference.

During the third week of that month Lizzie knew for sure that she was not pregnant, and offered an informal prayer of thanks to her Maker. Daisy Foster visited her on the Friday evening and brought along with her two bottles of stout. They brought each other up to date on their lives, and Lizzie was sad to hear that Daisy had called it off with Jimmy Powell. He would never marry her, she said. He was still doing his bit at Holcroft's, but was also busy keeping at least two deprived young wives happy and content while their husbands were soldiering in France.

Half way through February Lizzie received a letter in the familiar green envelope issued by the army to those men on trust, whose outgoing mail was not censored by superior officers. The handwriting it bore she did not recognise, and since she'd received no mail from Ben for three days she thought that it must contain bad news. As she opened it, trembling, she sat down, and braced herself for the worst. It read:

My dearest Lizzie,

At last I find myself in northern France. Ironic, don't you think, that in all my years in the army this should be the first time? Whatever Ben has told you about this place can only be half the truth, because words cannot adequately describe conditions here.

There are hundreds of thousands of our chaps here, so the possibility of me encountering him must be pretty remote, as I'm sure you'll realise. Should I bump into him, though, I'll naturally tell him how much you miss him! The truth is, though, I hope I don't.

Lizzie, since our time together on Christmas night my mind has been filled with very deep regrets. Regrets that I didn't stay till morning, and even for the whole of the next day. We parted fairly impassively I know, never expecting to meet again in quite the same way, and I hope you won't mind me saying it. But since that night you have been in my thoughts a great deal, reminding me of the adolescent dreams I had about you all those years ago. Of course, I wish Ben no harm as I'm sure you know. His fine children need a father, but if he were never to return to you, I would like to think you might consider allowing me to fill the void he would leave in your life, and in theirs.

I'll say no more. I hope it is enough to leave you in no doubt as to my feelings. It would be an honour if you were to reply to this letter.

All my love,
Stanley.

Lizzie read the letter through twice more, feeling even hotter than when she opened it, her heart still pounding. Guiltily she folded it up, put it back in the envelope and hid it behind the clock on the mantelpiece. She sighed in confusion. Why did he have to write something like that? It was just something more to prey on her mind. She knew, and so must he, that she was susceptible to other people's feelings and desires. She was especially susceptible to him. Now thoughts of him were rekindled when that lovely night was just beginning to fade from her mind. Was he deliberately teasing her now, having taken advantage of her then? It wasn't fair. It wasn't fair at all. He was still single; he could do as he wished; he could write to as many women as he wished, saying the same thing. In all probability he was. Now he wanted her to write to him.

She let Stanley's letter lie where she left it for a couple of days, while she pondered whether to reply or not. She was sorely tempted. But those couple of days enabled her to see it with a clearer mind. She'd been lucky that night; nobody had seen or heard Stanley come and go; the door had been left unlocked when anybody could have walked in. But nobody did; and she had breathed a word to nobody about it. Not a soul knew. So what would be the sense in starting a romantic correspondence with yet another man who was away in the army for God knows how long. What was the sense, when the one she was already writing to was breaking her heart by not being home? Could she really be so stupid as to fall for that? That would really be pushing her luck. So she screwed the letter up, and its envelope, threw it in the fire and watched it burn.

On July 3rd the Somme campaign opened. It was the biggest army – 26 divisions of volunteers – Britain had ever sent into battle, and all were comprehensively equipped. The following day there was a truce while the dead and wounded were brought in from the area known as No Man's Land. It took three days to collect the sixty thousand British casualties. In December David Lloyd George was appointed to succeed as Prime Minister after a smear campaign in the media, aimed at Herbert Asquith, achieved its aims. In March 1917 Czar Nicholas II of Russia abdicated and, in April, the Americans joined the war on the side of the Allies. By November the Russian Provisional Government had been ousted by a Bolshevik coup, and the Allies knew that Russia would pull out of the war in consequence.

During all this time Lizzie Kite paid less attention to the alarming news she read in the papers, and paid more to the survival of herself and her children. Every week she went to the post office to have her Ring Sheet stamped to draw the twenty-five shillings allowance to which she was entitled for Ben's service. There were promises of more from the government, and a good thing too, since trying to make ends meet was almost a full time job. Reluctantly she pawned some jewellery and a good pair of shoes that belonged to her mother, together with Ben's wedding suit, and the gold fob-watch that was her father's. In desperation she sought work at the bottling stores in Caroline Street, and was offered three hours each afternoon, Monday to Friday, which she was glad to accept.

May kindly agreed to look after the children, along with Emmie, while Lizzie was at work. But Lizzie needed money immediately to buy coal, and mentioned to May that she would have to pawn her mother's Coalport China tea service, which Tom Dando had given her as a wedding present all those years ago. She was utterly surprised when May claimed that Eve had promised her the tea service. Lizzie, of course, considered it her own, and knew May to be lying, but since the need for May's help in looking after her children outweighed the more immediate fiscal need she thought better of seriously challenging it.

'When did Mother tell you as you could have that?' Lizzie asked, very curious.

'When Henzey was born. She said I could have it for what I did helping when you were confined.'

Lizzie wanted to call her a liar and, that in any case, she hadn't done a fat lot to earn it. 'If Mother said that, then you'd best have it,' she conceded, bitterly disappointed in May. 'But she never told me any such thing.'

Before that moment Lizzie had only ever considered May to be a kindred spirit, good and kind, completely reliable and a true friend. Now she vowed she would never trust her again. From that moment she saw her in a different light. Lizzie pondered her own daughter's reluctance lately to go anywhere near May. Children were often more perceptive than adults, she was aware, and it set her wondering whether May had been at all unkind to Henzey. She would keep a weather eye on May Bishop, especially where her children were concerned. If ever she hurt one of them while they were in her care there would be hell to pay.

So Lizzie handed over the cherished tea service, said nothing, and simply watched for any signs. She knew it was futile falling out over children. As May's child grew, and her mental deficiency became more evident, there was no discrimination by Lizzie's brood. They spent hours playing happily with their cousin Emmie. In their eyes she was no different to them, and she tried to emulate them as best she could. May watched Henzey mothering the child, protecting her, as if she instinctively knew that she needed extra care. As the weeks and months passed May felt ever more guilty that she'd been so hostile towards her niece. She finally realised it was not her niece's fault that nature had dictated the way things were to be.

Early in April 1918, Lizzie received a letter from Ben. It was dated 30th March, and it read:

My darling Lizzie,
   Nobody will be more pleased than me when this lot is over. I've seen enough of human nature and human suffering to last me a lifetime. Yesterday we went forward. There were enough dead lying about to carpet the Albion ground – our own men, and Jerries. Some of them had been there so long they were yellow. It made me feel sick. We could see Jerries' front line, only about as far as from our house to the Junction. Our lads moved in later, but the trenches were empty, except for one young German soldier who come out with his hands up. He looked scared to death and I felt really sorry for the poor lad. Then some swine rushed him and stuck his bayonet in him. I've never seen anything so cowardly in all my life. It was nothing less than cold blooded murder, and I felt ashamed that our chaps should be that wicked. I know the Jerries sunk the Lusitania and that hundreds drowned, but that poor mother's son didn't do it. Two minutes after that some German prisoners guarded by some of our blokes came over the same spot. If that one poor devil had known, and waited

before he came out, he'd have been all right. Fate, eh? Then suddenly, shrapnel shells burst all around us. There was no time to duck, nor nothing. It copped a dozen of our lot. One bloke had a big hole through his thigh, so the Sergeant cut through his clothes. with a pair of scissors he took from one of the first aid men lying dead. He tied it up with bandage, then carried him back to the trenches. When he came back he said as how the trenches were full of wounded blokes. Blow me, if he hadn't been back two minutes when a bullet caught him and sent him reeling backwards. He was a goner as well.

I tell you, Lizzie, this place is hell. If you can imagine anywhere fifty times worse than the marl hole at the Coneygree on a wet day, or the brick works with all the mud and filth around, and an army of maniacs all trying to blow your head off, then that's what it's like here.

When I think of them barmy buggers on the Clyde who went on strike and stopped production of the guns we need, I feel like going along and playing hell up. When this lot's over I probably shall. They should be ashamed of themselves putting the lives of everybody at risk. It would do the buggers good to come and get amongst this lot. Then they would know what a soft time they've got of it.

Don't worry about me, Lizzie, because no Hun's going to get me after I've come this far. My thoughts are always about you and the kids, and they keep me going. I hope little Maxine's still coming on all right. I can't wait to see her. Is she as pretty as our Henzey? If so, I shall have my work cut out keeping them chaste when they grow up.

Sorry, my sweetheart, but I shall have to pack up

*now. We've just had the order to move back. Sounds
like we're retreating. I'll write tomorrow if I get the
chance.*
  Love to you and the children,
  Ben.

But Ben did not write the next day. The Germans were employing new tactics, and their army in France had been swelled by troops no longer required on the Russian Front. The British line in the Arras sector, where he was fighting, was shattered.

Having received no word from Ben for more than a week, Lizzie put her hands to her face in horror when she answered the door to the telegraph boy. She cast an anxious glance at him, and began to tremble as he handed her a telegram from the War Office. When she'd closed the door behind him her legs felt like jelly, and she thought she was going to faint. It could only contain bad news. They didn't send you telegrams to say your husband was better after a bout of flu; nor to say he'd been promoted. As she looked at it with dread and unutterable disappointment she felt tears burn her eyes. Gingerly, she fingered the unopened document. Her heart was thumping hard, she felt hot with perplexity. In her hand were tidings of widowhood; the prospect, after all, of a life devoid of the man she loved; of endless poverty with four children to bring up, in a world that cared nothing for those who had nothing. Everything she'd feared most had come to pass.

But she could not keep the telegram unopened.

It seemed to prickle her fingers, begging her to read it. Finally she plucked up the courage. She fell into a chair, shaking uncontrollably, tears flooding her eyes, a look of fearful apprehension on her face as she thrust her forefinger gingerly under the flap.

At first she could not believe what she read, so she read it again; then yet again. Ben was being sent home. He was alive. Thank God he was alive after all. But for some reason, perhaps because of some strange quirk in her nature, perhaps because of the unexpected joy she felt, the significance of the words 'wounded in action' did not have the full impact they might otherwise have had. Perhaps it was because she took it for granted that when he recovered he would be fit and active.

She wondered whether he would have changed after the atrocities he'd seen and suffered. It must have had some effect on him. The stories she heard about the changes in some men returning from the war were alarming, but she knew Ben to be level headed. She could hardly conceive of him being affected too badly.

She set about spring cleaning the house ready for his return. In Brown Street she bought wallpaper, and using paste made from flour and water, hung it on top of the old in their bedroom to brighten it up. She distempered the walls in the scullery so that it all looked fresh and clean, and while she worked her excitement mounted. She scrubbed the table, the red quarry tiled floor in the scullery and the oilcloth in the front room. She relined all the shelves in the cupboard, and at the top of the cellar steps. She begged a couple of Hessian bags from Percy Collins's corner shop that had been used for storing potatoes. Washed and sewn together they made an ideal backing material for a rag rug, which she podged while the children were in bed.

At last the day arrived when Ben was due back home, and Lizzie told her young family as they sat eating breakfast.

'Hip hip, hooray,' Henzey yelled; then more objectively, asked: 'What does my daddy look like, Mom?'

'Oh, he's tall and ever so handsome. You'll remember him when you see him.' Lizzie suppressed a tear. She had not considered that the children might have forgotten their father. Often she talked about him, but it had never once crossed her mind they might not be able to recall what he looked like. 'When you get back from school,' she continued, 'I want you to be nice and quiet. No dancing about and making a noise. And no showing off, either. Your daddy's poorly, that's why he's coming home, and we've got to make him well again. So he won't want any noise at all. All right?'

Henzey agreed. 'What's the matter with him?'

'Has one of his legs been shot off?' Herbert asked, influenced by the type of talk he was used to hearing.

'No, he's still got both his legs, I'm sure, but I daresay he'll have to rest for a week or two. So don't get bothering him. Come on now, you two. It's time you were off to school. Marge'll be here in a minute.'

Marge 'Ardmate called two minutes later to accompany Henzey and Herbert to the Board School. Lizzie kissed them, told them to be good and to keep out of the horse road; she would see them at dinnertime with their father. Then she proceeded to clear away the breakfast things, to dress Alice and Maxine, and finish the rest of the chores. Beccy Crump called round and said if there was anything she could do Lizzie only had to ask. She stayed for a cup of tea, then returned home with the curtains Lizzie had washed specially for Ben's homecoming. Beccy had offered to iron them.

Lizzie couldn't help looking at the black marble clock every few minutes to check the time. Even though she was in a spin the time seemed to drag. She was apprehensive and nervous. She didn't know what to expect. Ben had been wounded in action, that was all she knew. She'd prayed and prayed that his wounds would not be too debilitating; that he would soon recover. If he hadn't lost a limb she would give thanks to God. Yet despite all these fears she was excited, too. She hadn't seen Ben for three and a half years, and she'd dreamed and fantasised about their reunion. She couldn't help recalling how they met and fell hopelessly in love. She pondered the first fumbling time they made love, and afforded herself a smile. She recalled the day they married; how overjoyed they both were at the births of their children. And she wondered how soon it might be before another child was on the way, for it was certain that his return would sharpen both their appetites for love. After all, there was so much catching up to do, and Lizzie was looking forward to it with relish. She hoped desperately that it would be like it always used to be.

Shortly after half past ten May called to take Alice and Maxine out of the way and, at ten past eleven, Beccy returned with the curtains freshly ironed. She climbed onto the table with surprising agility to hang them back on their pole in the scullery, then went upstairs with Lizzie to help hang another pair in the bedroom. Lizzie thanked her wholeheartedly and wiped the windows, giving them a last minute buff.

She was satisfied the house was looking clean and fresh for Ben when she heard the steady thrum of a vehicle engine reverberating through the entry. She glanced at the clock again. It was five past twelve. The children would be back from school at any minute. She darted outside and, through the entry, saw the back end of an army truck in the street. Her heart leapt. She rushed down the entry and reached the truck just as the driver was climbing out of the cab.

'Oh, are you Missus Kite?' he asked when he saw her.

'I am.'

'We've brought your husband. We'll soon have him in the house, my lover. He ain't too grand, though. We'll have to be steady with him.'

Another soldier emerged from the other side of the lorry and opened up the back. As they manoeuvred the stretcher and began to draw it out Lizzie could see the two peaks in the blanket made by Ben's feet. A wave of relief rippled over

267

her that he at least still had both his legs. She moved so she could see the rest of him. He was lying on his back, and all she could see were bandages. As the men began carrying him she saw his head and part of his face was bandaged. Lizzie shuddered. Ben opened his eyes, dull and sunken, but they seemed to light up at the sight of her.

She smiled, tears blurring her vision. 'Oh, Ben ... thank God you're home.' She reached out to him, to touch him, but he was just about to be carried through the entry, so she had to wait.

As they reached the back yard the two men tried to turn the stretcher so that they could enter the house with it by the back door. But there wasn't enough room. Lizzie went in before them and commenced shifting the chair closest to the door, to clear an access.

'You'll never get him up the stairs on that,' Lizzie informed them.

So the soldiers laid the stretcher on the floor, and lifted Ben from it bodily. Lizzie noticed for the first time that he still had both arms as they hung limp from his shoulders; and indeed both hands. Thank God for that, too. His injuries must only be burns. As they carried him into the house Lizzie caught sight of Henzey, back from school, standing in the yard watching, a look of concern on her pretty young face. Lizzie smiled at her reassuringly.

One of the soldiers said, 'Easy on, old mate, we'll have you up them stairs in no time,'

Lizzie turned, opened the stairs door for them, and held it while the men struggled to convey

268

Ben upstairs. She was longing to be alone with him, to hold him, to talk to him after so long. But she must wait. In the bedroom she turned back the crisp, clean sheets of the bed, so that the men could place Ben in it without further ado, and she noticed how he winced with pain as they laid him down.

'Thank you ever so much,' Lizzie said sincerely to the driver, while fussing round Ben to make him comfortable.

'Our pleasure, Missus. He'll be better off here than where he's been. If you'd like to come back down to the lorry I'll hand you the rest of his things.'

Lizzie smiled at her husband lovingly. She told him she'd only be a minute, and lingered reassuringly for a second before she followed the two men out to the truck. 'Look after your daddy for me for a minute, while I go and get his things,' she whispered to Henzey, who had followed them all up the stairs.

Henzey stood and watched as her father, unaware that she was there, lay on top of the bed with his eyes shut. Tentatively, silently, she approached him, peering curiously at his face, trying to remember what he looked like beyond the bandages and the sores. Although she could not remember his face, she remembered how he used to toss her into the air and catch her just as she screamed with excitement, thinking she would hit the floor. It came back to her how he sometimes lifted her up and sat her on the back of Jesse Clancey's huge cart-horse when he brought their milk on a Sunday. She remembered how he used to take her on his bike, and she would have to sit on a cushion on the crossbar and hold onto his arms for dear life while he pedalled and steered. But she could not remember there ever being such a tortured look on his face. He had brought her joy, yet she had almost forgotten. As she got closer she leaned over the bed. For a few seconds she stood there and studied him. Then he shifted his head slightly and opened his eyes. She recoiled, then smiled tentatively as his eyes at once lit up with recognition, brightening his ashen face.

'Henzey! Oh, my little precious,' he gasped, and held his hand out to her. 'God how you've grown.'

'Daddy?' she whispered.

She hesitated for just a second then threw her arms about his neck. His arms, once so strong, hugged her in return, and she heard him wheeze alarmingly close to her ear. A faint, sweet smell of hair-oil lingered and it was so familiar, yet she'd forgotten that too. Memories flooded back of how his stubbly beard used to scratch her face, and she expected it now; but there was no stubbly beard this time.

'You'll never know just how much I've missed you,' he breathed, taking a good look at her.

She regarded him intently. His eyes were full and watery. He closed them again and a tear rolled down his left cheek.

'Are you goin' to get better?' she asked, 'so's you can ride wi' me on your bike again?'

He opened his eyes again and smiled. 'You remember that, my pet?' he murmured hoarsely, and she nodded. 'Thank God you do.'

Downstairs Lizzie put Ben's bags down on the floor. She could sort his stuff out later. As they reached the top of the stairs she heard him talking to Henzey. He spoke with great difficulty, as if the effort was consuming all his breath. Lizzie further discerned how weak he sounded as she presented Herbert to Ben.

'Hello, my handsome,' Ben sighed, and reached out for his young son.

Herbert was reticent about going to his father. He did not know him. But Lizzie thrust him gently forward with a nod of encouragement.

'D'you think they've grown, Ben?'

'Unbelievable.' He gently touched Herbert's cheek. Herbert smiled shyly. He had no recollection of his father at all.

'And you, our Lizzie. You still look beautiful. You're all slender again, like when we got married.'

'It's hardly surprising I'm slender, worrying about you and this brood. It's been a long three and a half years.'

'Yes, but it's over now, my flower.' He coughed painfully. 'I'm back home, and I'm going nowhere else... I've done my bit.'

Lizzie turned to Henzey. 'Take Herbert round to your Aunt May's, my pigeon. Your dinners will be ready. Alice and Maxine are already there. You can come back and see your daddy after. Now, I'm going to make him a nice cup of tea, and see if he wants anything to eat.'

Lizzie waited for the two children to disappear downstairs, then looked into Ben's blue eyes for a few seconds. She felt her own eyes fill with tears as he held his arms open for her. She embraced him, held him tight, tighter, and started to shake uncontrollably with sobbing. It was such a relief to have him back, but her tears were a mixture of happiness and despair. For three and a half years she'd entertained thoughts, hopes, of a resumption of the life they knew before. In those thoughts she envisaged only a fit man, capable and ready to continue where they'd left off. All the time he was gasping for breath as if perpetually climbing a steep hill, and his skin was covered in those awful, hideous burns. She was not mentally prepared to see him returned in such a poor state. He was a shadow of the man that went away. But by God, she would do her best to help him get better. She owed it to him.

Ben felt her silent sobbing as she leaned against him, holding him. He raised his arms and hugged her weakly. It was so good to feel the warmth of her body again; reassuring to see her so emotional for him. Then Lizzie wept aloud, releasing the long suffered distress of loneliness and confusion, of grief compounded by her mother's death, and the unrelieved guilt of one night of stolen love with another man.

'God alone knows how much I've missed you, Ben,' she wailed. 'Nobody knows.'

'Oh, Lizzie, my little flower.' He spoke hoarsely, as if he had a bad chest and was trying not to induce a fit of coughing. 'I've missed you as well. Sometimes, when I was in them trenches... I'd fall asleep and dream I was here with you, comfortable and warm, with the kids playing round us.' He stopped to cough, and a look of agony twisted his face. 'Your mother would be reading the paper and whispering every word, like she always did ... and the fire would be roaring its head off up the chimney... Then I'd wake up, aching, stinking and soaking wet, with shells exploding all round me ... and I'd feel ten times worse than when I fell asleep.'

'Oh, Ben.' She wiped her eyes. 'Try to forget it. You're home now. I'll look after you.'

'You've got enough to do, I should think ... I won't take much looking after, though. In a week or two I'll be up and about... I ain't one for lying abed.'

Before long all four children came up to see their father. He was growing tired, but he fussed them all, particularly Maxine whom he had not seen before. He went to sleep during the afternoon, woke up and picked half-heartedly at fish and boiled potatoes with parsley sauce, then slept again.

When Lizzie slipped into bed with him that night there was no lovemaking. She barely slept, thinking about it, but noticed how disturbed Ben's rest was. At one point he tried to get out of bed and she had to restrain him as he hoarsely tried to shout warnings to imaginary comrades. Then he woke up, fighting for his breath, gulping desperately for air. She calmed him down, fetched a towel to mop up the sweat from his chest and face, and wondered how long this would go on.

Next day, she sent for Donald Clark.

'So what do you reckon, Donald?'

Donald shook his head gravely, and accepted the cup of tea Lizzie handed him. As he took it she noticed how his hands were shaking.

'Lizzie, you must remember that Ben's experienced some traumas while he's been in the trenches. Mentally he's as sound as a bell, but don't expect him to have perfectly restful nights. Not for a long time yet. The war's had an effect on his mind as well as his body, and it'll take time to get over it.'

'What about his injuries? All those burns?'

'They're chemical burns, Lizzie. Mustard gas. I'm hopeful they'll heal satisfactorily, but they're likely to leave awful scars. But more significantly, his lungs have been irreparably damaged by breathing in the gas. Inside they've got blisters similar to those on his face – perhaps even worse. Frankly, I doubt if his poor lungs will ever recover. He'll never work again, Lizzie. That's for certain.'

'Never work again?'

'Nor even have the breath to walk more than a few yards at a time. I'm so sorry, Lizzie.'

'Oh, my God. This is terrible. I can't believe it.'

She sank into a chair, devastated. First it was one thing, then another. As if she hadn't had enough to contend with while he'd been away. Now this. Had she been so wicked that God had to punish her like this? And punish Ben, after he'd been so brave? Gassing was something she had never considered. It was inconceivable that the enemy could use mustard gas on her poor husband.

'There's nothing that can be done for him, except to see that he doesn't overtax himself. Rest and quiet is what he needs above all, and rest and quiet he must have.'

'Quiet might be a bit hard to find in this house with four kids, Donald.'

'I know, Lizzie, and I certainly don't advocate making the children's lives a misery by shushing 'em up all the time. They'll all be at school soon enough. The days'll be quiet then.' His cup chinked on the saucer as he replaced it. 'Nobody can tell yet the full effect this gassing will have had. Little is known. God knows what an evil weapon it is to inflict on your fellow man. Not only are his lungs ruined, making it difficult and painful to breathe, but it's likely he'll suffer from excruciating headaches as well. For all we know he might lose his sight in due course, and his brain might be affected. There's no sign of it at this stage, though, thank goodness. Trouble is, we just can't be sure. But we must be prepared. It's only fair, Lizzie, that I forewarn you of the possibilities.'

This was vastly worse than Lizzie had anticipated. Returning from the war with all his limbs intact was of no use at all if he had no decent lungs to breathe the air God had provided. He would never work again; barely be able to walk more than a few yards at a time. Poor, poor Ben. He would be an invalid for the rest of his days if what Donald said was correct. The injustice of it all! After he'd so willingly volunteered for service, to return a spent man, ruined for the sake of his country. It was a sin. He deserved better. He deserved a hero's welcome. He'd given himself for his country.

And his wonderful, good looks... They were doubtless gone forever, marred, spoilt, destroyed by those awful blisters and burns.

It surprised Lizzie how quickly they got used to their new way of life. Ben got no better, but neither did he get any worse. She was thankful for that, but she had to do every mortal thing for him, though she did it willingly enough, spurred on by the guilty conscience that still haunted her over that Christmas night making love with Stanley Dando; the guilty conscience, because she continued to relive over and over in her mind that brief evening, and the unexpected pleasure and romance it brought. She could not forget it. Before long she began to realise that she didn't want to forget it. And then she would remember the letter she subsequently received some six weeks later, saying that he couldn't get her off his mind either. This, now, was her penance. It was no less than she deserved.

Lack of money became the biggest material problem. Ben was due some weekly war pension, but it didn't go far. Soon, she was forced to seek extra hours in her part time job, and she realised how fortunate she was to be awarded them. With the war over, hundreds of thousands of men were returning to civilian life to find there were no jobs at all. At no time did she entertain the idea of going to ask either Donald Clark or the Reverend Mainwaring to sanction parish relief; her pride decreed she should continue to work. While she did, May would call round to make sure Ben was all right, and to make him a cup of tea. It hurt Lizzie's pride enormously to ask, since she still harboured resentment over her mother's Coalport China tea service, but May readily agreed to look after Alice and Maxine daily while she went out to work. The benefit for May, Lizzie realised, was that the children occupied her own daughter, Emmie, who was becoming ever more demanding as she grew older.

The extra money Lizzie brought in helped the Kites, but still it was not enough. She collected every scrap of left-over food for pig swill; stale bread, left-over vegetables, and boiled potato peelings. Jack 'Ardmate was eager to pay a penny a bucket for it to feed his pigs. On Saturday mornings she took the children to the Oakham colliery, or the disused Bunns Lane colliery, to glean pieces of coal from the pit banks. If they could fill a couple of buckets they would return grubby, but well pleased.

Lizzie somehow always managed to scrape up enough money to pay the rent. Since the war it had increased to five shillings a week. New clothes were out of the question, and the children had to walk the streets without shoes as they wore them down to little more than strips of leather. They were growing fast, and whilst kitting out the two younger girls was easier because of hand-me-downs, it was different with Herbert: he could no longer be dressed in a frock like a girl, which was normal till school age; he was at school now and had to wear proper boys' things. Lizzie was grateful when at a routine inspection the headmistress of his school deemed him *needy* and recommended him for a pair of boots from 'The Daily Mail Fund'. There was a stigma attached to having them, but this time she swallowed her pride.

Joe gave Lizzie a half sovereign when he could afford it, and many other families were kind. Realising their plight, those who could were happy to help by donating the outgrown clothes and shoes of their own children. It was a paradox in Lizzie's eyes that the poorer a family was the more clothes they wore, camouflaging the holes in the outer jersey with one underneath.

There was, however, one person to whom Lizzie could have turned, for anything, money included, though her pride would never allow it. That person was Jesse Clancey. During the whole time Ben was away he'd kept a discreet watch over her, like a guardian angel. If ever she'd been in any sort of trouble he would have been there to help her. She was never aware of it, even though he delivered her milk every day. Jesse kept his custodial distance, for fear of her reputation becoming tarnished. With so many men away from home, women were potential prey to the Romeos left behind wishing to exploit them.

Shortly after Ben's return home, however, when he knew she would be safe from such tittle-tattle, he decided to let his concern be known. It was eight o'clock in the morning and she was holding out her quart enamelled jug while Jesse ladled milk into it from a churn. Ben was still in bed.

'How's Ben, Lizzie?' Jesse asked.

'Oh, about the same, Jesse, thanks. But he gets so frustrated that he can't do anything. It's driving him mad ... and driving me mad as well.'

'Lizzie, if there's anything I can do to help – no matter what it is – you've only got to ask. I want you to know that. Anything at all. If you're short of money, or want any errands running, just let me know.'

'Oh, Jesse, that's kind of you. Really kind. But I can cope.'

He shrugged, and replaced his ladle, the hook at the end of the handle secure over the lip of the churn. 'As long as you can, all well and good. But just remember as there is somebody you can lean on if you need to.' He put the lid back on his churn.

'I shan't forget, Jesse. Thank you. I shan't forget.'

He could see she meant it. 'How would Ben take to me coming round occasionally to spend an hour with him – of a night time, say? I'd love to talk to him about his war experiences, not having had any myself. D'you think he'd mind?'

'Oh, I'm sure he'd love that, Jesse. He'd really love that. Come round any time. Come round tonight if you want.' Lizzie saw the warmth in his eyes.

'Right, I will. About eight o'clock. But I shan't make a nuisance of myself. I'll only come when I think it's right... Not every night. I wouldn't want to wear out my welcome.'

She smiled. The years had taken nothing away from Jesse. He must be close to forty now, but he was no less handsome. His filling out a bit had made him even more attractive, she thought; and his air of confidence and maturity now seemed to enhance it. There must have been some local, young war widows who'd benefited from his still being around.

'Whenever you want, Jesse,' she assured him. 'We'd both enjoy your company.'

Chapter 15

Jesse Clancey became a regular visitor. He would call, on average once a week, at about eight o'clock in an evening, and stay till ten. Lizzie would fetch a couple of jugs of beer, which he was always keen to pay for, and he and Ben would chat, exchange views, and hear about Ben's escapades in the war. Lizzie would sit and listen, too, since his stories were usually all new to her; mostly amusing tales; leaving out the horror and the sadness, and the wretchedness of being holed up in filthy, muddy trenches.

As Jesse listened he watched Lizzie, in her late twenties now, mother to four handsome, but increasingly threadbare children; wife to a shattered hero, disfigured through his desire to serve his country. He dearly wished he could do more for Lizzie. She was worthy of so much more. She was still as appealing as the day she got married, retaining her youthfulness. Her figure was still like that of a young girl, not in the least coarsened by bearing four children. Her face was as beautiful and round as ever, registering a few thin lines around the eyes now, and at the corners of her mouth, but not at all unbecoming, especially when she smiled. Her complexion was smooth as a lily, too, and free of blemishes.

Jesse saw in Lizzie a determined woman who had withstood heartbreak, boredom, tragedy, fear and grim poverty. He saw a caring mother, coping with the everyday dramas of her children's grazed knees and bleeding cuts; of lost buttons; of frayed and snapped boot laces. He saw a young wife tending dutifully to her sick husband's every need, yet retaining a dreamy, girlish demeanour, which to anyone else would suggest vulnerability. He knew that, despite this illusion, she made sure the rent was paid on time, that her family was fed and their clothes mended. She gave all her heart to her children and, in return, received the overt love of not only them, but of everyone else who knew her.

As the months passed he saw her sink deeper into depression. He began to understand that her apparent shyness was merely a cloak of protection, worn to hide her uncertainty from the prying eyes of less sensitive folk; folk who might bruise her gentle heart if she exposed it. He began to understand that she was sentimental, and needed the resolute love of someone, as much as she needed sleep, food, and breath in her body. She needed the resolute love of her husband, it was clear; but Jesse began to understand that Ben was not well enough to provide it.

Jesse found himself drawn to Lizzie all over again as he called at the Kites'. He admitted to himself that it was Lizzie he really came to see. Now, though, the attraction was double-edged. In the early days it was physical. Now it was more than that: it was also protective. But as he got to know her better, the more he admired her courage.

Lizzie, too, was glad of Jesse's visits. When husband and wife are limited by the finite space they share for the best part of twenty-four hours every day of every week, conversation inevitably becomes less stimulating, and even infrequent. Lizzie was becoming increasingly depressed by circumstances, too. There was no one to blame for the way things were but Ben. Ben was the one who decided in 1914 to go off and fight; not her. He was the one who needlessly gave up a good job to satisfy his own misplaced priorities. He alone created the circumstances that led to his irreversible uselessness. It wasn't her fault he was an invalid and would be so till the day he died. Of course, she would never dream of spelling it out, but look where his heroics had got them.

Yet she was the one who suffered most. He could shave himself and clean his teeth, but she had to wash him, help him dress, brush his hair. She had to walk him slowly to the lavatory and wait for him to bring him back. Every week she had to bath him in the tin bath on the hearth, and that whole routine was a fearful task. He could reach nothing for himself, and each day he wanted a hundred things handed to him, or fetched, so she was always running errands.

There were a thousand other jobs to do besides: rugs to beat; the grate to blacklead; the brass fender to polish; changing the beds; the washing; the ironing; the mending; the dusting; scrubbing the stairs; cleaning windows; peeling vegetables and cooking; getting four children ready every morning; getting them off to bed at night without a battle. The fire forever wanted making up.

And, of all things, Ben always insisted on wearing a starched collar when Donald Clark or the vicar were due to visit him, yet nobody ever knew where his studs or cuff-links were. So the arrival of another person, less familiar, but well liked, in the shape of Jesse Clancey, was a welcome relief.

When it was time for Jesse to return home to his widowed mother, Lizzie would walk to the bottom of the entry with him and they generally stopped and talked. She sometimes thought he wanted to take her in his arms; or was it just fanciful thinking? There were times when she ardently wished he would. Not necessarily to be loved sexually. She'd done without sexual love for so long now that she was acclimatised to it; all that was behind her; but just to be held close would be nice. Yet it did not happen.

The more Lizzie saw of Jesse, the closer she wanted to get to him. Oh, she'd always fancied him, but time and events had precluded any romantic liaison. Now she was irrevocably drawn to him again. At first she denied she was experiencing such feelings, but as time went by those feelings were undeniable. The problem was, she wasn't free to tell him, and she wouldn't

283

dream of doing so. She was a married woman, with clear responsibilities, and a husband and children who depended on her totally. It was all so frustrating.

When she asked herself whether she still loved Ben she was bemused by her own answer. She loved him, certainly, in the sense that he was the father of her children, and she wished him no ill. She loved him, too, simply because she'd always loved him. But she had to admit she was no longer *in love*. His good looks were gone. His face and body were covered in scars and weeping sores that would not heal. He was bent, frail, pallid, while Jesse was none of these things. Jesse was all the more attractive by comparison.

She did not like herself when she realised this truth. She could never have admitted it before, even to herself; but yes, when she looked at Ben she even felt some revulsion now. She was certain, though, that if he had returned from the war the same fit man that went away, her love would have been eternal. Yet the man who did return had the same soul as the man that departed – albeit he was far more worldly; he was the same caring, intelligent, opinionated man. Only his appearance had changed. His was a body racked with pain, scarred, weak, ultimately lacking the sweet, sensual vitality she'd always adored. It was that same sensual vitality that Lizzie, in her absolute prime, was sorely missing.

Lizzie was still of an age when physical considerations were uppermost. She was fickle, she told herself, greatly disappointed at the realisation of her own shortcomings. She was as fickle as a child craving chocolate, taking it from whoever's promised to be sweetest.

She couldn't help pondering that clandestine session with Stanley Dando. To justify her seduction that fateful night she'd tried to make believe she was with Ben. But it had not been Ben, and she had known it well enough. It had all been a charade, an excuse to try and make it right with her conscience. She scolded herself. The chance to taste Stanley's lips; the chance to thrill to his earnest seeking of those secret places inside her underwear that only Ben had known, had unexpectedly arisen, and she wasn't slow to take advantage. Dear God, she was no better than a common whore, except that she'd not charged money. Worse: she'd done it for pleasure; for self gratification; knowingly; wilfully being unfaithful.

Yet the memory lingered, and she yielded again to the warmth of desire that flowed through her; since it was not an unpleasant memory... But where was Stanley now?

May Bishop watched her own child, and those of Lizzie and Ben, growing up together. Although she could see a marked difference in the development of Lizzie's children, compared with her own daughter, it was a difference that the children either ignored, or in their innocence hadn't noticed. Emmie was nearly five by this time, and a real handful, but Henzey in particular seemed to revel in a self-imposed responsibility for making sure her younger cousin was well looked after, and not slighted or put upon by any of the others. May noticed this on many occasions, and it made her aware of her own past spitefulness towards Henzey. So she tried to think of some positive, material way she could redeem herself in the eyes of her Maker. It occurred to her that the Coalport tea service she'd lied to Lizzie about a while ago could help. If she could make some arrangement with Lizzie for it go to Henzey it would ease her conscience no end, and show some appreciation of her niece's care.

So, with Emmie at her side one sunny July day in 1920, she called round to see her sister-in-law. First she asked Ben how he was and, while Lizzie put the kettle on to boil, she passed the time of day with him. While the tea was steeping in the pot Lizzie suggested they take two chairs outside onto the yard and enjoy the sunshine.

'Lizzie, you know that Coalport tea service that was your mother's?' May said when the tea had been poured and they were both seated, with Emmie on her lap.

'The one Mother said you could have?' Lizzie was facing the sun with her eyes closed to better appreciate its warmth.

'Well, I've been thinking. Seeing as how I'm too frit to use it for fear of bostin' it to smithereens, I'd like our Henzey to have it – for when she grows up and gets married, I mean – not to play with here on the yard. We could keep it for her. You know – put it away till she gets married. What d'you think, Lizzie?'

Lizzie took a swipe at a hovering wasp that was

threatening to mar her peace, and spilled some tea into her saucer in consequence. 'Oh, damn!... Yes, I think it's a good idea, May.' She casually drained the sudden contents of the saucer back into her cup. 'Shall I keep it for her? It'd be safe in its box on the top shelf of the cupboard.' Lizzie knew that having got thus far May could hardly refuse to hand it back.

'If you like. It'd be a load off me mind.' She pulled a piece of rag out of her apron pocket and wiped her child's dribbling mouth. 'I'll fetch it when I've drunk me tea.'

While she waited for May to return with the tea service, Lizzie watched Emmie scraping moss from between the blue bricks paving the yard with a broken clothes peg. She smiled to herself. The reason for May's change of heart she understood perfectly well: her guilty conscience had got the better of her; and Lizzie welcomed it.

After a minute Lizzie heard footsteps in the entry but, expecting May's return, kept her eyes shut as she sat with her face tilted towards the sun – till she heard a man's voice.

'Bugger me, our Lizzie. Got nothin' to do but sun theeself?'

She turned to look, shielding her eyes. 'Uncle Tom! What brings you here?'

'Bad news, our Lizzie.'

'Oh, no. Not Stanley?' Her heart seemed to stop beating.

'No, not Stanley, thank the Lord. Our Sylvia's husband. He passed away sudden last night at ten to eleven. I thought you ought to know.'

'Sylvia's husband? Oh, I am sorry, Uncle Tom.

What on earth was the matter with him?'

'Heart failure, the doctor said. There was nothing wrong with him that we knew of. He hadn't been bad nor nothin'. He stood up to go to bed, and just collapsed. We sent for the doctor right away, but the poor chap was dead by the time he come.'

'And how's Sylvia taking it? Bad, I expect.'

'Well, it ain't sunk in yet, our Lizzie...'

'I never met him, Uncle Tom. Nor have I seen their son.'

'Kenneth.'

'Yes. Kenneth... Well, you know I haven't seen Sylvia for a good many years.'

Tom ran his finger round the inside of his collar. He was still panting after his strenuous walk up to Cromwell Street. Working all his adult life in a brass foundry had taken its toll on his chest.

'Oh, Kenneth's a bostin' little chap. I'll bring him up one o' the days so's you can see him. Anyway, how's Ben?'

'About the same, thanks. He's in the house. Go in and see him, and I'll pour you a cup of tea. There'll be one in the pot still. I'm just waiting for May to come back.'

'I thought as that was May's daughter sitting there ... poor little soul. How old is she now?'

'Coming six. She'll be six in September.'

He bent down and touched Emmie's cheek and the child grimaced, although it was her attempt at a smile.

'Where's Stanley serving now, Uncle Tom?' Lizzie tried to sound casual. 'Have you heard from him lately?'

'He's in Ireland, Lizzie. Dublin. He's due back on leave soon.'

'Oh? Well, promise me you'll tell him to come and visit me and Ben. We'd like to see him again. Ben would really enjoy talking to him, I bet.'

'I will. I daresay as he'd love to see Ben an' all. To talk over the war with him.'

'How much longer has he got to do in the army before he's finished? He seems to have been a soldier all his life.'

'He's just signed on for another spell, Lizzie. He won't be due out till nineteen twenty-six.'

'Struth! And d'you think he'll ever get married?'

Tom shrugged and gave a little laugh. 'I wish he would, Lizzie, but who knows? He's still only a young chap, really. There's plenty time – and plenty spare young women about these days. When he comes out he'll still only be thirty-eight or thirty-nine – a good age for a man to settle down.'

'Plenty of time to have sown his wild oats.'

Tom laughed at her candour. 'Wild oats? Well, he'll have had plenty bloody opportunity ... without me behind him.'

Lizzie blushed and wished she'd never said such a thing. Tom leaned over and fussed Emmie, and Lizzie felt relieved at the transfer of attention as she helped the child to her feet.

'Listen, I can hear your Mommy coming.'

Tom turned and saw May carrying a box. He greeted her, and Lizzie explained the reason for his visit.

Lizzie then remembered about the Coalport tea service. 'I bet you can remember this, Uncle Tom.' She placed the box on one of the chairs and opened it. 'It's what you bought my mother for her weddin' present ... in eighteen sixty-eight. A long time ago.'

'Oh, that tea set. Well I'm buggered.' He peered into the box. 'Is it still intact?'

'It's still intact,' May confirmed. 'We'm saving it for our Henzey – for when 'er gets wed.'

Two distinct emotions, both worlds apart, were existing symbiotically within Ben Kite's consciousness. The first was complete satisfaction, and it was evoked by the sight of his children as he watched them progress, intelligent and well adjusted.

Henzey was the apple of his eye, and always would be. She was the perfect cross between himself and Lizzie, inheriting her fine looks and mannerisms, but his colouring and temperament. Already it was evident she would grow up to be startlingly beautiful, with soft, long-lashed blue eyes and an abundance of raven hair. It pleased him greatly to acknowledge it. She also possessed a gift for art and, when she brought him her work to admire, hopeful of his praise, he was often amazed at her dexterity.

Herbert was more complex. Unlike his sisters he was not a particularly sensitive child, always keen to be in the thick of a rough and tumble with lads his own age. He showed no signs yet of any academic gift – indeed, his scholastic endeavours raised him only to the middle of his class at school.

Alice, on the other hand, was becoming a bookworm. She wasn't greatly gifted with common sense, and the arithmetic they tried to teach her at school went straight over her head. She seemed drawn noticeably to books for boys and men, relishing the hard bound compilations of Cassell's Magazine and Scribner's Magazine she borrowed from Jesse Clancey.

Already, music enthralled Maxine. The old piano that had stood redundant for years in the front room was given a new lease of life when Ben declared it should be tuned properly so Maxine could learn to play it. So they sent for Mr Mason, the blind piano tuner, and he spent half a morning tuning it, while Lizzie stood beside him with a feather duster and a damp rag, dislodging and wiping away the cobwebs and dead spiders of decades from inside its frame, and from between its strings. Jesse Clancey imposed on his mother, who was reluctant at first, to give Maxine an hour's tuition every week.

The second of the distinct emotions Ben experienced was bitter regret, which stemmed from his volunteering to fight in the Great War. Increasingly, he accepted that singular, rash act as the cause of his indisposition. More significantly, however, he recognised it as the virtual end of what had been as good a marriage as he could have ever hoped for. Oh, he was still married, to the same lovely girl, but he'd unwittingly destroyed that marriage. Now he was a burden upon Lizzie, and he sincerely felt she deserved more; much more than he was able to give. He loved her with all his heart and, because he loved her so much, he hated to see her selflessly devoting her time to him, barely ever complaining. He did not deserve such attention. Her life – her potential for living – was too closely tied to his own greatly narrowed existence for his peace of mind.

One Saturday morning, late in that warm July of 1920, the same two contrasting emotions became heightened more than at any other time since his return home. His children, full of the joys of life, asking his opinion on this and that, ate their breakfasts together, bubbling with conversation. Lizzie brushed the girls' hair in turn, plaiting Maxine's, piling and pinning up Henzey's dark tresses, and made sure they were all properly turned out. Then the children set off for the town where they could gaze in the shops, watch other folk and perhaps mingle with other children.

That done, Lizzie helped Ben wash and dress. Then she fed him, helped him struggle up the yard to the privy and back, washed the dishes, fetched coal from the cellar and made the fire up, swept the yard, scrubbed the front step, cleaned the windows, dusted the front room, prepared vegetables for their dinner, and then put the kettle on to make him a cup of tea.

'Lizzie, for Christ's sake, slow down,' he said. 'You're making me feel dizzy. You'll wear yourself out. You never stop doing things for me...'

'Things that have to be done, Ben. Things you couldn't do on your own.'

'Dear God! I wish I could do more. D'you

292

know how it feels sitting here like a mawkin ... can't do a thing ... having to watch you bugger yourself up doing everything ... not just for me, but for the kids as well?' He wheezed as the effort of speech robbed him of his precious breath.

Lizzie poured boiling water into the old teapot and gave it a stir, then left it to steep on the hob of the grate. 'I know how you feel, love,' she assured him gently.

'But you don't, Lizzie... You think you do, but you don't. You don't know half what's going through my mind.'

'Well I'll never know if you don't tell me.' She reached for two cups and saucers.

'Here, come and sit beside me.' He held his hand out to her. He was in his normal downstairs position, sitting across the sofa with his feet up, a light blanket over his legs.

'In a minute, when I've made the tea.' She poured milk into the cups. 'D'you want a piece of toast or anything?'

He shook his head. 'Sit down while the tea's a-steeping. I want to talk to you.' Her look was distant and troubled, he thought. She seemed grossly unhappy.

She sat down compliantly at one end of the sofa, shifting his legs over to make room. He took her hand and rubbed his thumb gently over the back of it.

'Go on, then,' she said, and looked into his eyes, serious, earnest. 'What d'you want to tell me?'

'For a start I want to tell you how much I love you...'

293

She turned away. 'I know how much you love me, Ben.'

'But I want you to hear it... Oh, it ain't just that, Lizzie. I know it ain't much of a life for you the way I am, but I want you to know I don't take for granted what you do for me...'

'Whatever I do, I do it because I want to, Ben. Not because I have to.'

'Will you stop interrupting me? As I say, I don't take it all for granted... Look... What I'm trying to say is this... Oh, I don't know how to put it.' He sighed with exasperation. 'Look, I know I ain't much of a husband ... particularly in bed, I mean... You know what I'm trying to say... Well, you're still a young woman, Lizzie, my flower, and still lovely with it ... and much as I love you ... I could hardly blame you if you took up with somebody else ... if you had a bit on the side... A lie-by.'

'A lie-by?'

'Somebody you could go to bed with ... for a bit of physical pleasure and comfort.'

Such a blatant suggestion warranted an equally blatant protest. 'Ben, do you know what you're saying? I've never heard anything like it. What d'you take me for? An old pro or something? As if I'd do such a thing.'

'I mean it, Lizzie. I've thought about it a lot. You're the most respectable woman I know, but I also know what you're like... You need loving and I can't oblige... And it grieves me as much as it grieves you, my flower... You must feel the need every now and again.'

She studied his scarred hand on hers, not

294

wishing their eyes to meet at that moment. God, an affair! He was right on target, of course; as if he could read her very thoughts.

'Yes, I do feel the need ... from time to time.' What was the sense in denying it? 'But such thoughts I have to put to the back of my mind, Ben. To think of me doing *that* with somebody else. I couldn't. It wouldn't be right. It'd mean me being unfaithful. I wouldn't want to be unfaithful, Ben.'

Neither spoke for a few seconds, each summing up the significance of what the other had said. Lizzie's eyes were still fixed on their joined hands.

'You can be unfaithful if I say it's all right,' Ben said eventually, 'if I release you from your vow of keeping thee only unto me. I see how Jesse Clancey looks at you, Lizzie. You know very well he's always had a soft spot for you... And he's single... What's more, he's decent with it... You could do a lot worse You don't think he comes here of a night to talk to me, and I don't know what's going through his mind, do you? He can't keep his eyes off you.'

Lizzie avoided looking at Ben in case guilt surfaced in her eyes. 'When we got married, Ben, it was for better or worse, in sickness and in health, as I remember. I made my vows then, and I intended to stick to them then. I still intend to. So I don't want to listen to you now driving me into another man's bed, because that's what it sounds like.'

'Oh, Lizzie, God bless you. What I'm trying to tell you is simple enough. If you feel the need to

295

stray, I understand ... and I wouldn't hold it against you. I ain't suggesting for a minute that you'd have to let me know about it... In fact, I'd rather not know ... so don't ever tell me... Just as long as you promise never to leave me, Lizzie... It'd break my heart if ever you left me.'

'Oh, Ben. Where would I go, for Lord's sake? I'll never leave you, you big gawby, you know I won't. So don't even think it.'

'Then you're free to do as you want.'

God! She effectively already had. She looked away, feeling ashamed and thoroughly guilty. 'No, I never will. I promise you that.' It was the least she could do.

'Hey! There's no need for tears, our Lizzie... There's no need to make any promise either. You never know who or what's around the corner... Anyway, what about when I'm dead and gone? Even if you never stray while I'm alive, I'd never expect you to stay unmarried for ever... You're a lovely looking woman and you've got your whole life in front of you. When I'm gone make the most of it... So long as the kids are content with whoever you decide on... Just so long as the kids are content.'

'Oh, stop it, Ben. Stop talking like that.'

She dried her tears, and stood up huffily, uncomfortable with this line of talk. She poked the fire into life and fished a spoon out of the table drawer for want of something to do. It was as if he could read her mind. Had he ever considered that she might have been unfaithful while he was away fighting the Germans?

'Tom Dando says that Stanley's coming home

on leave soon,' he said, breaking an awkward silence. 'There's somebody else you could have a little fling with. I reckon you've always had your eye on him, even though he is your cousin. Just as long as he ain't caught a dose of the pox on his travels... There's a lot of pox about after the war, you know.'

Lizzie felt her colour rise, and got up awkwardly from the sofa. 'What makes you think Stanley's interested in me?'

'He always used to be. He said so himself.'

'We were only kids then.'

'We were little more than kids ourselves then, Lizzie.'

She spooned sugar into his tea, and handed it to him.

He watched the bubbles spinning in the middle of the cup for a few seconds. 'D'you remember the day you were churched, and we stayed behind after the service ... and we sat in front of the altar with our Henzey?'

'I'll never forget it, Ben.'

'Nor will I. When I looked at you I could tell you were thinking the same as me – that I loved you with all my heart and soul, and that I always would ... no matter what.'

Lizzie looked up at Ben and saw his eyes, full and watery. She put down her cup and saucer on the table and threw herself across him, holding him as tightly as she dared. He understood her so well. Had he really perceived what had been on her mind for such a long time? If he had, and he was prepared to allow it, he was either a bigger, braver man than ever she'd realised, or the biggest fool. With such a big-hearted husband, could she ever be unfaithful again, with or without his blessing? It was out of the question. If the boot were on the other foot, and she were the invalid, would she be able to face the prospect of him being unfaithful to fulfil his carnal needs? It was too horrible to contemplate.

He ran his fingers through her hair lovingly, while she wept, unwilling to show her tears. 'Never ever leave me, Lizzie. Promise?'

'Oh, Ben, I promise. You know I'll never leave you.'

Chapter 16

It was the first Sunday in August that Stanley Dando called. Lizzie answered the knock on the door to see him looking as patrician as ever in his Captain's uniform. The children were at Sunday School, and Ben was dozing on the sofa after his dinner. She greeted him with a pleasant smile, feigning surprise, and he kissed her on the cheek which, to her quiet annoyance, made her blush. No sooner had they started to speak than Ben woke up.

It had been some years since Ben had seen Stanley, but he recognised him at once. Before long they were in easy conversation about the war, and swapping experiences. Lizzie took advantage of this to go upstairs and spruce herself up.

She'd been on tenterhooks for days wondering whether Stanley would call. At first she was keen that her Uncle Tom would pass on her invitation but, after Ben's confession that he wouldn't object to her taking a lover, she changed her mind. She wished for no temptation to be placed in her way. That unexpected discussion had elicited intense feelings of humility in Lizzie, pushing her closer to Ben again, if only spiritually. It pleased her, but it did not resolve anything fundamental. She still needed loving – but, at least, she'd become stoically resigned to remaining faithful. Since this reconciliation was non-physical, however, she knew deep in her heart that it would not be enough. It would be nowhere near enough. She still needed something beyond; something more than Ben's spiritual love and her own good intentions.

As Stanley talked to Ben his cool eyes frequently met hers, and unwittingly lingered. She could tell what he was thinking. He was mentally undressing her, and a secret stab of longing touched her, which she prayed would go away. Although she tried to avoid his piercing looks, vanity and a fatal wish for him to desire her, ensured that she could not. The very last time she had known sexual love, nearly five years ago, had been with him. Lord, had it been so long? As Ben told a humorous tale of the thin, hard mattress he called a 'biscuit', on which he slept in the trenches and how it provided fodder for ants in the form of fleas and bugs, Lizzie remained quiet, pondering how manly, how immensely more desirable Stanley had become.

So her earnest resolve to remain faithful evaporated like steam; as she knew it would.

Before long the children returned from Sunday School in their best clothes, noisy, and exuberant, glad to be released into the sunshine from that monotonous, weekly imposition. They were introduced to their Uncle Stanley, whom they only knew by occasional reference. He gave them each a shilling, for which he received four incredulous but grateful smiles in return, and their instant approval.

'You never had any more children then?' Stanley asked, and Lizzie thought what a pointed question it was.

'No, we never had any more,' she replied, lowering her lids.

He stayed for tea and, at about half past eight when the children had been put to bed, he suggested they send for some beer. Lizzie offered to fetch it and he gave her the money to pay for it. By the time they'd drunk it all it was dark, and Ben remarked that he needed to go up the yard, so would Lizzie help him?

'I need to go as well, Ben,' Stanley said. 'I'll take you. Then I must be off home.'

When they returned Stanley picked up his peaked cap and lingered at the door.

'Lizzie'll see you off,' Ben said, panting as he settled himself on his sofa. 'I would myself if I could.'

'It's all right, Ben, don't trouble yourself. I'll see you again soon, God willing.'

'Call and see us any time.'

So Lizzie, who had been fidgeting on her chair

like a cat with fleas waiting for this moment, too keenly went to the door with Stanley and out into the darkness of the entry. They stopped as they reached the street, and he turned to her. It was a warm, sultry night, with low clouds, and Lizzie fancied she saw flashes of lightning in the far distance.

'I never realised Ben was so dependent on you, Lizzie.'

'We manage.'

'You're a brick. And your children are a credit to you, you know. The eldest one – Henzey, isn't it? She'll fetch the ducks off the water...' He smiled, one of his dazzling smiles. '...just like her mother.'

'For all the good it's done me,' she replied experimentally.

'Well you're not over the hill yet, Lizzie. Far from it. You're as lovely as ever.'

'Oh, that's easy to say, Stanley. But none of us get any younger.'

'And you think life is passing you by, eh?'

'There's no doubting it, is there?'

'You've got a lot to be thankful for, Lizzie. You've got four lovely children... And Ben obviously thinks the world of you'

'Oh, and I think the world of him ... but...'

He took her hand and squeezed it, and she looked up into his eyes. 'Don't be too despondent, my love. I can tell you're despondent.' His voice had dropped to a whisper, but there was a pause while both concentrated on this caressing of hands. It told so much, and Stanley was encouraged by her acquiescence.

'Listen, can you get out at all? To meet me, I mean.'

'Oh, I don't know, Stanley.' She noted her own lack of refusal. 'When do you mean?'

'Whenever you can. During the day. At night? Any time.'

'I work in the day. There's only at night...' She was well aware that she was submitting too easily. 'Oh, but even that's impossible. There's too much to do. It's just too much with Ben and the kids. In any case we shouldn't, Stanley.'

'What about a Saturday? How about this coming Saturday. Would that be easier?'

'Saturday afternoon might be all right if I could get May to call in and see if Ben and the children were all right... I could say I was going shopping to the town. Where would we go, though? We couldn't be seen together.'

'We could go to an hotel.'

'An hotel?'

'I'd book a room. I might even stay the night, but I know you couldn't. I could meet you there in the afternoon. Nobody would know. What d'you say?'

She wrestled with her conscience for no more than a few seconds. Her mouth went dry and her heart started beating as if it were a big bass drum. It was going against her new resolution, but she was as driven to Stanley now as the birds are driven to build nests. This yearning was becoming an obsession, and Ben had promised he would turn a blind eye if she felt the need. How could she refuse? Why should she refuse? In a way it was a perfect set-up. Because Stanley

302

was a soldier, and would be for at least another five years, there was no chance of her being tempted away permanently. She could never leave Ben; she never would; and this way there was nowhere else to go; even if she wanted to. The only drawback, as far as she could see, was that she wouldn't be able to meet Stanley often enough.

So they stepped back into the discreet darkness of the entry, and he held her to him; and his lips parted hers with a hungry kiss that held so much promise. She pledged then to be at the front door of 'The Station Hotel' at two on Saturday afternoon. If the arrangement had to be altered the one would let the other know. With her mind racing back to that Christmas night of illicit love, she watched him walk away. Her heart throbbed so much with anticipation that she was hardly able to contain herself. Silhouetted against the light of a street lamp Stanley turned and waved, before he disappeared into the sultry night.

Getting out that Saturday afternoon was easier than Lizzie expected. Casually, during the week, she told May that she wanted to look for some new clothes for the children, and May instantly offered to see to Ben and the children for her, as she knew she would. But deceit on this scale was something new, and she felt a pang of guilt for telling the lie. All week she was increasingly preoccupied with the recklessness, the sordidness, the betrayal, the degradation of the approaching assignation, trying to imagine how it would be in some strange bed, with clean white sheets, in an hotel room. Oh, it was all so wrong, so sinful, so risky. If her mother were alive to see her there would be hell to pay. But it made no difference. It made no difference at all. She was like a bitch on heat. She'd been unfaithful once before, and it would be even easier a second time.

The weather that Saturday was set fair – perfect for a romantic tryst. Lizzie's mind was in a whirl but, all around her, life went on as calmly and, as surely as ever as she walked towards "The Station Hotel" carrying, for the sake of her alibi, her shopping basket. Housewives went about their business buying food for their families' dinners tomorrow, and girls in domestic service scurried from shop to shop with similar intent, complaining about the heat and how much they were expected to do. Workmen, thirsty from their labours, entered public houses, impatient for the taste of smooth, rich beer to slake their dry mouths. Children tripped across the cobbles ever hopeful of a sugar mouse or a toffee apple as they clutched their mothers' hands. Although Lizzie felt conspicuous, as if what she was about to do was written all over her, nobody except Stanley knew about that room today, and what might happen in it.

Stanley was already waiting when she arrived. He smiled and asked how much time she had. She must be home by six at the latest, she told him as they walked up the steps to the main door. While he paid for the room Lizzie tried to blend into the background, her eyes fixed to the polished wood block floor for fear of intercepting a curious or amused glance, or even recognition. Was this how a prostitute felt in similar circumstances? Her demeanour would certainly give her away. Lucy, her sister, used to work here; somebody might remember her and easily recognise her. So she was glad when they were out of the public area and climbing the oak bannistered stairs to their room.

Stanley unlocked the door and opened it, letting her in first. She looked about and heard him close the door and turn the key. Even if she changed her mind now and wanted to escape it was too late. But she did not want to escape. She was more than ready for this affair.

The room was much as she expected: plain, with a double bed, newly made up, with a brass bedstead; a wardrobe with a long mirror on one of the doors, a small dressing table, and a couple of wicker chairs. There was a rug at each side of the bed; save your bare feet getting too cold on the linoleum, she thought. A wash-stand, bearing a bowl and a jug of water stood near the window.

She turned to Stanley and smiled unsurely. 'Well, here we are, then,' she said, and waited for him to make the running.

Smiling, he took her basket from her and placed it on the floor. 'Are you going to take your hat off?' He put his hands to her waist and drew her to him. 'I should hate it to get crushed.'

She laughed at the thought and raised her arms to take out the pin. At the same time he started undoing the buttons on her blouse, since she wore no coat on account of the weather. She stuck the pin back into the hat, then placed both on the wicker chair at the foot of the bed. Submissively, she tilted her head forward, so that it was touching his chest, and he sniffed her hair, freshly washed that morning. He put a hand to her chin, gently lifted her face to him, then bent his head forward and kissed her luxuriously on the lips, dwelling, as if drinking her. Unlike their last encounter she was in total control of her senses, and the mere thought of his lips, the subject of so many adolescent fantasies, now full on hers and relentlessly probing her mouth, sent the blood swirling through her body. And after just one solitary evening and a long five year gap there was a strange familiarity in his kiss. This time, like the last, she tasted drink on him, possibly whisky, but she ignored it, sighing, tingling at his touch.

Her blouse was open and one hand was inside it. He must surely be able to feel the thumping of her heart beneath it, she thought. Then he concentrated on unfastening her skirt, and it fell to the floor silently around her. They broke off their kiss and, like the time before, he scooped her up in his arms to lay her gently on the counterpane. Without hurry he undressed her, kissing every inch of her body as it became exposed, till she was aching with longing.

Stanley sighed and reached into the pocket of his uniform, lying on the floor at the side of the bed. He pulled out a book of matches and a pack of Black Cat cigarettes, lit one and inhaled deeply, shuffling to make himself comfortable. All the sweet-talk had been spoken while they'd enjoyed each other.

'I suppose it'll be another five years before I see you again,' Lizzie remarked lightly, pulling the bedclothes over her nakedness.

'Not if you don't want it to be. I've still got another week of leave yet.'

'And what about after that?'

'I don't know. Probably about six months. We're due for a posting to Londonderry because of the troubles in Ireland. Will you write to me this time?'

'If you want me to...'

'I'd like you to,' he said. 'I'll write to you first so you'll know my address. It is okay to write isn't it?'

She caught his meaning at once. 'Oh, yes. I always get up first anyway, so I'm always the one to grab any post that comes. Ben doesn't get up till the children have gone to school.'

'Good.' He inhaled again on his cigarette, and flicked ash onto the rug unthinkingly. 'Why didn't you reply to the letter I sent you last time?'

'Things were different then, Stanley.' She turned to look at him. 'Ben was away and I was deeply in love with him and really missing him. I didn't want to start something with you that might muck things up. I didn't know he'd come back in that state.'

'I understand.'

'Besides, you were away as well, so what would've been the point? I expect you had lots of other women to concern yourself with, anyway.'

'Nobody serious. We move about too much in our regiment to get trapped by women... And after that first night we spent together nobody else had a chance.'

She smiled at his flattery, aware he was flannelling, of course.

'I kept thinking about the way you made love,' he said, 'the way you responded to me – your body.' He drew on his cigarette once more, savouring the taste and the memory for a few seconds. 'You know, Lizzie, considering you've had four kids, your body's still as fresh and firm as a young girl's.' He pushed the covers off her and ran his fingers over her naked belly, feasting his eyes on her. 'No stretch marks ... no sagging titties. You're amazing. Just like I imagined you to be when you were sixteen. And you're, what? Thirty now? Mind you, I think you've gained a pound or two since last time.'

'Nothing very much.'

'Oh, I think a few extra pounds suit you better, if anything... Anyway, you made me realise what I'd been missing all my life. Jesus, I really envied Ben.'

She laughed coyly, feeling very flattered. 'I bet you don't envy him now.'

'You might be surprised. Ben's still got you. I haven't.'

'But right now I'm lying here with you, not him.'

He looked her up and down. 'I know, and I'm counting my blessings. But when you go back home, you'll be with him. And tonight, you'll likely be naked making love with him.'

He was fishing, she knew, but why not let him think she and Ben still made love? It could do no harm. It could do no harm to let him believe he had some competition. It could do no harm to let him believe he was not the only one these days to have access to her body.

'Good God, Stanley. What do you think I am? I couldn't do it with Ben on the same day as I'd done it with you. I wouldn't. Anyway, he's not too demanding these days. I daresay it'll be a day or two yet... Can I pull the bedclothes up again now? I'm cold.'

He threw his unfinished cigarette in the empty fireplace and snuggled up to her. 'No,' he whispered. He began kissing her neck and his hand brushed gently up the inside of her thigh, sending delicious shivers through her entire body once more.

'I wonder what your father would say if he could see us now?' she remarked, smiling, feeling her desire rise again as she felt his supple body once more pressing against her skin.

Lizzie returned home in good time, albeit with an empty shopping basket. Ben teased her about it, but she replied indignantly that she'd only been to the town to see what was available and to check prices. She could always go next week, or even during the week, to get what they needed, when she'd paid it some mind. At once she set to work preparing the family's meal, and sang as she did so. Ben commented how chirpy she sounded. Later, they talked randomly before she put him to bed; and in bed together, they continued their disconnected conversation until Ben fell asleep.

She lay for a while, listening to the grunts of Jack 'Ardmate's pigs, to the soft cooing of pigeons which Joe had begun keeping in a loft he'd built near the pigsty, and to the intermittent wailings of a drunk staggering along Grove Street. She slipped Ben's protecting arm off her, slid out of bed and stood at the window in her night-dress looking out at the stars, like pin pricks of light shining through a sheet of blue black velvet. The light of a bright half moon floating low over the roofs of Grove Street lent a silvery sheen to the slates of the brewhouse roof.

Even though it was warm in the room she shivered as she considered the enormity of what she'd done that afternoon. She was scarcely able to believe she'd gone out and left her family, knowing she was going to be unfaithful to her husband; and not just to her husband, for she was being unfaithful to her children as well, inasmuch as whatever she did must also affect them indirectly. Of course, this wanton infidelity had been in the back of her mind ever since Ben returned home from the war. The memory of that unintended first time with Stanley had eaten away corrosively at her, undermining her acceptance of Ben's condition, his ruined looks and his inability to physically love and satisfy her. Now she'd allowed herself to slip into this prearranged adultery which, as a younger woman, she would have believed impossible in herself.

Almost from the first day of their courtship Ben had always been more than just a sweetheart, more than just a husband. They'd been more than just lovers, before and after their marriage; they'd been true soul mates. In that time she'd matured from a dreamy, adolescent girl into a practical woman. Always she made the best of herself, for Ben as much as for herself, and endeavoured to be lady-like, as her mother had always taught her to be. Ben had given her his love, his protection; he'd given her his name and four delightful children. Now she'd betrayed all that, wilfully, yielding to a man whom she'd known all her life, who was pretending to be Ben's friend. She'd given herself with consummate ease, too, affording him the same sensuous warmth she would at one time only ever have bestowed on Ben. It had happened sordidly, hidden away from the rest of the world in an hotel room, without any embarrassment or second thoughts. There must be something perverse in her subconscious that drove her to be like this; some flaw that had always been there.

Yet she did not regret it. Nor did she love Ben any the less. Stanley had had many other women, doubtless of all races and creeds; and she was just one of them. That in itself was stimulating; not because of a wish to be more desired by him than any of the others, but because she was convinced that all those other women almost certainly desired him as much as she did, thus endorsing her own taste. She felt no different toward Stanley because of it. She was not taken with him now like she used to be, but she was certainly stimulated by his expert lovemaking, and by her own response to it.

She'd lacked sexual love for years. For a long time it had been an important part of her life. And she'd missed it more than anything. It was something she needed; it helped keep body and soul together; it was addictive, like a drug. Without it she was moody and depressed; as dull and lacklustre as a heap of slack in the cellar.

Thankfully now there was opportunity; opportunity that had been contrived once the will had manifested itself. And once the opportunity had been devised, there was the expectation, the anticipation of something incurably, perhaps even ruinously exciting, and she had to pursue it at all costs. The reality was no disappointment either; and not just in the physical sense. The knowledge that she was locked in that room alone with him, as naked as the day she was born but for her wedding ring, tasting and savouring his naked body, yielded a wonderful unreality. She wondered whether it was all a dream; whether this thing could really be happening to her.

But she was well aware that one of the things that drove her to this affair was that, when they did it before, that notable Christmas night, she was in the depths of despair. And that act of physical love had lifted her, and enabled her to carry on, putting the world and all its woes into perspective. This time she expected it to do the same; and, thankfully, it seemed to have done.

A lifetime's drilling had brainwashed her into

believing that it was not right, that it was sinful in the eyes of God. Adultery only ever happened to other people who were depraved, and they were frowned on, condemned by society. But it made no difference. She was swept along in this current of craving for sexual satisfaction, and all other thoughts were negated absolutely.

Ben turned over painfully in their bed, grunted, and then began snoring. Lizzie turned away from the window momentarily, allowing the moonlight to fall on him, so that she could see him. Oh, Ben ... dear Ben ... poor Ben... She sighed, knowing it would have been better if ... if he'd never gone to war, of course. If he'd never gone to war they would still be as much in love as ever they were. Maybe they'd have six or more children by now. But he had gone to war, damn him; against her better judgement. It was all his fault. It had to be his fault.

She turned back to the stars and the moon. A cloud, like a black bag with a pale yellow lining, hovered over the tilting chimney pots of Grove Street. 'Your body's still as fresh and firm as a young girl's,' he'd said. 'I really envied Ben.' It might be Ben's fault, but she didn't like herself particularly after what she'd done, and was intending to do more. '...still as fresh and firm as a young girl's. Just like I imagined you to be when you were sixteen. And you're, what? Thirty now?' A shiver stole over her body in the warm night. This affair would be understandable if Ben had been seeing other women. But he had not. Or rather, perhaps he had when he was away in the army, but she wasn't aware of it, and now it was of no consequence anyway. But she regretted nothing. Not yet, at any rate.

They'd left that room at about half past five, in the full light of day, parting with a brief kiss at the main entrance, promising to meet there at the same time next Saturday. He would not call to see Ben again on this leave, so it was unlikely she would see him before next Saturday.

Lizzie drew the curtain at last, and slid in to bed beside Ben, as gently as a mouse so as not to wake him. For a few minutes she lay, wide awake, staring at the half dark ceiling, but seeing only what was in her mind. 'Will you write to me this time?' 'If you want me to.' 'I'd like you to.' Ben snuffled, gasped, and snored once or twice. 'But right now I'm lying here with you, not him.' Her knee itched and she scratched it. 'But when you go back home, you'll be with him. And tonight, you'll likely be naked making love with him.'

Fat chance.

Ben moved, as if aware she'd been away. He sought her hand, and found it while he slept.

While Lizzie waited for next Saturday she felt brighter and happier, more content than she had for years. She smiled more as she set about her daily chores, knowing that at the end of the week there was another gorgeous afternoon with Stanley to look forward to. Her attitude to Ben and the children was more tolerant; she showed a greater willingness to tend to his needs. In part it was guilt, but mostly it sprang from the joy of rediscovering the pleasure and contentment that hard loving could provide, magically soothing away tensions and pressures, lifting her.

And so the next Saturday came, and it was much the same as the last one, except that a whole week's anticipation moved them both to greater appreciation and enjoyment. This affair promised already to be highly physical. It was such a pity they could only meet on odd days, when Stanley was home on leave. Next time would not be so long to wait, though – only six months. And six months, although long enough, was not like another five years.

Ben never saw the letters that arrived for Lizzie. She read them, then burned them, envelopes and all, before he got up. Or she intercepted the postman with the second post. They were never wildly passionate letters, nor indecently frequent, and this pleased her. Stanley put no pressure on her with head-turning words of love, as she thought he might, and it rendered her deceit all the easier to contain.

The months passed and, in October, the miners went out on strike again, shutting every pit in the country. Ben Kite was predictably outraged. He complained to Jesse Clancey about it during one of his visits.

'I have to laugh at that bloody Smillie, the president of the Miners' Federation,' he scoffed, reaching for his newspaper. 'It says here, "Robert Smillie said in Lanarkshire last Sunday ... that this fight for an extra two shillings per man per shift ... was not a fight against the community or the government ... but a fight against the mine owners backed by the government." Jesse, I've never heard such a load of bloody clap-trap in all my life.' He put the newspaper down, his breath coming in rasps. 'If it ain't a fight against the community, then why is it the damn community has to bloody suffer, eh?... If their fight's with the pit owners then why don't they grab hold of the pit owners and shake seven bells of shit out of 'em?.. Rather than put their so-called brothers in lumber ... with the winter coming on and all... The railwaymen and the dockers'll be out next. They generally all like to have a go together ... just to rub it in.'

In November, Maxine went down with chicken pox and, in December, it was Alice's turn. Lizzie read with interest that martial law had been finally declared in Ireland in an attempt to curb the escalating violence and, in January, British tanks rolled into Dublin. She thought about Stanley. By February the number of unemployed had topped a million, and during the third week of March Stanley came home on leave again.

Chapter 17

Soon after his father died, Jesse Clancey realised that trying to cover two milk rounds by himself was virtually impossible. It was tiring, not just for himself, but for his poor horse, Ramsbottom, as well. It left him no time to relax and do the other things he wanted to do. So he hired Harry Skilbeck, a long time friend, whom he could trust. Jesse gave the Buffery and Dixons Green round to Harry, because it eliminated the likelihood of him ever meeting Sylvia Dando and, just as relevantly, her mother. When Jesse heard of the death of Sylvia's husband, he considered how judicious this decision had been.

Sylvia's marriage had been entirely satisfactory. Her husband, James, had provided the means for a standard of living vastly better than the one she'd been used to, since residing with her mother and father had presented an opportunity to save a useful amount of money. Sylvia took James' death philosophically, with great sadness, yet barely shedding a tear. His wife for more than seven years she would miss him, of course, as would her six-year old son, Kenneth. James had set up a partnership as an architect, and it had flourished. Because he was of a methodical nature he'd gone about it properly using a solicitor to draw up a legal deed of partnership. Consequently, Sylvia found herself reasonably well off once compensated with the insurance money that represented James's share of the business.

It had always been their intention to move into their own house; and the house of their dreams, occupying a plot of land he'd purchased in Oakham Road, was nearing completion when James died. This project was being financed by a mortgage, and one of the conditions of it, naturally enough, was that his life be insured to the value of the finished house. So, besides the partnership share, Sylvia was also the owner of an unfinished detached villa residence, paid for, in one of the most desirable, almost rural, areas of the town. The house remained unfinished for more than a year until the insurance claim was settled, but that done it was completed over the ensuing months, and Sylvia and her son eventually moved in.

Having just delivered milk to one of his regular customers in Oakham Road one bright March morning in 1922 Jesse stepped onto his milk float and flicked the reins to move off when he heard a familiar voice calling him. He looked up and was surprised to see, of all people, Sylvia, waving enthusiastically. Being the gentleman he was, he acknowledged her at once and drew the float to a halt outside the new house. She walked down the front path to meet him. He'd watched this impressive house being built, noticed it standing unfinished for ages, not knowing who was to be its inhabitant, and not unduly concerned, except that it was another prospective customer. Little did he expect that customer would be Sylvia.

'Sylvia! Damn my hide! Are you living here?'

She said she was, and explained.

'Yes, I was sorry to hear about your husband passing away. It must've come as a terrible shock. But it's been what? Nigh on two years now?'

'James died in the July.'

'And have you settled in now?'

'Well I've furnished downstairs, and our two bedrooms, and I've got curtains up in those rooms, but there's still such a lot to do. The trouble is, it needs a man's strength, and my

318

father's not strong enough these days. And Stanley's not expected home till the end of the year.'

'What needs to be done, Sylvia?'

'Oh, absolutely stacks of things. I need coat hooks putting up, I want a dado rail put up in the sitting room, a towel rail in the bathroom, wallpaper everywhere. The garden needs establishing. You know, lawns, flower beds, trees planted. I only wish I could do it all myself.'

Jesse looked at her with studied eyes. She must be thirty-six now, but the years had been kind. She still looked attractive and well dressed in expensive if matronly clothes. Her face was thinner, if anything, and like her mother she carried no superfluous weight. She possessed an understated elegance that was appealing; and she tried diligently to be refined.

'Your best bet is to get recognised tradesmen, Sylvia. All right, they might cost you a copper or two, but if you can afford it, it'd be worth it. Have the jobs done proper.' He thought he detected a flicker of disappointment in her eyes that he had not offered his own services.

'I suppose you're right. Do you know of anybody?'

'I daresay I do. Let me have a think about it, eh? I'm sure I could come up with somebody... Anyway, you stopped me. D'you want me to deliver your milk?'

'Oh, please, Jesse. And can I have a jug now?'

''Course you can.'

Sylvia went inside and returned with a white ceramic jug. She held it up while he filled it from his ladle, giving her a generous measure.

'I'd ask you in for a cup of tea...'

'That's kind of you, Sylvia, but I'm running a bit late, to tell you the truth. Some other time, eh?' He stepped onto his cart and flicked the reins again, touching his cap as he moved off. 'See you tomorrow.'

Over the ensuing months Jesse Clancey got used to seeing Sylvia, delivering milk to her every day except Sundays. His initial unease gradually dissipated and he became more relaxed in her company. One fine September morning when he'd completely dropped his guard, Sylvia succeeded in coaxing him into her comfortable lair. Jesse had been early to the station with Harry Skilbeck to collect his churns of milk, and thus had a flying start to his day. Normally, he took the churns back to the dairy house and Harry picked up his allocation from there, but this new way saved a fair bit of time. Jesse wondered why he hadn't thought of it before.

'You're early today, Jesse,' Sylvia observed, as he decanted milk ritually into her jug. 'Does that mean you've got time for a cup of tea? The kettle's just boiled.'

Jesse dipped a hand inside his cow gown and into his waistcoat pocket. He withdrew his fob watch and scrutinised it. Yes, he could afford ten minutes. It could do no harm. Besides, he was curious to see inside Sylvia's new house. It would be a talking point with Lizzie Kite.

He followed her inside and was invited to sit down on one of Sylvia's new sumptuously upholstered armchairs. So dusting off the seat of his cow gown he eased himself in. While he waited he looked around, admiring the fine velvet curtains, the Pre-Raphaelite pictures of Arcadian nymphs with long flowing hair, hanging on the walls over the lush, flock wallpaper. There was an expensive looking marble fireplace standing proud of the chimney breast, a thick carpet under his feet and immaculately trimmed wall to wall linoleum on which it lay. Yes, Sylvia had done very well for herself.

That evening Jesse called round to the Kites' house.

'Sylvia asked me in for a cup of tea this morning,' he said, after Ben had given his breathless opinion on the day's political and sports news. 'She's got it beautiful, Lizzie. Like a palace, it is.'

'She can afford it. Her husband left her a tidy penny, by all accounts.'

'Ivor Whistle's done a bostin' job paperhanging. There's velvet curtains up at the windows, plush carpets. Oh, and she's even got a bathroom upstairs with a water closet.'

'Huh! There'll be no newspaper hanging in little squares on a nail for her,' Ben commented.

'Damned right, Ben. It'll be best lavatory paper for Sylvia, and no two ways... What are you laughing at, Ben?'

'Sounds to me as though she's aiming for a new husband, Jesse. You could be in the firing line. You want to keep your head down.'

Jesse smiled and nodded, glancing at Lizzie. 'And if I didn't already know the wench, she might be in with a chance. But not me and Sylvia, Ben. It never worked out the first time. As sure as hell it wouldn't work out a second.'

'But you don't know, Jesse,' Lizzie urged, deliberately goading him, trying to glean whether he really meant it. 'People change, you know. Everybody changes. Sylvia might be a completely different woman to the one you knew all those years ago. I bet she'd make a perfect wife, especially as she's been married before. I haven't seen her for years, but I imagine she's still a fine looking girl. She was always the sort to look after herself.'

'Oh, she's smart still, Lizzie, and no mistake. Proper ladylike. But it'd be, "watch where you're putting your jacket, Jesse",' he mimicked, making the others smile. '"Get your shoes off afore you come in the house... Don't flatten them cushions"... Why, me life'd be a misery.'

'I can't believe she's that bad.' Ben's laughter was hurting him

'Oh, she's worse. Anyway, I don't think I'm posh enough for her now.'

'But there'd be no harm in taking her out once in a while, Jesse. You could take her to the Opera House of a Saturday night to see one of those shows they have on. You don't have to marry her... You could still get your feet under the table. A good many would be glad of the opportunity... If you don't, somebody else will.'

'And they're welcome as far as I'm concerned,' Jesse said, looking at Lizzie again; a look which Lizzie caught.

Yet, as time passed, Jesse continued to respond

positively to Sylvia's persistent offers of liquid refreshment halfway through his rounds, and she told him to walk right in if she didn't answer the door at once. After all, she might be pegging washing out in the back garden, unable to hear him. He was flattered, and accepted one invitation for Sunday tea early in December. He arrived as it was getting dark, wearing his best three piece Sunday suit and gold fob watch beneath his heavy winter overcoat. The welcome, warm air that embraced his chilled face bore the homely aroma of bread baking. For the first time he saw how pleasantly subtle the lighting was. It was all very appealing. Sylvia relieved him of his best bowler and his coat, before leading him into the sitting room. Her son Kenneth was lying in front of a glorious fire scribbling on a writing pad. Sylvia introduced them.

'What's that you're drawing?' Jesse enquired, trying to befriend the fair-haired boy.

'Oh, it's not a drawing,' he answered politely. The child was well spoken, like his mother. 'I'm writing a letter to Santa Claus.'

'I see. So what d'you want Santa Claus to bring you, eh?'

'Just some tin soldiers.'

'Tin soldiers, eh? Have you asked your mother to get you a Christmas tree, as well?'

'She says if I'm very good she'll get one.'

'Well that's fair. It always pays to be good, you know. Santa Claus always knows how you behave. And if you've been extra specially good he might even bring you some sweets.'

Sylvia broke into the conversation. 'I'll go and

get tea ready, Jesse. Do you like fruitcake? Funny, but I can't remember.'

'I used to love your mother's. I daresay yours'll be just as good.'

'How's your mother keeping, Jesse? Does she still play the piano?'

'From time to time, but she's got arthritis in her hands these days, so she can't play that well now. Still gives a few lessons though.'

'Well that's something. And is she still keen on sewing?'

'Not so much now. How are your mother and father, Sylvia?'

She sat down on the edge of the other armchair. 'Well, Mother's fine, thank you, Jesse, but Father's not so well. He's a proper old man now. Getting quite frail.'

'I expect you'll be spending Christmas day with them, eh?'

'Actually, no. I shan't see them over Christmas at all. Kenneth and I have been invited to spend a few days with James' parents. They live in Sedgley, so we don't see them very often. I thought it would be a good opportunity.'

'Give you a break, as well.'

Sylvia stood up. 'And it'll be welcome. I'll make that tea, Jesse. Kenneth, would you finish your letter at the table, instead of lolling on the floor? Else Mr Clancey won't be very impressed with you at all.'

Stanley Dando arrived at Dudley station shortly after two o' clock on Sunday the 17th. The day was still, with a clammy cold that pierced through to the bones, and a thick grey fog that reduced visibility to about ten yards. Damp unhealthy English weather, he told himself, lugging his kit bag behind him into 'The Shoulder of Mutton' for a pint of home brewed bitter to liven up his appetite for his dinner. Thank goodness he wouldn't have to suffer it much longer.

He wouldn't have to suffer it much longer because the European population of Southern Rhodesia had voted in a referendum to go their own way and not become aligned to the Union of South Africa, as its fifth province. Next September, therefore, the colony was due to become self-governing, annexed to the Crown. It meant they must organise their own defence forces, and Stanley had volunteered for secondment to Salisbury, the colony's capital, to assist them, along with other officers. He was to commence the long journey as soon as his leave was over.

His mother made a great fuss of him when he walked in, and his father shook his hand and said how well he looked. Within half an hour he was enjoying roast chicken, a rare delicacy, with creamed potatoes, sprouts, and carrots, which Sarah had been keeping warm in the oven under an upturned plate. That finished, they talked, and he sat in one of the armchairs to read the Sunday paper, then fell asleep. At eight o'clock he decided to have a wash and patronise 'The Shoulder of Mutton' again. Later he could visit Lizzie and pay his respects to Ben. But he fell among amusing company in 'The Shoulder of

Mutton', and so postponed his visit. No matter; Lizzie wasn't going anywhere.

He spent most of Monday with Sylvia, enjoying her hospitality and relishing the novelty of comparative luxury in her new home. There were one or two odd jobs she asked him to do, which he completed gladly, and offered to do more while he was home on leave. In the afternoon he went to Dudley Market and bought lots of Christmas decorations and a Christmas tree that he decorated that evening with Kenneth.

The next day, Tuesday, Stanley finally called on Lizzie and Ben, and took with him a selection of Christmas gifts, which enhanced further his standing with the children. He gave Ben a box of fifty Black Cat cigarettes, and Lizzie a bottle of Shalimar perfume, with instructions not to open them till Christmas Day. He took along, as well, some of the Christmas decorations he'd bought the day before, and delighted the children by getting them and their mother to help him put them up, while Ben offered jovial words of encouragement from his sofa. Henzey, ten years old, asked if her Uncle Stanley could stay for tea, and she smiled when her mother said of course he could, if he wanted.

So Stanley stayed for tea and played with the children until it was their bedtime. They kissed him in turn on their way upstairs, sorry to be parted from him. He was such good fun, Uncle Stanley. Ben invited him to stay for supper and he gladly accepted, so they played cards and drank beer. Occasionally, as they passed cards from one to the other, Lizzie's and Stanley's fingers would touch briefly, and it was difficult to avoid flashing secret glances between each other. Then they sat in front of the fire and talked, watching the coals burning in the grate. Ben was tired and fell asleep on his sofa and, when Stanley glanced up at Lizzie and smiled, she smiled back knowingly, feeling that familiar, warm glow of desire that had not been sated for months.

He offered to go so that she could get Ben to bed, and took his greatcoat from the back of the cellar door. As he put it on, Ben roused and opened his eyes.

'I'm just on my way, Ben,' Stanley said, picking up his cap. 'It's been good to see you again and looking so well. I'll try and get to see you again over Christmas.'

Ben yawned, thrusting his arms out in a feeble stretch. 'Come any time, Stanley... Come Christmas night if you want... I daresay Joe and May'll be here with their daughter. I don't suppose we'll be short of drink.'

'Thanks, Ben. But I think Mother and Father'll be expecting me to spend the night with them, worse luck. If I do get the chance though...'

'Well a merry Christmas to you whether or no. And thanks for the Christmas boxes. It was a kind thought, Stanley.'

'You're welcome, Ben. Merry Christmas, both. Goodnight.'

'I'll just see Stanley off, Ben. I'll only be a minute.'

As Lizzie and Stanley turned into the entry he immediately grabbed her and pressed her against the wall. She sought his lips urgently in the darkness, and sighed as she tasted him again after so long. God, this longing was like a disease.

'I thought this Christmas was never coming,' she breathed when their lips eventually parted. 'And when you didn't come to see me on Sunday, nor yesterday, I thought you weren't interested any more.'

'I got waylaid, Lizzie,' he answered easily. 'Couldn't be helped. Sorry. Anyway, I'm here now.'

'When shall I see you? If you still want to.'

'Yes, 'course I want to.' He pecked her on the lips once more.

'When?'

'Now.'

The cold breeze soughed through the entry and she felt its chill under her fashionably short skirt as he lifted it. She'd bought it specially for when Stanley came home.

'No, not now, you dope ... stop it,' she giggled, wriggling away. 'Not here.'

'Thursday, then. Listen, our Sylvia's going to stay with her in-laws tomorrow. She'll be gone a week. She's asked me to stay at her house and keep it aired. I'll be in residence for a whole week, just like royalty. All by myself.'

'But I couldn't go to Sylvia's house, Stanley. It wouldn't be right. I haven't spoken to her for years. If ever she found out... God, no, I couldn't.'

'Don't be daft. I shan't tell her. *How* could she find out? She'll be in Sedgley. It'll be perfect. It'll

328

be private... Whenever we want.'

She did not particularly relish the venue, but he'd said it would be all right. And she so desperately needed him. 'I suppose night would be best then. I'll try to slip out after the kids are in bed. Would that be all right?'

'Couldn't be better, my love. What time?'

'About nine. Earlier if I can.'

Sylvia waited till Jesse called before she left for Sedgley on the Wednesday morning. She had a Christmas gift, which she wanted to give him before she went away, because Christmas boxes given after the event always seemed like an afterthought. She must also tell him that Stanley would be staying there over Christmas and that he would need milk delivered. Stanley must pay him, too. She must stress that. She saw no reason why she should pay for his milk when he was getting the comfort of her house for nothing, and burning her coal, and using her gas. She knew what Stanley was like; he would always take what he could if he was allowed to get away with it; he never failed to take advantage. That he was to do some odd jobs for her was neither here nor there.

On Thursday it rained all day. Grey clouds hung low and from dawn till dusk there was no break in them. It was cold, too, and windy.

'Fancy going out on a night like this,' Ben Kite muttered. 'You must want your head looking. Surely Daisy Foster will never expect you on a night like this.'

'I promised I'd go when I saw her in the town last week.' Lizzie was ready with her hat and coat on. 'I don't like letting people down. You know I don't like letting people down when I've promised.'

'Well don't be too late back. And take the gamp else you'll get drenched.'

She kissed him on the cheek. 'All right. I'll see you later.'

She grabbed the umbrella and went out, thinking how, if Ben had been in their bedroom to see, he would be wondering why she'd changed her underwear just to see Daisy Foster. Over the months she'd bought some very alluring items; shorter white drawers, light, sensually smooth and frilly with wide leg openings. She'd invested in a new lace brassiere with elastic straps, and it was infinitely more flattering than any of her old ones, or the tight chemises some women still wore to keep their bosoms in check.

And all these things she was wearing on this cold, wet night; for Stanley's benefit.

She knew where Sylvia's house was situated. As she walked across the top of Hill Street and down into the Sixcore, with the rain squalling and almost blowing her umbrella inside out, she thought how grateful she was that Sylvia had not spotted her when she'd been to reconnoitre. A vindictive streak suggested there was something perversely appealing about going to Sylvia's house now, to do what she and Stanley were going to do. It would be even more pleasurable to do it in Sylvia's very own bed. Perhaps they would.

The Sixcore was poorly lit and it was difficult to see where to walk to avoid stepping into puddles and getting wet feet, so Lizzie was glad when she turned into Oakham Road. Oakham Road was no better lit, but it had a decent pavement at least. As she approached the house, she began to feel conspicuous. She opened the front gate, looking round to see if anyone had noticed her. But there was not a soul in sight. Who but thieves and lovers were out on a night like this? She walked nervously up the path to the front door. There was a light inside. She tapped tentatively with the knocker, half fearing it might be answered by Sylvia herself; so was ready to turn and run, if need be.

At once Stanley opened the door and let her in. She shook her umbrella outside, and he took it to the sink in the scullery to drip before he helped her take her coat off. Lizzie looked around her, taking in the warm ambience of Sylvia's home, and admiring the polished oak floor beneath her feet, now spotted with water that had dripped from her coat.

'Oh, I do like this house. I really do like it.'

'Come on, let me show you around,' he said, hanging her coat on the newel post. 'It's very imposing. I'm glad our Sylvia suggested I stay here. I feel like Lord Muck.'

He showed her the sitting room, and she sat in each of the armchairs in turn to try them out, bouncing up and down like an excited child. In the scullery she was impressed with the New World gas stove and the geyser, and the new white sink and hot water on tap; and uttered little gasps of admiration. It was so clean and fresh. There was lovely carpet up the stairs, gas lights and gas fires in the bedrooms, and a bathroom with the much vaunted water closet Jesse had mentioned.

'Oh, I do like this house,' she said again, but with greater feeling, deliberately re-entering the bedroom that was obviously Sylvia's. 'Are you sleeping in here?'

'I don't fancy sleeping in Kenneth's little bed when this one's available.'

He sat down on it and patted it to indicate that she should sit beside him. When she complied he put his arm around her and, when their lips met, he eased her backwards so that she was lying down. She felt his weight upon her at last, his hand sliding up the inside of her thigh. She smiled up at him, overflowing with tenderness, trembling with anticipation and the desperate need to make love.

The next day, Friday, Lizzie finished work early, it being the last working day before Christmas. The rain had eased, but it was still dull, and by four o'clock it was dark. She was aching for more stolen moments of illicit love. The previous evening's eroticism was uppermost in her mind and had possessed her all day, nourishing her desire. She definitely was not in love with Stanley, she told herself, it was just that she could not get him off her mind. Images of how he made love to her; how he made her toes curl; how she felt more like a woman than she could ever remember, were preoccupying her. Simply, she felt that she could not get enough of him. And since he was home for a few paltry days only, she had to make the most of whatever time was available. So instead of going straight home she made her way to Sylvia's house again, her whole body tingling with anticipation.

He was sitting with his feet up, reading a newspaper but, as soon he saw her standing at the door wearing an unsure smile, he grinned reassuringly back and let her in. Within five minutes they were in Sylvia's bed once more, writhing like two slippery eels.

On Saturday morning Lizzie made the excuse to Ben that she wanted to get some last minute Christmas things from the town and might not be back till the shops closed. Particularly she wanted to buy Stanley a Christmas box, she said, since he'd been so kind to them. Henzey and Alice both said they'd like to go with her to see the shops all lit up with fairy lights, to hear the carol singers and the Salvation Army band playing by the fountain in the Market Place. But Lizzie guiltily had to refuse. So she went to the town alone, rushed impatiently to buy what she needed and hurried back along Dixons Green, to Oakham Road. She and Stanley were to spend the rest of the afternoon together.

There was something about this clandestine relationship that was double sided. On the one hand it made Lizzie feel like a young girl again. She experienced the same exhilaration at making love with Stanley in secret as when she and Ben used to do it on the hearth, or on the sofa before they were married when her mother was in bed.

It was forbidden then, but even more so now, and all the more exciting for it. But on the other hand, there seemed to be a worm of lust within her that, once awakened, would not be sated. It was like a disease that eroded her will. It provided excuses for what was inexcusable, driving her to seize every opportunity to placate it; for it to have its way. And after this worm was appeased she felt relief, she felt so much better; so much more at peace with herself and with her lot. She felt a return of warmth and tolerance, and these feelings reflected on Ben, rendering him more at ease in turn. But only for a while. For when the balm that soothed this arrant wantonness ran out, as it must when Stanley left, so her discontent and lack of fulfilment returned. And discontent returned with increasing rapidity and intensity until it could be sated again.

Worst of all, she could not help it. She had no antidote for it. She no longer felt any guilt. She had this licentious flaw in her character, and she was stuck with it.

They stood in front of the fire in the sitting room that Saturday afternoon before Christmas. Stanley's arms went about her and he began kissing her passionately. This crazy longing must be the same for him, she thought, as the touch of his lips heightened her aching desire. These last three days they'd both seemed insatiable, and lost no opportunity, wasted no second to enjoy each other. He unfastened her skirt, her heart thudded and her head was filled with a strange humming; and at once they slumped in a fervent wriggling heap to the hearth-rug.

Saturday was the busiest day of the week for Jesse Clancey, since it was the day he not only delivered his milk to all his customers, but also collected the money. Since it was Christmas Eve tomorrow everybody wanted extra milk, and here and there he'd taken a nip of whisky or port, and stopped to wish his customers a merry Christmas; so he was even later than usual, and not entirely sober. He arrived outside Sylvia Atkinson's house at about half past three, remembering Sylvia's comment that he must collect his dues from Stanley Dando. So Jesse walked up the path, having decanted a quart of milk for Stanley into the galvanised jug from which he sometimes filled customers' own containers. The path headed for the side of the house, and then turned at right angles towards the front door, passing the sitting room window. Inside, the gas mantle was lit and he automatically peered through the window. When he saw two naked bodies writhing animatedly on the floor he thought at first that one of them must be Sylvia. His first instinct was to turn away before they saw him watching. But he could not. He was like a block of stone, cemented to the spot, petrified like a statue on a plinth, eyes staring, fixed. His grip on his jug slackened, and the sound of milk trickling onto his shoes brought him back to awareness. He looked again, scarcely able to believe what he was seeing. This was certainly not Sylvia. He was looking at the woman as if she were upside down, so it was difficult to determine who she was; and her face

335

was contorted with either ecstasy or pain, oblivious to everything save what she was experiencing.

But it was not Sylvia.

The man, however, was certainly Stanley Dando.

Then the woman moved her head to the side, almost facing Jesse. He saw her intense, open mouthed expression turn to a smile of fulfilment, her eyes closed, her colour high from exertion, her forehead glistening with perspiration.

It was Lizzie Kite.

Please, God, let it be anybody but Lizzie Kite.

Chapter 18

On the evening of Boxing Day Stanley Dando called with a bottle of whisky to celebrate what remained of Christmas with Ben and Lizzie. Only then did he make it known that he was being seconded to Southern Rhodesia and would remain there for the rest of his army career, including his furloughs. Lizzie was taken aback, but said nothing, keeping her own counsel, wondering why he'd chosen not to tell her before. If Southern Rhodesia was anything like South Africa he might be inclined to stay there, he said, deliberately avoiding Lizzie's eyes. He extolled the virtues of life there, and commented that if Ben had been fit they should definitely have considered emigrating to that fabulous land of boundless opportunity and wealth.

When it was time for Stanley to leave, Lizzie escorted him down the entry. This occasion ought to appear to Ben no different to any other night Stanley called, she thought, and she made it look as casual as she could, though inside she was as tense as a baited mousetrap.

'It was nice of you to let me know in front of Ben that you're going to Southern Rhodesia for good, Stanley,' she said acidly as they halted at the bottom of the entry. Lizzie's arms were folded across her bosom, her eyes burned into him and she tilted her head to one side to indicate her disdain.

He gave no answer.

'I suppose you were afraid I might be awkward if you told me while we were by ourselves?'

'It crossed my mind, Lizzie.'

'Then you flatter yourself if you think I care that much... And you're a coward, I hope you're braver in battle.'

'It's not a question of bravery. It's more a question of expediency.'

'More a question of me not going to bed with you when you fancied it, if you'd told me sooner,' she said sullenly.

'Look, Lizzie, I've enjoyed our times together, and every time I leave you to go back to my regiment I feel it more acutely than the time before. I'm loath to leave you at all, but what can I do? I'm a professional soldier. My job takes me all over the world. I can ill afford to be ... to be emotionally trapped. More especially by a woman who's already married.'

337

'But it's all right to sleep with me from time to time?'

'I can't help it if you're married. But I wish you weren't. I wish to God you weren't. Things might be different.'

'Oh! You're not saying you're in love with me by any chance, are you, Stanley?'

'Well ... I ... if I let myself be, yes, I could be ... if I lived at home... If I lived at home it would be easy to fall in love with you. If you weren't already married. But I don't want to lose you, Lizzie. We could still write. There's no good reason why we shouldn't write. It might be for the best to keep in touch.'

'And what earthly good would that do if you live on the other side of the world?'

'Well, you never know, do you, Lizzie?' he said pointedly. 'You never know what might happen.'

Lizzie decided to make no comment. She knew he was referring to Ben's dubious health; that he might die at any time. Deeply she resented his inferences. But, inside, she was seething that he'd informed her so unconcernedly, in front of Ben, as if by so doing he could receive no reproach. It seemed to underline an immaturity in him she'd not really noticed before. He was like a little boy confessing to his mother, in front of the local vicar, that he'd agreed to trim grass in the churchyard for sixpence when she wanted him to run an important errand, knowing he couldn't be chided. It told her how heedlessly he regarded their affair; what little consideration he really had for her despite his constant innuendo; how easily he released himself from the half promises and suggestions he'd mooted about the future.

She felt as if she'd been jilted, treated like an old shoe to be discarded; and she was indignant. She was indignant that he had not considered her worthy enough to have mentioned it before, as if she would cling and make it awkward for him.

'No, please don't bother to write, Stanley,' she said coolly. 'If you do I won't answer. I just don't see the point now.'

He shrugged. 'I don't understand your attitude. I just hope you don't live to regret it.'

She bid him good-bye, the last one ever as far as she was concerned, and turned away huffily as he set off down Cromwell Street for the last time.

So this was it. This was the end of their relationship. It had to end sometime. Nothing lasted for ever. She'd often wondered how and when it would happen; who would instigate it. It was a milestone for her, but probably an everyday thing for him. He was probably always saying goodbye to women.

But, deep down, Lizzie's feelings were mixed up. On the one hand she was relieved that she was freed of this drawn out longing, however abruptly it had happened; freed of endless waiting, of anticipating their times together. But on the other hand she was sad; sad that the pleasure would never be repeated. Her greater sadness though, was that those shared hours, which had meant so much to her, seemed to have meant so little to him. They'd brought her torment, turned her into a dishonest, deceitful woman, but they'd brought her release when she needed it. Yet it seemed that for him they were no more than routine; as if his every furlough, anywhere, had yielded some similar diversion with somebody.

This shock to Lizzie's system also triggered some harsh assessment of herself. She berated herself for being drawn into a tenuous, dangerous relationship, which put everything that really mattered at risk. When Stanley was around she had stupidly put him before her family, lying, making excuses, just so she could spend a few sordid hours on her back with him. And for what? Why had she allowed herself to become so obsessed for so long when she was not in love with him? Was it just lust? Had it been stimulating merely because of its forbidden nature? Or was she in love with him after all?

Whichever, it had been at the expense of her children and her husband, and they were all that really mattered. Now Stanley was gone and there would be no more distractions. From now on only her family would have her complete attention. She would concentrate wholly on them. She would try her utmost to be more understanding of Ben's situation, and view it from his standpoint for once. Ben needed her help and, above all, he needed her love. Furthermore, he deserved it. He deserved it infinitely more than Stanley Dando. Nothing would ever again stand in the way of that. She had played away; she had not been caught; now that was an end to it.

For the whole of that Christmas Jesse Clancey was preoccupied with what he'd witnessed at

Sylvia's house. He could neither sleep properly nor eat. He guessed long ago that Lizzie and Ben Kite had little to do with each other in the matrimonial bed, because of his poor physical condition, but for her to seek comfort in the arms of her own cousin was scandalous. Jesse didn't like Stanley Dando to begin with. If you offered him a pinch of salt he'd take a block. He knew well enough from Sylvia what Stanley was like.

Jesse was painfully disillusioned. He'd always considered Lizzie to be virtuous, so never tried to prosper his own interest in her. Nobody was more aware of her wretched situation than he was. He knew how she strove to make certain Ben was cared for, that he wanted for nothing. But Jesse also realised how it all disheartened her. He understood why she was prone to becoming overwhelmed and depressed by it all. Despite that, she was always pleasant when he was there. It was always a pleasure to be in her company.

Stanley Dando, if there were any virtue in him at all, should never have taken advantage of the situation. Jesse knew from old that as a youth he'd always fancied Lizzie, and was a rival for her affection in the early days. But not lately. Just how long had this unspeakable affair been going on? What abominable secrets were locked in each other's hearts? The more he thought about it, the more he felt sick to the pit of his stomach.

Had he come to know Lizzie too well over the last few years? Had he overlooked what was staring him in the face? Why hadn't he recognised that she needed the physical love of a man? Why hadn't he seen that her heart was screaming out for love? Her poor husband loved her, there was no question of that, and she knew it better than anybody; but evidently she needed something more. And that something more had driven her to recklessness, seeking from Stanley what wasn't available from Ben. Yes, that must be it.

He'd noticed her looking at himself from under her lovely long-lashed eyelids, flirting, it seemed, but he could never ever have taken advantage, since he believed that was simply her nature. There was also the question of Ben. Now he decided that perhaps he should have done something; if only to prevent such attentions from that parasite, Stanley Dando.

But Jesse gradually came to the opinion that Lizzie was not entirely to blame; that what had happened might be forgivable after all. He began to regard Stanley as the ruthless hunter, Lizzie as the susceptible prey. Jealousy crept in, hand in hand with grudge. Better himself the lover than Stanley; at least he wouldn't use her and abuse her. He was a fool for not exploiting her need himself. He was a fool for not spotting earlier what was really going on, when he might have been able to do something about it. Stanley was only at home odd weeks at a time. What about all the months he was away? He could have been her lover himself every day of the year, if only he wasn't shackled by this cock-eyed conscience, this self-denying nobleness that would not allow him to cross Ben Kite, but which had allowed his heart to be wounded yet again.

Once more he'd missed his chance.

It was towards the end of February that Lizzie realised she was pregnant. She missed her monthly bleeding in January and was distraught, praying it was because of tension. In February she missed again, but worse, she was feeling downright sick in a morning and her stomach felt hard, her breasts tender. This sickly feeling was something different; something she'd never experienced with her other four pregnancies. When she awoke in a morning, she resisted the urge to vomit until she'd rushed outside to the privy in her dressing gown, to do it out of Ben's sight; out of earshot.

She'd made a big mistake nurturing that affair with Stanley Dando. She'd made a grievous mistake and she was profoundly sorry. Now she must live with it and take the consequences. She should have known she could not do what she'd been doing, so recklessly, so deceitfully, and not have to pay the price. There was no way out, either. There was no way out at all, unless she could get rid of it. Yet how could she do that? Donald Clark wouldn't help. He *couldn't* help; abortion was punishable by a long prison sentence. Nobody in their right mind would risk that, even if they agreed with the reason. In any case, if she asked Donald Clark to get rid of it for her he would want to know the top and bottom of it, and she would have to tell him. Nobody must know. Nobody at all must know that Ben was not the father of the child.

Oh Lord, what a reckless fool she'd been.

She was too honest to pretend that this child growing in her belly was anything but a catastrophe in her life. But she did not weep. She did not deserve the relief that weeping might bring. What utter shame she would bring on her husband, on herself, and on her children. What indeed would her children think of her when they grew up and came to know the truth from every foul-mouthed gossip who gleaned satisfaction from spreading mischief? None of her family deserved such persecution because of her immorality. She would have to give up her job as well. How would they ever manage on Ben's pension with five children to clothe and feed? Oh, God!

From somewhere she must find the courage to carry on. From somewhere she must find the extra courage to tell Ben. Sooner or later she would have to confess and plead for his forgiveness. And if he wouldn't forgive her who could blame him? Tongues would wag, fingers would point, and the whole of Kates Hill would know what a loose-legged whore Lizzie Kite really was and always had been. She would be a social outcast, shunned by all who claimed to live by that code of honesty and decency and virtue they called respectability. For she could hardly be called respectable.

Yet it was partly Ben's fault. To some extent he'd brought it on her. Who was it that made himself an invalid by going off to war in the first place? Who was it that said he would turn a blind eye if she felt the need to stray outside their marriage? Who was it that seemed so keen to drive her into the beds of other men? And how could you guarantee not to get pregnant when you were so mindlessly, blindly driven to do the very thing that makes a woman pregnant? Maybe she should have thought of that before; to have ensured that *he,* whose name she could not even bring herself to say anymore, was careful to prevent this happening. Naïvely, she'd believed he would afford her the consideration of being careful; that he would consider her position and protect her. Lord, how stupid she'd been! Now, even if he knew and was challenged, he could turn round and, with an easy conviction, say it must be Ben's child she was carrying, especially since she'd always allowed him to believe that she and Ben still enjoyed marital relations.

Easter weekend arrived, 1923. There was little change in Ben's health, and he decided that perhaps he ought to smoke more. He'd read in *The Daily Sketch* that, according to French scientists, smoking was beneficial because nicotine formed antibacterial chemicals in the system. Fearing yet another epidemic of Spanish flu, the last thing he wanted was to catch it. He suggested to Lizzie that to do so really would see him off. And, besides, he'd just run out, so would she go and fetch him some?

Henzey could go. And since the others were playing, it might just provide enough time to tell him she was in trouble. So she walked down the entry and called Henzey who was doing toss-ups against the wall in the street with her dress tucked into the elasticised legs of her drawers.

'Henzey, stop doing that at your age and come here.'

'Oh, Mom. What this time?'

'I want you to run an errand. Come on in, so's I can give you the money.'

Henzey followed her mother into the entry. One of Beccy Crump's hens stalked through the back door and into the room in front of them. Lizzie shooed it out and it flapped its wings in panic, departing hastily. She grabbed her purse off the mantelpiece, gave Henzey two half crowns, then took a string bag hanging on the back of the cellar door.

'Fetch your dad ten Woodbines and a *Daily Sketch,* and on your way back call at Jack Hardmeat's for a small joint of pork, about three shillings.'

But just as Henzey left, Alf Collins called to collect Ben's bet, and he stayed chatting, thwarting Lizzie's plan. She must tell Ben soon. It was more than three months now and her waist was thickening. Before long her belly would bulge and it would be obvious to everyone. She hadn't told a soul she was in trouble. At one time she could have talked to May, but poor May had enough troubles of her own with Emmie the way she was, so it was grossly unfair to burden her more. She could have told Daisy Foster, but decided not to. The only other person she could tell was Ben. He'd always been her closest friend, without exception, yet this was one thing that affected him more than anybody, and she hadn't mustered the courage to break it to him till now.

Alf took Ben's bet and left. She waited till the

sound of his footsteps in the entry had faded, and sat down, bracing herself to confess everything to her husband. She had no idea how he would take it, but he had to know. Doubtless he would be furious, and she did not relish the thought of an argument. They had never had a serious argument in all their married life and she did not know how it might affect him in his poor state of health. She would break it as gently as she could, with meekness, repentance, and humility.

'Ben,' she began, 'there's something...'

There were footsteps again in the entry.

'There's something what?'

'There's something ... in the brewhouse I'd better fetch in,' she said, abandoning the idea, and stood up to go onto the back yard.

The back door opened and it was Joe, grimy from his work, but grinning with self satisfaction.

'Hey, guess what. There's a trip to Rhyl on Easter Monday from "The Shoulder of Mutton". I've bought some tickets.'

Lizzie forced a smile. 'A trip? By charabanc?'

'I reckoned it was about time you all had a change of scenery, even if it is only for a day. And the kids'll love it.'

'But what about Ben, Joe? I doubt if he'll feel up to it.'

'No, I don't want to go, Joe,' Ben said, 'but it's a grand idea if the women and kids go. How much do I owe you?'

'Nothing, me old mate. It's my treat. I ain't going either, Ben. I'm stopping here to look after you. We'll have a right old party with the women out the way, eh? I'll get some beer in, and we'll

347

ask Jesse Clancey over as well, and Alf Collins.'

Ben chuckled. 'Damn my hide. I'll look forward to that. And you, our Lizzie. That'll be a lovely day out. Let's hope the weather holds, eh?'

'That's just what we could do with, Joe.' Lizzie's smile was one of real pleasure. 'Just wait till the kids know. They'll be thrilled to pieces.'

No, this definitely was not the right time to tell Ben of her trouble. Best leave it a couple more days. This trip was fate. There was just a chance that the bouncing and jolting of the charabanc might induce a miscarriage. That could save them all a great deal of heartache. There was no point yet in being panicked into a confession she could not retract.

When Joe had gone she busied herself with renewed hope, polishing the brass fender and the hearth set with Brassoline till she could see the whole room reflected in it. She dusted the mantel-shelf, moving the black marble clock, the picture of her father, the pin-cushion, the pair of flint vases she'd been given as a wedding present, the letter rack and the two brass candlesticks. She moved the japanned tea-caddy and a bottle of Ben's medicine into the cupboard, her purse into the pocket of her pinafore, then she heard Henzey walking up the entry. She looked at the clock; Henzey had been a long time; but still not long enough to discuss with Ben what she'd thought of discussing. And a good thing too.

At about the same time that Lizzie was considering confessing her plight to Ben, Sylvia Atkinson was peering through her sitting-room window, waiting for Jesse Clancey. He was due to collect his money, and the kettle was on the boil over a low gas ready to drench the tea leaves in her best electroplated teapot. Since Christmas Jesse had seemed noticeably more responsive, more amenable than at any time since they'd renewed their friendship. It gave her fresh hope. A few days earlier she suggested, casually, that with the weather picking up it might be an opportunity for the two of them to take Kenneth to the castle grounds one Sunday afternoon. She told him how the lad had asked if Mr Clancey could go with them, and Jesse had warmed to the idea. 'Bless him,' he'd said. Today, when Jesse arrived, she would suggest that since tomorrow was Easter Sunday, and the weather was set fair, it might be an ideal opportunity.

Sylvia was not averse to using Kenneth as a means of gaining Jesse's attention for herself. As the months and years drifted by she was growing more afraid at the prospect of extended widowhood. Spending the rest of her life without a man did not appeal. When you were the wrong side of thirty – nearing thirty-seven, to be more precise – the likelihood of trapping an eligible man became increasingly remote. No doubt it would be easy to ensnare a fancy-man; at the crooking of a finger any number of married men would come scurrying clandestinely to her bedroom with its flouncey feminine drapes. But why should she settle for sharing? She wanted a man to herself; a friend; a companion; a handyman; a mentor; not just a lover.

Jesse Clancey was probably as good as she

would get. He was after all a man of great integrity. She often thought about the times, years ago, when they were courting. He was never quite attainable then, rendering him all the more attractive. He was elusive, frustratingly non-committal, while she was turning mental somersaults devising ways to secure him. More than anything she wanted him to marry her, and was heart-sick when they parted. She'd had such beautiful dreams about spending the rest of their lives together. Then came that bitterly cold New Year's Eve in 1907 – good gracious, was it really more than fifteen years ago? Fifteen years since Jesse confessed his feelings for Lizzie Bishop? Eventually, when she met James Atkinson and committed herself to him, she lived out those dreams with him instead. But she never loved him as intensely, or as whole-heartedly as she loved Jesse Clancey. Jesse Clancey was her first real love; she first knew womanhood at the hands of Jesse Clancey. After all these years she'd forgiven him his puerile preoccupation with Lizzie Bishop, though she'd neither forgiven nor forgotten Lizzie for having such big, alluring hazel eyes, such a beautiful smile and a feminine slenderness she could not then help admiring herself. Yet Lizzie had slipped his net, to be caught in another – thankfully. Sylvia was content that Lizzie would not be a rival nowadays; not after all this time. So, using feminine wiles and any other devious methods she could devise, Sylvia decided that she would marry Jesse Clancey.

The glorious aroma of home cooking, timed to

coincide with his arrival, greeted him.

'Sit down a bit, Jesse,' she suggested. 'The kettle's on and I've made some beef stew. Have some. It'll keep you going?'

'Sylvia, you're as good as gold,' he said, warming his hands in front of the fire. 'How did you know as I'm clammed to death? If that's the stew I can smell I could do justice to a dollop. I've had nothing to eat since pig squealing this morning.'

'You must be starving.'

'Well, I could give a plate of stew some bell-oil, Sylvia... What's tickling you?'

'Oh, Jesse, you do come out with some expressions. We'll eat together. There's today's paper over there if you want to take a look at it while I'm in the scullery.'

Jesse reached the newspaper from its rack. While he was half way through reading about Germany's continued failure to pay war reparations, Sylvia called him. He put down the newspaper and joined her in the scullery, but she suggested that they eat together in the dining room. It needn't keep him more than a quarter of an hour, then he could be back at work again. So she swiftly laid the table and carried in two bowls of stew and a loaf of home-baked bread, all on a silver tray.

These little touches impressed Jesse. Sylvia had certainly changed over the years, and it had been for the better. She was much more a lady now, and not without some style, he thought. She had mellowed wonderfully and knew how to please a man. And if this show of consideration was anything to go by she was patently still interested in him, which flattered him enormously, although he was a bit wary still of her intentions.

'There you are, Jesse. Let's see if that lot will stretch your waistcoat.'

'You come out with some tidy expressions yourself, Sylvia. Stretch me waistcoat, eh?'

She began to cut a thick slice from the loaf. 'It's what my father often used to say to our Stanley when he was a boy.'

'How is Stanley, by the way? Have you heard from him?' He took a spoonful of stew and put it to his lips gingerly, testing it for heat before committing it to his mouth.

'I had a letter from him in February, posted in Egypt. Just to thank me for letting him stay here over Christmas. He said how he enjoyed being here all on his own.'

Jesse swallowed hard, almost choking. 'He must've felt like a bloody hermit not seeing a soul all that time. Mind you, I did see him going round to spend an hour with Ben Kite once,' he said experimentally, and took another spoonful.

'Oh, I think he took quite a shine to Ben these last few years. Said he always enjoyed talking to him. Said what a decent chap he is.'

Jesse looked at his bowl of stew thoughtfully, dipping a piece of bread into it while he chewed a lump of beef. 'I suppose he never mentioned Lizzie?'

'No, never. I don't think he'd got much time for Lizzie.'

'Fancy. Who'd have thought it?'

His regulated cynicism went over Sylvia's head. She was rearranging her meal, seeking to locate a piece of carrot to go with a piece of parsnip already on her spoon. 'Oh, he used to be sweet on Lizzie years ago. So had you, Jesse, as I recall.' She gave him a knowing look. 'But that's all water under the bridge.'

He avoided the remark. 'I'm surprised he's never married, you know, Sylvia.'

'Never married? Our Stanley? Oh, Jesse.' She gave a little laugh of derision. 'Of course he married. He married in South Africa.'

Jesse looked at her and gasped. 'Well bugger me. I never knew that ... and neither did anybody else.' The image of Stanley and Lizzie writhing naked on the floor of Sylvia's sitting-room plagued him yet again. 'How come he never brought her home?'

'Because Mother and Father never knew. It was all a big secret. I'm the only one he told, Jesse. Now you know as well, so I trust you to keep it to yourself.'

'But why should he want to keep it secret? Was he ashamed of the wench, or what?'

'I think it was the other way round. Her family were bitterly opposed to her marrying him. They thought she was too good for him, I suppose, and it would have hurt his pride to admit it to Mother and Father.' She shrugged. 'Oh, something was wrong, Jesse. She left him in the end. Maybe she was made to leave him. I don't know.'

'Has he got any kids by her?'

'One. I imagine he'll go and see the child – and her – when he gets time off in Rhodesia. I suspect it's one of the reasons he volunteered for secondment out there.'

Jesse at once began to wonder whether he should tell Lizzie, but just as quickly decided against it. Best not to interfere in something like this; best not infer that he knew about her affair. In any case, if Stanley was reasonable and honest he should already have confessed he was married while they were lying together. But knowing Stanley, it was more than likely he'd not, especially if he hadn't even told his mother and father.

'Let's not talk about our Stanley, Jesse.'

'Suits me.'

'Do you remember we agreed it might be nice to take Kenneth to the castle grounds one Sunday?'

'Yes, I remember.'

'If you're not doing anything this Sunday, it might be a good time to go, being Easter. There's bound to be something on. Would you be able to?'

'I'm doing nothing else, Sylvia. Mother'll be all right on her own for an hour or two.'

'Good. I thought, if you'd like to come back here afterwards I could cook us all an evening meal instead of eating at midday. How does that appeal to you?'

'Sounds good to me. But I should hate you to go to any trouble on my account.'

'It's no trouble at all. Kenneth and I still have to eat.'

Jesse finished his stew, drank his tea and declared he must be on his way. Next day, wearing his best Sunday suit and bowler hat, he called for Sylvia and young Kenneth at two o'clock. They walked to the entrance of the Castle grounds and began their perambulation up steep paths winding to the keep and the courtyard. The day was fine, but cool, and there were crowds of people, wrapped up warm, but all in holiday mood, enjoying the walks and picnicking. Kenneth asked if Jesse would take him to the top of the keep, so Jesse obliged, leading the way. By the time they negotiated the worn, spiralling stone steps to the castellations at the top, they were panting for breath.

The view was tremendous. Trams and cars, like perfect toys, glided along the Georgian streets below them. Beyond the hills of Dudley the landscape seemed to sink into a smoky basin, which was Tipton and West Bromwich. Jesse pointed out where he lived, beyond the grey hulk of St. John's church on the hill across the valley. On the opposite side of the town, at Eve Hill, they saw its sister church, St James', almost identical. To the south another basin, housing the forges and foundries of Old Hill, Cradley Heath and Halesowen, the iron and steel works of Brierley Hill from which the infernal fires of hell seemed to discharge. Yet this murky, fume-bound area was rimmed by the pleasant, green hills of Clent and Romsley in the distance, a contrast as picturesque as could be found anywhere.

'How high are we, Mr Clancey?'

'Ooh, nearly nine hundred feet above sea level, they reckon.'

'Is that high?'

'You'd think so if it was a wall and you fell off it. Look east ... over there.' He stooped to the child's height and pointed. '...there's ne'er a town or village higher than Dudley till you get to the Ural Mountains in Russia – hundreds and hundreds of miles away. How about that, eh?'

'But look down there, Mr Clancey,' the boy yelled. He pointed to the foot of the castle keep. 'There are some old cannons. See? Some boys are sitting on them. May I?'

'If you're ready to go back down now.'

At the foot of the keep Sylvia was waiting for them, sitting on an outcrop of limestone that was part of the ruins. Jesse sat beside her and she smiled at him affectionately while Kenneth climbed onto one of the ancient cannons to join another boy sitting astride it.

'Did he enjoy the view?'

'Oh, young lads ain't interested in views, Sylvia. As soon as we were up there he wanted to come back down to sit on one of the cannons.'

'I expect you were the same when you were his age.' An errant wisp of hair was blowing about her face appealingly in the breeze. She swept it behind her ear.

'I might've been a sight worse. It's been that long I can scarcely remember.'

'I must say, Jesse, Kenneth seems to have taken to you,' she said speculatively.

'Well, he seems easy enough to please. He's a likeable chap, an' all.'

'If things had turned out differently he might have been your son, you know, Jesse. But it

356

wasn't to be, was it?'

He shrugged. He had no answer. Or rather, he had no answer that he wished to discuss.

'How come you never got married?'

''Cause either me or the right women were never in the right place at the right time.'

'You must have had other lady-friends after me.'

'Nobody I wanted to wed.'

'I often wonder what it would have been like married to you, Jesse ... how many children we might have had ... who they'd be like. Do you ever wonder that?'

'Something I never think about, Sylvia. I can't see the point.'

She uttered a self deprecating laugh. 'Oh, Jesse. Humour me, why don't you? Here am I, nearly three years a widow, trying to reintroduce a touch of romance into my dull life.'

'God's truth, Sylvia,' he chuckled, 'I admire your forthrightness, but you and me are as different as silk and glass paper. Even more now than then.'

'But that's what makes it all the more interesting.'

'Maybe it depends on how you view it. For a start, you speak beautiful, Sylvia. No Black Country twang for you. But hark at me. I'm as broad as they come and I can't alter it. I'd show you up in company. You'd cringe every time I opened me mouth.'

She couldn't help but laugh. 'No, I wouldn't. The way you speak hardly matters. It's the person that matters. In any case, I'd have you speaking the King's English in no time.'

'And all me customers would think I'd swallowed a bloody Oxford dictionary. No, my wench, we're worlds apart now. It ain't just the way we speak. You've got style and class... Me? I'm as common as muck. There's a world of difference.'

'Oh, Jesse, don't belittle yourself. We are different, you and I. But it doesn't matter.'

'It matters to me, Sylvia.'

'You're wrong, Jesse. The difference would make it all the more interesting. It's when two people are the same that life gets boring. Think about it.'

Kenneth slid off the cannon and came running over to them. 'There's a man on an ice-cream cart down there,' he yelled excitedly. 'Can we go and buy one, please?'

Jesse smiled affectionately at the boy. ''Course we can,' he agreed. 'Run to him and order one for each of us. We'll soon be along to pay for them.'

Chapter 19

The bumping and shaking of the charabanc on Easter Monday failed to do the trick for Lizzie. All the way to Rhyl, and all the way back, she fancied she could feel the unwanted child shaking loose inside her. But another week passed and her skirts felt ever tighter round her waist, and her brassiere tighter under her breasts.

Maybe if she threw herself down their narrow, bent staircase it would shake this cuckoo free and leave her clean and whole again.

When she first realised her body was sustaining this obstinate growth she should have sought one of those back-street women who could rid her of it. But, doubtless, some blabbermouth would find out and gossip. It was too late in any case, and too dangerous; not that she cared much for her own well-being – she had no great desire to even live through all this and the shame that was inevitably to come – but her children and Ben depended on her too much to contemplate any such risk now.

Inevitably, fate offered Lizzie the ideal opportunity to confess to Ben that she was in trouble. Herbert disturbed her in her sleep by gently shaking her, trying to wake her, early one Sunday morning in April.

'I'm off fishing with Trixie Jukes, Mom,' he informed her in a whisper, concerned not to wake his father. 'I'll be back dinnertime.'

She opened her eyes and, at once, felt the familiar nausea that in itself was often sufficiently intense to wake her. 'What time is it?'

'Quarter to seven.'

Lizzie heard the back door open and shut, followed by his footsteps as he ran down the entry with his home made fishing rod. She rolled over, trying to defeat the awful sickly feeling and recapture her sleep. But it persisted, and she felt uncomfortably hot, perspiring. She heaved a sigh of frustration as she pushed the covers back and forced herself out of bed. The floorboards creaked under her feet as she emptied the jug of cold water into the bowl on the washstand and splashed it on her face. As she grabbed the towel to dry herself she felt as if she was going to faint, so she padded over to the window and parted the curtains a little to open the sash for a breath of cold air. Outside, the sky, though overcast, seemed bleached out and white.

She collapsed to the floor.

Ben's insistent tapping on her shoulders and hoarsely whispering her name eventually roused her, and she looked about, surprised to find herself lying in a heap on the linoleum.

'You must have fainted, Lizzie.' He fought for breath after the shock and the subsequent exertion of trying to wake her. 'A thump woke me up... It must've been you falling. Are you all right, my pretty wench?'

She eased herself up, clutching the bedclothes for support, and sat on the bed, still feeling sick. All at once the nausea was impossible to contain. 'God, I need the chamber pot.' She reached under the bed and retrieved it. Thankfully it was still unused. She retched into it at once, and immediately felt better, except for the bitter taste of vomit lingering in her mouth. She sat quietly for a while, head bowed, till she felt confident of standing up again. Ben watched intently. Once more she went over to the bowl of water and splashed it on her face and around her lips, then dried herself, leaving the towel hanging on the rail at the side of the wash-stand.

'I might as well get dressed now I'm up,' she said feigning a brightness that was eluding her.

She pulled her night-dress over her head and reached for her brassiere lying on the ottoman, her back towards Ben so he should not see her belly. She glanced round awkwardly and saw with alarm that he was watching her, a look of disquiet in his eyes.

'Don't look at me getting dressed.'

'You used to like it. Watching you undress, at any rate.'

She couldn't think of a suitable reply. Of course, he was right.

'Have you got something to tell me, our Lizzie?'

At once she felt herself flush. 'Such as what?'

He eased himself back on his pillow and put his hands behind his head, almost casually. 'Well, adding two and two together I can generally make four,' he said, with an evenness that she found unnerving.

'I don't know what you mean.' She stepped into her drawers and pulled them up. 'Stop talking in riddles.'

'Please don't take me for a fool, my flower.' His voice was low, to save waking the children. 'Over the last few weeks I've noticed your waist thicken up ... and your titties and your belly getting rounder... I've watched you get up in a morning looking pale and fretted... I've watched you run downstairs, outside to the privy – to throw up, I reckon... Now if you aren't pregnant, what's up with you?'

So he knew. Dear Lord, he knew already.

She caught a glimpse of her belly in the dressing table mirror. It was rounder; not by much, but it was there; hard, like a football. And he, knowing every inch of her so well, could tell. She sat on the bed again and looked into his eyes with a candour that had been missing for too long. There was no sense in denying it. No sense at all.

So this was the moment. This was the disastrous moment she'd been dreading. The inevitable crisis, that had loomed ever since she'd felt the weight of this bastard child in her belly, was about to be resolved at last, one way or the other.

'Yes, I am pregnant, Ben.'

Ben's sigh was heartfelt. 'How long have you known?'

'Two months, I suppose.' She looked down at her knees now, unable to face him; utterly ashamed.

'About the same as me then. Have you seen the doctor?'

She shook her head and her eyes brimmed with tears at his surprising placidity.

'Why didn't you tell me sooner, Lizzie? Why the hell didn't you tell me before this happened, and I had to coax it out of you?'

She sat on the bed, her back erect, her hands clasped together between her thighs taking this unaccountably passive scolding, knowing that only something infinitely more severe was deserved. She felt like a naughty schoolgirl being reprimanded for a minor misdemeanour by an unruffled teacher irritatingly sure of his standing. Yet this was infinitely more serious. Why didn't he shout and rage? That was what she really deserved; that was what she would have expected; that was what she desperately needed; not this composed, unwarranted, disturbing reasonableness. Why didn't he take her by the shoulders and violently shake her till her silly, senseless head fell off. Why didn't he slap her across her stupid face for being so recklessly foolish, and for putting him through a silent agony he'd obviously endured for weeks? Tears fell down her cheeks and she let out a great sob of a sigh. The pent-up anxiety and fear of months was released, and her tears flowed in a torrent as her face locked, contorted with emotion and self-pity; and an ardent desire to be thoroughly, humiliatingly punished.

'Why didn't you tell me, Lizzie? You know I like things straight. Am I such a big, bad ogre?'

She shook her head and bit her lip to stop herself wailing out loud. 'Why do you think?... Because I was ashamed... Oh, Ben, I'm so ashamed.'

She wanted to throw herself upon him for forgiveness, but she did not feel worthy of it. Easy forgiveness would be too kind. She remained sitting, facing the window, uncompanionable, craving fire and brimstone and anything else his justifiable retribution could sling at her. She felt utterly miserable, wretched, but grateful that it was all out in the open at last. Her confession could not now be unsaid. Her sin could not be undone.

'Does he know?'

She shook her head again, still avoiding his eyes, and a tear fell onto her bare thigh. 'I don't want him to know ... ever. It's not his business now. It's mine. It's mine alone.'

'Grab the towel off the wash-stand and dry your eyes. There's no need for all these tears.'

She stood up deferentially and reached over, taking the towel, then buried her face in it as she sat down again.

'Have you heard from him since Christmas?'

She looked up at him apprehensively, her eyes dry for a second or two after wiping them, but red from her tears. Just how much had he deduced?

'Not a word. Nor do I want to.'

'Well, perhaps that's because it takes such a while for the mail to come from Southern Rhodesia.' There was a hint of cynicism in his voice. 'On the other hand, perhaps he didn't intend to write to you any more, for fear of hearing for certain what he already assumed.'

Lizzie broke down in tears again, her shame greater than ever because he'd evidently known about her condition for some time; even known who her lover was. Her deceit clearly had not worked, and she felt contemptible, humiliated at having tried to fool him. Her covering of tracks had been remarkably unsuccessful and, even if it had worked, she still had this lump of irrefutable evidence growing inside her to give her away.

'I told him not to write. There was no point in him writing. Anyway, how did you find out about him?' Her tears were abating now it was all in the open. It was assuming the shape of a reasonable, but serious discussion.

'I asked you a minute ago not to take me for a fool, Lizzie. It was obvious from the outset.

364

Every time he came home on leave you were like a cat on hot bricks till he went back, and you were always making excuses about going shopping of a Saturday afternoon, but never coming back with anything; or saying you were off to see Daisy.'

'But you never said anything. You never questioned me.'

'Well, wouldn't I be a bloody hypocrite if I had? It was me that told you to get your leg over somewhere if you felt the need. If I said that much, then I have to take the consequences. As I see it, I'm as much to blame as you. But I wish to God now as I'd never said such a thing.'

'It wouldn't have made any difference, Ben.'

'Well, that's as maybe. The fact is, you're carrying another man's child and we're both lumbered with it.'

'You don't have to be lumbered with it, Ben. You don't have to be lumbered with it if you don't want to be. I could always go away. If you want me to, I'll go away. It's no more than I deserve.'

'D'you want to go?'

She shook her head. 'No. Even though I've been wicked my children still love me. They don't know I've been such a wicked woman. They need me. And I need them.'

Neither spoke for a minute. She stood up and went to the window again, feeling sick no longer. In the back yard Ben had lifted a small circular area of paving bricks – before he'd joined the army, when he was fit and well; there he'd made a flower bed and bordered it with coping stones

– the same ones that Henzey and, later, Eve, had fallen over. It was infested with weeds and long grass now, neglected for years, but every spring a few daffodils that obstinately remained, forced their way through, brightening the whole yard with their yellow flowers. So it was now, and Lizzie gazed at their fresh, bright trumpets absently, preoccupied with the moment.

Then Ben spoke. 'The kids need never know anything about your little fling.'

She turned to look at him, daring to hope what he meant.

'Did you love him?'

She took her time answering, measuring her words. If she said she didn't love him she would appear cheaper than she already did. 'I suppose I must have loved him to let it go so far. I must have loved him because I always longed for him to come home on leave.'

He closed his eyes momentarily and sighed. 'And do you still love him?'

'Oh, Ben, I don't know... I honestly don't know ... Maybe that tells me that I don't. If I did still love him, I suppose I'd feel it. But I don't feel anything now. Just shame ... regret.'

Lizzie's red, watery eyes scanned his face for a clue as to his innermost feelings. This had hurt him so much, and yet he took it, with all the rest of his ailments, without complaint, with unfailing dignity. What kind of man had she married? What other man could be so tolerant and so forgiving over something as devastating as this? Why had she not appreciated him more? Why had she felt the need to betray such a good and honest man?

'Lizzie,' he said decisively, 'as far as anybody else is concerned the child you're carrying is mine. Nobody knows what goes on between our sheets except us two, so even the way I am, nobody could gainsay it. Not even Stanley Dando. Is that true?'

'Yes, it's true, Ben. I've never led anybody to think any different.'

'There you are then.' He put his hand out to her, and she took it, sitting down by him. 'Now stop your werriting and let's get on with our lives. So we'll have another mouth to feed. What's an extra mouth when there's already six of us?'

It was in May that Ben broke the news to Jesse Clancey that he was going to be a father for the fifth time. Jesse forced a smile and congratulated him, shaking him by the hand. It came as no surprise, and Jesse was not fooled. He perceived that Ben's apparent enthusiasm was laboured. After he'd witnessed Lizzie and Stanley together last Christmas, the thought of her being pregnant as a consequence frequently plagued him, and almost daily he scrutinised her for clues. He'd noticed Lizzie had put weight on round the middle, when she was normally so small-waisted. He saw her preoccupied, touchy and looking distinctly wan. This child she was expecting had to be Stanley's, and he pondered whether Ben had been forced to accept it.

He would mention to Sylvia tomorrow night that Lizzie was expecting another child. Sylvia, he was certain, had absolutely no knowledge of Stanley's recent affair with Lizzie, and he did not intend enlightening her, but if she had any inkling at all she would express it at this news.

The pleasantness of Sylvia's home, the mouthwatering smells of sumptuous home cooking, her fussing him and making him comfortable and, not least, the affection her son Kenneth gave him, all contrived to weaken Jesse into submission. From the outset he was afraid he might eventually have to submit. He did not love Sylvia, but perhaps deep, emotional, fulfilled love was something that would always elude him. He was getting no younger, his ageing mother wouldn't always be around to cook for him and iron his shirts. So courting Sylvia made sense. It made a lot of sense.

Marriage would make even more sense. Lizzie Kite was no nearer him, nor ever likely to be. He'd spent too many long years yearning for her, wondering if she might ever be free. Of course, he hadn't actually waited for her; that would have been stupid in the extreme; but he couldn't help feeling the way he did about her. She was his *femme fatale*, yet he was destined never to be with her, and at last he felt he could accept it. At forty-two, what women would be attracted to him, despite the nest egg he'd accumulated? At his time of life the proverbial bird in the hand, Sylvia, was surely worth two in the bush. It was sensible to settle for what was on offer. It might be his only chance.

Sylvia, too, was satisfied that the dreams she'd so fancifully woven, the devices she'd so diligently exploited to make those dreams a possibility, were at last yielding results. Jesse was not rushing into this reconstituted affair headlong, and she had not expected him to, but the signs were positive. He'd spent many long evenings with her since Easter, and they'd talked easily, even of the old days. But Jesse was right about one thing: they were worlds apart when it came down to refinement and social grace. Sylvia realised that whilst he might have a successful dairy business with scores of loyal customers who thought the world of him, those very customers were keeping him down, at their level, with their low ideals, their commonness and their awful broad speech. At least James had succeeded in lifting her a rung or two up the social ladder, whereas Jesse would only help drag her back where she started. Therefore, she had some serious remedial work to do on him. She was determined that he could and should raise himself above the level of the folk he was used to.

Lizzie's illegitimate daughter was born, on Saturday 29th September 1923. Although she carried it full term, in a pregnancy that was singularly unlike any of her others, the baby was born dead. Its unusually long umbilical cord had been strangulated by a fatal twist created when the baby turned, the doctor later explained. She told Donald Clark, who attended her, that she hadn't felt the child move for more than two weeks before the birth, and he feared the worst, forewarning her that it might be still-born. She didn't have such an easy time of it, either, unlike all the previous occasions. Rather, she had an awful time of it. Labour was protracted and Lizzie was poorly and weak for days afterwards.

When she was well enough again to think properly she took its loss with mixed feelings. After Ben had accepted her pregnancy she regarded the forthcoming child as less of an evil, and more of a just punishment upon her; a punishment she would have to endure every time she set eyes on it. Yet she knew deep in her heart that she would grow to love it as much as she loved the others, so the loss of it saddened her, especially when she thought of how it might have grown up, and the joy it might ultimately have brought. Certainly Henzey, Herbert, Alice and Maxine were all excited at the prospect of a new baby in the house, and made all sorts of plans. They looked forward to it with such excitement. It was pitiful to witness their grief now, especially the girls. On the other hand, it meant that neither Lizzie nor Ben would be tied to a child conceived out of wedlock. Ben had agreed to pretend the child was his to protect her reputation and their children from malicious gossip, but he would never be able to countenance the child as if it were his own, and Lizzie knew it. He might even have grown to resent it. The child would have perceived such negative feelings, and maybe even have turned against him eventually.

On a more practical level, Lizzie could try to get her job back, so they could at least have some comfort in their lives from the money she earned. Without that job they would barely exist. At best they would exist in poverty.

The passage of time healed the wounds of that

traumatic year. Lizzie and Ben resumed their lives with more accord, closer in spirit than they'd been for years. She decided that she'd strayed enough for one lifetime and concentrated on the wellbeing of her family, cleansing her mind of all thoughts of infidelity and Stanley Dando absolutely. She and Ben conversed more than they had done for years, getting to know each other all over again. She grew to admire him all the more for his forthrightness, his honesty, his tolerance of his worsening condition and his surprising intellect. Yet her reborn reverence brought her no greater contentment. Oh, she would remain faithful, for she dare not ever think of straying again. The humility her wantonness had brought upon her would haunt her for ever more, and she never wished to experience it again.

But contentment would elude her for the rest of her life, and she must bear it. She was stuck in a marriage that offered spiritual love in abundance; love she could talk about if she wished to; but not physical love that could caress her where it had that magical explosive impact she'd always craved.

Four entities managed to sustain her: her children. She would die for her children. They were growing up at an alarming rate, relieving her of much of the hard work, and for that she was thankful. And the faster they grew the faster the months and the seasons flew by.

At thirteen Henzey still showed enormous promise as an artist, and both Ben and Lizzie encouraged her. The prospect of earning a living from drawing and painting, though, was very limited, they told her, so it wasn't a talent that could be taken seriously. The only possibilities for employment in that line were as a commercial artist in Birmingham, and Ben was never likely to encourage her to work there with all the travelling. So Henzey was to resign herself to a more mundane occupation when she left school.

Herbert's sole talent was talking. He was aware that he could charm anyone with humour and affability. Sometimes, to his father, he appeared flippant, but Ben realised that this was a ready wit in course of development. He had a different best friend every week and, at twelve years old, already had an eye for a pretty female face – except his sisters', of course, who were a constant source of embarrassment to him. Always he was working on some project or idea, sometimes two at a time, but seldom did he have the patience to see any of them through. He wanted once to build a pigeon loft like his Uncle Joe's, but only got as far as collecting half the wood he needed. But he was popular and there was a constant stream of friends, both male and female, tapping on the back door, asking if he was coming outside to join them.

Alice relished her books, but only saucy ones. Lizzie picked up one from under her pillow one day, called *Sons and Lovers* by D. H. Lawrence. She'd never heard of it, and put it back where she had found it, shaking her head, and none the wiser, unaware of the images it was fixing inside her daughter's impressionable mind. Alice was a quiet girl. She would sit and marvel at Henzey's ability to draw whatever was in front of her, or at Maxine's piano playing. But in some ways, Alice was like her mother: she needed to feel loved, to feel wanted, to feel a part of the family. If she was ever scolded she would sink into depression and sulk for hours. She seemed to react strongly to atmospheres within the home, and she was particularly depressed and touchy the whole time her mother was carrying that last child.

Maxine was proficient at the piano for a ten year old, and always enjoyed her lessons with Ezme Clancey. One evening, though, she went across to the dairy house for her lesson to find a cello leaning against the pianola. She asked Ezme if she could have a go on it. Ezme said she could, and watched her pupil experiment intelligently with the instrument, putting her arms around it as if it were a long lost pet. There was an instant rapport between Maxine and the cello. It had been in the Clanceys' attic for more years than anybody cared to remember, and it was Jesse who found it one day whilst having a clear-out. At once he thought of Maxine. If she took to it, there was no reason why she shouldn't have it. So have it she did and, after she cleaned it thoroughly and polished it, its warm, mellow tones began to take precedence in her life over the tinkling of the piano. The only problem was that whilst she discovered from books how to tune it they knew of nobody who could teach her to play it, so what she did play was at first self-taught.

With all this going on around her, Lizzie barely noticed the insidious decline in Ben's health. It was brought home to her after they realised it was necessary to move his bed downstairs into the front room for his convenience. He had been finding it more and more difficult to climb the stairs without feeling utterly exhausted and traumatised by the effort of it. Furthermore, he could not manage to shuffle up the back yard to the privy nowadays, and so weak was he that she even had to clean him after using the chamber pot. That was a job she especially hated; the worst job of all for her. It got so bad that she began to feed him eggs and dry cakes to make him constipated. Unfortunately for Lizzie, when it seemed to work he would ask for an infusion of sennapods in his tea to loosen his bowels, and she would be back where she started. She saw the funny side of it, and she and Henzey laughed when she told her what she'd done. But despite Lizzie's resolve to afford Ben all her care and attention, the romance had long since gone from their marriage. Henzey helped her mother whenever she could, and Alice was becoming more useful, but only lately was Herbert able to be of help. Till a year ago he had neither the natural, caring ability of his sisters, nor the strength of a grown man to lift his father when it was needed.

Nearly eight years of looking after Ben had more than taken its toll. Lizzie felt deeply sorry for him. But she felt sorry for herself too. She continued to blame him. If he hadn't gone off to war everything would have been all right; she would never have dreamed of having an affair; so she would never have given birth to an

374

illegitimate child. It was not all her fault. She could not be blamed for everything.

Instinctively aware of all this, and not heartened by it, Ben duly blamed himself. He blamed himself over and over again for his uselessness, and understood Lizzie's disenchantment. He understood more acutely what had driven her to find a lover in the first place, and feared she might yet be tempted again. And who could blame her?

As far as the children were concerned, their father was a loving man who spent hours talking to them when they were not at school. They loved him and did all they could for him. His disability they accepted without question, since his wisdom and knowledge made up for it. Always they found him interesting and they learned to value his opinions. For hours he would hold them spellbound, telling them amusing, amazing stories about his exploits during the Great War, and Henzey especially saw him as something of a hero.

But, in the last few months, she'd noticed a marked decline in his health. The spark of vitality had left his eyes and he'd become dull and morose. He still read the newspaper every day, but the distressing things he read seemed to have a detrimental effect on him. Henzey believed that the economic and social problems about which he read, and which he witnessed in his own household, depressed him more than he showed. And they all understood how sensitive he was to such things.

Chapter 20

In 1926, January and February between them bestowed nearly three weeks of continuous rain on the land. There was a danger of flooding in many low lying areas but, as February matured and the water and its latent perils subsided, so the weather grew decidedly colder. In the small hours of Sunday the 21st it began to snow in earnest. By ten o'clock, when the fall ceased, it covered much of the Midlands and the North. The blue slate roofs of Kates Hill were heavy with it.

Henzey slipped gingerly out of bed and shivered as the bitter coldness of the room seemed to claw at her. Snow was lying on the outside window sill. Quickly she swirled her dressing gown about her and tied the cord, her breath rising as steam. Downstairs the others were eating breakfast in front of the warm coal fire. Lizzie placed a slice of crisp fried bread crowned with a fried egg before her.

She looked at her father. He was picking at his breakfast with a singular lack of interest, and it seemed that the cold was making his breathing more difficult. Henzey ate her own breakfast quickly, downed her cup of tea and made an excuse that there was something she wanted to show her mother in the bedroom. Lizzie followed her upstairs.

When they were in the front bedroom she

376

closed the door. 'I'm worried about dad, Mom. He don't seem well at all. These past few months I've noticed he's got no interest in anything.'

Lizzie peered out into the street absently through the frost that coated the inside as well as the outside of the window panes. 'I know. I've had my eye on him.'

'Do you think I should fetch Donald Clark?' Henzey started to get dressed and shivered as she took off her dressing gown ready to put on her best Sunday clothes.

'He can do nothing, Henzey.'

Lizzie pulled the net curtain to one side and scratched the frost on the inside of the window panes with her fingernails. Outside everywhere was silent. The fields around Turner's Farm, visible between the brass foundry and the dairy house, were white over, and the hawthorn trees bowed under the weight of snow. The hills to the east wore their new, white dress like a shroud. In the street below, Beccy Crump was trudging to Holy Communion in her best coat, a shawl around her shoulders and a pair of Albert's thick socks over her boots to stop her slipping. Smoke curled up leisurely to the grey sky from every back room chimney.

'Donald can do nothing for him,' Lizzie repeated with conviction. 'He can only ever get worse, not better. He's not stupid, your father, and he knows what's what. Sitting on that sofa day in, day out, upsets him more than he ever lets on. He blames himself for the state he's in, and the fact that we've got no money nor decent clothes to wear. It bothers him, our Henzey, and

I reckon he's had enough, comfortable as we try to make him feel... And much as we care for him.'

Henzey pulled her clean dress over her head and, as she wriggled to get it on, she tossed her head to redistribute her thick, dark hair.

'But don't he see that we don't mind being poor just as long as we've got him?'

'Oh, I reckon he knows that. He knows that well enough, but it doesn't alter anything. If things had been different we'd be well off now. He reckons it's his fault that we're not.'

'Do you think it's his fault, Mom?'

'He was the one who decided to join the army in the war. I didn't want him to go, but he wouldn't listen. He gave up a good job in a reserved occupation. There was no need for it, Henzey, that was the annoying bit... But what I think is neither here nor there now. It won't alter a thing.'

'But it's no good him sulking about it, Mom.'

Lizzie picked a stray piece of cotton from Henzey's dress and dropped it into the small, empty fire grate. 'Your father's too sensible a man to sulk. Over the years he's had a lot to contend with one way and another. Now, besides, he reckons the world's going mad and isn't worth living in anyway.' Her eyes filled with tears. 'Just be kind to him, our Henzey. Be kind to him while we've still got him.'

Henzey bit her bottom lip and tried to stop her own tears. But it was in vain. The tears rushed forth and would not be stemmed.

'Oh, Mom, I don't want my dad to die. I love him... I love him so much.'

Ben Kite was taken seriously ill on the 4th of May 1926; ironically, the day the General Strike started. In his fever he was vaguely aware of Donald Clark examining him, of Lizzie giving him drinks, of his children sitting with him quietly, of night and of day. Most of the time he dozed, drifting in and out of consciousness, his world alternating between the real and the fantasy. When darkness came he was aware of Lizzie lying beside him, her arm welcome around his waist, her soft, warm body snugly fitting his. For more than a week he lingered in this twilight world of semi-consciousness, tortured with pain in his chest, in his head, and in his heart. He saw his father, black faced and stinking of beer, leaning on his shovel: 'Ben, Ben. Wheer'st thee bin? Wheer's thy slut of a mother? Ast brung me fittles?' Those victuals were a basin of broth wrapped in a muslin cloth, and a chunk of bread. He saw his mother, as he remembered her when he was a child, pushing him in a second-hand bassinet as she took him to watch some top-hatted dignitary lay a foundation stone for a new Methodist chapel in Tipton. Then, he was running along a muddy tow-path with Cedric, his eldest brother, chasing him playfully. But this pain in his chest as he drifted back into sentience...

...An idea: if only he could hold his breath for long enough ... if only ... oh, God, it hurt so much, but he would try... Yes ... oh, yes... A magnificent garden ... sunshine, masses of beautiful flowers, red, blue, orange, yellow. He'd never seen such brilliant colours before ... a grotto of moss covered rocks, overhung with weeping willows, ivy, and vines, and the sun penetrating in blinding shafts of yellow and blue light. But this extraordinary beauty was marred by excruciating pain within him. His chest was about to burst. *Oh, God... Please, God, release me from the misery of it...* Then he began to choke violently, blowing, heaving, and the pain was even greater, intolerable, returning him to consciousness to see Lizzie hovering over him, alarmed. It was as if death itself had woken him, cynically cheating him of its final comfort. The automatic responses of even his poor, ruined body were denying him peace. But why, when he wanted so much to exit this constricted life? Why, when he needed to die?

On the day the General Strike finally crumbled – the 12th of May, Ben Kite passed away peacefully. He was visited in his last days by his brothers, their wives and their children. His ageing mother prayed tearfully at his bedside. In his final hour the Reverend Mr John Mainwaring poignantly recited the commendatory prayer for a sick person at the point of departure, while Lizzie wept quietly.

During his eight years as an invalid there was little Ben could do; the Kaiser's gas warfare at Arras had ensured that. Yet his mind remained signally alert and, to compensate for his physical disability, he studied the newspapers from front to back and became a knowledgeable man. He knew the name of every footballer in the football league, every cricketer in the county sides and every horse and jockey that was placed in any race since 1918. Not least of his interests was politics. He'd always held strong views, and he'd grown more bitterly opposed to what he saw as trades union abuse of power, and the fostering of discontent among their members. To his mind it was abject nonsense that anyone could gain anything by striking; he believed it was nothing more than their leaders' attempts to force a misguided ideology down the throats of an apathetic people, and thus tear to shreds the fabric of ordered society; he was certain that it was a plot, no less, to create the chaotic conditions that would haul them and their beloved Communism to power at Westminster. He would have given anything to have been fit enough to go out and combat it.

But it wasn't just politics that concerned him. He saw futility in everything, including his own confined life, and he was utterly frustrated at his inability to do anything about it. He was perpetually angry with himself that he'd messed up the lives of his family by his rashness when the Great War began. He'd been a fool, but he realised it too late. He'd been an even greater fool for driving his wife into the arms of another man, and her resulting pregnancy had wrought its own intolerable hell. It was all his fault. He could no longer live with himself. Such a fool did not deserve to live. Thus, he lost the will to fight the depression that engulfed him. He willed himself into his grave. But he left a widow, three daughters and a son, who adored and respected him, and who had brought him so much joy.

In many ways it was a relief. Lizzie's life had declined into drudgery; she had no life; she never ceased working; she never ceased worrying; the dinner table bore the cheapest meals; poverty stared them continually in the face and the things she had to do to nurse poor Ben stretched the bonds of marriage to breaking point.

Yet they had been happy once; and she was thankful for that.

At the funeral, John Mainwaring had much to say about Ben; much that his family didn't even know. He told how many years ago he had saved a young child from drowning in the Birmingham Canal at the back of the Coneygree Collieries; how he was the best boxer at his school at Burnt Tree; how as a youth he'd even written to the then Prime Minister, Arthur Balfour, expressing his fears about Keir Hardie's plans for the trades unions. But how he'd felt the need to volunteer to fight for his country in the Great War, leaving behind a pregnant wife and three growing children, was well known to all.

'Thus was Ben's sense of duty,' John Mainwaring said. 'Thus was Ben's appreciation of what he perceived was right, and what he perceived was wrong. Thus was Ben's understanding of what was good and what was evil. If we ourselves, and I mean the whole human race, could determine right from wrong, good from evil, with the same clear perception as Ben Kite, then the world would indeed be a far happier, and a far better place in which to live.'

The two families, and some close neighbours, turned out for the occasion. While Lizzie and

Herbert attended the service and the poignant lowering of Ben into his grave, Henzey and her two sisters remained at home making sandwiches, pies, and cakes for the mourners afterwards. They borrowed an enormous kettle and an equally enormous teapot. Early that morning Jesse Clancey ladled several pints of milk into several borrowed jugs, and they were all standing on the cold shelf above the cellar steps. Price's bread cart delivered four loaves of fresh bread, still warm, and smelling divine, all of which they sliced and buttered.

For Ben's children the sorrow of the day was offset somewhat by the appearance of their aunts, uncles and cousins; all totally different; some of whom they had not seen for months or years. They were fond of them all in varying degrees.

In the scullery Jesse Clancey made a point of catching Lizzie as she was hanging the kettle over the fire. She turned to him, and he saw that her eyes were still red from crying at the funeral, but at least now they were dry.

She smiled bravely. 'Hello, Jesse. Thanks for coming. He would've appreciated it.'

'It's the very least I could do. He was a character, your Ben. It's been a privilege knowing him. He was a good friend. I'm just sorry he's gone.'

'He was good to me, Jesse.' Tears flooded her eyes again, so she took a handkerchief from inside her sleeve and wiped them, trying to regain her composure. 'He was as good as gold to me, but the more I think about him the more I think he was his own worst enemy, God bless him. Only he knew what the pain was like. He suffered unmercifully, you know. At least he feels no pain now, Jesse. And that's a blessing.'

The burning coals slipped, and she turned momentarily to check the fire.

'Listen, Lizzie, I want to tell you something. I've said it before, but I'll say it again – if you need any help at all – it don't matter what it is, send for me, ask me. I want you to feel you can rely on me for anything. Don't be too proud to ask... I mean it.'

'Oh, Jesse, you've always been kind to Ben and me – and the children. I do appreciate it. Ben always appreciated it as well. But I've no desire to bring down the wrath of Sylvia on myself again.' She smiled through her tears, aware that Jesse would know what she meant.

'It's nothing to do with Sylvia.'

'But if you're courting her again it wouldn't go down very well if she thought you were doing something to help me.'

'Like I said, Lizzie, it's nothing to do with Sylvia. If I want to help you, I'll help you, and nobody'll stop me. I don't belong to Sylvia. We're not betrothed. Not yet at any rate. We're only friends.'

'Only friends?' She gave him a knowing look. 'I bet she doesn't see the two of you as only friends.'

He tilted his head from side to side as if weighing up the facts of the matter. 'No, I don't suppose she would. Neither would she see me and you as only friends, but that's all we are, Lizzie.'

'And I hope we'll always be friends, Jesse.'

In August Henzey left school to the envy of her brother and sisters. Straight away she found a job in George Mason's provisions store in the Market Place. Edie Soap, Annie's granddaughter, had suggested she apply. There was a vacancy to be filled as one of the girls was leaving to get married. Wally Bibb, the store manager, duly impressed, offered Henzey full time employment at a starting wage of seven shillings a week. That extra money would help alleviate the extreme financial hardship the family were experiencing since Ben's death.

In the late afternoon of the same day that Henzey started her new job, Lizzie walked home from the shops in Brown Street. She could hear Jesse Clancey singing in the yard of the dairy house as he cleaned out churns with a hose pipe. She smiled to herself, and decided she would go over and say hello. After all, she had half an hour or so to kill. Just so long as Ezme wasn't about. She had no wish to see Ezme. Jesse's trousers were tucked into his rubber boots as he worked, and his cow-gown was spottled with water. When he saw Lizzie his big moustache widened in a delighted smile and, at once, he turned off the tap in the brewhouse.

'Lizzie! I was just thinking about you. I was going to come and see you later.'

'Why, why? What have I done?'

Jesse looked very solemn. 'When Harry Skilbeck got back from his round he told me that Tom Dando was taken ill this morning. Your

Aunt Sarah's had the doctor in to him. Sylvia reckons he's very poorly.'

'Oh, no. What's the matter with him, Jesse? D'you know what's the matter with him?'

'Heart attack, apparently.'

The colour seemed to drain from her cheeks. 'Oh, Lord. I'd best go and see him. I'll go and see him tonight.'

'Well don't forget as Sylvia'll very likely be there, as well.'

'Oh, I couldn't care less about Sylvia, Jesse. If she's there, she's there. If my Uncle Tom's poorly I want to see him.'

Jesse smiled. 'That's the spirit.'

'Poor Uncle Tom. He wasn't well last time I saw him. That's old age, Jesse. It gets you like that if you live long enough. I don't know which is worse – to die young or to live long and suffer.'

'Or worse still – die young and suffer – like Ben did.' He hoped she wouldn't regard it as a tactless remark. 'How are you now, Lizzie, anyway? Are you coping?'

'Well enough, thanks, Jesse. Our Henzey's started work today, and Herbert's going red mad to leave school and find a job. He can't leave yet, though. Not till he's fourteen. But I do wish he'd find himself something to do in the holiday and at weekends. He's a bundle of energy, but all he wants to do is go fishing and play football.'

'All lads are the same, Lizzie. So how d'you think he'd take to a little job of a Saturday?'

'I daresay he'd love one. Where, though?'

'Well, you know, I could do with some help of Saturday when I collect the money. The round don't warrant taking anybody else on full time, just a Saturday. I never thought about Herbert, though. It'd suit him, and suit me.'

'Oh, he'd love that, Jesse. Helping you on your float.'

It so happened that Sylvia had left her father ten minutes earlier when Lizzie arrived at the house in Grainger Street. Tom Dando was very poorly, and Donald Clark had ordered complete rest. Another such heart attack would kill him, he warned. So Lizzie did not stay long. But while she was there her Uncle Tom held her hand tightly.

'Yo'll never know how grateful I am as yo've called to see me,' he said weakly. 'Yo'm that much like your mother was at your age ... a picture.'

'But my mother was a lady,' Lizzie answered self-deprecatingly.

'Ar, your mother was a lady all right. And so am yo', our Lizzie.'

Lizzie smiled, grateful for his kind words; especially grateful for the consideration and affection he'd always shown her, as well as her mother.

'...Now yo'm a widder ... and yo'm no age. It's a sin. How old am yer now, our Lizzie?'

'Thirty-six. Clocking on a bit now, Uncle Tom.'

'Thirty-six. Lord's sakes, how the years have fled...Thirty-six... It's a sin, it is. Your mother was forty-two when'er had yo', God bless 'er... So there's still time, yer know. Somebody'll come along and sweep yer off your feet again. Yo'd be a worthy bride at thirty-six.'

She laughed. 'And who'd want me with four kids in tow?'

'Many a one,' he said feebly. 'But pick a bloke careful like, our Lizzie. The one yo' had was a good lad – a damn good lad. Yo'll do well to match him.'

'Any suggestions?'

'Suggestions?'

'Well, how about our Stanley? He's still single.'

'Our Stanley? Good God, no! Our Stanley's no good for yo', Lizzie, my wench. Have no truck with our Stanley whatever you do. He's too fly... Too thoughtless... Him? He's like a fart in a colander – out one hole, straight in another.'

Lizzie felt herself blush. 'Let's hope they've got plenty colanders in Rhodesia then,' she said, for want of a more suitable reply.

''Tis to be hoped.' Tom sighed, and was silent for a few moments while Lizzie adjusted his pillow. 'Am the children all right?' he asked eventually.

She confirmed that they were well, and that Henzey had started work that very day.

'They can be a big comfort, children.' He sounded emotional, but also very tired.

Lizzie stroked his forehead gently. 'I hope nieces can as well...You're tired, Uncle Tom. I'd better go now and leave you in peace. I'll call again in a day or two.'

He shook his head lamely. 'Doh goo yet, our Lizzie. Sit wi' me a bit longer. Yo' doh know just how much it means to me for yer to come and see me.'

She kissed him on the cheek. "Course I'll stay a bit.'

'Bless yer. Oh, yo' do remind me o' your mother, Lizzie... An' I did love 'er.'

She sat with him, all the time holding his hand, and Tom seemed at peace, a look of contentment on his pale, drawn face. As the minutes ticked by she felt his grip loosening, and she watched him as he drifted into sleep. Outside dusk was falling and the sun's red ink bled profusely into the western sky. Lizzie stood up quietly, slipping her hand gently away from his. She heaved a sigh of sadness as she tip-toed to the door and, opening it, leaned her head against its edge to take another look at her old Uncle Tom in the gathering gloom of his bedroom. Then she turned, reluctantly, to go home.

It was the last time Lizzie saw her Uncle Tom Dando alive. He died on the 3rd of September after another massive heart attack. He was eighty years old.

While Lizzie was bringing comfort to her Uncle Tom, simply by being with him, Herbert Kite called to see Jesse Clancey about the possibility of Saturday employment. Jesse said he was prepared to give him a try, and the arrangement was that while Jesse collected the money from one customer, Herbert would deliver the milk to the next, thus alerting them to get their purses ready. At the end of their first day together Jesse confessed it was the earliest he'd ever finished his round on a Saturday, and gave Herbert three-pence bonus, on top of his shilling.

389

As far as Herbert was concerned Jesse was a likeable man. His soft grey eyes, fair hair and blonde, walrus moustache seemed to bestow a look of compassion on his fine-featured face, inspiring people to confide in him. Everybody liked Jesse, everybody stopped to pass the time of day with him, and Herbert enjoyed working with him and his chestnut horse, Ramsbottom.

People got to know Herbert Kite, too, as he rode on the milk float, working the cobbled streets. He turned out to be a willing worker, polite and conscientious. Jesse soon learned that he could trust him with money and, together, they worked out an even more efficient system of collection and delivery. Mutual admiration waxed between them, and Jesse began to have a great effect on Herbert. Hitherto he'd always vexed his sisters by his seeming intolerance. He was a boy, so they were naturally inferior, he believed, though rarely did he get the better of any of them. But Jesse spoke about them with such respect that he wondered why he, himself, was so lacking in it where they were concerned.

The girls noticed a gradual change in their brother. It was more evident at weekends after the milk round. His attitude to them and to their mother was more considerate and genteel. Lizzie noticed it, too, and recognised it as Jesse's influence. It made her wonder about him staying on at school where he was picking up all sorts of anti-social habits.

The contribution Henzey made to the family's fortunes helped meanwhile, and was noticeable on the dinner table. Lizzie was able to afford fresh meat every now and again, or bacon, and she began visiting the wet fish stall on Dudley market every fortnight to give the family a very special treat for supper. It was soused herrings, cooked in vinegar with chopped onion rings, done in the oven. The aroma was utterly irresistible.

As they all sat down to such a supper one Friday evening in December, Lizzie put a thought to Herbert. 'I've been thinking, you know...' They all looked up expectantly as she addressed her son. 'You know you said you wanted to leave school at the end of next year?' Herbert nodded in acknowledgement. 'Well, if I thought Jesse could find you full time work as a milkman I wouldn't be against it.'

Herbert beamed. 'I'll ask him, Mother, shall I? It's funny. Only last Saturday he was talkin' about expandin' the business – gettin' another chap besides Harry Skilbeck. He said he wants to canvass down by the gas works.'

'Well, see what he says tomorrow, then. If he'll have you it might be for everybody's benefit.'

Chapter 21

Christmas Eve was dismal, dank and grey, with a persistent cold mist that seemed to cling to your clothes. It would have been tolerable, but it shrouded the lovely candles and Christmas decorations in the other shops in the town. Yet it still felt seasonal, as the soft, almost comical rasps of the Salvation Army brass band playing carols in the Market Place drifted towards George Mason's. Revellers, some who couldn't take their drink, were noisy, singing and wishing all a merry Christmas, sometimes stumbling legless past the shop windows. Today had been more than usually exciting for Henzey. While she was taking out the hams and sides of bacon to hang around the windows of the store, Arnold Jennings, one of the young lads with whom she worked had asked her out that very night, and she'd agreed, on condition that he could bring a friend to keep her own friend, Florrie Shuker, company, as well.

That evening she arrived home, cold and hungry. She handed her wages to her mother, who thanked her, handing her a shilling back as pocket-money. Then Lizzie went upstairs to share the remainder between the separate jars she used in her accounting. Herbert was already home, eating a lump of fruit cake. His expression suggested he'd found a half sovereign in it.

'Guess what, our Henzey?'

'Surprise me.'

'Jesse Clancey's takin' me on full time.'

'Oh, that's good... Here, give us a bite of your cake.'

'Get off! Cut your own.'

Instead, she cut a slice of bread from the loaf standing upturned on the table, and smeared it with dripping. 'It'll bring some more money in, you working.'

'Our mother deserves it.' Herbert laced his cup

of tea with several spoonfuls of sugar, then stirred it vigorously.

'Mother deserves even more, Herbert, don't you think?' Here was an opportunity to confide some thoughts she'd been having. They didn't often share secrets, but this was something that affected them both; that affected them all. And Lizzie was upstairs, out of earshot. 'Don't you think so, Herbert?'

'What d'you mean?'

'Don't you think she deserves some happiness as well?'

'She seems happy enough to me.'

'What I mean, Herbert, is I wouldn't mind seeing her married again.'

'What?' He sounded incredulous, and ceased stirring his tea. The idea was awful. 'I don't think I fancy that.'

'But what if *she* fancied the idea? What if somebody *she* liked asked her to marry him? She's still really nice looking even if she is a bit old now. And what you should remember, Herbert, is that she's had no life looking after Father – and we're all growing up. We shan't always be here for her. In three or four years time I might be married myself, for all you know. I'd most likely go and live somewhere else. Even you might get married and do the same someday ... if anybody will have you. See what I mean? When we all go – our Alice and Maxine as well – how's she gonna get on with no husband? She'd have to live with one of us.' She tore a piece off the bread with her teeth.

Herbert pondered Henzey's words. He'd never

considered the possibility. Always he'd thought of them as a total unit. The likelihood of them splitting up had never crossed his mind. It was only recently that he started to feel drawn to girls, though he'd been surrounded and antagonised by them all his life. They were a strange species, girls, and never had he considered the implications of marrying one, even less, the significance it might have on his mother. But yes, he might wed; he almost certainly would in time. Henzey had a point. 'I see what you mean.'

Henzey sipped her tea, satisfied that her idea had been presented well and received favourably, and they sat silent for a few seconds while she adorned another slice of bread with dripping.

'What are you doing tonight, our Henzey?'

'Going for a walk with Florrie.' She took a bite and put her bread and dripping down.

'Can I come?'

'No, you can't. We're meeting some chaps.'

'Chaps? Does Mother know?'

''Course not. And don't tell her, either.'

There was a knock at the door and they glanced at each other.

'Come in,' Henzey called, thinking it might be Beccy Crump, or even Jesse Clancey.

The door opened, and a smiling face appeared; familiar; a face they hadn't seen for a long, long time.

'Uncle Stanley!' Henzey was surprised, but pleased to see him after so long. 'Fancy seeing you back, Uncle Stanley. Come in, come in.'

'You must be Henzey?' He looked from one to

the other with apparent surprise as he closed the door behind him. 'And you're Herbert. My word, how you've both grown.' He placed a bag he was carrying on the floor by the table. 'You know, I don't think I'd have recognised either of you. You're grown up. Last time I saw you both you were just kids. Merry Christmas.' He offered his hand, and Herbert was first to shake it. Henzey smiled self-consciously, and blushed. 'Is your mother not in?'

'She's upstairs. I'll get her, shall I?'

Henzey stood up, opened the stairs door and, with her eyes, beckoned Herbert to follow. Half way up the stairs she turned and whispered melodramatically, 'It must be an omen. Uncle Stanley could be a husband for our mom.'

'I'll put a good word in for him as well if he keeps bringing Christmas boxes. Did you see what he was carrying?'

'What are you two whispering about?' Lizzie queried sharply from her bedroom.

'You'll never guess who's just come, Mom. Uncle Stanley. He's in the scullery.'

'Stanley Dando?' She did not know whether to welcome him or ask him to leave. Why had he suddenly shown up after all this time? It was a visit she could well do without. She'd been in his thrall for too long before, and she did not want her guilt and shame over the last time to muddy her clear thoughts again. Those stark emotions were fading from her memory and the last thing she wanted was that they should be revived.

But her curiosity, driven by vanity, began to get the better of her. She moved the oil-lamp towards the mirror so she could see to titivate her hair. Best not be too offish with him. Be civil. She took off her apron and threw it on the bed, then rearranged her pleats and the belt on her dress. She straightened her back and glanced in the mirror again to check that she looked presentable and, satisfied that she did, descended the stairs; but at a respectably sedate speed.

'I think she fancies him,' Henzey whispered when her mother was out of earshot. 'See how flustered she got?'

'He'll do, as well. I like getting Christmas presents. The more the merrier.'

'Christmas presents don't mean anything. But he is nice looking, isn't he?'

Lizzie appeared round the stairs door apprehensively.

'Lizzie!' Stanley greeted warmly, a confident smile on his handsome face, as ever.

She kept her distance, unsmiling. 'I had no idea you were expected home, Stanley,' she said evenly.

'I certainly didn't plan to be, but when Father was taken ill Sylvia sent me a telegram, and I left Salisbury as soon as I got it. It's a damned pity it takes so long to get here, but there it is. By the time I arrived back he'd already passed away. I never even had the chance to see him one last time. I regret that... Anyway, how are you, Lizzie? It's been a long time. I'm bound to say, you don't look a day older.'

'It's nice of you to say so.' She tried not to heed Stanley's flattery. But her emotions had suddenly been stirred into conflict. 'I expect you'd like a cup of tea.'

Stanley smiled to himself. He remembered that Lizzie was always putting the kettle on. 'Coffee if you've got it. I've taken the liberty of bringing a bottle of brandy to go in it, since it's Christmas. I take it you'll join me?'

'Well ... since it's Christmas.' There was a hint of a smile on her face. 'How long are you back home for?' She hung the kettle ritually over the fire.

'Four weeks. I was sorry to hear about Ben, Lizzie. It must have been a terrible shock for you.'

Lizzie turned and steadily met his eyes. 'It was no great shock, Stanley. He'd been ill for such a long time. We miss him terribly but, at least, he's not suffering any more.'

'I heard you lost a child as well. That must have been distressing.'

'It was. Very.' She reached in the cupboard for the bottle of Camp. She poured a small amount into two cups, anxious not to expand on the subject of her still-born child. 'So how's Southern Rhodesia?'

'Oh, fine. It's a wonderful country. With a fine future.'

'I assume you want your coffee made with water, not milk? I'm sorry, I should've asked.'

'Water's fine. Thank you. I prefer water... Actually, I prefer coffee made from ground beans...'

'We make do with Camp. We don't have a coffee grinder.'

'Perhaps I should've got you one as a

Christmas box.'

There was an awkward pause when neither spoke, and Lizzie finished making the drinks, all the time feeling his eyes on her.

'What are you doing this Christmas, Lizzie?'

'Oh, nothing fancy. We can't afford anything fancy.'

'Look, Lizzie.' His tone was suddenly different, more businesslike. 'How would you like to come for a Christmas drink with me down at 'The Shoulder of Mutton' tonight? There's things I want to talk over with you. I bet Herbert and the girls wouldn't mind.'

Lizzie handed him a cup and saucer, then the sugar bowl, without even looking at him. 'I don't think that'd be a very good idea. Ben's barely cold in his grave. I couldn't be seen out with you yet. It wouldn't do much for my reputation... Or doesn't that worry you?'

He shrugged. 'Nobody's going to judge you in that light, Lizzie. It *is* Christmas ... and we *are* related.'

For all the difference it makes, she felt like saying.

'Nobody'll think any the worse of you. There'll be a lovely Christmassy atmosphere. Here, I've taken the liberty of bringing you all Christmas boxes. I hope you'll like them.' Stanley delved into his bag.

'Well you shouldn't have done, Stanley.' The last thing she wanted was to feel beholden to him. 'You've got no reason to bring us Christmas presents.'

He smiled as he took out five beautifully-

398

wrapped parcels, putting them on the table. 'There's a present for each of you.' He took out the threatened bottle of brandy and opened it, pouring a stout measure into Lizzie's cup, then into his own. 'Cheers! Merry Christmas!'

The sweet smell of the brandy blending with the aroma of the coffee was heady, and evoked warm memories of how Christmas used to be. Stanley certainly had a way of getting round her. She would have to beware. But she allowed herself a smile, and returned the toast, lifting the cup towards him in acknowledgement.

The stairs door opened and Henzey appeared, lingering on the bottom step. She was in her best dress, and a pair of silk stockings, and looked every inch a grown woman, despite her tender years. Her lush, dark hair shone, and her blue eyes were big and bright. Stanley gawped at her in overt amazement and admiration.

'See you later,' she said to her mother. 'I won't be late.'

'Be back here for half past nine, madam, and no later.'

With a charming smile Henzey said good-bye to her Uncle Stanley. She grabbed her coat and disappeared before Lizzie had a chance to ask where she was bound, followed by Herbert.

'My word, Lizzie, your eldest daughter's a fine-looking girl,' Stanley said, running his forefinger round the inside of his collar. 'She'll even give you a run for your money.'

'And you can keep your eyes off her,' Lizzie replied knowingly. 'She's far too young for the likes of you.'

He laughed. 'You're wrong, you know, Lizzie. No grown girl's too young for a man, no matter his age.'

'Then you're a sight too old for her.'

'Ooh, you're sharp today. Now, what about coming out with me for a drink?'

'I've got too much to do here as it is. It is Christmas.'

'Another time, then?'

Lizzie hesitated. 'No, I don't think so, Stanley.'

He picked up his cup and sipped the coffee. 'Last time I saw you, you were keen enough to meet me, Lizzie,' he baited. 'Has the spice gone out of it now there's no one to deceive?'

She glared at him icily. 'That's unfair. What happened between us was a long time ago. A lot of things have happened since, not least of which I lost Ben only six months ago, and I've got no intention of getting mixed up with anybody again. At least not yet, and certainly not with you. I've got four growing children to think about.'

'You had them to think about before, if you'll pardon me for saying so, Lizzie, but they didn't stop you then. What happened?'

'Well, you suddenly saying you were going off to Southern Rhodesia without a word of explanation didn't help.' Her eyes were wide with indignation. 'I thought I warranted some consideration, even if I was only one of your affairs.'

Stanley smiled to himself with apparent amusement. 'Oh, I see. But at the time I thought it was the easiest way – for you as well as for me

– I was afraid we might both get too emotional. Telling you just before I went left no time for that.' He shrugged. 'Perhaps I was wrong.'

'Oh, you were wrong on a good many counts, Stanley, especially if you believed I was in love with you.' She relished the opportunity at last to unleash her pent-up resentment. 'And I know you're lying if that's your way of saying you were in love with me.'

'But I was in love with you...'

'Then why did you never say so?'

'...Once – I was about to add, Lizzie – I was in love with you once. And it wouldn't take much rekindling, it's a certain fact. Let's spend a few more hours together, like we used to. We'd soon get the taste for each other again.'

She shook her head emphatically. 'No, no, Stanley. Those days are long since gone. That sort of arrangement isn't for me, ever again. I learnt my lesson.' At once she knew she'd given away too much.

'Learnt your lesson?' He drained his coffee and put his cup down, eyeing her intently. 'The child you lost, Lizzie. Was it mine?'

She turned away, and edgily began clearing things from the table, feeling hot, aware she was blushing. 'Good Lord, no,' she said scornfully. 'What makes you think that?'

'Oh, just a feeling. I calculated that it was about the right time, after what I heard. And I remember we were never especially careful.'

She had to pull herself together; she had to appear calm. 'You flatter yourself, Stanley.' She smiled, turning to him with an assurance she didn't feel. 'No, the child I lost was Ben's all right. Conceived and born in wedlock... You can rest assured. She was the image of him.'

'Ah, well. I'm pleased about that.' He took his fob watch from his waistcoat pocket and glanced at it. 'I'll go then if you're not coming out to play. But I hope I'll see you again before I go back. Would you mind if I called again?'

'I can hardly stop you, can I? But what's the point?'

He smiled once more, that enchanting, dangerous smile. 'Perhaps just to get to know your children better. They are my relatives, after all.'

Stanley did call again. It was on the Sunday after New Year's Day. He arrived unexpectedly at about half past three. Outside it was cold and raining, so all four children were in the house, occupying themselves. They welcomed Stanley, made a great fuss of him, and thanked him for their Christmas boxes. Lizzie was less enthusiastic at his presence.

Henzey sat beside him, looking at him in wide-eyed admiration. He was eminently suitable as an eventual new husband for her mother. He had all the attributes. He was handsome, congenial, generous, always smart, even in the civilian clothes he wore now, and altogether well-groomed; qualities that all appealed to her own awakening sexuality. If only he didn't have to return to Southern Rhodesia.

They all squeezed companionably around the scrubbed table, which was wearing its best tablecloth today. As the time flashed by the small talk developed into something more serious, about Stanley's adopted country. All four of them wanted to know about Southern Rhodesia, and Stanley relished the opportunity to enlighten them.

'It's magnificent,' he began. 'Hundreds and hundreds of miles of savanna, without a city in sight. It's a new land of opportunity, of endless sunshine, of wild animals roaming free...'

'What sort of animals?' Alice interrupted.

'Oh, impala, hartebeest, water-buck, bush-babies, monkeys...'

'Aah!' the girls chorused soulfully, recalling these appealing creatures from pictures they'd seen.

'Any lions and tigers?' Herbert asked.

'Lions, tigers, leopards, cheetahs. Oh, and elephants, hippos, giraffes.'

'Does it get very hot, Uncle Stanley?' Henzey enquired.

'It's pretty warm most of the time, Henzey, but although it's in the tropics, most of the country's on a high plateau, so it actually stays quite cool. Salisbury's nearly five thousand feet above sea-level, so it's never too hot. The warmest season is spring, between July and October when it's very dry.'

'July and October ain't spring,' Maxine mocked.

Stanley shook his head and smiled. 'No, no, it's spring, Maxine. You see, that part of Africa is in the southern hemisphere. Right now it's midsummer over there – the rainy season.'

'Cor, it'd seem funny being warm at Christmas,' Herbert conjectured.

'We usually eat Christmas dinner outside, on the verandah in the shade.'

'Even in the rainy season?'

'Even in the rainy season we get at least six hours of sunshine a day. Not like here, where it drizzles for days on end.'

'Do you live in a nice house, Uncle Stanley?'

Henzey felt warmth in his smile, and when he matily rubbed shoulders with her. 'I do now. You see, my secondment to the colonial government ended when my British army service finished. That was earlier this year. I'd been able to save a lot of money in the army so I decided to buy a house there, with a good sized piece of land – about a thousand acres.'

'A thousand acres?' they sang, in unison.

'That's not such a big area over there, and land is cheap.'

Lizzie joined in this conversation for the first time. 'So you intend to stay there?'

'There's no place on earth I like better.'

'So what are you going to do with all that land?'

'I shall try growing tobacco and coffee. Perhaps cotton. The climate's ideal.'

'Have you got servants?' Alice wanted to know.

'Oh, everybody's got servants, Alice. I've got a cook, a housekeeper, a maid, a lad I call my batman, besides all those who work on the plantation.'

'Darkies?'

'Yes, darkies.'

'And do they live in your house, Uncle Stanley?'

'All except the plantation workers.'

'Then it must be a damn big house,' Lizzie remarked.

'It's a damn big house, Lizzie.' He turned to her, pleased that at last she was showing some interest. 'A typical colonial house, big and spacious.' He felt in his inside pocket and drew out a folder containing some photographs. He passed them first to Henzey, and winked at her. 'And all the young girls out there, Henzey, have their own horses, and ride to other plantations and farms, to parties and gatherings. It's a great life for colonials...' Secretly, familiarly, he squeezed her thigh under the table. 'Especially for the girls.'

Lizzie wondered why Henzey had blushed and had given Stanley a dewy-eyed look as she turned to smile at him.

Alice looked at Henzey and sighed as they scrutinised the photographs together, asking who this was, what building that was, and a host of other questions, before passing them one by one to their mother.

'D'you go hunting wild animals?' Herbert asked.

'Sometimes. You might get a rogue lion, or a hyena, that preys on farm animals, so you have to destroy it. Sometimes you go on specially organised hunts, just for the sport.'

'You've got a gun then?'

'Oh, certainly, Herbert, I've got a gun. All young lads learn how to use a gun.'

'And fishing?'

'Fishing galore!' Stanley was aware he was

405

enthralling them with his descriptions of the country he loved so much. 'Fishing in the Zambesi in the north, or the Limpopo in the south, and any number of rivers in between. Massive fish. Absolute whoppers. Loads of 'em. And you should see the Victoria Falls...'

The very names conjured up pictures of warmth and sunshine, of wide open spaces and the freedom to explore them, of blue skies, and of an endless round of jolly parties.

'Oh, I'd give anything to go fishing there ... on the Limpopo,' Herbert decided, enjoying the sound of the name on his tongue as he spoke it. 'Or hunting wild animals with a gun. Can I go back with you to Southern Rhodesia, Uncle Stanley?'

Stanley glanced at Lizzie, but she avoided his eyes, pretending to concentrate on his photographs. He knew, and she knew, that her children were on the hook. Now he had to draw them irrevocably into his net.

'You could all come if it were up to me. I could use some extra help – some personal assistants to help run the place. I'm fairly new to it, even though I get plenty of help and advice from friends out there. I have some good friends out there now – some very influential.'

'You should ask our mom to marry you, Uncle Stanley,' Alice suggested innocently. 'Then we could all go and live with you in Southern Rhodesia. We'd all love...'

'Alice!' Lizzie snapped. Then, with greater composure, she said, 'I don't really think Uncle Stanley would appreciate having us lot round him all the time.'

'On the contrary, Lizzie. I'd enjoy having all five of you there.' He winked at Henzey. 'You're all so damn beautiful, it'd be like having a muster of peacocks around me.'

'Peahens, if you don't count Herbert,' Henzey chuckled.

They all laughed, except Lizzie.

'But far be it from me to try and persuade your mother.' He looked at Lizzie tauntingly. 'I think her roots are far too entrenched in the Black Country.'

'Yes, they are, so let's get back down to earth.' Lizzie was anxious to change the subject. 'I'll get the cake and jam, and butter the bread. Henzey, you make the tea. When we've eaten you can get on learning your catechisms, else the Bishop of Worcester will never confirm you.'

Lizzie made sure that Henzey and Herbert stayed with her till Stanley had gone. Aware that he wouldn't easily get rid of her unwitting chaperones, since they were so drawn to him anyway, Stanley decided to leave at about nine o'clock; time enough for a couple of pints of home brewed at 'The Shoulder of Mutton'. But when he'd gone the conversation about Southern Rhodesia continued, to Lizzie's frustration.

'It sounds beautiful, Mom,' Henzey said dreamily. 'I'd love to go … away from these drab streets, away from all this cold and rain.'

'I'd fish for whoppers all day in the sunshine in the Limpopo,' Herbert added. 'I can just imagine it.'

'I'd ride around Uncle Stanley's plantation on a beautiful white stallion,' Henzey mused, her blue eyes glistening with an ardent longing, 'like a lady riding round her country estate.'

'And be waited on hand and foot by obedient servants,' Herbert said. 'It's a dream.'

Lizzie picked up some mending that was waiting to be done. 'Well, you can stop your dreaming, all of you, because it'll never happen.'

'But why? Uncle Stanley would marry you tomorrow if you said yes. Just think of the life.'

'Oh, yes, he makes it sound like paradise on earth, I grant you. But I don't want to marry your Uncle Stanley. Had that crossed your mind?'

'But why not?' Henzey pressed. 'He's ever so handsome and smart. And he's got plenty of money by the sounds of it. What more d'you want?'

With one eye shut, Lizzie aimed the end of a length of cotton at the eye of her needle. 'Henzey, I couldn't care less how handsome he is, or how smart he is, or how much money he's got. It's no nearer us. I don't want to marry him, not for all the coffee or tobacco on his damned plantation. Not if you were to crown me with gold. Besides, your father isn't cold in his grave yet. What would the neighbours say?'

'They could say whatever they liked when we were in Southern Rhodesia,' Herbert commented astutely. 'I bet they'd all swap places, given the chance.'

Henzey said, 'We all grieved over our father, Mom. There was never a man like him. I don't think any of us have got over his death yet, but that doesn't mean life has to stop. We know how hard you worked for our dad, and we both feel you deserve more out of life now he's gone. This would be an ideal opportunity. A chance to get away – to start afresh – for all of us, not just yourself.'

'Our Henzey, stop trying to make me feel guilty, that I'm holding you four back.' She put her mending on her lap. 'You're pressing me to do something I've got no intention of doing. I know Southern Rhodesia sounds tempting to young folk like yourselves. So does America, Canada, Australia. But when you got there it might not be all parties and riding on horseback everywhere, and fishing in the damned Limpopo. If I know anything about life and the world we live in, it's that nothing comes for nothing. You have to work for what you get, and the work would be hard. And there'd still be no guarantee that we'd be any better off there than we are here.'

'But it might be worth a try...'

'Listen, I know your Uncle Stanley a lot better than you. If things went wrong, and they might well, we'd be cut off, weeks, months, from England where we know we belong, even if we could afford the fares back. I don't think you two understand the risks. You only see the glamour, and I blame Stanley for trying to turn your heads.'

'But it'd be better than what we've got, Mom. Better than all the grime, the smoke, the tumble-down buildings, the crowding – being on the breadline all the time.'

409

'The weather might be better, I grant you, Henzey. But like I said, there'd be no guarantee of anything else. So let's hear no more about it. We're not going, and that's that.'

'But why? Why?' There was exasperation in Henzey's voice.

'Because I'm not marrying him, that's why. Not for you. Not for him. Not for anybody.'

Bitter cold weather ushered in 1927, and a continued shortage of coal meant that many families suffered miserably. The Kites burned whatever they could get hold of to keep warm and to cook. Herbert collected wood, and sneaked the odd cardboard box full of coke from the dwindling pile that still remained outside the stoke hole of the Board School. Occasionally, Georgie Malpass, the coal merchant in St John's Street, would have a consignment, but as soon as word got round there would be a queue for it. He was generally known as Georgie Slack, because of the damp slack he sneaked in everyone's orders to make up the weight. Herbert was often first in any queue for coal, but the stuff he was allotted was invariably blighted with bats, which spat like jumping jacks when burned.

One inclement afternoon Lizzie was trying to liven up the meagre fire with off-cuts from the timber yard on East Street, holding a draw-tin over the fire opening. The back door was open to improve the draught, and the fire had just started to roar when Lizzie felt two strong arms around her, and the bulk of a man's body warm at her back. She jumped, startled, letting go the draw-tin, which slid off the hob into the hearth with a loud clang, only to be arrested with an equally resounding clang when it hit the fender at her feet.

Stanley Dando laughed at his surprising her, but Lizzie was not amused.

'Stanley, that's a terrible thing to do to a woman. It could've caused an accident.'

'Sorry, Lizzie.' He threw his hat on the table. 'Just a bit of fun.'

'Fun for you, maybe,' she said acidly. 'So what brings you here again?'

'Ooh, you sound as cold as the weather. I wanted to catch you while the kids were at school. I can't talk to you properly while they're about, let alone do anything.'

'You can forget doing anything, that's for certain.' She picked up the draw-tin. 'What do you want to talk to me about?'

'About this coolness towards me. That's not how I remember us. I only remember warmth and positive responses, but all that seems to have disappeared, like that smoke disappearing up the chimney. Why?'

'Stanley, I lost my husband little more than six months ago, and you expect me to forget him and jump into bed with you? Can't you get it into your head that I'm not interested anymore?'

'And is it just due to Ben's death, this change of heart?'

'I suppose it is.' The handle of the draw-tin was getting hot, so she changed hands, and leaned over for a rag by which to hold it.

'Ironic, isn't it? A pity, too. I came to ask you to

come to Rhodesia with me, without your family hearing. To ask you to make a new life there for yourself and your children. With me. They'd love to go. You know they would.'

'Oh, I know they would. And I know who's turned their heads. I don't thank you for it, Stanley.'

'So it's you I have to persuade now.'

'You're wasting your time.'

'Come with me, Lizzie. You know how good it would be.'

'No. I don't want to marry you. I'm not...'

'I'm not asking you to marry me. Not yet anyway. Just come with me. We can live together, as a family. Marriage could come later.'

'Live in sin, you mean? I was never brought up to live like that, lowly as we were.'

'Only the six of us need know – you, me, and the children. Everybody would just assume we were married.'

Lizzie shook her head emphatically.

'Look, let me whisk you away from all this ... from all this drabness. From this filthy hole where you can't even get enough coal to light a bloody fire. Look around you, Lizzie. What do you see? Fog, and more bloody fog, rain, smoke, grime, dirty cobbled streets dotted with muddy puddles, row after row of bloody redbrick terraces with slates missing off the roofs and more smoke pouring out of the crooked chimneys. Just look about you. There are awful pit banks everywhere, enough to depress a saint, a million chimney stacks all belching out even more black smoke, kids with no backside in their trousers and no shoes on their feet. It's a dump, Lizzie. There's more out of work in this God-forsaken country than the whole population of Rhodesia. Come with me to somewhere beautiful, where the sun shines all year long, where it's warm, and where life is easy; where there's space. I need you Lizzie. I need you out there.'

'Oh, honestly!' She removed the draw-tin and placed it on the hearth so that it was standing up against the grate. The wood fire was burning cheerily now.

'You'd live the life of a lady, Lizzie. You are a lady, you know. You just lack the money and the social connections to live like one. I can provide that for you. I'm well off. Look, you'd have all new clothes. Everything. All the years I've been in the army I've saved and saved, and I've invested my money wisely. Since I've been in Rhodesia I've done some unbelievable deals and made a fortune. How else could I afford this place I've bought out there? That's where my future lies, and I want you to be a part of it, little Lizzie. The potential for your kids is limitless. If you wish to deny it yourself, you shouldn't deny it them. Come with me for their sakes. But once you're there, I warn you, you'll love it. You'll never want to leave... What do you say?'

Oh, he was very convincing.

'You make it sound perfect. But I'll be thirty-seven this year – too old to think about uprooting.'

He sensed her resistance was weakening. 'Oh, nonsense, Lizzie. That's a lame excuse if ever I

413

heard one. There's no age in you at all. You're still in your prime. God, you're more beautiful now, in that old black dress and that awful apron with the holes in it, than anybody I can think of in their finest silks and gold.'

She faced him, her arms folded, amused, pleased by his flattering words. 'Such flannel!' She permitted herself a smile. 'I never heard such flannel in all my life.'

'It's not flannel, Lizzie. Listen. Out in Rhodesia we have servants to do everything for us – lovely warm-hearted people – you wouldn't have to lift a finger if you didn't want to. No more mangling and maiding in the brewhouse on cold winters' mornings, no drying, no ironing, no black leading these ridiculous fire grates, no lugging coal up from the damp cellar, no whitening the front step, no changing the bedclothes, no raking out ashes and gleeds from the fire in a morning, no more setting mouse traps. You wouldn't even have to do your own hair, or bath yourself. Everything would be done for you. It's paradise. What do you say, Lizzie?'

'Oh, you make it sound very tempting, Stanley, you really do. But I don't know. Honest, I don't know. What about if we didn't like it? What about if you and me didn't get on?'

'Then you could come back here. Simple.' He held his hands out, palms up, as an expression of openness and candour. 'Look, d'you want to think about it? D'you want to talk it over with the children? It's more than a week till I leave.'

'Oh, I don't know. Really. There's so much to think about. What about schools? Maxine's mad keen to become a cellist, daft as it sounds. Henzey would love to be a commercial artist.'

'Pah!' he scoffed. 'Schools are no problem. There's a good English school in Salisbury, not so far away from the house. A kid can become whatever he or she wants to be over there.'

'But our Herbert's already got his heart set on a job with Jesse Clancey. Henzey's already working, and loves it. They have their dreams here as well, you know.'

'Whatever they can do here they can do there, Lizzie. The sky's the limit. The potential is limitless. Will you think it over?'

It all made reasonable sense. And he was so persuasive. 'All right, I'll think it over. I'll think it over very seriously, but don't expect anything to come of it. Anyway, how soon would you want us to go out there? Next week, when you leave?'

He laughed. 'That would be nice, but it wouldn't be possible. There'd be lots of papers and documents to organise. I'll advise you on all that. And I'd see that you received the money for your fares and all expenses.'

'I see. And how would we travel?'

'By land and by sea, of course. How else? There are railways across the whole of Africa nowadays. Travel wouldn't be a problem. But we can sort all that out later.'

'All right, Stanley. I'll give you my answer before you leave.'

'Good. Now, any fear of a cup of tea?'

''Course, now the fire's ablaze.'

Chapter 22

Alice Kite kept her head down, feigning devout worship that first Sunday evening in February 1927. As she knelt on the hassock she couldn't help peering to her left to watch the Bishop of Worcester performing his laying-on of hands for their Confirmation. Alice waited, while it was Henzey's turn, wondering whether she would feel vastly different after it, wondering who had placed these hard, wooden chairs and hassocks between the front pews and the chancel steps before Evensong began. Now it was Herbert's turn to receive the Episcopal hands. She knew by heart every word of the catechism, but not the Order of Confirmation, yet she'd heard this short prayer the Bishop was reciting in his deep, cultured voice so many times in the last few minutes that she felt she could recite it alone already. Herbert gave his response clearly. Alice continued to look down, and caught a glimpse of the Bishop's red sanctuary slippers beneath his long, red cassock as he shifted sideways to stop in front of her. She wanted to look up into his face, but she dare not.

He laid his hands gently on her head and took a deep breath. *'Defend, O Lord, this thy child with thy heavenly grace,'* he intoned with pious sublimity, *'that she may continue thine for ever, and daily increase in thy holy spirit more and more, until she come unto thy everlasting kingdom. Amen. The Lord be with you.'*

'And with thy spirit.'

Alice breathed a sigh of relief that it was all over, and as the Bishop shuffled towards Maxine she listened to the proceedings no more.

Since their father's death Lizzie had insisted that they all be confirmed, so it was opportune that the vicar had decided to hold confirmation classes in the vestry for all those interested, starting in autumn. Before Alice knew it the Bishop had finished with Maxine, the last candidate. There were more prayers, including one for the twelve thousand British troops under orders to sail for China and the forty thousand British nationals in Shanghai, whom they were to defend from an upsurge of xenophobia, intensified by the Chinese civil war. They returned to the sitting position; the choir sang an anthem; the Bishop preached a sagacious sermon; they sang another hymn; said more prayers. Then finally the entire clutch of clergy and the choir moved out in procession. There was a general murmur of approval from the congregation standing in reverence, wearing best Sunday clothes and most affable Sunday smiles. Everybody began filing into the aisles from their pews, carrying the *Book of Common Prayer* and *Hymns Ancient and Modern* for surrender to the church-warden as they left. The church was full, and warm, and bright, and the atmosphere was of a special occasion, and Alice was sad that it was all over. Confirmation had been painless but, no, she did not feel any different as a result of it.

She made her way down the centre aisle with Maxine at her side, nodding here and there with pleasant but unassertive greetings to other parishioners she knew. Halfway down, their mother, who had been sitting with Beccy Crump, met them and smiled proudly.

'Will you come with me to Holy Communion next Sunday, Mom, so's I can have some bread and wine?' Alice asked, with a cheeky grin.

Lizzie laughed and said that all four of them could escort Beccy to church next time, since she was the only one they knew who attended regularly nowadays. Beccy agreed she would like that. They shuffled slowly down the aisle, waiting patiently for each in turn to be addressed by either the vicar, the new curate, Bertram Bebb, or the Bishop.

Lizzie and Beccy clicked for the vicar.

'Lovely to see you, Mrs Crump,' John Mainwaring said, greeting the senior parishioner first. 'A lovely service, you'll agree.'

'Beautiful. It's grand to see these young 'uns commit theirselves to the good Lord.'

'Indeed, indeed... And Mrs Kite...' There was a look of benign admonition on his face as he shook her hand. 'We haven't seen you for quite a while, Mrs Kite.'

'Not since my husband's memorial service. I'll try and do better, Mr Mainwaring.'

'Ah, but not for long, I hear. Rumour hath it you're leaving the parish for foreign climes.'

Lizzie glanced guiltily at Beccy. She had not mentioned it to her neighbour. 'Yes, it's true, Vicar, but goodness knows where you've heard

418

it,' she said. 'We're going to Southern Rhodesia to live – next month, all being well.'

'Aha! They say it's a beautiful country, Mrs Kite. We shall sadly miss you and your lovely girls. Still, I hope you'll all settle and be happy there. I understand there's a thriving Anglican church where you can continue your worship, so your girls' confirmation won't have been in vain.'

'Thank you,' Lizzie said, and moved on so that the girls and Herbert could all be spoken to in their turn.

As they stood outside waiting for the children to come out Beccy huddled inside her coat. 'I dai' know as yo' was hemigratin', Lizzie. Yo' never said.'

'It's only just been arranged,' Lizzie replied apologetically. 'It seemed pointless saying anything till it was fixed.'

'How come? How yer fixed that? Yo'm a brave wench hemigratin' by yourself with four kids.'

'Oh, I won't be by myself, Beccy. My second cousin, Stanley Dando's arranged it. You know? Tom's son. We're going out to join him. He's got a plantation out there. He wants us to go and help with it.'

'An' where d'yer say it is?'

'Near Salisbury in Southern Rhodesia.' Lizzie pulled her collar up to fend off the cold wind that was gusting round the monolithic graves of wealthier families. 'There's nothing to keep us here any longer. It'll be a new life for us. A new start. And I daresay it'll be a sight warmer than here. I wasn't that bothered about going at first,

419

but the offer was there, and the kids talked me round in the finish.'

'With Tom Dando's son, you say?' Beccy sounded concerned.

'Yes. He's doing ever so well out there.'

Lizzie's family all shot out of church, laughing among themselves, and found their mother and Beccy. Lizzie suggested they go straight home out of the cold and get supper ready.

'Give me the key then, Mom,' Henzey suggested. 'We can run on and give the fire a poke, and put the kettle on.'

Lizzie duly took the key out of her pocket and gave it her. They all headed through the lych gate, bidding goodnight to folk they knew. Lizzie continued walking at Beccy's leaden pace, holding her arm to steady her. Beccy was seventy-seven and, although she was still active and went to church regularly, she was careful to do everything unhurriedly. Rushing about was for the young and the insane.

'I should think twice about buggerin' off abroad to live if I was yo', Lizzie.'

'Oh, I've given it a lot of thought, Beccy. It wasn't a five minute decision, believe me.'

'An' am yer gunna marry the chap?'

'I might, later on. It's been suggested. At my age beggars can't be choosers.'

'But yo' ai' bin a widder five minutes.' Beccy's tone was cold. Evidently she did not approve, but Lizzie was not surprised.

'By the time we get there Ben will have been dead nearly twelve months,' she said defensively. 'I know it's not a long time, but it's circum-

420

stances. He wouldn't have minded.'

They crossed the road junction at 'The Bird in Hand'. The fact that her father, Isaac had been killed at that same spot twenty-five years ago seemed to have been forgotten, since neither mentioned it.

Beccy spoke again. 'Twelve month ai' long enough, Lizzie.' There was an urgency in her tone that made Lizzie take more notice. 'Your mother'd goo mad if 'er knowed, God rest her soul. And besides, I ai' at all sure as Stanley Dando's the right chap for yo'. Think again, my wench, afore yo' do summat as yo' might live to regret.'

'Why d'you say that, Beccy? Stanley's all right. Oh, I know he's been a bit of a lad in his time, but he's mellowed now. He's shaping forty after all. He thinks the world of the kids as well. Where else would I find a man who'd take four kids on?'

'I know,' Beccy croaked. 'But what yo' gorra remember, Lizzie, is them kids o' yourn am all but growed up now. Your Henzey is proper growed up. They ai' gunna be no trouble to man nor beast, they'm lovely kids. Any chap'd be prepared to tek 'em on... And I reckon as yo' can do better for yourself than Stanley Dando. By God, I do.'

They stopped walking so that Beccy could catch her breath.

'You sound adamant that you're right, Beccy. How come you're so certain?'

'I know I'm right, Lizzie my wench. I know I'm right. Tek a tip from me, and have bugger-all to do with Stanley Dando. Yo' could've married Jesse Clancey, if yo'd wanted him.'

Lizzie smiled again, amused. 'Except that he's marrying our Sylvia in a few weeks.'

Beccy realised that her words, no matter how insistent, were not compelling enough. This young woman, whom she'd known since birth, had to be warned off Stanley Dando. She must be deterred at any price, even if it meant losing her respect or her friendship. Although Beccy didn't know Tom Dando's son well, she knew he was totally unsuitable. Her old, but agile mind raced to find some convincing way of dissuading Lizzie. There was perhaps only one way, and she prayed it would work without causing dissension.

'Anyroad,' Beccy went on, trying to mask her anxiety, 'how d'yer know it ai' Henzey as he wants?'

'Why would he want Henzey? It's me he wants.'

'Am yer sure, Lizzie? I know about men like Stanley Dando, and I know his reputation. Men like him am always after young madams – young flesh. Yo'm still a fine lookin' wench yourself, Lizzie, but that wo' last forever, an he knows that. Pooh, it's a damned certain fact as he wouldn't ask me to hemigrate with him. And nor would I goo, neither. For all yo' know he might be temptin' yo' out there just to get is hands on young Henzey, cause 'er's gunna be a rare beauty, and no mistek. In a year or two, Lizzie, when 'er's sixteen or seventeen, that Stanley Dando wo' gi' her a minute's peace. Yo' wo' dare turn your back.'

They began walking slowly again, in silence now. Beccy's comments had unnerved Lizzie. There was certainly a ring of truth in her perception of Stanley. Lizzie herself had noticed how he'd gawped at Henzey with lingering, lusting eyes last Christmas Eve when she was all dressed up to go out in her new short dress and silk stockings. And since, too. But she was barely fifteen, even though she looked and acted like an eighteen year old. Surely it was unthinkable. He'd not denied it, though, merely passing it off with his usual chauvinistic bravado.

What was it about Stanley that he could always get his way with her? Lizzie didn't fool herself that she was in love with Stanley. Not any more. Yet still he could manipulate her as if she were his puppet. She was forever falling into his traps; and perhaps this was just yet another. He could manipulate any female with his bright, expressive eyes, his virtuoso smile and his easy, amiable way; Henzey as well according to the way she looked at him with her big, blue eyes agog. If only she could glimpse the future and see herself and her children in ten years time, she would know then whether or not it had been the right decision. Unfortunately, few people are gifted with foresight, and Lizzie wasn't one of them. Common sense and her tenuous trust in Stanley were her only guides.

But was Stanley to be trusted? Could you trust a man who seldom seemed to have thoughts higher than his groin? Could you trust an inveterate romancer? Patently, you could not. Yet she'd foolishly agreed to risk all for his half promises. She was prepared to take herself and her four precious children to a strange land, as yet undeveloped, not really knowing what awaited them; not really knowing the truth of any of Stanley's words. Perhaps he meant well – oh, she was certain he meant well – but he was prone to romancing, to exaggerating, especially over something as emotive as this. No, she could never trust Stanley. She could not trust him when something as important as the well-being of her family was at stake. Stanley was not like Ben; never would be. Stanley was not dependable, and she knew it of old. Even her Uncle Tom had warned her about getting mixed up with him just before he died. Had he foreseen the future in his dying days? Why on earth should he try to warn her off Stanley? Now even Beccy Crump was trying to frighten her off. Why did everybody seem so set against him? What did they know that she did not?

As they walked up Cromwell Street arm in arm Lizzie and Beccy remained silent, but for the calls of goodnight to passing neighbours and acquaintances. Beccy hoped she'd given Lizzie something to think about; profoundly hoped she'd planted some seeds of doubt in the mind of her late best friend's daughter. If she'd not tried she would have felt unworthy of Eve's friendship; a friendship that had spanned all those years of trauma and uncertainty, and emotional hardship.

They reached the entry, and Lizzie followed Beccy into it.

'Would you like to come in and have a cup of tea with me, Beccy?'

'If yer doh mind, my wench, I'll goo' um. I've gorra nice bottle o' stout on the cellar steps as I'll have mulled with a bit o' sugar in. I've got some bread and cheese for me supper an' all, as I've bin lookin' forward to. 'Sides, yo'll have to be up early in the mornin' if yo'm a-washin'.'

'All right, Beccy. I'll see you tomorrow.'

'Tomorrer, ar. And think on what I've told yer. Good night, Lizzie.'

Lizzie waited till she heard Beccy's key turn in the lock and her door open before she went indoors herself. The room was already bright from the gas light, the fire was burning welcomingly, and the kettle was exhaling a wisp of steam, almost boiling. Alice and Maxine, she guessed, were upstairs changing from their best white dresses into their night-dresses, while Henzey and Herbert sat at the table, each reading a half of the same Sunday newspaper spread out between them. They exchanged a few pleasant but irrelevant comments while Lizzie cut slices of bread, and buttered them. Henzey got up and made the tea and, when Maxine and Alice came down to join them, they ate their suppers, talking mostly about the confirmation service and the Bishop. Shortly after ten o' clock, they went upstairs to bed; all except Lizzie.

She knew she would not sleep. Her mind was too lively for sleep, mulling over Beccy's words. Yet she leaned back on the couch on which Ben had spent so much time, and closed her eyes. She closed her eyes as a means of escape from the awful ugly truths of life, wishing she could sleep, wishing she could wake up only when the date they were due to sail had passed, and she could honestly say they'd missed the boat. What was she to do? Whatever she decided would be wrong. If she refused to go to Southern Rhodesia she would suffer a serious rebellion from her children that could lose her their respect forever; and if she decided they should go they might find themselves wallowing in a nightmare from which there would be no awakening. How had she got into this mess? Why had she allowed herself to be railroaded into this situation when she knew she should have remained impassive to Stanley in the first place? Now it was too late. Everything was arranged. It was just too late.

As she sat with her eyes closed, resigned to her own weakness and to her fate, she saw Stanley's face vividly in her mind's eye. Of course, he was smiling, so charming, so desirable, so affable; every woman's best friend; every woman's dream man. He came close and she felt his breath as light as a summer breeze. He kissed her full on the mouth, parting her lips easily with his tongue. The sensation of his gorgeous lips on hers was so satisfying, so soothing, that she sighed deeply with the pleasure of it. Then he opened her blouse and loosened her skirt at the waist, and she felt his skilful hand caressing one firm young breast, his tongue teasing the nipple of the other till she was ready to scream with longing. She felt his hand up her skirt, and she raised her backside so he could slip her drawers down easily. And while she was allowing all this she was aware that

426

she was still only a slip of girl; no more than sixteen; a virgin. They'd just come out of church and it was the first time he'd showed any adolescent interest in her. They'd sat alone together for the first time ever in a pew at the back of the church, and he'd daringly held her hand, and she smiled dreamily at him and sighed with a young girl's longing. Now, with Eve away, enjoying the company of his mother and father in 'The Shoulder of Mutton', she was stripped naked on the hearth. She was lying beneath him, and his deep gentle thrusts were mesmerisingly sweet. A glow like a bright light ignited her lower belly, tingling, hot and satisfying. Then she was floating above herself, looking down at his bare, heaving backside as he drove remorselessly into her now like a pumping engine. But the sixteen year old girl wriggling beneath him was not herself anymore; it was some other girl, even younger, very slender, with long legs, unblemished skin and sleek, dark hair that was almost jet black save for the fine strands of red that caught the flickering firelight. The girl turned her face toward her, smiling dreamily, and Lizzie could see that she was extraordinarily pretty, but so very young.

The power of the image was such that it brought her back to consciousness with a start. It was Henzey. Dear God, it was Henzey! How could he? How could he take advantage of a girl so young? It was too vivid to be a dream. She could touch him, smell him, feel his hot breath, hear his grunts and groans – hear her own daughter whimpering. It was too much to bear. It

427

was far too much. Henzey had to be protected from that. They all had to be protected.

Lizzie sat up, her back erect. She looked at the old, black marble clock. It was almost half past eleven. How long had she been asleep? A good hour, it seemed. She was thirsty. She got up and opened the cellar door, seeking the bottle of home-made ginger beer Beccy Crump had given them yesterday. She poured herself a glass, and drank.

Somehow she felt as if a weight had been lifted off her shoulders. It had only been a dream, but it was a dream she could not allow to happen in real life. It was a portent of the future. Beccy's desperate suggestion had elicited a glimpse of what might be. There would be no emigration to Southern Rhodesia for them now, rebellion or no rebellion. Her mind was made up.

Lizzie felt the desperate need to talk to somebody. But Beccy would have been in bed ages ago, and she couldn't wake Henzey without waking the others as well. She took her glass into the front room and parted the nets, peering out towards the dairy house, wondering if Jesse Clancey had come home yet. She could always talk to him. She saw the faint glow of an oil lamp still burning in the hall, which meant he hadn't yet returned. She went back into the scullery and found her coat among the others lining the cellar door, and put it on. She would wait at the bottom of the entry for him. Besides, she needed the luxury of cold air on her face.

There was such a vibrancy about her now that she did not mind the cold. She sniffed the air and looked up into the sky. There were no stars tonight. The sky, lightened a shade by the street lamps from the distant towns, was a threatening charcoal grey, and the blackness of St. John's tower in the middle distance stood against it like a monolith of coal. She felt a snowflake flutter against her cheek ... and another. From the top of Cromwell Street she heard footsteps, then the vague, dark figure of a tall man. It was Jesse. She felt her heart start beating faster the closer he got. Just as he turned into his wide entry she called him in a hoarse whisper. At once he stopped, and Lizzie stepped out of her entry into the paler darkness of the street.

'Lizzie?' He walked straight over to her. 'Struth, you frightened me to death. What's up?'

'Oh, Jesse, can I talk to you? I need to talk to somebody.'

''Course you can talk to me. Whatever's the matter?'

'Come inside. It's cold out here.'

She turned, and he followed her through the entry. Back in her scullery she shivered. The fire was dying down, so she poked it and fed it a bundle of dried wood from the hearth. From sheer habit she lifted the half-full kettle onto a gale hook to boil, then sat down at the table, inviting Jesse to do the same.

'Come on, tell me what's up, Lizzie?'

She hesitated, wondering how to begin. 'I need your advice,' she said at last.

'If I can give it I'll be glad to.'

'But I need to talk, as well. I do need to talk, Jesse.'

So she told him how Stanley's persuasive words had tempted them all. How she'd finally, against her better judgement, agreed to go to Southern Rhodesia to join him; to live with him, with the half promise of marriage.

'All in all it seemed we'd be better off there in the sunshine,' she said, 'protected by all his money – better off than living here in poverty, always struggling to make ends meet. So just before he left to go back I told him, yes, we'd go. I've had to arrange all sorts of papers, passports, and everything. I really got into the spirit of it all, looking forward to a brand new life. I've thought about little else since.

'But even then, Jesse, I started to get doubts. I've known Stanley all my life, and you know as well as I do that he's been a devil in his time. I started making excuses to myself that he was older now, so he'd be wiser... That he'd settled down... Not so keen to chase other women.'

Jesse rolled his eyes in disbelief.

'Anyway,' she went on, 'they say a leopard never changes its spots. I realise now that Stanley'll never change his.'

'What made you realise that, Lizzie?'

'Believe it or not, it was the way he looked at our Henzey last Christmas Eve. She'd just got herself ready to go out, and I must be honest, she looked a real bobbydazzler – a lot older than her years, at any rate. Well, Stanley couldn't take his eyes off her, and I could read exactly what was on his mind. The last thing I want, Jesse, is to put us all in a situation where we're beholden to Stanley, so that he thinks he can do as he likes

430

with my daughters, when my back's turned.'

'Lizzie, I had no idea you were planning to go to Southern Rhodesia. But if you want my advice – and that's what you asked for – I think you'd be a fool.'

Lizzie waited, watching him, thinking how well he'd retained his looks and his demeanour, feeling a pang of jealousy that her estranged cousin Sylvia had been the one to finally win him. Jesse was the only other man she'd ever known, besides Ben, whom she knew she could trust without question.

'Oh, God,' he groaned, struggling with his conscience. 'Lizzie, there's something I know about Stanley, but I've been sworn to secrecy... But damn it, I'm going to tell you, 'cause I reckon as it wouldn't hurt you to know. In fact, it might hurt you *not* to know.'

'Oh, Lord. What is it?'

'Well, you obviously didn't know... Stanley's married, Lizzie. He's been married years – to a South African woman – and he's got a child by her. That's why he wanted to get back there in the first place, Sylvia reckons. I bet that's why he volunteered for secondment.'

Lizzie slumped back in her chair, but there was a smile on her face. 'Well hang me... I oughtn't to be surprised, had I? How d'you know this?'

'Sylvia told me.'

'But why were you sworn to secrecy?'

'Because his mother and father never knew. He didn't want 'em to know.'

'But why ever not?'

'Because her family didn't approve. The shame

431

of rejection. Only Sylvia knew.'

'So, who did he marry?'

'A wealthy colonial's daughter. Somebody who looked down on him. Somebody who didn't approve of the marriage in the first place. Somebody who evidently was potent enough to make sure she didn't follow him here. They might even have bought him off, for all we know – paid him enough to bugger off.'

'But d'you know whether he's still married to her? I mean, he might be divorced, or she might be dead. He might have gone back there for his child. Anything could've happened.'

'Well I agree, but d'you want to go all the way out there and take that chance?'

'Oh, no. Not now I know that. That's settled it altogether. Whether the kids like it or not we're not going. God knows what trouble we might find ourselves in.'

'You'll never know how happy I am to hear you say that, Lizzie.' He scratched the tablecloth nervously, pensively, with his forefinger.

'Oh? Why should it make any difference to you now?'

'It doesn't matter.' He smiled reflectively, leaning back.

'Yes it does matter. Why should it make any difference to you?' But she felt that she sensed his meaning.

He laughed, a self-conscious little laugh for a grown man.

'Tell me, Jesse. Or do I have to drag it out of you?'

'Oh, because of the way I feel about you – the

way I've always felt about you.'

'Jesse!' She could hardly believe her ears. 'Still? After all these years, you still reckon you feel the same for me as you did, what – sixteen, seventeen years ago?'

He sighed. 'I know. After all these years.'

'You ought to be ashamed, you getting married and all to Sylvia in a week or two.'

'I know, I know. Daft ain't it? I've watched you grow from a flighty young madam to a woman. I've watched you get married, to one of the nicest chaps imaginable, and never begrudged him you. I've watched your belly grow big and wished they were my babies you were carrying – five times, now, Lizzie – five times. I've watched your kids grow up, and I think the world of them, as well.'

'Oh, Jesse, I don't think you'd feel like that if you knew what I was really like – if you knew some of the things I was capable of doing – some of the things I've done in the past.'

'I know a sight more than you might think, Lizzie. I've watched you wasting your time on Stanley Dando, if that's what you mean – and that's never made any difference.'

She felt herself blush. 'What d'you mean, you've watched me wasting my time on Stanley Dando?'

'I know that you were having a fling with him whenever he was home on leave.'

'Oh,' she said, unprotesting. There seemed little sense in denying it. 'Well, I'm not very proud of that, Jesse. Not very proud of it at all.'

'And yet you've been thinking about going to live with him in Rhodesia?'

433

'Because there's nothing else for us here. Particularly for my kids. We're fed up to our back teeth living in poverty. It was an escape for us – an escape for me... Anyway, how could you possibly know about me and Stanley? Unless he told Sylvia, and she told you.'

'Sylvia knows nothing. I'm certain of that.'

'Well, thank God. So how d'you know?'

'Because I saw you, Lizzie.'

'Saw us? When?'

'Oh, I'd gone to collect my milk money from Sylvia's one Saturday before Christmas, and you were ... you were lying on the hearth with him in the sitting room. Going the game, you were, the pair of you. Neither of you had got a stitch on. I never felt so devastated in all my life.'

'Oh, Jesse! You mean you watched us? Through the window?' There was no sense in trying to deny that either. Horrified, she blushed to her roots again.

'No, I didn't stop to watch. I couldn't have watched, it upset me that much. I just turned round and went on my way as quick as I could.'

Lizzie was quiet for a few moments, weighing up the implications of all this, and all they could hear was the peaceful tick of the clock on the mantelpiece and the soughing of the kettle. So all along Jesse had known about Stanley and her. And he'd said nothing, silently, secretly grieving over what she was doing. If only she'd known. Jesse Clancey was the last person in the world she'd want to hurt, the kindest, most generous soul. Why had she not jumped at the chance to be his woman when he first confessed his feelings for her all those years ago? Things would have turned out so different. At least she would still have a husband; one who cared for her, too, as much as Ben did. She would never have sought an affair with Stanley Dando, nor anybody else; there would have been no need. Her life would have been settled, stable, fulfilled. And they would have had children; different children of course, but they would have been loved just as much as the children she'd had by Ben.

Yet she could never regret marrying Ben. They had been so much in love, and he'd brought her so much happiness. Only later, when he'd been gassed and was invalided, was he so helpless, so useless, so visually repulsive. Only then did their world really begin to fall apart.

She looked up at Jesse, and their eyes met. It was time to be totally frank with him. She could confide anything in him. She wanted to confide in him; to tell him everything; to absolve herself of her past. If he still felt the same about her after that she would be surprised, but she would also be very happy; and inclined to take advantage of it, Sylvia or no Sylvia.

She said, 'Then you very likely realise, Jesse, that the child I had nine months later was Stanley's, not Ben's.'

'Oh, Lizzie.' The sadness in his voice touched her. It was neither accusing nor judging, but compassionate, deeply concerned. 'Give me your hand.' Hers moved to meet his, and he held it reassuringly, and he recognised the warmth for him in her eyes. 'Oh, Lizzie, my poor darling, I'd guessed as much. When Ben told me he was about to become a father again, it crossed me mind he was just protecting you.'

'He was as good as gold about it, Jesse. I couldn't have wished for more support than he gave me. And I certainly didn't deserve it.'

'But that was typical of him. He thought the world of you, Lizzie.'

'I know, and I deceived him. When I first started seeing Stanley we used to meet at "The Station Hotel" of a Saturday afternoon. He'd book a room for the night, and I'd tell Ben I was going shopping.' She gave a sad, little laugh as she recalled it, ridiculing it. 'But it never fooled Ben, you know. He told me after, when it all come out into the open, that he used to wonder why, if I'd gone shopping, I never came back with anything. He knew all along. He was never fooled for a minute.'

'So did it make any difference to your … you know … to your married life?… I'm sorry, Lizzie, I shouldn't ask.'

'But that was the trouble. We had no proper married life after he came back from the war. He was incapable. That's why I sought it elsewhere… But he told me to, Jesse. He told me to.'

'Huh! I wish that you'd come and sought it with me, Lizzie. I dearly wish you had.'

Lizzie squeezed his hand. 'Oh, I thought about it, believe me. But you could never have gone through with it. Your conscience would never have let you do the dirty across Ben. You're too honest for that. And I admire you all the more for it. You're not deceitful like Stanley Dando – or me. I've been a terrible person.'

She looked absently at the table. 'Sylvia said I was a whore once. D'you remember?'

Jesse continued to stroke her hand. 'Oh, I remember. But who takes any notice of Sylvia?'

She looked at him intently, pleased that she detected scorn for Sylvia. 'Jesse, if you think like that why are you intending to marry her? You shouldn't. It'd be wrong.'

'I can see that now, talking to you. The truth is I always held out for you, Lizzie, but I started to realise I never had a chance. I'm getting no younger, and I reckoned it was about time I was wed. I suppose I've just gone along with the idea of marrying Sylvia, without really questioning it too seriously. Courting her now is no different to how it used to be, except now she's got more about her, and a sight more to say for herself.'

'Don't do it, then. I should really hate to see our Sylvia get you. She's too snotty. Thinks too much of herself.'

'Well, I ain't really content, Lizzie. At my age I ought to be content.'

'If you're not content, give her up. There's no sense in prolonging the agony.'

Jesse chuckled. 'I seem to recall having a conversation like this with you once before – a long time ago. Remember?'

'But a lot of water's passed under the bridge since then.'

'And it has. And yet nothing's changed, for all that. We're right back where we started. Except this time I'm on the verge of getting married...'

'Last time it was Ben, wasn't it, Jesse? Ben was the reason we never really got together then.' She smiled appealingly, looking straight into his eyes. '...But this time, Jesse, I've got nobody...'

'If you've decided not to go out to Stanley...'

'I've definitely decided. I'm not going out to him.'

He squared his shoulders and breathed in deeply. 'Lizzie, if I was to give Sylvia up now, d'you think there might be some sort of a chance for you and me? It's always been you, you know. There's only ever been you.'

Lizzie remained silent for a few seconds while his hand tightened around hers. He watched her intently, the spit thickening in his mouth as he awaited her answer. He saw tears of emotion well up in her eyes, and he silently prayed for a positive answer. Lizzie was worth ten Sylvias.

Chapter 23

So Jesse Clancey once more became a regular visitor to 48 Cromwell Street. Lizzie didn't blatantly encourage him, but enjoyed his unforced attention and always made sure she looked her best. Since Ben's death she'd had neither the means nor the inclination to make the most of herself, but with Henzey earning something, and Herbert on the brink of his full-time job, things were beginning to look up. Now, with Jesse's rekindled interest in her there was somebody worthwhile to trouble herself over. Even after five pregnancies she was only six pounds heavier than the day she got married, according to the weighing machine in Boots in the Market Place.

This new relationship was what she needed to shut Stanley Dando out of her life forever. She wrote to him of her decision not to join him in Southern Rhodesia, and promised to return all the money he'd sent to pay for their passages just as soon as it was refunded. Alice and Maxine took this news with sulky disappointment but, to her surprise, neither Henzey nor Herbert seemed to mind. For Herbert, of course, it meant that he could concentrate his efforts on his new job, on which he was keen. Henzey already had an inkling that there was something promising afoot with Jesse, and some young beau had refocussed her own interest more locally, so she accepted the cancellation philosophically. That Lizzie seemed no longer interested in Stanley she did not question.

Lizzie now realised she'd been far too hasty in deciding to emigrate so soon after losing Ben; in even considering marriage to Stanley. Her judgement had been clouded by sweet memories of those stolen hours of pleasure. Now she wanted time to acclimatise herself to her new situation. She was enjoying Jesse's gentle courtship increasingly. She wanted to savour it; to relish the little things he did for her; to see his smile at things she did for him; to revel in a pulse rate that increased whenever she saw him. These things reminded her of the way she used to feel when she was younger. She wanted time to appreciate them for what they were, untainted by any pressure to escalate the affair with sex. To rush things would have been to mar the gentle pleasure of it, to have cheapened it. They discussed this at length and Jesse understood. He'd waited nearly twenty years for her. A few months more wouldn't hurt.

Jesse had finally despatched Sylvia, the wedding had been cancelled, and she was grossly put out about it. She sobbed with disappointment and frustration. Twice she had failed to secure the man of her dreams; but this time she did not suspect it was because of Lizzie. Jesse was concerned, however, that once she did, and sooner or later she was bound to, then all hell would be let loose. But they'd deal with that when it arose, if it arose, and not worry about it yet.

So life moved on. Lizzie's thirty-seventh birthday came and went, as did Easter, when Herbert left school to take up full time employment with Jesse. The weeks seemed to fly, and before they knew it April was out. They sat around the tea table one evening in early May, Lizzie preoccupied.

'Listen, there's something I want to talk to you all about,' she said, looking very serious. Her family looked up at her in anticipation of some great revelation. 'It's something I've been considering for a while now. You see, I fancy a change. I really fancy going away for a bit, somewhere different, now I haven't got your father to worry about. So I thought, this September, our Alice, our Maxine and me, could all go to Bromyard for the hop picking. That way we could earn a bit more money. I'm sure I can get the time off at the bottling stores, and it'd mean you having a week or two off school. If you all agree I'll go and see the woman who does the hiring. She'll be about in a day or two.'

'I think that's a smashing idea, our Mom,' Herbert said. 'We don't mind, do we Henzey?'

'It'd be a nice change. Will Jesse be going as well?'

'He'll be too busy with his business. But he doesn't mind me going.'

And soon enough hop picking time was upon them. On the morning of the 27th August they carefully packed up everything they were taking to Bromyard, checked it off against the list Lizzie had made, and put it all securely into the old tin trunk they'd borrowed from Beccy Crump. Jesse started his round an hour earlier than usual so he would be finished in time to transport them and the trunk to the station on his milk float. They were due to catch the two o'clock train. Henzey wished them a nice time as she set off for work, certain she would miss them, but excited at the prospect of getting her first taste of independence and freedom. A lad called Harold Deakin had walked into her life and she had expectations of spending some time with him, without being questioned continually about it by her mother.

'Keep your eye on our Herbert, Henzey,' Lizzie said. 'Don't let him fall into bad ways. And mind what you're up to yourself.'

They set off, Jesse and Lizzie and the trunk up on the cart, with Alice and Maxine following on

441

foot. The station was teeming with families waiting for the same train. Half of Dudley was there, it seemed. Ten minutes later the longest train Lizzie had ever seen came steaming and clanking into platform two. It was longer than the platform itself.

'Have a nice time, then, Lizzie,' Jesse said, lingering.

Alice and Maxine jostled their way into the carriage to claim three seats.

'I shall miss you, Jesse. I'll write just as soon as I can.'

He took her hand. 'See if you can write fifty pages.'

'I'll try. I'd better get on the train now. Thanks for the lift, Jesse.'

Jesse stood and watched her board the train, then made his way home, heavy hearted. He would miss Lizzie. The next few weeks would be hard. While he knew he had Lizzie's affection, he still found it hard to believe that, after so long, she was finally his. He, too, loved their easy, mellow relationship. They could talk about anything and had no secrets. He didn't yet believe the time was right to start pressurising her to consummate it, though he longed for her. That in itself would present problems, for there was nowhere they could be alone long enough. At her house the children were always hovering, if only outside, and at the dairy house his mother would be doing likewise. But he was in no rush. The time and the place would present itself surely enough; and both would recognise it.

It was certain, though, that the dairy house

would not be the venue. Whilst Maxine had cause to visit his mother frequently, by virtue of her music lessons, Lizzie never did. There always had been, and there still was, an invisible barrier between her and Ezme Clancey. Jesse was aware of it, but could not comprehend it. It was, he knew, a legacy from the old days, when he used to hear his mother make bitchy remarks about Eve. Such professional rivalry over dressmaking should have died with her, but evidently it had not. It was bitterly frustrating. He wanted to tell his mother how happy he was that he and Lizzie were courting, but her reaction would not be favourable. She expected him to settle down with somebody a cut above Lizzie Bishop. Eve's daughter would not be good enough. Tom Dando's daughter was, however, and Ezme could not understand why Jesse was unable to commit himself to that fine girl.

Whenever Jesse called to see Lizzie he never confessed to Ezme where he was bound, unless it was to say he had a message for Herbert. It was easier to lie, and to tell Ezme he was going to 'The Junction' for a pint, or 'The Dog and Partridge'. Ezme, though, was not stupid. She had her suspicions, but was unwilling to ask Jesse outright whether there was anything going on for fear the truth was confirmed. She would not have been able to countenance the truth. So while she sometimes watched him cross the road, and turn into Lizzie's entry more times than might be considered decent, she cast it from her mind, telling herself it really was young Herbert he was going to see. She believed what she wanted to believe. There were times when she couldn't help saying unkind things about Lizzie, but those times merely succeeding in alienating her son, for whenever Ezme made some such comment, he would counter it vehemently and think what a stupid, twisted old woman his mother was.

Jesse was forty-six, and his heart was set on settling down sooner or later with Lizzie. If he could manage to do it with his mother's blessing, all well and good; if he could not, then so be it. He wanted nothing more than Lizzie to be his bride, and neither his mother, nor anybody else would be allowed to stand in the way of that. And with Lizzie, of course, came a ready-made family. It would please him more than anything if he could father a child of his own but, at his time of life, he would hardly grieve if he didn't. He and Lizzie were now enjoying each other's company on a regular basis, and there was no earthly reason why they shouldn't eventually become man and wife. It was up to him to let her know the extent of his hopes and dreams.

In Bromyard, Lizzie and the girls were met from the station, along with all the other hop pickers, by a train of wagons and carts pulled by massive shire horses. The tin trunk and all their belongings were piled onto the wagons with everybody else's, but they had to walk the couple of miles to Pickett's Farm alongside the wagon. The living accommodation was primitive. First, the overseer took them to a vacant cow shed, and pointed out the space allocated to them. A few bales of straw had been provided for bedding, and Lizzie decided that they should make one big bed to accommodate all three. Their own blankets laid over the bales lent a vague feel of home. They'd been advised to bring along extra sheets to use as screens between them and the living areas of other families, thus creating a little privacy, for there would be little enough of it.

Alice suspiciously watched the family garrisoned adjacent to them. Few men went hop picking, but the head of that particular family was present, lining a galvanised bucket with straw.

'What's he doin' that for, Mom?' Alice whispered.

Lizzie laughed. 'So's it doesn't make a noise when they pee in it.'

'Does that mean we have to pee and that in here?' Maxine asked, looking around the cowshed, fearful that they would have no privacy at all.

'Only at night. There's proper earth closets during the day, but they're locked at night for some reason.'

Next morning they befriended other families as they got used to their new environment, familiarising themselves with the cooking and feeding arrangements. Lizzie saw that experienced hop pickers had taken steamers, in which they cooked several dishes at a time. It was all done on a communal open fire outside, adjacent to the living quarters. Everyone dined at trestle tables, and some families used sheets of newspaper as a table-cloth. It was rough, but it promised to be good humoured.

Work started on Monday morning. The Kites soon learned how. First they were allocated a section of a field, referred to by the overseer as a 'house'. They were to pick all the hops in their house. The hop vines were trained to grow up strings attached to a series of wires stretched at different heights between posts, the highest about eighteen feet. Alice wasn't the tallest, but she had the job of pulling the vines down from the netting using a long pole with a hook attached. Lizzie and Maxine would then strip off the hops and throw them into a crib, which was a hessian sack slung between wooden supports. From time to time a man known as the busheller would come along and transfer the hops from the crib to a wicker basket. Volume was the method of measuring the amount of work done, and thus the amount they would be paid. But Old Sourface, as Alice decided to call him, annoyed her tremendously when he squashed down the hops as far as they would go in his basket to produce as little volume and as much weight as he could, to their detriment.

It was hard, rough work. Their appetites were voracious, fuelled by the heady smell of hops drying in the kilns no more than a hundred yards from where they worked. After they'd eaten they often accompanied other families to one or other of the local pubs, and relaxed with a drink and a singsong. It was a way of life entirely different from the one they were used to, but they were enjoying it. The holiday atmosphere and the comradeship rendered even the work pleasurable, and time flew.

446

Lizzie wrote to Henzey and Herbert, and received a reply saying what a lovely time they were having at home without their mother's discipline. Jesse, in his letter, said how much he was missing her. The only impediment now to their future was his mother, seventy-two years old, and strong as a horse.

On the third warm and sunny Sunday morning in Bromyard a smartly dressed man appeared at Pickett's Farm in a taxi-cab. He wore a dark, three piece suit and a starched collar. A gold fob watch sat in his waistcoat pocket, its gold chain hanging loosely across his chest and secured through a buttonhole. On his head was a black bowler hat, and in the lapel of his jacket was a red rose. He walked up to the farmhouse and tapped on the door with the silver knob of his walking cane. When it was opened he introduced himself as Jesse Clancey.

'I'm looking for a Mrs Lizzie Kite. She's working here with her two young daughters.'

'Ar, there is somebody o' that name, sir,' the portly farmer Pickett replied, scratching his groin. 'Moind you, oi'm 'anged if oi know what she looks like. She's one o' them new 'uns. Oi got that many families here, oi can't 'ope to get to know 'em all, specially the new 'uns.'

'Any idea where they might be?'

'Well, she ain't workin' today, that's for certain. None of 'em works of a Sunday.' He sauntered along the path that ran under the front window and, on tip toe, peered over the hedge at the side of the house. 'Here, if you come here, sir, you can see some byres. See that caravan there? I'll lay a shillin' she's with all them folk standin' round it.'

'What is it? What's going on? Is it gypsies telling fortunes or something?'

'It's the gospel van, sir. We always observe the Sabbath. Mr Archibald Smedley comes here every Sunday durin' hop pickin' and conducts a service. They've been at it nigh on an hour already. One more hymn should see to it.'

Jesse pulled his fob watch out of his waistcoat pocket and checked the time. 'Thanks very much. I'll toddle over to 'em then.'

The farmer pointed to a gate further down the lane. 'That's the way in, sir.'

Jesse made his way briskly along the lane, through the gate, and into the field. He headed along a rutted track towards the gospel van just as a stirring version of 'We plough the fields and scatter' rose up, disturbing the magpies in the trees. He put his hand up to shade his eyes as he sought Lizzie among the congregation; and then he saw her, singing lustily, Alice and Maxine at her side. He watched for a few seconds, smiling to himself, savouring the welcome sight of her. Then, Lizzie spotted him and her eyes lit up, and with a broad grin he raised his hat. He saw her whisper something to the girls, and leave them to make her way unobtrusively through the chanting congregation, towards him.

She looked well and happy, and her face and bare arms were tanned. It seemed natural to want to embrace her, but he decided he must exercise some self-control in front of the other

448

hop-pickers – especially on a Sunday – especially during a religious service. After the months of undemanding wooing, of kind attention, and enjoying the companionship of this handsome, young woman, he missed her more than he thought possible. Never would he find anyone more suited to him, and he was sure she now felt the same about him.

He could never have guessed just how much their fortunes would meander before he might ever have a chance with her. He recalled her years ago, dressed up in her Sunday best, walking elegantly past the dairy house. How he used to long for her. Sometimes he would wait for her to walk back, pining for her as she stopped to talk to her friends. He would see her laughing, her eyes bright, and always with a charming look of devilment in them as if she were about to shock everybody with a scandalous display of some sort. Now, twenty years and five children later, as she hurried over to him, dressed for roughing it, but still with that engaging look in her eyes, she was no less beautiful.

As she reached him, he slipped his big hand around hers and squeezed it.

'Jesse, this is a nice surprise, and you looking so smart as well,' she cooed. 'Why didn't you say in your letter you were coming?'

'I wanted to surprise you. Oh, you look a treat, my darling. What have they been feeding you on? Here, let's have a look at you.' He stood back a step and eyed her up and down. 'I reckon you're just about right. I've never seen you looking better.'

The congregation continued singing their hearts out, fifty yards away.

'Well that's a blessing. Anyway, how's our Herbert? Have you seen Henzey?'

'They're fine. They send their love. But listen, I haven't come all this way to talk about Henzey and Herbert. I've missed you, you know, Lizzie. I couldn't keep away any longer. Oh, it's good to see you.'

'Oh, Jesse. It's good to see you as well. How's your mother?'

'Fit as a fiddle... Lizzie, if it weren't for Mother I'd ask you to marry me straight away. You know that, don't you?'

She sighed. 'Oh, Jesse, I'm that flattered, but I'd reckoned as much. There's nothing I'd like better, either, than for us to be married. But let's not think about it yet, eh? Not while your mother's alive.'

'I know, my darling. But I want you to know how I feel. I love you, Lizzie. With all my heart and soul I love you. I can't wait to marry you.'

The congregation were just finishing their *amen*, and the only sound for a few seconds afterwards was the gentle rustling of the leaves in the trees.

She looked into his kind, grey eyes. 'I've thought about it a lot – you and me, Jesse. There wouldn't be anything amiss in it would there? I mean me being a widow less than eighteen months and all that?'

'Nothing amiss at all. But I don't want to saddle you with my mother. Not after all you've been through these last ten years. The trouble is, she's ever likely to live till she's a bloody hundred.'

'Well, there's no rush. I wouldn't think of it till Ben's been dead two years, anyway. And that isn't till next May.'

He sighed, a frustrated sigh. 'As long as we both know where we're headed.'

'I think I've known all along. Ever since that night I decided I wasn't going to Southern Rhodesia I've known...' She squeezed his hand. 'Listen, they've finished singing hymns now, and we've got rabbit stew for our dinners. Shall we go for a couple of halves at the Red Cow when we've fetched Alice and Maxine?'

'Sounds like a good idea.'

Chapter 24

In May 1928, the second anniversary of Ben Kite's death passed poignantly. It was a day when memories of him crowded Lizzie's thoughts. Even the weather, sunny and warm with white racing clouds, was similar, rendering those memories more vivid. The children were unusually subdued that day. Henzey talked about her father at the tea table, and wondered what on earth he would have thought about the Equal Franchise Bill giving the vote to women over twenty-one. Lizzie replied that he would have approved.

Things had improved materially. Three of the

451

family were now working, so they were better off. Also Lizzie felt free; not only from Ben's confining disabilities, but also from Stanley Dando's thrall. The only dark spot on her horizon was the prospect of old Ezme Clancey standing bigotedly in the way of marriage to Jesse. But Ezme would not live forever, though Lizzie wished her no harm.

On the first Saturday of June, Jesse was due to call at eight o'clock to take Lizzie out. Usually, they went to 'The Shoulder of Mutton', and all their friends and neighbours were aware of the romance that had blossomed between them. Most wished them well, and nobody made any reference to Ben in their company. Everybody knew Jesse and respected him, and everybody knew that Lizzie deserved some pleasure in life. No one begrudged either their happiness.

At half past eight Jesse still hadn't arrived and she, sitting ready in her best frock, began to think something must be wrong. But a few minutes later she heard footsteps in the entry and she stood up, eager to go. The door opened, and Jesse appeared, looking overwrought.

'It's Mother,' he said breathlessly. 'I think she's had a stroke. Can you get Herbert quick to help me get her to bed. She's too heavy to shift on my own. Then I'll have to fetch the doctor.'

Lizzie was suddenly flustered. 'You'd best go back, then, Jesse. I'll get Herbert. We'll be there in a minute. Henzey will fetch Donald Clark.'

He disappeared at once and she directed Alice to fetch Herbert from upstairs where he was listening to the crystal set Jesse had given him at

452

Christmas. Henzey duly rushed to fetch the doctor, and Alice was told she must stay home with Maxine in case they needed her. As soon as Herbert came downstairs, he and Lizzie went to the dairy house.

In the verandah, rows of potted plants stood on shelves that were badly in need of a fresh coat of whitewash. A marmalade cat, said to be a good mouser, sat and watched, unconcerned and half asleep while Jesse bent over his mother. She was slumped on the quarry-tiled floor. He looked up as soon as he heard Lizzie and Herbert arrive. Ezme was conscious, but she was dribbling saliva uncontrollably down the side of her face and neck, her eyelids were half-closed, and her face was contorted. Since she was such a hefty woman there was no way Jesse could have lifted her by himself. The three of them together managed to man-handle her through the hall and upstairs to her bedroom, though not without a gargantuan struggle. They put her to bed and Lizzie did her best to make the old lady as comfortable as possible, and wiped away the stream of saliva while they awaited the doctor.

It was the first time Lizzie had been upstairs in the dairy house, and she scanned the bedroom quickly. It was large, cold and bland, with no pictures hanging from the rail. Sun-bleached curtains and nets hung limp with age and dust at the sash window. Old Ezme was evidently not a tidy woman, and strewn all over the rugs and linoleum were off-cuts of material and stray threads of cotton. Mannequins as old as Moses stood spookily erect in a corner, connected by cobwebs, looking like headless, limbless corpses. A treadle sewing machine stood under the window alongside an ancient, wooden spinning wheel. Lizzie could scarcely believe that this collection of junk was the material substance of the continuous feud with her mother. It was all so different from the image of competence and regimentation Ezme evoked as a piano teacher. A tin of Mansion Polish, a broom, and a pair of dusters wouldn't come amiss, Lizzie thought. When she and Jesse married, there would have to be drastic changes in this house.

Lizzie tended to the old lady for about twenty minutes before they heard a motor car turn into the entry and lurch to a halt in the yard. Jesse looked out of the window and saw Donald Clark and Henzey step out of a black Morris Cowley. His hair was grey and his alcoholic flush was surpassed only by the glory of his nose. Henzey looked pleased with herself, having had her first ride ever in a motor car. They knocked twice on the verandah door, then entered.

Jesse hailed them, guiding them to the right bedroom. The doctor entered first. He put his bag down on the chair at the side of the bed and opened it as Henzey followed him in. His hands were shaking more than ever as he took out his stethoscope and opened the front of the patient's blouse to listen to her heartbeat. Jesse waited anxiously for the diagnosis while Donald conducted several simple tests on Ezme.

Eventually, Donald put his instruments away and closed his bag. 'Severe stroke, I'm afraid.' Jesse could smell drink on his breath. 'It's taken her left side and, for the time being, she can't open her eyes properly, though I've no doubt that'll rectify itself. So will her ability to swallow properly. I'm pretty sure she can't hear, either.

'Another stroke like this would see her off good and proper. Just keep her comfy and see she gets plenty to drink. In the morning try her with some solid food. Her eyes might have opened all right by then. Try and get her to talk as well... I can't tell yet, but she might have lost her speech as well, see? And er ... something else I was going to say... Damn, I've forgotten what it was now... Ah, yes ... look for signs that she can hear all right.'

'Is there anything you can give her, Donald?'

'I don't think there's anything she could take, yet, Jesse. More than anything she needs complete rest. I'll drop by in the morning. If she shows no sign of an early recovery I'll arrange for the district nurse to come in every day.'

Without mentioning it to anyone, Henzey arranged to have her hair cut after work on her half day. She had it styled in an Egyptian bob and was delighted with the result. The fringe framed her face beautifully, and accentuated the slant of her big blue eyes, whilst the straight cut at the neck heightened her elegance and enhanced the youthful inclination of her head. She felt good, and it was exactly the tonic she needed to perk her up after a crisis with the latest young man in her life.

'What have you done to your hair?' her mother asked when she saw her.

455

Henzey twirled around and her hair flared out, following in a spiral, then fell back perfectly into place. 'Don't you like it?' Her smile was vivacious.

'Well it won't be any trouble by the looks of it. How much did it cost?'

'Oh, that's a secret. It doesn't matter how much it's cost; I like it. At least it's modern.'

Lizzie laughed. 'You're getting to be a proper flapper, our Henzey.'

Henzey laughed too. 'How's your mother-in-law? Still hanging on?' The gentle sarcasm was well-intentioned.

'Oh, she's a lot better. I went round dinnertime. She's got her appetite back, and no mistake. She'd eat a man off his horse. There's no wonder she's the size she is.'

'Can she see now as well?'

'Yes, her eyelids are back to normal, and she's talking all right, but she still can't hear. She hasn't got the use back in her left side, either. Nor do I think she ever will. I reckon she'll be bedridden for the rest of her life. It'll be no life for poor old Jesse.'

'Yes, poor old Jesse. Perhaps you ought to marry him now.'

'Let's wait and see how the old duch goes on first, eh? I'll pop round tonight and clean for him again. I've been cleaning there the last two nights. Jesse's done his best over the years, but that house was in a terrible state. It was absolutely riffy. I'll take some Sunlight with me again, and my scrubbing brush. I don't think it's had a good clean since the old queen died. Poor

Jesse shouldn't have to live like that. I'll take some clean sheets over for his bed, as well.'

While Lizzie cleaned and polished the living room at the dairy house, Jesse assisted eagerly and ably. Soon, she was satisfied it had more of a woman's touch. Jesse returned, having just filled the coal scuttle in the cellar.

'I'll go and settle your mother for the night, Jesse. Then I'll change your bed for you.'

'You're as good as gold, Lizzie. I'll pop round to the outdoor licence and fetch a jug of beer while you're doing that.'

She climbed the stairs and tiptoed into the bedroom that she'd made clean and tidy two days before. Ezme was resting, motionless, her eyes closed, her silver hair glistening by the reddening evening light from the window. Lizzie stood and watched her for a few seconds. The old lady did not budge, nor even appear to breathe. She looked peaceful, and Lizzie guessed that she'd passed away quietly in her sleep.

So Ezme had met her Maker at last. She'd always been a tyrant. Always partial to a drop or two of whisky, a loyal member of the Mothers' Union, and devout churchgoer and stand-in organist. Yet so devout in her Christian fellowship as to take enormous pleasure in riling Eve over something as trivial dressmaking.

So the time was fast approaching when Lizzie herself would take the name Clancey, and her joy for her own good fortune was greater than her sorrow for Ezme's demise. Over the past few days and evenings she'd got to know her way around the house, and she reckoned that with a bit more cleaning and some decorating she could happily settle there with Jesse. It was big, with plenty of room for all of them.

She tip-toed over to the window and looked out, excited about the future. The sun had almost set over to her left, and the western sky glowed orange and purple, and was streaked with ribbons of green. Its blaze of vibrant colour matched her own new mood of excitement. Dark clouds loomed, tinged with gold and, as she contemplated marriage and what she should wear for it, she tip-toed back to take another last look at Ezme Clancey lying finally at rest.

'Heft me up, Lizzie, wut? I'm bostin' for a piddle.'

A wry smile spread over Lizzie's face. 'You had me fooled that time, you crafty old devil,' she said under her breath. But she failed to stifle a chuckle. She put her arms under the old lady's armpits and struggled to heave her up, then pulled the bedclothes back and helped her swing her huge, dimpled legs round. After a gigantic tussle she managed to get Ezme to her feet, and shuffled her, like five hundredweight of cataplectic blubber, an inch at a time over to her commode next to the bed.

There was an oil lamp on the bedside table and, beside it, a box of matches. Lizzie lit the lamp and trimmed it. As it glowed, Ezme hitched up her night-dress about her backside and peered around her from her throne.

'I see as that district nuss's bin doin' a bit o' cleanin.'

458

'District nurse my foot! It's me that's done all the cleaning, never mind the district nurse. My God, you need be glad I don't hold all your old spitefulness against you.'

But of course, Ezme could not hear her. Lizzie, however, heard Jesse return and open a cupboard door. The chink of glass told her he was bringing the jug of beer and two glasses upstairs.

'Cost help me off, now, Lizzie?'

Together, they reversed the procedure, and Ezme was settled into her bed for the night. Lizzie took the chamber pot from the commode to empty it downstairs. Jesse met her at the bedroom door carrying the beer and two glasses.

'Why don't you strip your bed while I empty this up the yard, Jesse?' she suggested. 'Then we'll put some clean sheets on. I've just settled your mother for the night.'

When she returned, Jesse had lit the gaslight and stripped his bed, and was stuffing his pillows into fresh, clean pillow cases.

'I can do this myself,' he said. 'Pour the beer and let's have a drink now.'

She did as he suggested. While she sipped her beer Lizzie watched him expertly change the bedclothes, as deftly as any woman could.

'You know, Jesse, I thought your mother had passed away when I first came up,' she said softly. Her voice sounded young and clear. 'She looked that peaceful, and I started to think we could soon be married. But it was a false dawn. Next thing she was wide awake. She wanted a pee.' She sat on the bed and laughed at her mistake, just as he'd finished smoothing it out. 'But I'm so

459

annoyed at her. All these years of persecuting my mother – and me for that matter – but she's not too proud to accept my help now she's poorly. Convenient, isn't it?'

He made no reply. He knew Lizzie's comments were justified. But he was glad of her help. He reached up and pulled the chain on the gaslight, dimming it. Then, he took his own glass of beer from the dressing table, drank, and sat beside her. Lizzie looked into his eyes, smiled, then reached over to put her glass down. His hand gently stroked the back of her neck, and she shivered at the delightful sensation. He put his own drink down, his eyes never leaving hers. It was easy to see what was on his mind.

'I want you, Lizzie,' he whispered.

Lizzie swallowed hard. 'I want you as well, Jesse. I was beginning to wonder if we'd ever get round to it.'

'I've always wanted you.'

Slowly their lips met, and she kicked off her shoes, anticipating the next move. He eased her backwards gently onto the bed, and she felt the welcome weight of his body upon her, cautiously at first, then urgent. Her heart started pounding then as it had not done for a long, long time. She felt him undo the row of buttons at the front of her dress, and in no time the floor was strewn with their clothes. At last she was lying naked beneath him, and her arms were around his neck. Her eyes were closed, and she was smiling with anticipation, and she heard herself breathing his name and saying, 'Love me, Jesse. Love me.'

And he did.

And after they had made love again they lay still, content just to be in each other's arms. They spoke little, thinking their own identical thoughts, weaving their own identical dreams.

Old Ezme Clancey showed little improvement over the next three months. The stroke had taken the use of her left side completely, and her hearing had not returned, though that didn't stop her talking all the more. The district nurse called every morning, and Lizzie brought Ezme her dinner, and helped her onto her commode every dinner time. When Jesse finished his round, usually early in the afternoon, he would do whatever was necessary after he'd stabled and fed Ramsbottom. Donald Clark called every week, and examined Ezme, but his advice was always the same: don't allow her to exert herself, nor over eat. *Some hope of that,* Lizzie thought.

Every evening now, Lizzie would send either Alice or Maxine to the dairy house with two plates or basins, covered in white tea-towels, containing dinner for him and his mother. It was as easy to cook for seven as it was for five, she maintained, and Jesse gave her extra money to buy food because of it.

The extra bit of cash was useful, but no longer were the Kites as impoverished as when Ben was alive. Jesse had also given Herbert a handsome rise and he was earning good money now for a lad of fifteen. Henzey had just received another rise and, next Monday, Alice was due to start work in the offices of Bean Cars at Waddams Pool, just half a mile away. It meant that Maxine

461

could stay on at school till she was sixteen. She entertained ideas of becoming a professional cellist and, if Lizzie could afford for her to go to a college of music when the time came, she said she would be happy to allow it.

Alice found working for a living entirely preferable to being at school. Eventually she wanted to become a private secretary; it held such glamorous appeal. To begin with, however, she was content to do filing and running into the factory with memoranda and works orders. Even for a girl it was fascinating to watch motor-cars at various stages of construction.

Alice was not without admirers herself. She was petite and pretty. Although she and Henzey were sisters, you could have been forgiven for not connecting them. Henzey was about four inches taller at five feet six inches, and their colouring was different. Even at fourteen, Alice, like Henzey, was a fine-looking young woman, but more like her mother than either of her sisters.

When it came to dancing, the new national obsession, Henzey and Alice were no different from other young people. Due to their ever-increasing interest they practised, listening to dance music on the wireless in the front room, with the sofa and the table moved to one side. Roller skating offered similar pleasures. Henzey had been to the rink many times with Jack Harper, her latest boyfriend, and Alice with her school friends, so both could roller skate reasonably well. They decided to go together one Friday evening in early September when Henzey, in crisis again with Jack, had declined an invitation to go for a walk with him in the castle grounds. At the skating rink they met two other young men, well heeled and well spoken.

The following Saturday, Lizzie found herself in the street at the bottom of the entry being charmed by the same two charmers, both in their early twenties, standing by a gleaming black motorcar. They were taking the girls to the twenty-first birthday party of one of them.

'Don't forget what we agreed, Henzey,' Lizzie called as Henzey climbed into the car. 'Alice is in your charge, and I want you back here by midnight at the very latest.'

She saw Henzey roll her eyes with embarrassment as the car pulled away.

Lizzie was concerned about Henzey. She was sixteen, and her stunning looks ensured that practically every man she passed in the street turned his head. Men would always be attracted to her, and that was her worry. Not all men were honourable; not all men were gentlemen. She hoped, prayed, that Henzey would not be like her. Lizzie saw herself as a woman of easy virtue, even though her virtue was corrupted with the best of intentions. Thus, she was beginning to judge Henzey by her own past behaviour; beginning to fear that Henzey was old enough, physically and mentally, to find herself in situations where she could be taken advantage of. If she got into trouble it would be calamitous; an utter tragedy. She must grab every opportunity, therefore, to coach her, and ensure that she was in no doubt what could happen.

463

So it was ironic that, whilst her two oldest daughters had been ferried back home before their deadline – albeit after a thoroughly eventful evening – and were now tucked up safely in bed, Lizzie entered the back door with her own stockings in her pocket, adamant that one wayward woman in the family was more than enough.

On the third Tuesday in March 1929, Donald Clark was called to the bedside of young Emmeline Bishop. She'd been suffering from a bout of influenza. Prior to his visit, May had not been feeling well either, and she reckoned that a hot bath would do her and her daughter the world of good. Accordingly, she fetched in the tin bath from the brewhouse and put it on the hearth. When she'd filled it with water she helped Emmie in first, telling her to have a good soak. May saw to it that they both had a stiff measure of brandy beforehand to make them feel better and, unfortunately, as a result, they both fell asleep, May in an armchair, Emmie in the bath. When May awoke two hours later, the bath water was as cold as if it had been drawn from the Dudley Canal, and Emmie was lying in it comatose. The girl was overweight, but May, unable to wake her, managed to lift her out onto the rug and dry her off. She warmed her in front of the fire, and when Joe returned home they put her to bed and sent for Donald Clark.

'Pneumonia, I'm afraid, May,' Donald said. 'Keep her warm, apply hot linseed poultices regularly to her chest and her back and, when she coughs anything up, don't let her swallow it under any circumstances. Get her to spit it into a rag, then throw it in the fire straight away.'

'D'you reckon as she'll wake up soon, Donald?' Joe asked. 'It's as if she's had a bang over the yed and been knocked out. I don't like seeing her like that.'

'It's my opinion, Joe, that she'll wake when she's warmed through thoroughly. She's actually suffering the effects of shock from the cold right now.'

'You'll have to tell me, Donald,' May cried, wringing her hands, 'whether she'd already got the pneumonia afore she went in the bath, or whether the bath's caused it. I feel that guilty I could break me heart. Tell me the truth, Donald. I want to know the truth.'

'Oh, May, there's no need to feel guilty. Pneumonia was present before she had the bath. It's my opinion she's had a bout of flu and it's weakened her considerably. It's hard to say how much she was weakened amidst all her other problems. And she can't tell you either. Now it's developed into this. Have you two been feeling ill as well?'

'I've been off the hooks, Donald,' May confessed. 'It's as if me legs have been kicked from under me, and I've had the headache summat vile.'

'You've had the headache summat vile every night since our Emmie's been born, May, to hear you talk. That's nothing afresh.'

'It strikes me you've had this flu as well, May. Look, I'll call in tomorrow morning and have another look at Emmie. Till then, do as I've said.'

As Joe escorted Donald down the stairs and to the back door May remained with Emmie, sitting anxiously at her bedside. She'd never said anything to Joe, but she'd often wondered whether Emmie's mental state might have been avoided in the first place. Deep in her heart she blamed Annie Soap and her lack of competence at being able to deliver a child into the world unless it was a straightforward birth. She recalled the animosity she'd felt towards Lizzie for insisting on having Donald Clark to each of her confinements, and saw now that Lizzie had been wise. If only she'd been as wise herself. If only she'd been less defiant to common sense, less eager to criticise her sister-in-law as over-cautious, less disparaging of the abilities of Donald Clark, her daughter might be well today, and normal. The more contact she had now with the alcoholic doctor, the more she admired his ability and his manner, and overlooked his drinking. Profound feelings of guilt would occupy her till her dying day because of Emmie's condition, whether she recovered from the pneumonia or not.

Outside on the back yard, Joe and Donald were deep in conversation, their voices low. 'What d'you reckon, Donald? I know pneumonia's enough to frit you to death, but d'you think she'll pull through?'

'I can't see into the future, Joe. You know as well as I do that as many people die from it as get over it. Sometimes the stronger ones die and the weaker ones survive. Look after her as best you can, and pray that she recovers. You can do no more. And convince May not to blame herself, whatever happens... And Joe ... if you feel unwell yourself, get to bed and rest.'

'Thanks, Donald. We'll see you tomorrow, then. I'd better pop round our Lizzie's and tell her the news.'

A week and a half later Henzey sat and recalled dreamily two hours she'd spent earlier that Wednesday afternoon in 'The Station Hotel's' lounge bar with a wealthy young man called Billy Witts. Ever since she'd met him Henzey cherished a dream that this would grow into something more than mere friendship. She'd had two glasses of Champagne today, celebrating her birthday a day early, and it made her feel so romantic. It made them both feel romantic. They'd talked and held hands, and she felt close to him. She imagined romantic evenings over candlelit dinners, visits to smart night-clubs in Birmingham, to theatres, art galleries. She imagined hot summer days with picnics in green meadows dotted with daisies and buttercups in the Worcestershire country-side; walks in parks among beautiful flowers and shrubs, and garden parties at the smart homes of his well-to-do friends. A whole new world could be opening up.

'I'm just popping round to see Donald Clark, our Henzey,' her mother said, interrupting her day-dream. 'He's next door.'

Henzey tried to gather her senses. 'Oh. Is Beccy

467

Crump poorly then?'

'Wake up, Henzey. How long has Emmie been poorly?'

'Oh, 'course. Sorry, I wasn't thinking. How's she been today?'

She felt guilty that she hadn't thought about poor Emmie once because of Billy.

'I don't know. That's why I'm going round.'

'Shall I come with you?'

'No. Peel the potatoes for me, please.'

So as Henzey sat, euphoric, Lizzie went out worried. She walked into the street and saw Donald Clark as he was getting into his car. She called him, and he leaned his elbows on the roof of the Morris and peered over the top with a pleasant smile.

'Hello, Lizzie! Nice to see you. How are things?'

'That's what I want to see you about, Donald. How's our Emmeline?'

He shook his head. His lank, grey hair ruffled in the breeze, and there was concern on his florid face. 'Not good.' His voice was little more than a whisper. 'There's little I can do, and God knows, May and Joe are doing all they can.'

'Oh, it's a crying shame,' Lizzie said. 'Donald, d'you mind if we sit inside your motor for a minute? I won't keep you.'

''Course I don't mind.' He walked round and opened the passenger door for her, and Lizzie sat inside. He got in beside her. 'Normally the tenth day is critical, as you know. In Emmie's case that's tomorrow.'

'Oh, Lord! Our Henzey's birthday.'

'Yes, of course. I ought never to forget it, had I? Your first confinement. Good God, Lizzie, how long's it been?'

'Well she'll be seventeen, and quite the young lady now, as I daresay you've noticed.'

'Oh, I've noticed all right. You can't help but notice her. You must be proud of her, Lizzie.'

'Oh, I am, I am. Our Henzey's grown up too quick, though. I do worry about her.'

'What worries you?'

'Oh, that she's ever likely to turn out like me. I see myself in her when I was a young madam. Breaking my neck to get at lads, I was. How I never got pregnant with Ben in the days before we got married I'll never know. It was more by luck than common sense. We always intended to be careful, but you know how it is when you're young and in love. Too often we'd get carried away. Lord, the shame I would've brought on my mother is nobody's business.'

'Well now, Lizzie, that's quite a confession for a woman to make, even to her doctor. And you think that Henzey will be the same?'

'Maybe not, Donald. I hope not, at any rate. I just worry in case she is. I don't think she's got a sweetheart even at the moment, but I don't want her to turn out like me.'

'She strikes me as being very level-headed, Lizzie – very sensible. I honestly don't think you've got much to worry about. Besides, girls are so much more aware of the risks these days, and less inhibited about doing something about it – even talking about it to the likes of me. We live in a different world to when you were a

469

young girl, Lizzie. There's been a war, and times have changed. Moral values have changed. In any case, you've made certain she's been brought up properly, despite the hardship and the handicaps.'

She smiled at Donald wistfully and nodded. 'It'll worry our Henzey to death about Emmie, specially it being her birthday. 'Tis to be hoped the poor soul gets better.'

''Tis to be hoped she does, Lizzie, but she's losing ground. I've seen a fair few of these cases, but Emmie's really poorly. She's been weakened so much already.'

'Maybe this isn't the time to mention it, then, Donald, but I want to come and see you at your surgery one of the days, if you don't mind.'

'Of course, Lizzie. Whenever you want, you know that. What's the problem?'

'I think I'm pregnant again.'

Chapter 25

Emmeline Bishop died, aged fourteen, on Henzey's seventeenth birthday. It was a bitter blow to Joe and May, who nursed her and tended her with the utmost devotion throughout her restricted life. They loved their daughter dearly. The Kites, too, mourned her death and, according to the number of houses in Cromwell Street that had curtains drawn, so did many others.

The one person, though, whom Emmie's death

had clearly not yet touched, as everyone thought it would, was Henzey. Lizzie expected it to be particularly poignant for her since the death occurred on her birthday, but her eldest daughter seemed to have withdrawn to a world of her own. A happy world, too, by the looks of it, for she kept smiling unaccountably for such a sad occasion. The unexpected appearance of a beautiful pearl necklace, about which she'd said nothing, and a birthday card from somebody called Billy taking precedence over the rest on the mantelpiece, suggested her daughter must be in love. It was not difficult to recognise the signs.

Lizzie, perplexed with worry and disappointment at her own predicament, awaited her impending visit to Donald Clark's surgery. At thirty-nine, and her youngest daughter now fourteen, she was unhappy that the whole world would sneer at what she and Jesse had been up to. Fancy being caught out at her age! The jokes and mockery would be unmerciful, however good-humoured, and it was certain that her son and daughters would be the innocent victims of plenty irreverent gossip. And all because of last Christmas Day; because she would have bet anything that that was when she caught. Jesse was to have his Christmas dinner with the Kites, but together they'd taken Ezme a meal and a glass of sherry. They'd already had a tipple with May and Joe, and were feeling frisky. It seemed as good a time as any. They were alone in the dairy house – the only time they were likely be alone for days – Ezme couldn't hear, and she was safely in bed wolfing her Christmas dinner. Lord, if only it were possible to turn back the clock and undo it. It was almost as silly as being caught with Stanley Dando's child.

Her biggest worry was how her children would take it. The shame of having to confess that she and Jesse would have to get married would be unbearable. Most of all she felt for young Herbert. He was coming sixteen, and she could imagine the sort of leg-pulling he would have to put up with, about his mother and the milkman. She tried not to think about it. The truth was, she didn't want the responsibility of another child; not at her time of life, when her children were grown up and she was waiting for them to get wed in their turn and move on. She didn't want another child when she was so looking forward to spending the rest of her life comfortably and quietly with Jesse. Maybe it was a selfish attitude, but the next child in her arms ought to be a grandchild, and not for a few years yet. At least a grandchild could be handed back. The thought of another grizzling baby at her breasts, restricting her for years, did not appeal. It did not appeal at all.

The situation was worsened by the grim prospect of having to care for old Ezme when they married. Jesse, to his credit, but also to his detriment, had tried to avoid that. He knew that in some ways it would be like the old days for Lizzie looking after Ben and the children. They had both assumed all that was behind her.

The following day, Friday, Lizzie called to see Donald Clark at his surgery. He agreed she was almost certainly pregnant and, with a roar of misplaced laughter, congratulated her. Lizzie wasn't particularly amused, but she did not condemn Donald for seeing the funny side. He made a note in his diary of the likely date of her confinement and promised to be on hand. Next, Jesse had to be told. It was only fair that he should know when she did, so from the doctor's she walked directly to the dairy house.

This could not have come at a worse time. Not only had it come to a head right on Emmie's death, but Alice had brought bad news that the Bean factory might be shutting due to a lack of orders. She would be out of work. To cap it all, Henzey was mooning about like a lovelorn doe over this damned Billy and wanted to invite him home for tea on Sunday. Something told Lizzie that he, whoever he was, was going to be a source of concern... And all too soon she would be worrying about what Alice was getting up to.

Despite her reservations about Henzey and her likely carryings on, Lizzie sensibly believed that condoning her having a boyfriend was more likely to achieve conventionality and good moral behaviour than would prohibiting it. Any constraint would only fuel their ardour, and she had no wish to induce wilful stupidity. Lizzie knew that if Henzey was going to be wayward it was already within her, and she would be so with or without her mother's blessing. The consequences of having one wayward woman in the family was soon to be made manifest to them all, and she sadly realised she would not have set them a good example.

When Lizzie arrived at the dairy house, Jesse was putting shelves up in the brewhouse.

'Come in the sitting room, Jesse. I've got something to tell you,' she said calmly. He duly placed the screwdriver he was holding on top of the wash boiler and followed her. 'I should sit down first, if I were you.' Her level tone made him apprehensive, and he sat down uneasily in the armchair facing the grate, where a coal fire was burning untroubled. 'I've just come from Donald Clark's surgery, Jesse.'

'Why, what's up, my darling? Are you poorly?'

'No, I'm pregnant.'

'Oh, Christ! You're what?' He stirred as if to stand.

Lizzie gently put her hand on his shoulder. 'You heard. I'm pregnant.'

He gave nothing away in his expression. He did not know whether to show happiness or sorrow. He did not really know how Lizzie felt about it for, although she'd told him she'd missed a couple of periods, it did not seem feasible that she should be pregnant; she had not seemed unduly concerned either, so they'd never discussed the possibility in any depth. He'd considered it many times, though, and he wasn't sorry. He wasn't sorry at all. In fact he was relieved, for this was less of a trauma than he might have expected from Lizzie's ominous tone. The thought of a child of his own, presented by the woman he loved, did not appal him. Rather, it appealed.

'Well thank the Lord for that. It means we can get wed straight off. But you don't look very

474

pleased, Lizzie. Don't you want the child?'

'I can do without it, Jesse.' She sat on the arm of his chair, her hand still on his shoulder. 'I hadn't exactly counted on having any more. No, Jesse, I don't want it, but if you're happy about it, I reckon I can accept it. What really bothers me is what folks'll say. We shall come in for a lot of sarcasm, and I certainly don't want my kids upset.'

'I reckon the kids'll be pleased. The three girls will bring up this baby. We won't get a look in. All young madams are as soft as tuppence when it comes to babies.'

'Well let's hope you're right. They say the Lord works in mysterious ways. He takes one away with one hand, and gives back with another. It's only a pity it isn't May who's having it. It'd take her mind off Emmie a bit. I feel that sorry for her and Joe.'

'Its a crying shame, Lizzie, and no two ways.' He paused, allowing time for this great news to sink in. 'When shall we tell everybody we're about to get wed?'

'We could've told them tomorrow night at our Henzey's birthday party, but we'd best postpone that till after the funeral now. Let's tell your mother first... But I don't want my kids to know yet that I'm pregnant. I'll tell them that when I feel ready.'

He said, 'In the meantime I'd better sort it out with the vicar. The sooner the better, eh?' He tapped her right knee and winked boyishly at her, and his huge moustache stretched across his handsome face as he grinned.

'The sooner the better.' Her expression was less intense now. 'There's a lot of work to be done getting this house ready before we can move in. I mean, look at this room. It's hardly homely, is it? It's bare, hardly any furniture in it, bar this old three piece. Look at the curtains as well. Mind you, at least it's clean now.'

'Well, I ain't short of a bob or two, Lizzie. We can soon remedy all this. Do with it as you will. The kids can muck in, and all. I'll get Bert Foxall to come an pipe running water into the scullery, save going to the brewhouse for it. We'll have a new gas stove put in, and while we're at it, we might as well have a new water geyser over the sink.'

'Is there any chance of having one of them inside lavatories, Jesse? Or even a proper bath-room like Sylvia's got? We could turn one of the bedrooms into a bathroom, couldn't we? It's enough to freeze your backside numb having to sit on a cold plank of wood outside in the privy... What are you laughing at?'

'The thought of you with your frock up round your back and the wind whistling under the door, ruffling your drawers. My God, we don't want your drawers billowing out like a spinnaker and blowing you to the top o' Cromwell Street, do we? Like a ship in full sail.'

She laughed with him but, after a second or two, she was serious again. 'I wonder what your mother'll have to say about it when we tell her, Jesse? I'm dreading it.'

'There ain't a lot she can say, Lizzie. Whatever she might say won't alter anything.'

The following Sunday at tea, Sylvia Atkinson picked out an egg custard from the silver cake-stand on her spotless, white damask table cloth and placed it delicately on her Minton Willow Pattern tea plate. She took a knife and cut it into segments, then put one in her mouth. As she tasted its sweet richness she refilled her elegant cup that matched the rest of the fine bone china adorning her table. She looked up at Kenneth.

'More tea?'

'Yes, please, Mother.' He slid his cup and saucer closer to her, and she poured.

'What would you do this evening, Kenneth, if I said there was no need for you to go to church with me?' Sylvia asked, holding another segment of egg custard between her well-manicured fingers.

'I might read.'

She put down what was left of her egg custard and wiped her fingers on her napkin. 'Well, you needn't come to church if you don't want. I have some sick visiting to do afterwards. I doubt if it will interest you at all.'

'Grandma Sarah again?'

'Not this time. You remember old Mrs Clancey? She's long overdue a visit. She had a stroke months ago, and she's still bedridden, poor dear. I'd like to see her again. I always got on well with her. Will you be all right by your-self?'

'Of course I'll be all right. I am fifteen you know. Will Edgar go with you?'

'I was hoping he'd take me.'

477

'And he won't mind?'

'Why should he mind?'

Kenneth didn't like Edgar very much, but he used to like Jesse Clancey enormously. Jesse always had such a casual, easy way about him, a far cry from the uppishness of his mother. Kenneth often privately wondered what Jesse used to see in his mother. They were so different. He was approachable, obliging, but she was always stand-offish. and formal; he spoke with an accent like everybody else, as if it were the most natural thing in the world, while she always tried to sound posh like those people on the wireless. Jesse was cheerful, always ready to share a laugh and a joke, but she was usually serious, superior, as if laughing was common. It got on Kenneth's nerves a bit that his mother was the way she was. She seemed so affected, so detached from real life. And Kenneth felt ashamed sometimes when other boys followed behind her in the streets, imitating her by swinging their backsides and thrusting their noses in the air.

For years now Sylvia had been a regular churchgoer at St. Thomas's at the top of the town. It was the church in which she married, and it was more expedient to worship there than at St. John's. There she was introduced, shortly after James's death, to Edgar Timmins, a widower some ten years older than herself. They'd been on friendly terms ever since, both giving much time to the church, until Jesse Clancey once more let her down so badly, when the pace of their friendship seemed to accelerate and their meetings became more secular.

Edgar was a businessman, with his own successful haberdashery shops in Dudley and Wolverhampton. He was well-spoken, which Sylvia much preferred, and he was, she knew, an honourable man. His wife had died tragically during surgery eight years earlier, and now his only daughter was married to a pit manager and living in Cannock. Edgar shared many of Jesse Clancey's qualities, like affability and candour but, whereas Jesse was well read and didn't manifest his culture, Edgar flaunted it. He was refined, smartly conventional and, perhaps, even old fashioned in his outlook as well as his dress; he still wore spats and a bowler hat for church. But more to the point, Edgar was seeking a wife. Coincidentally, Sylvia was seeking to give up the job she'd felt obliged to take in order to maintain the standard of living she'd grown used to. After all, work was unbecoming. Work did not befit a lady.

Now she wondered what the dickens she had seen in Jesse Clancey all these years. Being her first real love wasn't everything after all. Their differences were unbridgeable. Oh, she had believed that with some gentle coaching he could have been exalted to her standards, but she'd tried and tried, and Jesse resisted exaltation. Furthermore, she could not see herself swilling out milk-churns or washing down his milk floats in rubber boots and a cow-gown, nor living in that dilapidated mausoleum they called the dairy house. She could not see herself willing to be woken up at four in a morning when he roused for work. She deserved a more genteel, more civilised way of life, and with Edgar that's exactly what she would get.

It came as no great surprise to learn eventually that Jesse had finally taken up with her second cousin, Lizzie Bishop, although it riled her to contemplate it. Strange how she never thought of her as Lizzie Kite. She must be thirty-nine now. Funny how she never saw her. She was most likely fat these days, like old Aunt Eve, and held together by stout corsets. Good Lord, what must Jesse see in her? They lived little more than half a mile apart, and yet she had not set eyes on her for years. She wouldn't know Lizzie's children if she saw them, except for Herbert, of course, who used to collect the milk money.

So Lizzie had finally got Jesse. Who'd have thought it after so long? Maybe she'd been carrying a torch for him ever since that New Year's Eve at Joe and May Bishop's, all those years ago. Sylvia didn't have to remind herself that she was heartbroken then because of her. She had never forgiven Lizzie for it. Never could. Never would. It hardly mattered now, of course, now that she had Edgar. It was so long ago. Yet the bitterness lingered in her heart, like rancid butter lingered on her tongue.

'Damn this weather,' Sylvia exclaimed, throwing herself inelegantly into the passenger seat of Edgar's black Clyno. They'd just left Evensong at St. Thomas's. She shook her umbrella forcefully to rid it of the rain clinging to it, closed it up, and shut the car door. 'You're sure you don't mind taking me to see Ezme Clancey?'

480

Edgar adjusted his bowler hat, glancing at himself in the rear-view mirror, and pulled the starter. 'Not at all. I'm curious to meet the old girl.'

The engine rattled into life and they began moving forward, away from the church. Sylvia waved to the verger in his black cape as he pushed his bicycle across the shining, wet street in front of them, scurrying to get out of their way. Edgar switched on the windscreen wipers.

'Oh, Ezme's quite a character – or at least she was. Calls a spade a spade, and she's not too concerned about who she might upset with her forthrightness. She used to be quite a pianist and organist, too. I remember she used to play the organ occasionally at St. John's years ago, and I believe she was still giving lessons up until her stroke. Very active woman.'

'You evidently liked her.'

'I've always admired her. She liked me, as well. Just because I no longer have anything to do with her son doesn't mean I have to forsake the friendship I had with her.' She turned to look at him for reassurance. 'Don't you think so, Edgar?'

He wiped the inside of the misting windscreen with the back of his leather-gloved hand. 'Oh, I agree. If you get on well it's a miserable shame not to keep in touch. Good relationships are often so hard to form.'

'I wrote to her, you know, when Jesse and I realised nothing could come of our ... relationship. I explained that although I would only be able to see her very occasionally I would often think about her.'

But Sylvia, deep in her heart, wanted to know what Ezme thought of Jesse's relationship with Lizzie. She knew Ezme had no love for Lizzie, nor Lizzie's mother, and curiosity about how she was handling the situation was consuming her. After years of contempt, could Ezme suddenly turn and confess to liking the woman after all? Sylvia thought not, and it would give her immense satisfaction to know it for sure. It would give her enormous pleasure to be assured that there never could be any woman but herself worthy of Jesse.

'And she wrote back, Sylvia?'

'Oh, yes, she wrote back. Said how distressed she was that Jesse and I had parted. I wouldn't be surprised if the stress of it all didn't induce her stroke.'

'You never know. But if Jesse is there tonight, are you going to mind?'

'Oh, I'm a bit apprehensive, I have to admit. I don't want that to get in the way of my regard for Ezme, though. Mind you, it all ended hugely amicably.'

Edgar changed down a gear to turn into the wide, climbing street known as Waddam's Pool. Spray from the narrow wheels was hitting the underside of the car and sounded like running water within.

'Is Jesse stepping out with anybody else yet?'

It was a question Sylvia did not welcome. She had not volunteered any information before because she felt it might reflect badly on herself – that Jesse had rejected her for her cousin, who was as common as muck. But now, since she had

482

been asked, she had to answer.

'Oh, yes, didn't I tell you? He's courting my widowed cousin now, Lizzie Bishop.'

'Ah, well. Keep it in the family I always say.' Edgar laughed at his own joke as the car chugged up the hill.

'Distant family, Edgar,' she said scornfully. 'I haven't seen Lizzie for years. I wouldn't know her now, and I don't want to. Frankly, I don't admire her... Never have... Take the next turning on the left, Edgar.'

Lizzie did not like Billy Witts when she met him. He was in his middle to late twenties – hard to guess exactly – but far too old and too experienced for Henzey. To his credit he was polite, even charming, and it was easy to see why her daughter was drawn to him. He was not a bad-looking fellow, she thought – not that looks were everything – but did he really have to show off his acquired wealth with a tasteless display of gold rings? He was much too flashy. And, of course, he had a motor-car; a rakish rag-topped contraption, which must be a waste of time in this weather. Herbert admired it covetously, as did Alice and Maxine. But Lizzie was apprehensive; Henzey was still impressionable enough to be seduced by the trappings of wealth.

So she was pleased when Jesse arrived to accompany her to church. It wasn't a common occurrence nowadays, but the banns were to be read at Evensong. Because of the wind and rain, which had not ceased all day for the second Sunday running, Billy nobly offered to drive them to church, save them having to sit through the service soaking wet. Afterwards they intended to break the news to his mother that they were to be married on the last Sunday in April, and Lizzie was growing more nervous about telling her. She had not yet mentioned to her own family that there were to be wedding bells in a month; she wanted to survive the ordeal of telling Ezme first.

As they left the church afterwards, the Reverend Mr John Mainwaring warmly congratulated Lizzie on the splendid news, and said how much he was looking forward to her wedding day.

'Well, 'tis to be hoped the weather's picked up by then,' she commented.

'Indeed, indeed,' was the vicar's stoical reply. 'But April can be a treacherous month weatherwise.'

On the porch steps Jesse unfurled his big, black umbrella, and Lizzie took his arm as they began the puddle-ridden walk back to the dairy house. She told him of her concern and her mistrust for this chap Billy Witts, and that Henzey's affection for him was worrying her.

'Don't be judge and jury yet, my darling,' Jesse counselled. 'The lad's got some good points. Just 'cause he's made a shilling or two don't mean he's a thief and a liar. He was thoughtful enough to bring us to church in all this rain, wasn't he?'

'I'd have been a sight more impressed if he'd been thoughtful enough to fetch us back.'

Jesse chuckled. 'And then you'd have sworn he was trying to get round you. No, the lad seems all right to me. If he's come from nothing and made a pile of money I don't begrudge it him. At least it shows he's got a good head on his shoulders.'

'Yes, but it's not his head I'm worrying about, Jesse... I don't want to see our Henzey blinded to his faults by money. I think he's fly.'

As they walked on the narrow footpath past Westley's Brass Foundry, they saw a car pass along Cromwell Street at its junction with Price Street, the splashes from its wheels glistening momentarily by the light of the gas lamps.

'He's no more fly than that other chap she used to see. Him from Holly Hall.'

'Jack Harper?'

'Jack Harper. Except he was as poor as a nailer's bribe. Your Alice was sweet on him, as well, I could tell. Couldn't take her eyes off him.'

'Oh, Lord. Alice as well. 'Course she's getting to that age. I shall be well hoped-up with three daughters to worry about.'

'Yes, and who knows you ain't carrying another?'

'Oh, let it be a lad, please, dear Lord. Lads are never such a worry. Look at our Herbert.'

'Well, he gets more like his father every day. You can't deny as he's a good-looking lad. Works hard and all. I shall take him into the business. As a partner, I mean. When he's older.'

Rain was still drumming incessantly on the umbrella when they reached the top of Price Street. It was a shorter route than going by way of Brown Street, but a steeper climb at the end.

'Two cars in our street, Jesse,' Lizzie com-

485

mented easily. 'We must be on the up and up.'

'Well, one's that Billy's – at your house,' he reminded her.

'And the other's at yours, Jesse.'

'It looks like the one what just passed across the top of Price Street.'

'How can you tell? They all look the same to me.'

'I wonder who it can be, Lizzie? There's only the doctor as I know who's got a car.'

'Well, somebody's paying you a visit. It means we shall have to put off telling your mother again that we're getting married.' She sighed with frustration. 'Oh, Jesse, I did want to get it over and done with.'

'Well, it can only be somebody we know. If we tell her while somebody else is there, she won't pull her jib quite so much.'

'No, she'll just make our lives hell afterwards.'

'But we'll have to tell her. The banns have been called. Folk will be talking about it to your children tomorrow.'

They approached the dairy house without saying another word. When they drew level with the car Jesse stopped to look at it.

'Well, it ain't the doctor's car. The doctor's got a Morris. This is a Clyno.'

They walked through the entry and opened the verandah door. Jesse shook his umbrella outside while Lizzie took off her coat, leaving on her new cloche hat. She wore a knitted dress Jesse had bought her for her birthday, very fashionable, knee-length and like a tube. It was cream, a colour that suited her, with a row of small brown buttons at the back and a brown band an inch above the hem. The waistline was low, and her bosom was modishly flattened. Her slenderness, belying her years and the fact that she'd given birth to five children, gave her the look that all women were striving for. But of course, it would not be for long.

She went into the scullery where Jesse had left the gas light to burn when he went out. He followed her, having shaken his wet coat and left it hanging in the verandah.

'I'll put the kettle on seeing as we've got company,' he said, and went out to the brewhouse to fill it.

When he returned, Lizzie said: 'Whoever's come must have let themselves in and gone straight upstairs to your mother. We ought to go up and say hello first, and make sure she's all right.'

So she followed him upstairs, across the landing, and he opened the door to Ezme's room, which was unusually ajar. Normally it was left wide open.

At first Lizzie did not recognise Sylvia.

'Sylvia!' Jesse exclaimed. 'This is a surprise... I never expected...'

'Hello, Jesse.' Sylvia coloured up, but maintained a dignified smile. 'I thought it was time I called to pay my respects to your mother. She looks well, I think... Oh, this is Edgar Timmins, a friend of mine... Edgar, Jesse Clancey.'

Edgar got up from the wicker chair he was occupying and shook Jesse's hand.

'Nice to meet you, Edgar. And this is Lizzie.'
He turned to her and winked reassurance.

Lizzie stepped forward. She smiled tentatively, and shook Edgar's hand.

'Delighted to meet you, Lizzie,' he said pleasantly. 'I understand you and Sylvia are related.'

'We're second cousins.' Lizzie's eyes met Sylvia's for the first time. 'Hello, Sylvia,' she said uneasily. 'It's been a long time.'

'A good many years, Lizzie.' Her tone was impassive, giving nothing away as to her feelings. 'And how are your family?'

Sylvia studied her cousin briefly. But, for all her indifference, she couldn't help but admire what she saw. She wanted to tell Lizzie she'd barely changed in all those years; she wanted to say that she expected she'd have aged considerably. Yet she said no such thing. Such compliments to Lizzie Bishop would never come from her lips.

'They're grown up now,' Lizzie replied economically. 'And yours?'

'Kenneth's grown up, too. All too quick.'

Lizzie felt uneasy with Sylvia and did not really wish to pursue this forced conversation. Jesse sensed the chill and, to break the brief embarrassed silence, he turned to his mother.

'I've put the kettle on, Mother. D'you want a cup of tea?' He pretended to put a cup to his mouth so she would understand.

'And a cheese an' onion sandwich. I'm clammed to death.'

'I'll do it,' Lizzie said, glad of the excuse to be away from Sylvia's cold scrutiny. 'Would everybody else like tea?'

Sylvia looked at Edgar for his response. 'I think maybe we should be going.'

'You've only just got here,' Jesse protested. 'Stop for a cup of tea, at least.'

'We're in no rush,' Sylvia said. 'Thank you. That would be very nice.'

Lizzie trotted downstairs and into the scullery, and started putting out the crockery and preparing Ezme's supper. While she worked, she pondered Sylvia. The years had been kind to her. She was still lean, like Aunt Sarah, if a bit thicker at the waist and broader at the backside, but she had an undeniable grace. Her face was still attractive, although carrying a few more lines. Her nose was bigger than she remembered it, though, and emphasised by the way she wore her hair brushed back tightly and pinned in a roll at the back, in the old fashioned way. Her dress, too, was old fashioned and quite long, but redeemed by its excellent quality. Sylvia seemed to be stuck in the style of the days of the war when she was a younger woman, making few concessions to current fashion. In the same way, Edgar suited her. His appearance suggested he was stuffy, but he seemed pleasant enough, and Lizzie felt she could not dislike him just because he was with Sylvia.

She returned to Ezme's bedroom carrying a tray, and placed it on the dressing table. She began arranging the cups and saucers and spoons, conscious that Sylvia was watching.

'The district nuss is as good as gold, Sylvia,' Ezme croaked, breaking the focus. 'Good as gold.

489

Comes in every day.'

'And Lizzie's as good as gold,' Jesse affirmed, knowing his mother would never admit as much. 'She sends a cooked dinner round for her every night, and does all the cleaning.'

Lizzie was pouring out the tea. 'Everybody take milk?'

'How often does the doctor call?' Sylvia asked Ezme, and had to repeat herself.

'Oh, every wik. Comes in every wik. He's bin as good as gold, an' all.'

Lizzie handed the plate of cheese sandwiches to Ezme, and placed a cup of tea on her bedside table. Then she picked up the tray bearing the other cups and offered them around. Sylvia took hers, thanking Lizzie pleasantly, and poured in a spoonful of sugar.

Jesse was as determined as Lizzie to tell his mother that very night that they were about to get married. He was proud of the fact, and he was also keen to assert his love for his bride-to-be in the face of Sylvia. This presented a golden opportunity. This way, Sylvia could hardly claim that he still had his cap set at her, which he believed she was ever likely to do. To tell his mother now, with Sylvia unexpectedly present, would leave her in no doubt as to where his real love lay. There could be no misunderstanding.

'There's er … there's something me and Lizzie want to tell Mother tonight, Sylvia, and it'd be unfair on her to wait any longer to tell her,' he began. Lizzie felt the tray trembling in her hands as she proffered tea to Edgar, who looked up and smiled. 'So as I see it, you might as well hear it as well.' He, too, took a cup and saucer from the tray, spooned in sugar, and stirred it nervously as everyone waited to hear what he wanted to say. He waved to gain his mother's attention. Ezme looked up, a crust hanging out of her mouth, about to be savaged by the uneven, discoloured tombstones that were once a decent set of teeth. 'Lizzie and me are getting married next month.' There. The truth was out.

'What say?'

'I said, Lizzie and me are getting married next month.'

'Well, congratulations, Lizzie,' Edgar said with a look of genuine pleasure.

Lizzie smiled self-consciously, but couldn't help glancing at Sylvia. But Sylvia avoided her eyes and scrutinised Jesse instead, her gaze as cold as granite.

Ezme had still not heard, but she had picked up everybody's reactions: Edgar's smiling face; the bitter resentment in Sylvia's glance; Lizzie looking abashed, but with bright, expectant eyes; and Jesse, her only son, watching her own expression with apprehension. Something monumental was being announced. She dearly hoped it was not what she had dreaded more than anything else in the world.

'What did yer say?' she asked again, suspiciously. 'I aer' catched what yo' said.'

Jesse sighed with frustration and put down his cup and saucer. 'Married,' he yelled. 'Christ, it's like talking to the bloody wall.' He wanted to get this over and done. He pointed to Lizzie, and then to himself, and his mother watched his telling movements. He took Lizzie's hand and drew an imaginary ring around the third finger of her left hand.

'Yo'm gettin' wed to Lizzie?' Her face bore a look of absolute horror.

He nodded, relieved. She knew at last.

Ezme shook her head and choked as if from shock, sending wet pieces of bread and cheese over her counterpane. 'No, yo' ai',' she barked. 'Yo' cor'... Never.'

Jesse nodded back in cool defiance. 'Yes, we can.'

'Over my jead body.'

Jesse let out a little laugh of frustration and shook his head, signifying that this was the response he'd anticipated. He took Lizzie's hand and squeezed it reassuringly. 'We're getting married, and there's nothing you can do about it.'

Ezme couldn't hear, but his challenging look gave her the gist of it. 'If yo' think yo'm marryin' 'er...' she wagged what remained of her sandwich contemptuously at Lizzie, 'yo'd best think again. I'll mek sure yo' doh. I'll get to the church some road or other, and shout out as I've got just cause and himpediment why yo' shouldn't.'

Lizzie wanted the floorboards to slide open and consume her, presuming Sylvia's intense satisfaction at witnessing her excruciating ordeal. Why was Jesse so adamant in choosing this moment when Sylvia was right there? Was it just to snape the girl? He could easily have waited till she'd gone.

'I knew she'd be like this. Cantankerous old

492

bugger.' He turned to his mother. 'What just cause and impediment? It's nothing to do with you. I was only telling you out of common courtesy, 'cause the banns have been read today. We're getting married and that's that.'

'I'll stop it' appenin',' Ezme shrieked. 'I'll send for the vicar and tell him.'

'You're too late, Mother. We've already seen the vicar. The banns have been published. It's all fixed.'

'The banns? The banns, did yer say? The banns am so as anybody with just cause can spake up again' it. An' I shall.'

'You can speak up till you're blue in the face.' Jesse's anger was rising. 'You're a bit too late, though. Lizzie's already pregnant. We've got to get married.' With a look of satisfaction he signed a rounded belly on Lizzie, and Ezme understood at once.

Lizzie thought she heard Sylvia gasp.

'Oh, yo' pair o' bloody fools,' Ezme snarled.

Then Edgar stood up, and hovered hesitantly. 'I think maybe it would be best if Sylvia and I left. I'm sorry to have witnessed this, Lizzie. It must be most embarrassing for you. It certainly is for us... But you can depend on our utmost discretion, I can assure you... Sylvia...'

Sylvia stood up. She sighed heavily. It was such a pity to leave now, just as things were getting so interesting.

'Sit down, the pair o' yer,' Ezme ordered, and the couple sat down again compliantly. 'I want witnesses to this, for fear of anythin' 'appenin' to me. And yo'll do, Sylvia. In fact yo'll do better

493

than anybody. If he'd a-married yo' in the fust place there'd be no need for any o' this malarkey.' She turned angrily to Jesse again, and he noticed a bead of water form in the corner of her eye that begin to trickle down her overwrought face. 'Yo', yer big saft bugger, why d'yer think as I never encouraged yer to goo with Lizzie Bishop, eh? Why d'yer think as I dai' want yer to have anythin' to do with her? Why d'yer think I was so bloody keen for yer to marry Sylvia and get yer out the road, eh? Well, I'll tell yer now, wi' these good folk as me witnesses. Our Jesse, it's 'cause Lizzie's your own flesh and blood. 'Er's your own sister, as God's me judge. Isaac Bishop was your fairther as well as hers'n... And may God forgi' me for me sins.' She broke down, weeping piteously, her face an icon of misery. 'It's a cardinal sin to lie with your sister, our Jesse.'

'My God! And I thought it was because of the dressmaking,' Lizzie said, stunned.

Chapter 26

The rain was ceaseless. It seemed to slap Lizzie's face as if it was her own unforgiving mother, blending with her tears as it ran down her anguished face. She bit her lip to stop herself screaming out into the darkness over what she'd just heard. The whole situation was irredeemable; her love; his love; their whole lives. As she

494

trudged up Cromwell Street she was unaware that she was stepping in puddles, stumbling on uneven cobbles. There was an ice-cold numbness in her mind, and yet her mind was focused, more acutely than ever before, on her own private hell. Her chest stung inside, like bile rising, and her poor heart was hammering, hammering sickeningly in her ears. There was a dull, miserable ache ravaging the pit of her stomach; it was not the child she was carrying, but alarm, fright, and unbounded horror.

She had no idea where she was heading, yet she walked on up Hill Street, oblivious to the downpour, to where it flattened out and you could see for miles on a clear day. She stopped, and stared out into the darkness. On the plain below she could discern just a few twinkling lights; just a few lights out of the many thousands that must be there, but masked by the foulness of the weather. Through the filter of her tears and the driving rain they looked like long pointed stars stretching and contracting animatedly. She sighed, a heaving, desolate sigh, hunched inside her coat, her hands in her pockets. She saw nobody; she heard nobody. The only sounds were the heavy rainfall, sibilant as it splashed the ground, turning puddles into streams, and yet more water spewing onto the footpath from broken guttering on the terrace of houses fifty yards away. She was alone, utterly disorientated, utterly bewildered. As she looked out across the saturated night she realised where she was, but could not remember walking there. It triggered thoughts of that first evening she spent with Ben;

an evening that was to change their lives; an evening that was to change the lives of Jesse and Sylvia. They'd stood here on this very spot. Ben had asked to kiss her, and she'd allowed it; their first ever kiss. She'd huddled to him to keep warm in the crisp, biting cold of that frosty night twenty-one years ago, and they'd looked out across this same valley and watched the clear, bright stars in the sky, had seen the fires of distant furnaces, heard the rumble of far-away machinery, and had been enchanted by it all, and by each other. They had no idea then what the future held in store; what elation; what disaster; what heartache.

An hour or two earlier than that, Jesse had surprised her by expressing his love for her. It was just as well he hadn't told her a week sooner, else she might easily have been tempted. But what good would it have done? What chance would their romance have had then, to be nipped in the bud just the same? Under no circumstances could it have been allowed to flourish. It was always destined to be repressed. Yet prohibiting it might also have brought defiance; an ardent will to meet secretly; and who knows what might have followed from that? She was a young girl then, and love promised so much. It promised so many good and wonderful things. She did not know then that love could also bring unbearable pain and suffering, and scars that time itself could not always heal.

She let out a shuddering sigh, and felt for another handkerchief that she knew was in her pocket. She found it and blew her nose, and then began walking again, slowly, back down Hill Street, towards home. But she could not go home. She could not show herself to her children looking like she felt, with puffed eyes, weeping tears that were impossible to stem. She thought about this love-child growing unbidden in her belly; this poor, incestuous bastard. Who could be to blame? Neither had not known Jesse was her half-brother. Anyway, how could they possibly have known? The shock of that knowledge wrought unmitigated torment. It was impossible to cope with. It might take weeks or months to sink in. But somebody was to blame for the agony this revelation brought, and that somebody had to be her father – or Ezme.

Over the years she had heard rumours and tolerated snide remarks about her father and his womanising, but never had she thought it amounted to anything this serious. He really had deceived Eve, and made a cuckold of old Jack Clancey. How ironic that Jack Clancey's horse had killed him. No wonder there was no remorse in Jack. No wonder he was said not to have grieved. He must surely have known the truth. He was not about to grieve. If he'd planned it all it couldn't have wreaked a more warranted revenge. By all accounts Jack was never fond of Isaac. Now it was plain why. It was plain why nobody else was particularly fond of him either. Except Ezme, of course, who must have been only in her twenties when it all happened.

Lizzie found herself walking past 'The Junction' again, all sorts of possibilities crowding into her mind. One thing was certain. She would

497

have to arrange an abortion. The law allowed it if a child was conceived in incest. It must allow this. This was totally different to the time she was pregnant by Stanley; she had no husband now to assume fatherhood; Jesse was her half brother; she could not marry him. It would be a sin. It was against the law.

She walked past the dairy house, looking, hoping that Jesse might see her and come running out. Before she had left him, after Sylvia and Edgar had gone, he'd cried with her, sobbing pitifully that his dream of spending the rest of his life with her was so cruelly crushed. Then he agreed to let her go. He wanted to find out more about this hideous disclosure from his mother. But he did not come running out now, and she did not go in after him.

She did, however, know where she ought to go to try and seek some peace of mind; to try and find some answers.

The rain was seeping through her coat. She was cold and wet. She could feel a clammy dampness in her hair where it had soaked through her hat. Her stockings clung to her lower legs with a gripping wetness that was rising to her thighs now. Yet it hardly mattered. It was nothing to the discomfort, the degeneration she felt in her heart. She had no idea of the time, but Billy Witts's motorcar was still outside the house. She wouldn't dream of returning home while he was still there. So she hurried past, lest they saw her.

Somebody passing on the other side of the street bid her goodnight as she turned the corner into Price Street, down the steep slope by the brass foundry. Sometime this week she would have to pluck up the courage to see Donald Clark and arrange this abortion. He would be as shocked as she was to learn why. Would the offspring of brother and sister, or father and daughter, be any different from the rest? Why should society be so eager to dislodge from the womb a child thus conceived? Was there something unspeakably evil about such a child? She would ask him. Not that she wanted it. But she would like to know.

Before she knew it Lizzie was walking through the lych gate of the church, past the bell tower and the main door, and into the graveyard beyond, as if drawn to it. In the valley below a locomotive whistled and huffed, and seemed to sigh in profound sympathy as it shunted wagons into a siding. The clatter of its buffers seemed to echo her own life; shunted from relative contentment to abject misery in the time it took to say she was Jesse Clancey's sister. The muddied, overgrown pathway descended, and she picked her way in the darkness between the graves. Fronds of wet, limp grass clung to her legs like tentacles, but she hardly noticed. What little light there was, was being reflected from the distant streets, but there was sufficient for her to find the grave of her mother and father. She felt no fear, alone, surrounded only by the dead; and the dark skeletons of trees dripping water incessantly.

'In loving remembrance of Isaac Bishop,' she recited from memory as she peered into the gloomy void of the headstone, 'who died tragically *and unexpectedly 15th March 1902, aged 59 years. Also of Eve, his wife, who passed away peacefully 3rd December 1915, aged 67. At rest. They have sown the wind. Thy Will be done.'*

Lizzie sat on the soaking wet grave and another spate of tears stung in her eyes, so that she was barely able to discern the bunch of daffodils she'd placed on the grave a few days before. She wondered what other indiscretions, what other heartaches, were so blithely withheld by bland, engraved words on surrounding headstones. *They have sown the wind.* What on earth did it mean? She recalled asking her mother its significance years ago. 'Just a saying from the Bible,' Eve had answered dismissively. So did her poor mother know about her father and Ezme? How could she not know, living so close? And watching Ezme's belly grow big, Eve had stood by him, loyally, no doubt deflecting any criticism or suggestion of infidelity.

'Isaac Bishop, you didn't deserve her,' Lizzie cried out aloud. 'And while you were lying with Ezme, taking your ill-gotten pleasure, did you spare a thought for the likely consequences? Did it ever cross your deceitful, dirty mind that a daughter by your lawful wedded wife might fall in love with a son by your lie-by?' She paused, heaving with distress, her scorn for her father increasing inexorably with every sobbing breath she took. 'I wish to God you were here now so's you could see just how much Jesse and me are hurting.' She snivelled, and wiped her nose again. 'We were to be married, *Father.*' She uttered the word scathingly, contemptibly, her voice rising, quivering. 'I'm carrying *his* child ... my own brother's child... God help me. If only we'd known. If only somebody could've warned us. Mother, Mother, why didn't you warn me?'

She broke down again, her howling sobs overwhelming her words, her handkerchief pressed against her mouth lest her crying be heard. Her eyes were streaming, her nose was running, she shivered with cold and felt utterly demolished. Any chance of happiness was gone. From now on there would be only shame and ridicule.

And then she likened herself to her father. Maybe she'd inherited her wantonness, her easy virtue, from him. She'd behaved no differently. Was one generation ever any different from another? Was not human nature now the same as when Adam had lain with his Eve? And because of this same despicable wantonness, had she not tortured poor Ben over Stanley Dando, in exactly the same way that her father had tortured her mother? Of course she had.

She blew her nose again as her crying subsided. Somehow, this brief communion with her mother and father had elicited some comfort. Her relationship with Jesse could never be the same again, but she realised they would always be close, they would always love each other, if only as brother and sister. Perhaps they could never be lovers again, perhaps they could never wed, but as brother and sister they could live in the same house, be eternal companions... Except that there was a flaw in this assumption: if nobody else knew they were brother and sister they would be deemed to be living in sin; and if word got out that they were brother and sister, then they would be under eternal suspicion of committing incest anyway.

The hard, cold stone of the grave was hurting her backside, and she was wet through to the skin. She shivered and stood up, wondering what time it was. She needed to sit in front of a blazing fire now with hot cocoa laced generously with whisky. A couple of those might enable her to sleep. She thought of her dry night-gown warmed in front of the fire, and her bed snug with clean white sheets. So she picked her way back between the graves, back onto the path, through the lych gate and onto the dimly lit street. As she turned into Cromwell Street from Price Street she could see that Billy's car had gone. With any luck, her family would be in bed.

As she neared her house, Jesse was there to meet her. He'd seen her walking up the street, and decided to intercept her. At once they fell into each other's arms.

'My God, Lizzie, you're wet through.'

She looked up at him, her eyes puffy. 'I've been out in the rain ever since I left you. I've been to Mother and Father's grave – talking to them. D'you think that's the first sign of madness?'

'No. I guessed that's what you'd do. Come in the house and dry out. There's still a lovely fire in the sitting room.'

She was glad of the offer, and nodded. He took her hand and led her through the verandah. In the scullery he took her coat and draped it over the laundry rack. He sent her to the sitting room while he put the kettle on to boil, then joined her and poked that fire to liven it up. Lizzie stood in front of it trying to get warm, but even her knitted dress was wet through.

'Will you unfasten me frock at the back, Jesse? I'll have to take it off a bit to let it dry.'

He did as she requested, moved by their intimacy, heartbroken that it was so futile. She removed her dress, and stood in her camisole and high heel shoes.

'Have you talked to your mother any more?' She hung her dress over the fire guard, realising that it might shrink as a result, but too devastated to care.

'I think she's as upset about it as we are, I honestly do. At first I thought it was just a ruse to stop us getting wed, 'cause she can be a crafty old bugger. But now I know it ain't. There's no doubt as it's the truth, Lizzie ... more's the pity.' His eyes filled and he turned away. 'Oh, what a bloody mess. I still don't know what to make of it.' He seemed utterly defeated.

Lizzie sat in the armchair in front of the fire. 'Did she say anything about my father?'

'You mean our father.'

'Yes, our father which art in heaven ... or hell, more like. That would be the best place for him... Yes, Jesse, our father.'

'Mother's told me quite a bit. She got married when she was twenty – well I already knew that – and she'd been married five years when she started having it off with him. So how old would your father be then?'

'What year were you born, Jesse?'

'Eighteen eighty-one.'

'So if she conceived you in eighteen eighty, say, that'd make Father ... what? ... thirty-seven or thirty-eight. Quite a bit older than your mother.'

'Maybe that was the attraction. You wouldn't think it to look at her now, but she was a fine-looking woman when she was young. Long, fair hair – long enough to sit on – and big, blue eyes.'

'Did she say why she never had any children by your father? – Sorry, I mean by Jack.'

'She reckons he hadn't got one in him. They tried hard, she just said, but in nearly five years she never caught. And then she went and caught with Isaac.'

'Did she say whether Jack knew?'

'He knew all right. She confessed the lot, and he told her if she kept her mouth shut he'd be a father to me.' He sighed heavily.

'Like Ben with that child of mine...'

Jesse nodded, acknowledging the similar circumstances. 'He was a good father to me, you know, Lizzie. He was a good husband to Mother, as well... You know, it don't matter what happens from now on, I shall always think of him as my father. I don't think as I could ever get used to thinking of Isaac Bishop as my father.'

Lizzie shivered and rubbed her bare arms to increase circulation. Jesse remembered the kettle heating up in the scullery, and went out to make a pot of tea. He came back carrying the teapot, two mugs and a half bottle of whisky.

'Let that steep for five minutes, and we'll have a decent cup o' tea,' he said, sitting on the edge of the same armchair as Lizzie. 'It'll warm you up a bit.'

He put his arm around her and she rested her head wearily on his shoulder.

'What shall you do about the child?'

'I shall go to Donald Clark's tomorrow after work and see about getting rid of it,' she answered candidly, looking up at him. 'There's no alternative, is there?'

'Oh, Lizzie, this is a bloody nightmare. I was that happy you were having my child.'

Jesse couldn't help but kiss her. It was sheer force of habit. And with the same force of habit she responded, lingering, savouring his lips. But it was wrong. She knew it was wrong. It was forbidden. She was kissing her own brother ... like a lover again, and she ought to break off. But they had already been lovers. His child was in her belly. Hell would be no hotter for tasting him just once more.

'Oh, Jesse, I know I shouldn't, but I want you.' Shamelessly she eased herself back in the armchair.

'But, Lizzie, my flower,' he sighed, struggling with his conscience.

'Nothing's changed inside me, Jesse. I love you just the same. I wanted you before, and somebody suddenly saying you're my brother doesn't stop me wanting you still... I'm sorry ... It just seems so right.'

'Don't be sorry, my sweetheart. I want you as well... It's just that...'

'I don't think I'll ever feel any different. God, I can't stand to be plagued like this for the rest of my life. Maybe it's a mortal sin, but I can't help feeling the way I do. You're too deep under my skin... Oh, I'm sorry, Jesse.'

'Oh, Lizzie,' he howled, agonised. All these years of longing for her seemed so pointless; such a waste of time. Yet here she was now; his, of her own volition, devoted to him, wanting him.

But cruelly, he must not have her.

She slid down further in the chair wantonly, clinging to his waistcoat as if she were drowning, too desperate to care. Her satin camisole slid up exposing the tops of her stockings and the smooth flesh of her thighs. It was the only stimulus he needed to give up the fight with his conscience.

They both knew such carryings on could not continue, but they made love that night with such ardour, driven to wilder intensity than ever by the certain knowledge that what they were doing was forbidden by law and by convention. Because it was wickedly incestuous, morally and sinfully wrong, this one occasion would linger forever in their hearts, overshadowing till eternity the memories of any other love-making.

Such carryings on must not continue, however. Sylvia, damn it, knew the truth about them, and although Edgar had promised to be discreet, whether *she* could remain so was another matter. Sylvia for too long had held this grudge against Lizzie, and Lizzie realised that she would not be able to keep such a juicy piece of gossip to herself for long. Sooner or later she would have to tell somebody. She was vindictive by nature, and it was the ideal snippet with which to get even with Lizzie. Never could she have dreamt up such a glorious bit of scandal. And how she would enjoy using it.

Donald Clark was shocked. 'If you're absolutely certain of the facts, Lizzie – if you're certain beyond doubt that your father is also Jesse's father – then, yes, I can legally abort the foetus myself, or authorise it to be done. Let's see, you're less than sixteen weeks, aren't you?'
She dried her tears and sniffed, trying to regain her composure. 'Yes.'
'I could do it at home, but you'd need some nursing afterwards.'
'No, not at home, Donald. The last thing I want is for the children to know.'
'Of course. Then I'll book you a bed in hospital. You'll have to stay overnight, at least. I daresay you could dream up a suitable yarn to explain your need to be away?'
'I suppose so. The children are old enough to look after themselves now. And I could always ask Jesse, or May, or even Beccy Crump to keep an eye on them. I'll ask Beccy. She won't mind.'
'It's a distasteful business, abortion. It's a sight more unpleasant than actual childbirth, too. It won't be a tea-party, I warn you.'
Lizzie shrugged, twisting her handkerchief through her fingers. 'It has to be done.'
'And I'm desperately sorry, Lizzie. Talk about visiting the sins of the fathers upon the children! Please give Jesse my kindest regards... Good gracious! Old Ezme Clancey and your father. It

sounds preposterous now. Who ever would have thought it, eh?'

'As you say, who ever would have thought it? So how soon can I expect to go into hospital, Donald? I need to make arrangements for the children.'

'I'll see if I can get it fixed up in a day or two. I'll be in touch as soon as I know.'

Lizzie drew comfort from the knowledge that if it were not for Sylvia and Edgar actually witnessing Ezme's revelation, she and Jesse would have ignored the truth, got married anyway without telling Ezme, and taken a chance with the child she was carrying. But Ezme knew what she was doing when she asked Sylvia and Edgar to witness her words. Jesse had subsequently turned up his birth certificate, and his father was actually named as Jack Clancey, dairyman. Nobody therefore could dispute it, except Sylvia. But because they feared she would, given the opportunity, they could not afford to take the chance. Lizzie started having bad dreams about her wedding day that could never be: with Jesse at her side she wanted to hide in the vestry when Sylvia shouted from the back of the church that they must not get married, that they were brother and sister. It was a vivid dream, too. Sylvia then walked up the aisle, dressed as a bride herself; she took Jesse's arm, and he slipped his ring onto her finger, while Edgar watched smiling as best man.

On the Thursday evening of that week Donald Clark called round to see Lizzie. She walked outside with him to his car for privacy, and he told her that a bed was available at the Guest Hospital tomorrow, Friday, and that she should report there at ten in the morning. She should take her overnight things, and be prepared to stay a couple of nights.

She swallowed hard at the news. 'I'll be there,' she said resolutely. 'I haven't a clue what to tell the kids, though, to save them worrying.'

'Well, I can't help you there, Lizzie. Whatever you tell them needs to be plausible. Anyway the best of luck. I'll find out when you're due to be discharged, and I'll call round to see you.'

'Thanks, Donald. You're as good as gold.'

He waved as he climbed into his car and Lizzie turned to go back up the entry. But she did not re-open her own back door. She walked straight past, to go to Beccy Crump's house. She opened the door and called out.

'Come in, my wench,' Beccy invited. She was sitting at her scullery table, tucking, with her fingers, into conger eel and chips from Iky Bottlebrush's. They were still wrapped in newspaper, and smelled divine. A jar of pickled onions and a saltshaker were at her elbow. 'Get yourself a cup and saucer out the cubbert, and pour yourself a cup o' tay.'

Lizzie found a mug. 'Where's the milk?'

'Top o' the cellar, where it always is.'

Lizzie located the jug of milk, and took it to the table. She sat down and poured a few drops into her tea.

'Mind yo' doh sheed it on the cloth,' Beccy said, mocking her own lack of a tablecloth. 'Here,

509

have a chip.'

Lizzie took a chip from the newspaper. To have argued would have been pointless. 'Are you keeping all right, Beccy?'

'Yes, 'cept I seem to have the wind a bit. Keeps givin' me the ballyache. I could do with a drop o' whisky after to help settle it.'

'I'll send you a drop round after, Beccy, if you'll do me a favour.'

'A favour? Oh, I'll do yer a favour if I can, Lizzie, yo' knowin' that. What is it?' She picked up three or four chips and worked them into her mouth.

'I, er ... I've got to go to Manchester to our Lucy's. She's poorly, and there's nobody to look after her. I'll only be away a couple of days, but I wondered if you could just pop in and make sure the kids are all right. I'll let May know as well, but you know how she's been, what with Emmie's death and all that. I don't want to burden her with anymore.'

''Course I will. But it looks to me like yo'm the one who wants lookin' after, Lizzie. Yo'm as white as a ghost, and yo' look mythered to jeath. What's up, my wench, eh?'

'Oh, nothing that a day or two away won't put right,' she answered ambiguously.

'Is it Jesse?'

Lizzie shook her head unconvincingly.

'I sid yer walkin' up and down the street in the pourin' rain last Sunday night. Yo' looked as if yo' was lost. Nobody in their right mind would've bin out on a night like that. I was gunna come and ask yer what was up, but I thought it was no

510

business o' mine.'

'Oh, we'd had a row, Beccy,' she lied. 'It upset me and I didn't want to go home with our Henzey's new chap there.'

'It must've upset yer a lot, I should think, if yo' wouldn't goo 'um. What did yer row about? His mother, I reckon?'

Lizzie ran her fingers through her hair, and her anxiety showed.

She wanted to be honest with Beccy, but could not bring herself to tell her the truth. The fewer who knew, the better.

'Was that Ezme causin' trouble?'

Lizzie nodded sadly.

'By God, 'er can be a nasty bag o' washin', that Ezme. 'Er'd always got it in for your mother an' all, yer know. If your mother's arse had bin on fire Ezme would've tried to put it out with lamp oil. An' yet your mother wouldn't hurt a fly. A real lady, your mother was.'

'I know my mother was, Beccy ... but what about my father? What about my father, eh? Would you say he was a gentleman?'

Beccy stoked the last bit of conger eel into her mouth, relishing it as she chewed. Lizzie awaited her answer, curious.

'He always turned his money up,' she replied evasively, and wiped her mouth on the tea cloth that was on her lap. 'None o' yer ever went short.'

'That's not what I asked, Beccy. I want to know whether you think my father was a gentleman?'

'A gentleman?' The cat emerged from under the table, arched its back and sprung onto Beccy's lap. It sniffed tentatively at the bits of food remaining in the newspaper. 'Your father could be a gentleman when he'd a mind to be.'

'But not always?'

Beccy shoved the animal back down to the worn linoleum, then put the newspaper containing the scraps on the floor in front of it. The cat began licking at the bits of batter and the grease, purring contentedly.

'Sometimes he was a bit brusque. Liked his drink, your father, and he was vile when he was drunk. He was never a well-liked man, though God forgi' me for spakin' ill o' the jead.'

'Oh, never mind that. I want to know the truth about him. I was only twelve when he got killed. I thought the sun shone out of his backside, but what girl doesn't idolise her father? It's only when you get older that you get to realise what they're really like. I can't say as I ever really knew him.'

'What's brought this on?' Beccy queried, as if she could see into Lizzie's head.

'Oh, I was just thinking... Jack Clancey's horse killed him, but Jack Clancey never so much as said he was sorry. I remember Uncle Tom at the time telling my mother how they fetched Jack out the pub when it happened. He must've looked at my father lying there dead, and said he wouldn't grieve over him. It seemed that strange to me. That callous. Even as a child. I often wondered why it was. Didn't Jack Clancey like my father for some reason, Beccy?'

'Like I said, Lizzie, few men liked your father. If yo' want the truth, then I'll tell yer the truth, especially if this is what's mytherin' yer. Your

512

father was a womaniser, and no two ways. No bloke's woman was sacred. He tried it on with me once, till I told him where to get off, in no uncertain terms. There was a stink about him and Ezme, years ago. Ezme was only a young woman then – before Jesse was born. Praps that's why Jack dai' like your father. Praps that's why Ezme dai' like your mother.'

'Hmm. I thought it might go deeper than that, though,' Lizzie suggested, plumbing the depth of Beccy's knowledge.

'Well, if it does I know nothin' about it. But what makes yer say that, my wench? What yer drivin' at, eh? Summat's mytherin' yer.'

'Oh, I don't know, Beccy. It's just my imagination running riot... On their gravestone it says, *"They have sown the wind"*. I suppose Mother must've had it inscribed. It must mean something. Do you know what it means, Beccy? Did she ever tell you what it meant?'

'Never. But I can imagine.'

'Tell me then.'

'It's from the Bible. *"They have sown the wind, and they shall reap the whirlwind"*. Yo' could say as Isaac sowed the wind, p'r'aps. I daresay that's what your mother meant.'

Lizzie picked up her mug of tea, and drank it, and Beccy finished off hers. 'Well I know who's reaping the damn whirlwind, Beccy, and it isn't my father... Look, I'd best be off, else they'll wonder what's happened to me. I haven't told them yet I'm going away... Now, you're sure you don't mind keeping your eye on them for me?'

'They'm no bother, Lizzie. Doh fret theeself.

513

They'll come to no harm.'

'Just be sure that if our Henzey's new chap comes, that his motor's gone by eleven. I don't want her to harbour him.'

'Oh, I'll soon get rid of him, Lizzie.'

Chapter 27

Beccy Crump retired to bed that night preoccupied. She pinned up her wispy, silver hair for the night and contemplated Lizzie's insistent questions. There was something badly amiss, and no mistake. Poor Lizzie looked like death warmed up, as if she were carrying the world on her shoulders, and on top of that she was expected to rush to Manchester to look after her ailing sister, who hadn't been a-nigh Lizzie for years; not even for young Emmie's funeral. Ezme Clancey, as temperamental as a starving flea on the rump of a rocking horse, was the cause of Lizzie's worry, that much was certain. What happened with old Isaac was years ago; before Lizzie was born. Lizzie had nothing to do with it, so it was no reason to hold it against Lizzie. But you couldn't expect Ezme to take kindly to her only son courting her. That would be almost like Eve coming back to haunt her. It was all up to Jesse, and Beccy hoped he was strong enough to stand up to his mother.

It was strange how Lizzie was eager all of a sudden to know about her father. It was strange how she wanted to know why old Jack Clancey disliked him. *'I thought it might go deeper than that'*, she'd said. What was she getting at? Jack was jealous of Isaac, for obvious reasons; like a lot of men on Kates Hill; and beyond if the truth be known. So what did she mean by suggesting it might go deeper? Was there some deeper, hidden mystery that she, Beccy, had not been privy to? She believed she knew everything there was to know about all her friends on Kates Hill. Had something occurred so secret that it must be kept from everybody? If she didn't know what it was, nobody knew.

Beccy put on her hairnet, then pulled her frock over her head, dislodging her spectacles. 'Damn and bugger it,' she cursed, and slid them back into place again. She unfastened the pouch containing her purse that was tied around her waist, and put it on the tallboy. Then she unlaced her corset. As she wallowed in the welcome freedom from constriction, scratching the loose skin of her belly ecstatically, she pondered further Lizzie's probing. *'I thought it might go deeper than that'*. Deeper than what, for God's sake? Deeper than Jack Clancey's mere dislike of her father? What had Ezme said or done that could cause poor Lizzie to ask such a question, and cause her so much anguish? What could cause Lizzie to roam the streets alone on a night so wet that even a rat wouldn't venture out.

Lizzie and Jesse had had no row. That was just her excuse. Beccy had seen Lizzie and Jesse embrace in the street late that Sunday night in the pouring rain through her bedroom window. If they'd had a row, they'd soon made it up. No, Lizzie had been told something that had upset her more than anything; that had upset Jesse as well.

Could it have been something to do with Isaac? Something from so long ago? That inscription on his gravestone that Lizzie had queried: *'They have sown the wind'*. What exactly had Eve meant by it? And Lizzie saying, *'I know who's going to reap the whirlwind, Beccy, and it isn't my father'*.

What whirlwind? What could be a consequence of Isaac sowing the wind? *'I know who's going to reap the whirlwind, Beccy, and it isn't my father'*.

Beccy rolled her corset into a bundle, and placed it on the ottoman. She tugged at her chemise, pulled it over her head, and shivered. As she reached for her thick, winceyette nightdress an intriguing thought crossed her mind. The more she pondered it the more sense it made; the more it answered many, many questions; the more the pieces seemed to fit. Why had she never considered it before? Why had she missed it, till now? What if Jesse happened to be Isaac's son?... What if Jesse was the consequence of that affair all those years ago? Oh, it was far too outlandish... It couldn't be... Yet it could be. It must be. Jesse must be Isaac's son. Damn it, there was even a resemblance now she had made the connection: the fair hair; the steel grey eyes; the big moustache.

So that's why Lizzie was so upset. She was upset because Ezme had told them they shared the same father. Why hadn't Lizzie said so, for goodness sake?

Beccy lifted the cover of her commode and eased her voluminous bloomers down her legs, shaking her head. She'd better try and catch Lizzie before she went off to Manchester in the morning.

But Beccy Crump overslept next morning. Her mind had been active till the early hours, and she believed she would not sleep at all. She eventually did, however, and did not wake up till half past nine. She got up wearily, dressed herself, and attended to her ablutions as quickly as she could, but it was difficult to break the leisurely routine of many years thriving in measured widowhood, and pampering herself in her old age. She went downstairs, raked out the ashes from the fire and lit a new one. She held her draw-tin against the grate opening till it set alight properly, then grabbed the kettle and took it to the brewhouse to fill it. It could be heating up while she went round to see Lizzie. She tapped on Lizzie's back door, and lifted the latch to open it. But it was locked. Damn and bugger it. Lizzie must have gone already. Never mind. The thing she wanted to tell her would keep. It would keep till she got back.

She returned to her own fireside. The fire was drawing well and the coals had caught. Beccy reached for her Dutch oven in the bottom cupboard and placed it on the strides over-hanging the grate. As the residual fat began to melt she peeled a couple of rashers of bacon from her small stock, and hung them on hooks in the Dutch oven to cook. Next she cut a couple

517

of thick slices of bread, spooned tea leaves into her teapot, then sat for a few minutes, watching. When she got her breath back she picked up the coal scuttle and tottered to the cellar to fill it. She preferred to go down there just once a day, so the scuttle, holding sufficient coal, was heavy to lift on the way back up. But she managed it, in her own unhurried way, resting it on each step for a few a second or two as she ascended. She washed her hands, then returned to the scullery and turned the bacon. It was sizzling beautifully, and the aroma made her feel hungry. The kettle boiled, and she brewed her tea, enough for two large mugs. The bacon looked perfect now, so she lifted the Dutch oven and placed it onto a sheet of newspaper that was covering her scrubbed table. She took the two slices of bread, dipped them in the fat, and with her toasting fork held them in turn in front of the fire to crispen the liquored side. Then, with a blob of HP sauce smeared over the bacon, her breakfast was ready.

When she'd finished she wiped her mouth. Now she would visit Ezme Clancey. Beccy made a habit of calling to see her two or three times a week, usually while Jesse was working. So she wrapped her shawl around her shoulders.

As she walked through the wide entry of the dairy house she saw the doctor's car. Damn. Friday was his day for visiting. Never mind, you could talk in front of young Doctor Clark. She opened the verandah door and called out, then made her way through to the stairs. 'Stairs, stairs, it's all damned stairs,' she mumbled, gripping the bannister as firmly she could. Eventually, she reached the top, and presented herself at Ezme's bedroom door, to be greeted by Donald Clark's ruddy, smiling face.

'How is she this mornin', Doctor?'

'Not so well, Mrs Crump. A bit under the weather, it seems.'

She looked at Ezme, and asked her how she felt. The two women had known each other for years, and although Ezme had lost her hearing she still understood from Beccy's facial expressions exactly what she was saying.

'I doh feel too grand, Beccy,' she moaned, with a pained expression.

'Has young Lizzie bin to see yer?'

'Young Lizzie, did yer say?' Ezme shook her head. 'No, 'er ai' bin a-nigh since last Sunday. Our Jesse and Lizzie have fell out.'

Beccy looked at Donald Clark in disbelief. 'What did they fall out over, Ezme? I said, what did they fall out over?'

'I doh know for sure.'

'Yes, you do.' Beccy straightened her friend's counterpane. 'Now tell me. What did they fall out over?'

'Oh, Lizzie wanted to get wed, but our Jesse said as he dai' want to.'

'Well that's a damned lie for a start,' Beccy remarked to the doctor.

Donald frowned with concern. 'I believe so, too.'

She turned to Ezme again and shook her head. 'I doh think as they've fell out at all, Ezme. I reckon it was yo' meddlin'.'

'No, it was nothin' to do with me.'

'Had it got anythin' to do with Isaac Bishop, then?'

Ezme cupped her hand to her ear and frowned. 'The fish shop, did yer say?'

'No. Isaac Bishop,' she yelled precisely. She turned to Donald again. 'I realise as yo' cor' say nothin', Doctor, 'cause yo'm bound to keep confidences, but I can say as I'd a mind.' Donald smiled and nodded. 'Well, it's my belief as Isaac Bishop was Jesse's father, you know, not Jack. And because of it 'er's seen fit to use it to put a stop to their courtin'.'

'Mmm! That's my understanding as well, Beccy. But if it's true, then Jesse can't marry Lizzie.'

'I know that an' all, Doctor, but yo' 'ang on a minute.'

Ezme shuffled nervously, looking from one to the other. 'Isaac Bishop, did yer say? What about 'im?'

Beccy addressed Ezme again. 'Isaac was Jesse's father. Am I right?'

Ezme began to weep silently. 'Yes,' she confessed with a wheeze, 'he was, and I hope as the good Lord'll forgive me for the terrible sin o' lyin' with him. But I loved him, Beccy. Oh, I loved him all right.' She took the handkerchief that was on her bedside table and wiped her tears. 'I loved him more than anybody'll ever know. But when he found out as I was carryin', he dai' want to know me, the swine, and I was in lumber good and bloody proper. Mercifully, Jack was as good as gold about it.'

'So yo' told Jesse and Lizzie so's they wouldn't get wed, eh?'

'They cor' get married, Beccy. They'm brother and sister. It'd be a cardinal sin. Yo' ask the vicar.'

'I've no need to ask the damned vicar. The trouble is yo' only know half the story, as bloody usual. Still, yo' war' to know, I reckon.' She leaned closer to Ezme, shaking her head. 'Jesse an' Lizzie ai' brother an' sister at all. Tom Dando's Lizzie's father. D'y'ear what I say, Ezme? Tom and Eve was havin' it off for years.'

Donald gulped. 'Mrs Crump, are you absolutely certain of this?' His expression was grave.

'As certain as I'm standin' 'ere. I know it for a fact, Doctor. What's good for the goose is good for the gander, Eve always used to say. I tell yer, there was some tidy shenanigans gooin' on round here in them days – there was no sittin' in th'ouse pullin' faces at the parrot then. Me and Eve was ever so close. Two friends have never bin closer. 'Er used to tell me everythin'. Absolutely everythin'. Enough to open my eyes wide, I can tell yer. And I do know for certain as Lizzie's Tom's daughter, and no mistek. Eve always told me 'er was, and I got no reason to misbelieve her. Why yo' only 'ave to look at the wench to see the resemblance to Tom. Lizzie's nothin' like Isaac. Nothin' like Jesse.'

'Thank you, Mrs Crump, very much,' Donald said. 'That's near enough. It means they can get married after all.'

'That's what I wanted to say, Doctor. It's what I wanted to tell Lizzie this mornin' afore 'er went off to Manchester.'

Donald looked at his watch anxiously. It was quarter to eleven. He snatched up his bag. 'Mrs Crump, I'll tell Lizzie for you, but I'll have to go this very minute. Can I leave you with Ezme? See if you can make her get used to the idea of Jesse and Lizzie being married, will you? I'd take you with me, but I fear you'd slow me down, and I might be too late already.'

'Yo' carry on, Doctor,' Beccy consented, her face set in a puzzled expression.

'What's he took short?' Ezme asked as Donald hastened out of the room. 'He ai' examined me nor nothin'.'

'Listen, Ezme, there's one or two things I've got to explain to yer.'

Donald Clark was normally a steady driver. He was a hardened drinker, and excessive use of alcohol had taught him never to trust his own reactions, especially when inebriated at the wheel of his Morris. This morning he was stone cold sober, however; or to be more precise, he was as sober as you would ever expect to find him. He drove therefore, with a little more alacrity and purpose than usual, all the way to the Guest Hospital, taking risks he would not normally take, praying he would be in time to prevent the termination of Lizzie Kite's pregnancy. As he swung violently into the hospital grounds the car lurched to one side, and the tyres squealed momentarily, while a passing nurse feigned disdain at such appalling driving. The car juddered to a halt at the entrance to the building.

He leapt out and rushed along the corridor to his left, seeking the ward where he hoped she would be. A few seconds later he presented himself at the entrance to the women's ward, panting for breath.

'I'm looking for Mrs Elizabeth Kite,' he gasped to the first uniformed woman he saw, a short, dark-haired nurse with a squint. 'Most likely gave her name as Lizzie. Is she still here?'

'Is she supposed to be in this ward?'

'She's in for a pregnancy termination.'

'An abortion? Fancy. What did you say her name was?'

'Elizabeth or Lizzie Kite.'

'Elizabeth Kite? Hang on, let me check.'

Donald wanted to tell her to hurry up. These moments stalling by the nurse could be the difference between saving Lizzie's child and losing it.

'Am you sure she's supposed to be here? We got nobody here called Elizabeth Kite. Nor Lizzie. Not according to this.' She waved a record of the days admittances in front of him. 'Oh, yes, she's expected, but she ain't been admitted.'

'Look, nurse, she has to be here. I'm her doctor. It's vital I find her before they operate on her. There's been a dreadful mistake. Find out where she is, woman, and take me to her at once.'

The urgency in his voice prompted the nurse to find the ward sister, who listened intently to his story. She slid some papers across the desk and paused, scanning one of them. 'I'm sorry, doctor. Her name's down here, but she certainly isn't here.'

Donald scoured the streets of Kates Hill for sight of Jesse or his horse and float. Jesse might know where Lizzie was. If not, he feared she might have done something drastic. It was vital they track her down. When she'd called to tell him about her plight she was distraught. He'd never seen her in such a state before. Depressed and over-worked, yes, but never utterly defeated. The fact that she had avoided going to hospital suggested something was wrong. Donald drove up and down every street searching, his anxiety rising by the minute. A new council estate had been built – the Roseland. Jesse might be around there. To his relief he spotted Jesse's unattended float just as he turned the corner into Bunns Lane. He pulled up behind it and waited for Jesse to return. Fortunately he did not have to wait long. Jesse came walking down the path of one of the houses, and Donald at once leapt out of his Morris.

'Jesse, thank God I've found you. I've been looking everywhere for you.'

'Blimey, Donald, what's up? Is it Mother?'

'No, no, your mother's all right. It's Lizzie.'

Jesse instantly paled, and a look of dread clouded his face. 'Oh, Donald, what is it? If she's... What is it, Donald?'

'She seems to be missing, Jesse. I thought you might know where she is.'

'But she was due to go into hospital this morning. You ought to know. You fixed it.'

Donald put his hand on Jesse's arm as a calming gesture, but inside he was simmering with anxiety. 'Yes, I know she's supposed to be in hospital, but I've just come from there, and she hasn't been admitted. I thought maybe you might know if she's changed her plans.'

'Why should she change her plans, Donald? There's no alternative, is there, the way things have turned out?'

Donald smiled. 'I need to talk to her, Jesse. I have to talk to you as well. It's not all bad news, you see. But we must find her to let her know.'

Jesse put his jug and ladle into a churn and sighed. 'What are you on about, Donald?'

'I was attending your mother earlier, and Beccy Crump came over. I got the impression that Beccy had got a point to make. She evidently knew, or rather had guessed, who your real father was, and she asked your mother if that was the reason you'd abandoned your intention to get married.' Jesse was listening intently, his eyes fixed on Donald's. 'Well, when your mother confirmed it, Beccy told her off for meddling.'

Jesse forced a smile. 'Good old Beccy.'

'But you see, Jesse, Beccy maintains that even though Isaac Bishop was your father, it doesn't make any difference. It just doesn't matter.'

'Doesn't matter? Of course it matters. It's the very reason we can't be wed.'

'But, Jesse. Isaac wasn't Lizzie's father.'

'Eh? You what?' This was going to take a second or two to sink in. 'Well if Isaac wasn't her father, Donald, who the bloody hell was?'

'Tommy Dando.'

'Tommy Dando?'

'Apparently Tommy and Eve had been … how

525

shall I put it? ... very close for a number of years. Very close indeed. Beccy, God bless her, had been privy to all the intimate details – from Eve, of course – and she's adamant that Lizzie is Tom's daughter. That being so, there's nothing to stop you getting married after all.'

'But what about if she's wrong, Donald? What if she's got it all wrong?'

'Jesse ... if I were you I wouldn't argue with it.'

Jesse's face lit up and his blue-grey eyes sparkled. He threw his arms about Donald, and started jumping up and down, whirling him round in a sort of spontaneous dance, for all to see.

'Jesse!' Donald tried to shove him off, but laughed all the same. 'Stop it, stop it... Ouch! Pack it in... Christ, you've trod on me blinking corns!'

'Tom Dando and Eve Bishop! Yippee! Who'd have thought it? Who the bloody hell would have thought it?'

'Keep still, for God's sake. Remember Lizzie still doesn't know. We need to let her know. We need to find her.'

'Oh, she'll be back by tea time, I'll bet you any money. As soon as I've finished my round I'll go and look for her. She's probably gone to see Sarah Dando, or Daisy Foster, one of her old mates. She might be with May Bishop. I'll find her, don't you fret, Donald.'

'I'll help you look if you like.'

'I'm sure you've got patients that could do with your attention, eh? No, leave the searching to me. But I'm grateful to you for finding me, for letting me know. I tell you, it's the best news I've ever had, bar none.' He laughed again.

Donald laughed too. 'You know, Jesse, it's the best news I've ever been able to give anybody... Bar none.' He shook Jesse's hand amiably. 'One thing's for certain, you know...'

'What's that?'

'Lizzie's certainly Eve's daughter, and no mistake.' Donald got back in his car, waved, and drove off.

With a broad smile, and with thoughts that excluded everyone and everything but Lizzie, Jesse stepped back up onto his milk float to finish off his round.

Jesse was not in Sarah Dando's best books. Hadn't been for years, but he called there in his endeavours to find Lizzie. He also tried Daisy Foster's house in Tividale, and May's and Joe's in Cromwell Street before her realised he was alarming them all as to her whereabouts, and decided he'd asked enough. But perhaps he ought to see what Beccy Crump might know before he gave up all hope of finding her and induced himself into a panic attack. But all Beccy knew was that Lizzie had to go to Stockport to tend to Lucy, which he knew full well was merely the excuse she'd made to put everybody off the scent. However, Beccy took great pleasure in relating the events of the morning, and how humble Ezme was after hearing that Tom Dando had fathered Lizzie. It left Jesse in no doubt, and he thanked her with all his heart before leaving to ask Henzey if she knew anything.

'All I know is she's gone to look after my Aunt Lucy,' Henzey said in the scullery, her hands in a bowl of water, peeling potatoes. 'Didn't she tell you?'

Jesse banged the heel of his hand against his forehead, feigning a terrible memory. 'Oh, God. Fancy me forgetting that. I'd forget my head if it was loose. It's just that I could do with talking to her... But say if she hadn't gone there, Henzey ... where else might she have gone?'

'If that's where she said she was going, that's where she'll be. But she won't be back till the day after tomorrow.'

'Has your Aunt Lucy got the telephone in?'

'The telephone? I don't think so, Jesse. Why should she have a telephone?'

'It was just a thought.'

'She'd never have a telephone anyway. She's too much of a skinflint.'

If it were necessary to take a trip to Stockport just to satisfy himself that Lizzie wasn't there, he would do it. But he would wait till morning. She might well turn up in an hour or two. She could not have gone far.

So Jesse went home. He ran upstairs at once to see his mother, and broached the subject of Lizzie's parentage. Ezme said she could scarcely believe it, but it shouldn't surprise her, really. Eve Bishop was capable of anything, bar handling needle and thread, she said spitefully. And she'd always thought that Tom Dando had a shifty look about him whenever Eve was around. Come to think of it, Tom always used to be stuck at the Bishops' house when Isaac was out on the booze, especially on summer evenings when the kids were all out. There's never no smoke without fire, she said. At any rate, Jesse was convinced. Lizzie bore no resemblance to Isaac.

He pondered the last few traumatic days, when it seemed that the only woman he had ever really loved was finally being denied him. He shuddered, remembering vividly the sheer desolation and hopelessness he'd felt. Somehow, even in all that heartache, he'd had a gut feeling that all would be well; an illogical impression that he could not substantiate. Now it had come to pass, thank God. It was little more than hearsay about Eve and Tom, but Beccy had sworn on her life that it was true.

So Jesse was happy to be persuaded. He went to bed, having sat in the front room all evening, watching for signs of Lizzie's return. But she had not returned, and something was gravely amiss. He lay awake most of the night trying to think where she was hiding, what she was feeling.

But he knew what she was feeling. She was feeling what he had felt. If only he could tell her everything was all right. He was desperate to free her of her anguish. But she had evidently changed her mind about having her pregnancy terminated. Maybe she had accepted her lot, and was prepared to have the child, come what may. But maybe she did not care anyway, since life was ... not worth living...

He prayed earnestly to his Maker. Oh, dear God. If ever she had done something stupid... But she wouldn't. She was too resilient. The years had proved that. And besides, she would never put her children through the trauma of losing her... But the idea returned, and again he tried to dismiss it. She was somewhere. She had to be somewhere. Seeking counsel perhaps. But where? Who could be harbouring her?

Eventually he drifted into a fitful sleep. At five o'clock next morning his alarm clock woke him and he got up. After he had tended to his mother and breakfasted he went to the stables to wait for Herbert. While he tacked up Herbert's horse by the light of an oil lamp, Herbert himself came sauntering into the yard, ready to start his day.

'Morning, Herbert. Has your mother come back by any chance?'

'She's not due back till tomorrow.'

'Look, d'you think you could manage my round today as well as your own? I've got to find her. I'll pay you extra.'

'What's the rush, Jesse?' Herbert patted his horse on the neck. 'Can't it wait?'

'It can't.'

'But she's at Manchester. You'm never going all that way when she'll be back tomorrow?'

Manchester... Stockport... Just her alibi. But he'd tried everywhere else. She might just *be* at Lucy's. Just for the change of scenery; a change of company. He had to go there to find out. It was the only logical place she would go. 'Do you happen to know the address, Herbert?'

'Twelve, Thorny Lane, Reddish, Stockport, Cheshire,' he recited. 'I know that 'cause I generally post Mother's letters to Aunt Lucy.'

'I have to go there, Herbert. It's important. Can you manage my round if I give you the book?'

''Course.'

'Good lad. I'll see you later, when I get back.'

'I wish I knew what all the fuss was about.'

'Nothing to concern you, my lad,' Jesse said equably. 'But it does concern your mother. Oh, and would you ask Henzey, or May, or even Beccy to drop in and have a look at my mother?'

'Yes, 'course I will, Jesse.'

'Good lad.'

So Jesse caught the Dodger from Dudley Station to Dudley Port, and took the L.M.S. line from Dudley Port to Victoria Station in Manchester. With every mile he grew more apprehensive, more concerned for Lizzie's welfare. What if she were not at Lucy's? What then? Where else should he look? It would mean going to the hospitals to see if she'd been brought in; reporting her missing to the police. He felt hot and fearful at the thought.

After a long and tedious journey the train pulled in to Victoria Station and he hopped out hurriedly. Once outside he managed to grab a taxi-cab and asked to be taken to Thorny Lane, Reddish.

Jesse had never been to Manchester before. It was bustling, full of Victorian buildings. As they headed out of the city towards Stockport he saw the mills that spun and wove the cotton, the factories that produced the dyes that coloured them, the engineering and locomotive works. Chimney stacks pointed to the sky at every turn. So much like Brum and the Black Country. It was not long before he was paying the taxi driver. That done, he looked about him. Thorny Lane was little more than a dirt track, with houses on one side only, a field on the other. He found number 12 with its square bay window, and walked to the front door, his heart in his throat. He knocked the door and waited.

Chapter 28

Jesse did not see the figure that appeared at the window to see who was knocking the door. He seemed to be waiting ages. Then, the door flew open, taking him by surprise, and in a flash Lizzie flung herself at him, and her arms were around his neck.

'Jesse, Jesse!' She burst into tears instantly, sobbing piteously, her head against his chest.

'There, there,' he breathed, hugging her tight, relieved to see her, desperate to feel her in his arms again. 'My God, I've been worried to death over you, ever since Donald told me you hadn't been to the hospital. Are you all right, my pet?'

'All the better for seeing you,' She looked up into his eyes, and they told him she'd been crying a long, long time. 'What brings you here? How did you find me?'

'Here, let me dry your tears.' He took his clean handkerchief from his pocket, and dabbed away the tears before he held her tight again. 'I found you, that's all that matters. I found you.'

'Oh, Jesse, I'm that miserable. I had to get away. I had to. I couldn't stand being so close to you and not being able to be with you.' Her eyes filled again, and she wiped them with the back of her hand. 'Come on inside.'

'Where's Lucy?'

'At work. And her husband. I've got the house to myself till they get back. I said I'd cook the tea for them.'

He followed her inside, into the living room. A fire was blazing cheerily in a low, tiled grate, and he could hear the measured tick-tock of a brass clock on the mantelshelf. A French window looked out onto a long back garden, still winter dead, depressing in the dull afternoon.

'Oh, Jesse, I'm that shocked to see you I'm still shaking. Here, feel me.' She placed her trembling hand on his, and he could indeed detect it. 'But I'm that glad to see you. What's made you come here for me? I'd have thought it the last place anybody would've looked.'

He gave a little laugh. 'That's why I came here. If I'd have sent Henzey or Herbert to find you they would have come straight here. I just had a strange feeling you might have come here, just so that you knew they could find you here if need be. You weren't really lost, were you?'

'No, not really. I just had to get away, Jesse. I just couldn't go to that hospital and go through with an abortion. I thought about it long and hard, and I just couldn't do it. I kept thinking about that poor little daughter I had before. The one that was born dead. I didn't want it at first, you know, Jesse, but as time went on I started to look forward to having it, to holding it in my arms, to feeling it at my breast. And when it was

533

born dead I was so sad. Oh, I was ever so sad, because I know I would have loved it no less than I love the others. It would have been part of the family. I know I'd feel exactly the same about this child I'm carrying now. You're my brother and all that, but it makes no difference. I want to take the risk with this child. There's no reason why it shouldn't be all right. I know I'd grieve over it if I had it aborted, I know I would. I wouldn't be able to live with myself. So when I was walking past the station on my way to the hospital I just couldn't help it. I bought a ticket to Dudley Port and waited there for the first train to Manchester.'

'Sit down, Lizzie,' Jesse said kindly.

She sat biddably on the arm of the settee. 'What are you smiling at? I can see nothing to smile at.'

'Some good news,' he said, and took her hand.

'God, that would make a change.'

'But just brace yourself, because it might come as a bit of a shock. It was certainly a shock to me... It's come to light that your father isn't your father.'

'Well that's Irish.' Lizzie frowned in puzzlement, but there was a flicker of hope in her eyes; hope that had been missing for too long. 'You'd better explain what you mean, Jesse. If you're saying Isaac Bishop isn't my father, then who is?'

'Tom Dando. Tom Dando's your father, Lizzie.'

For a second or two she looked utterly bewildered. And then, at the realisation of what it meant she smiled; a radiant smile that lit up her face with relief and happiness. She did not question the truth of it. It really came as no surprise. Her mother had told her years ago how they used to be sweethearts. She had seen with her own eyes the knowing glances that used to flash between them. If Tom Dando was her father it was no great disappointment. She'd loved him and admired him like a father.

'This had better be the truth, Jesse Clancey.'

'I swear.'

'So how did it come about? I mean, how did you find out?'

He explained.

'So we'll get married as planned?'

'As planned. The banns are already published. The church is booked, the vicar ain't been told no different. It's still on, my darling.'

'Oh, Jesse.' She began weeping again. But tears of joy this time. 'Why does life play such cruel tricks and then make everything right again when you think there's no hope? I just thank the Lord for my mother. I wish to God she was here right now so's I could fling my arms round her neck and thank her for having me by Uncle Tom.'

He gave her his handkerchief and she wiped her eyes again. 'I'd fling my arms round her neck as well, you know.'

She managed a chuckle through her tears. 'You know what this means, though? It means that Sylvia's my sister... God... Just fancy!... And... Oh, Lord! Stanley's my brother...' That realisation hit her hardest. 'Stanley's my brother, Jesse... Christ almighty! No wonder Beccy didn't want me to go to Southern Rhodesia with him.'

'Nobody wanted you to go, Lizzie. Everybody knew what Stanley was like.'

'Everybody except me. God, what a fool I was to even consider it.'

'Don't think too badly of yourself. And you weren't to know Stanley was your own flesh and blood.'

'Nobody knew, except Beccy, God bless her.' Lizzie stood up. 'And she said nothing then about us being brother and sister... Oh, I'm sorry, Jesse. I bet you're parched coming all this way, and I haven't even offered you a cup of tea. I'll make you one.'

'Oh, I'll live. It was more important to put you out of your misery first. Tea can wait.'

'Well it needn't wait any longer.' As she got to the door to go into the kitchen she stopped, rested her head against the edge and said, 'You know, Jesse, on my mother's and father's grave are the words, *"They have sown the wind"*. Mother had them inscribed. For years I wondered what significance those words had. I used to think it was something to do with her sewing – you know – her dressmaking. As if you could sew the wind. Now I realise it wasn't. Now I realise why she'd had a gap left under Father's epitaph. Room enough for her own. So the words could apply equally to her. She'd sown the wind the same as him. Maybe those words were her way of letting us know. I'm certain she would have wanted me to know eventually.'

'I can well imagine, Lizzie. Anyway, what time do you suggest we leave for home? You might as well come back with me, eh?'

`Yes, let's leave tonight. When we've had some tea with Lucy and Jim. We've got some good news to tell them after all.'

The following night Jesse and Lizzie paid a visit to Sylvia Atkinson. Politely, almost patronisingly, she invited them in. As they sat down they enquired if Edgar was with her, but she replied that he was not. Not tonight. Jesse commented what a nice chap he seemed to be, then Sylvia bluntly asked the purpose of their visit.

'Sylvia, it must have been very embarrassing for you and Edgar last Sunday, to hear about who my father really was,' he said, and there was a ready smile on his face, which to Sylvia was unaccountable, and thus very disconcerting. 'It's took me till now to come to terms with it. But we wanted you to be first to know, that as it happens, it won't make a blind bit of difference.'

'Oh?' She looked from Jesse to Lizzie, surprise and abject disappointment written on her face. 'What do you mean?'

'I mean we're still getting married.' He allowed a few seconds for the news to sink in.

'But you can't be serious? I thought it was against the law for brother and sister to wed.'

'Oh, it is, and no two ways, Sylvia.'

'You mean you're going to ignore the law? You're going to break the law?'

'No, we aren't about to break the law.'

'Well what, then?'

Jesse smiled benignly. 'The truth is, Sylvia, Lizzie and me ain't brother and sister, after all.'

Sylvia looked doubtful, unable to believe such

nonsense; as if it was some cock and bull story they'd trumped up between them to try and fool her. But she would not be fooled. 'But I heard your mother state quite categorically that Isaac Bishop, Lizzie's father, was your father as well.'

'Yes, you did, and there's no doubt it's the truth – the last bit anyway. I accept that Isaac Bishop was my real father. But what we've come to tell you, Sylvia, is that Isaac Bishop wasn't Lizzie's father.'

'But that's preposterous. Who are you suggesting was her father?'

'Now this might come as a bit of a shock, Sylvia, so prepare yourself. Your own father, Tom Dando, was Lizzie's father.' Jesse realised that his bluntness might be insensitive, yet he felt it justified nonetheless, and revelled in the moment. Sylvia, they both knew, would have done it with no less rancour if their situations had been reversed.

Sylvia looked at Lizzie in horror. 'I ... is this true, Lizzie? Do you set any store at all by this nonsense? Surely it's only hearsay?'

'Oh, I'm certain it's true, Sylvia,' she answered, smiling easily, amused by Sylvia's reaction. 'I do know that my mother and your father were sweethearts long before she met and married Isaac ... I was about to say married my father, but I suppose I'll get used to not saying it. Anyway, it seems they were lovers again years after. Our next door neighbour, Beccy Crump, can verify it. She and Mother were very close. They confessed everything to each other.'

'I'm not sure whether I should set much store

by such gossip. That's all it is, surely. Besides, it doesn't put my own father in a very good light. Nor your mother, Lizzie.'

'Even so, I think you'll find there's no doubt about it,' Lizzie said.

'The two best kept secrets on Kates Hill, Sylvia,' Jesse remarked. 'My father, and your father.'

'But I'm flabbergasted. If it's true, it means you and I are sisters, Lizzie.'

'I had worked that out, Sylvia. And that Stanley's my brother.' She glanced at Jesse.

'The point is, Sylvia,' Jesse said, 'I'd be surprised if you wanted every Tom, Dick and Harry to know, eh? The scandal, I mean. I respect that you might not want such a scandal about your father to be common knowledge. So as far as we're concerned there's nobody else need know. I'm thinking particularly about your poor old mother, and Kenneth... And Edgar, for that matter.'

'Yes,' Sylvia replied thoughtfully, 'I wouldn't want them to know any such thing. Edgar would have to know, of course, but I'd appreciate it if you could make sure that as few people as possible know – that I could count on your discretion, Jesse. I'd be very grateful.'

'I take it you've said nothing about last Sunday night to anybody else?'

'Well of course not,' Sylvia was very eager to confirm. 'Edgar and I would never breathe a word. We gave you that assurance.'

Jesse smiled. 'Good. The wedding's on the twenty-eighth. You and Edgar are welcome to come. Bring Kenneth as well. You needn't let us know for sure as you're coming till the week before.'

'That's very kind of you, Jesse – Lizzie. I'm sure that ... yes. Thank you. I accept.'

Jesse stood up. 'Right. Well we'd better be off. There's a lot to do, Sylvia.'

So they left, and laughed together at Sylvia's stunned reaction.

'Why did you invite her to the wedding?' Lizzie asked when they were out in the privacy of the street again.

'Because it'll be nice to see her looking bloody humble for a change. And she will, after all that's transpired.'

The following Friday Jesse Clancey finished his milk round early. He called at the Kites' house to see Lizzie, who had come home during her dinner break to put a stew in the oven so it would be ready for their tea when they all returned home.

'Why are you back so early?' she said when she saw him.

'I fancy a pint at "The Shoulder". I want to try and catch Donald Clark. I thought you might like to come with me.'

'But you know I've got to go back to work.'

'No, you haven't. I want you to pack it in as soon as we're wed. You'd have to pack it in anyway afore long.'

'But I get my wages this afternoon.'

'Get 'em Monday. Come on.'

Lizzie didn't need much persuading. She

closed the oven door in the grate, and donned her hat and coat.

'The Shoulder of Mutton' was their favourite public house these days. The beer was home brewed, noted for its flavour, the company was good, and it was always immaculately clean. One of the things Jesse liked about it was the Tap Room. There was no bar counter; beer was served from pumps on one side of the room and Patty, the resident barmaid, served it directly to the table without the patrons having to stand and wait. All you had to do was call her and she would attend to you as soon as she could. Beyond the arrangement which housed the beer pumps there was a hatch for service to a tiny snug, and a smoke room, both of which looked out onto Dixons Green, and there was always a welcoming fire in each room.

'A pint of bitter, Jesse?' Patty asked politely as he entered. She was a pretty girl, about twenty, with auburn hair, personable, always smartly dressed, and was one of the reasons why many hopeful young men frequented the place.

'If you don't mind, Patty, and a half for Lizzie.' He saw that Donald Clark was in residence, as expected. 'Put a double in for the doctor as well, and have one yourself.'

Donald duly raised his glass.

'Come and join us, Donald. We've come here specially to see you.'

The doctor pulled a stool from an adjoining table and sat with them.

Talk at first was about Emmie's funeral, then Donald asked how Ezme had been this week.

541

Jesse replied that she seemed much better.

'Yes, I thought she was better when I called in this morning. All that worry from last week is behind her, that's why.'

Before long the conversation centred on the wedding and inevitably, Lizzie's condition.

'We'll have to keep an eye on you, you know, Lizzie,' Donald said in a low voice. 'Having a child at your age can present problems you don't get at twenty-two. We'll have to make sure you're well all through.' Lizzie looked a little concerned, and he at once realised he'd alarmed her. 'Just a precaution, Lizzie. I doubt if there'll be anything to worry about, but it pays to err on the side of caution.'

'It'd have paid Jesse to err on the side of caution last Christmas,' she said sardonically, though Jesse saw the humour in her eyes. 'It'll cost a mint of money to have the house knocked about to make it comfortable.'

Donald Clark smiled. 'You're having the house altered?'

'Oh, yes. A bathroom with a proper water closet upstairs, and a proper kitchen where the scullery is at present. It'll be like a palace once it's done.'

'That's going to cost you a bob or two, Jesse.'

'What else have I got to spend my money on, Donald, apart from Lizzie here? She's worth it. She's worth every penny.' He smiled at her.

'So what date's the wedding?'

'Twenty-eighth of April. A Sunday. I've come here today specially to ask you, Donald. Since I've known you all me life, would you be me best man?'

Donald laughed. 'Delighted, Jesse. Cor, what a privilege, eh? Here, Patty, can we have another round of drinks, please?'

Chapter 29

Right up till the day before the wedding the dairy house was alive with the hustle and bustle of tradesmen. Bert Foxall, the local plumber, plumbed furiously with his mate to have the new bathroom and kitchen sink ready. He employed a navvy to dig a trench to accommodate the new waste pipe that had to run through the yard from the old scullery to the field behind. Ivor Whistle, so called because he was a football referee in his spare time, was the local dab-hand at paper-hanging and he, together with a gas fitter from the gas company, darted about like swifts building a nest, sometimes climbing over each other to get their work finished. But just in time everything was ready, and Lizzie was delighted.

It had taken her a while to come to terms with the information about her parentage. She spent a long time recalling the past, her relationships with her mother and with Tom Dando; and with Isaac, the man she'd always assumed was her father. She and Jesse discussed it at some length, and at first were in two minds whether to inform her brothers and sister. But as Jesse suggested, such a revelation might cause them to doubt their own pedigree.

Beccy had been the soul of discretion, keeping all this to herself for forty years, and only then revealing the truth for the sake of Lizzie's happiness. Even when Lizzie told her she was planning to join Stanley in Southern Rhodesia she hadn't let on. There was no reason to suppose she would divulge anything to anyone else. And Sylvia was unlikely to tell anyone and risk upsetting her mother. It also ensured that she would regard Lizzie with some respect now, not just because she was her sister, but because she didn't want Lizzie to broadcast the truth.

So their secret was safe. The only professional man to know was Donald Clark, and he was ethically bound to say nothing. The Reverend Mr John Mainwaring was none the wiser. He knew nothing of the crisis that had plagued them. Their birth certificates gave nothing away; in the furore the banns of marriage were never withdrawn; the original wedding date was never cancelled. As far as the vicar was concerned it was a perfectly normal, happy event. They would have to see whether he raised his eyebrows when Lizzie went to be churched only six months or so after her wedding.

But more than once Lizzie contemplated her escape from Stanley Dando. They'd been ardent lovers, yet he was her brother. She'd even had his child. Often she'd wondered who the child would have been like. Now she wondered more than ever. And the irony of her carrying another child now, which, for a few days she'd believed to be incestuous, was not lost on her. Thank God for Beccy.

Ezme, too, was by this time acclimatised to the facts. She even apologised to Lizzie for being so outrageously unkind and unfeeling, especially on the night she revealed who Jesse's father was in front of Sylvia and Edgar. Lizzie, of course, forgave her. She also knew what it was like to have a child out of wedlock, and the anguish it wrought. Lizzie and Ezme tolerated each other equably now.

Lizzie gave the landlord plenty of notice that they wanted to vacate their house by the 4th of May, thus giving them time to shift everything over to their new home. Henzey was also quick to point out to her brother and sisters that for the first few days after the wedding, they, the children, should continue to sleep in the old house for a day or two, giving their mother and Jesse a brief honeymoon alone; except for Ezme, of course, who was hardly likely to intrude. They were all happy to comply, even though they were keen to move.

Just a few close friends and relatives were invited to the wedding. It was never intended to be a lavish affair, but they wanted to make certain that they provided a good spread after the ceremony.

Getting their mother ready was by far the most important event of the day for Henzey and Alice. They fussed her, and took great pains to see that her make-up was perfect, that not a hair on her head was out of place. When they struggled to fasten Lizzie's wedding dress Henzey couldn't help noticing that her mother was definitely gaining weight.

'It looks like you slimming after the wedding, Mom,' she advised. 'You're starting to get podgy. You'll regret it.'

'I know,' Lizzie answered evasively. She would not be able to disguise it for long, but this was not the time to confess her condition.

And so the wedding took place at St. John's at twelve noon, after matins. Lizzie wore a short cream satin dress with a fashionable, uneven hem line. She looked significantly younger than her years, and quite radiant. Maxine was the only bridesmaid. Henzey wore a short, straight dress in cinnabar red with a row of pearls, and Alice, a beige, flouncey dress and a borrowed fox fur. They all looked exquisite, enhancing their reputation as the best-looking girls in the parish, though that elite group also included Lizzie in the eyes of a great many. Jesse and Herbert each wore a new three piece suit, new shoes and new shirts. Donald Clark, having treated himself to a haircut especially for the occasion, looked resplendent, as did his nose.

For May and Joe Bishop the day brought some welcome laughter into their lives, seeing again the relatives they seldom saw. Lucy and her husband Jim travelled from Manchester, and Lucy was puzzled when they all, in their turn, asked if she was better. They were due to return by train that night so that Jim could go to work next day. He was at pains to remind Herbert that he built locomotives at Peacock's works. Brother Ted, his wife and family, and brother Grenville, with his incumbents, were all made welcome. Dear old Beccy Crump was guest of honour.

Many well-wishers, friends, acquaintances and customers of Jesse also turned up at the church to witness the event and offer their congratulations afterwards, while the photographer set up his camera and tripod, and organised his plates.

It was commonly accepted that John Mainwaring did not approve of the throwing of confetti outside in the church grounds, since it had to be swept up. Rice, however, was perfectly in order, since it softened in the rain, and the birds would eat it.

While guests and well-wishers flung grains of rice over the newly weds, Beccy Crump turned to Joe Bishop and said, 'This throwin' good rice is criminal, Joe. It'd make a grand puddin'.'

'Maybe we should've waited till it was a pudding, Beccy, and then throwed it,' he replied dryly.

Back at the dairy house, everybody, especially Sylvia, was amazed at the transformation that had taken place, and she actually complimented Lizzie on a magnificent achievement in getting Jesse to part with some of his money. Lizzie smiled generously and thanked her. 'If I'd known he'd got any money, Sylvia, I wouldn't have offered to pay towards it myself,' she said.

During the morning Herbert transferred all the available chairs from their own and Joe's house. With the new furniture Jesse and Lizzie had bought there were just enough seats. They borrowed sufficient crockery, glassware and cutlery to make up the numbers, and asked Iky Bottlebrush's wife, Hilda, to organise the catering. She did so with enthusiasm and expertise.

John Mainwaring was invited to the party after the ceremony and he graciously accepted. At two o'clock the informal feast began and everyone set to eating and drinking. They sat in groups in the big, front room, eating from their laps, and in the refurbished sitting room that was also to serve as a dining room from now on. Donald Clark had kindly delivered, in his black Morris, a firkin of best home-brewed bitter Jesse had ordered from 'The Shoulder of Mutton'. With it were two bottles of gin, three bottles of whisky, one of which Donald guarded possessively, and two bottles of sherry. The vicar himself polished off nearly a whole bottle of sherry. Henzey and Alice took it in turns to tend to the needs of Ezme Clancey upstairs, though there was a steady procession of people taking food up to her, along with their good wishes, including Donald Clark, who took her a glass of stout. Sylvia Atkinson and Edgar made themselves comfortable, but kept a low profile, and Sylvia watched with unease as her son befriended Lizzie's daughters. Kenneth seemed quite taken with them, but especially with Maxine. None of them knew Sylvia, apart from Herbert, but Henzey recognised her, not realising who she was, because she often called into George Mason's for groceries.

When the eating finished, Donald Clark got to his feet and asked for everybody's attention. His whisky glass was in his hand, his ample nose was shining like a hurricane lamp and his greying ginger hair was still typically tousled, despite the recent attention to it.

'It has been my privilege,' he began, with no evidence in his speech of how much whisky he'd drunk, 'to know Jesse and Lizzie Clancey for a good many years...' There was a cheer as they all acknowledged Lizzie's new surname. 'Both families, the Bishops and the Clanceys, have been good to me in the past, and I shall always be grateful for it. I hold them all dear to my heart. Yet there's been a sort of reciprocal arrangement too, for while Jesse's been delivering milk to me over the years, I've delivered of Lizzie a family. A family for him, as it now turns out, ready made, in the form of three beautiful daughters and a handsome son.' Another cheer went up, and the Kite girls and Herbert looked at each other and giggled. 'And who's to say that I shan't deliver Lizzie of more children now that she's tied the knot with this handsome fellow, who was always Kates Hill's most eligible bachelor?'

A roar of approval and laughter went up at the suggestion, and Lizzie blushed – the first time for a long time.

'And here I should add, that Jesse must be complimented on his choice of wife, for Lizzie always used to be the prettiest girl on the Hill, with absolutely hordes of admirers.'

Lizzie glanced at Sylvia. This was not the most tactful thing Donald could have said, but Sylvia caught Lizzie's apprehensive glance, and smiled forgivingly, raising an amused eyebrow.

Donald continued, oblivious to his gaffe. 'I recall how I used to visit the Bishops' home with Ted, my old pal there, before he married Ada from Gornal. Lizzie, in her Sunday best was always a sight to behold. So it's not surprising that when her first husband, Ben, whom we all respected and admired, sadly passed away, she should become a very alluring young widow.'

There were murmurs of approval that Ben had not been forgotten, and Lizzie cast her eyes down so as not to meet anyone's glance. She was not certain it was the appropriate moment for Donald to mention her late husband either, but Jesse took her hand and gave it a reassuring squeeze.

'And I'm sure you'll all agree, that Jesse's just the man to make Lizzie a deservedly very happy woman. Jesse and I have been friends for years, and I know of no one more down to earth and more honest. Moreover, I know of nobody else who's totally unflappable. Never have I known him get flustered. But I do know that his steadying influence, his considered advice, his always having time for people, has helped many a poor soul over difficult times. I believe that these two fine people deserve each other.

'So I propose a toast. I give you the health, the future happiness and prosperity of Lizzie and Jesse.'

'*Lizzie and Jesse*,' came the reply, and everybody drank.

Jesse replied, thanking Donald for his kind words, and the rest of them for attending and witnessing the happiest occasion of his life. He said how much he was looking forward to married life, and settling down with his ready made family. 'I love 'em all as if they were my own.'

Everybody cheered and, after another toast, they all fell into general conversation. One or two guests drifted back to the sitting room and Joe started playing the pianola. Some began singing, feeling sentimental after the speeches, full of beer or gin. A few ditties that were none too savoury could be heard coming from Lizzie's brothers, before they started on the more serious stuff.

Lizzie was happy, but the mention of Ben earlier was a poignant moment for her. However, she smiled and looked at Jesse adoringly as their guests came up in their turn to speak with them while the singing continued.

By six o'clock Hilda Bottlebrush had cleared away and washed up all the crockery and cutlery from the dinnertime feast, and had brought out tea and cakes. Many ceased their drinking, by virtue of sleep imposing itself upon them. But those whom sleep side-stepped continued raucously, sometimes hushed by the more abstemious wives who were afeared of waking others' husbands, or of upsetting the vicar with doubtful language. At five, the said vicar departed to sober up for evensong. Come eight o'clock the relatives who lived furthest away had also left, as had Sylvia, Edgar and Kenneth, together with Donald Clark. Donald had some serious solo drinking to do at home, where every glass was not being counted by fearful patients. Beccy Crump said goodnight shortly after nine, since she had to rise early in the morning to light the boiler in the brewhouse, now that she was going to do her bit of washing on a Monday instead of a Tuesday.

One by one the hangers-on left, and Alice, Maxine and Herbert drifted back to number 48. Just after midnight Billy Witts announced he ought to leave, too. Henzey duly fetched her best hat and coat from the hall, and gave Jesse and her mother a goodnight kiss.

'It's been a happy day for me seeing you two married,' Henzey confessed. 'I know you'll be happy.'

Lizzie wrapped her arms around her. 'Thanks, my flower. You don't know how much that means to both of us.' A pang of guilt struck her that she'd said nothing to her about the child in her belly.

'Goodnight, Mom. Goodnight, Jesse.' Henzey took Billy's hand. Billy raised his free arm in a gesture of goodnight, and they left the newly-weds to their first night together.

As Henzey and Billy walked across the street, Lizzie watched them from the front room window of the dairy house. They stood by his car holding each other in a clinch for about five minutes, pecking at each other's lips occasionally, looking into each other's eyes and laughing. *Unless she gets rid of him and goes to bed soon she won't be up for work in the morning,* she thought.

'Are you coming to bed, Lizzie, or are you gunna stand ganning on them pair all night?' Jesse called from the bedroom, after settling his mother for the night.

Lizzie dragged herself away from the chink in the curtains and went upstairs. 'I just wanted to make sure Billy hadn't gone in the house with her at this time of night.' She kicked off her new shoes with relief and slumped onto their new, supple bed. 'If they do, I'll know they're up to no good. I just don't trust that Billy, Jesse.'

Jesse peeped through the curtains. He saw Henzey and Billy going into the entry boisterously, holding hands. He turned away, and said nothing of it to Lizzie to save her worrying. He shifted his braces from his shoulders and they hung down at his sides. 'Billy's all right, don't malign the chap,' he said. 'You can't be Henzey's guardian angel every hour of the bloody day and night. And anyway, let her have her fun – you've had yours.'

'And look where it's got me. Pregnant and nearly forty.' She hitched her dress up and unfastened her suspenders.

'What d'you mean, Lizzie? You only married the most eligible bachelor on Kates Hill,' he laughed. 'The doctor said so, so it must be right. Anyway, Billy's gone now, so stop your werriting.'

'You know how I am about her, Jesse. I don't want her to get into trouble.'

He chuckled. 'Like you, you mean?' She hit him playfully. 'Lizzie, be ruled by me.' He was removing his rear collar stud. 'She won't get into trouble. She's got a sight more sense than you give her credit for. You've got to let go of her sometime. God knows how you'll be when the other two are her age.'

She slid her stockings down her legs and hung them over the bedrail, pondering his words. Jesse detached his collar, took off his shirt and unbuttoned his trousers.

'Unfasten my frock, Jesse, will you?'

She stood up, turned her back towards him and his fingers nimbly undid the fastenings. As her dress fell to the floor around her, he kissed the back of her neck and she shivered at the sensation. She turned her face to him and smiled saucily, like the young girl he remembered.

'Hurry up into bed, Jesse, and warm it up. It is our first night, you know.'

'Race you there,' he said.

This Large Print Book for the partially sighted, who cannot read normal print, is published under the auspices of

THE ULVERSCROFT FOUNDATION

Other MAGNA Titles
In Large Print

LYN ANDREWS
Angels Of Mercy

HELEN CANNAM
Spy For Cromwell

EMMA DARCY
The Velvet Tiger

SUE DYSON
Fairfield Rose

J. M. GREGSON
To Kill A Wife

MEG HUTCHINSON
A Promise Given

TIM WILSON
A Singing Grave

RICHARD WOODMAN
The Cruise Of The Commissioner